SO-AAC-747

POUL ANDERSON

"...creator of some of the most superb and memorable characters in Science Fiction."
—FRANK HERBERT

Winner of five Hugo and two Nebula Awards, Poul Anderson is one of the great names of contemporary Science Fiction. Author of more than fifty books, he lives in California, where he is active in the Society for Creative Anachronism and has won a Knighthood for prowess in medieval combat.

THE EARTH BOOK OF STORMGATE

"Pure unadulterated enjoyment...for readers of the rousing tale well-told, this is the genuine, the hand-grown!"
—ALGIS BUDRYS

Berkley Books by Poul Anderson

THE AVATAR
THE CORRIDORS OF TIME
THE DARK BETWEEN THE STARS
THE EARTH BOOK OF STORMGATE
THE ENEMY STARS
THE MERMAN'S CHILDREN
MIRKHEIM
SATAN'S WORLD
SHIELD
THE STAR FOX
TAU ZERO
TRADER TO THE STARS
THE TROUBLE TWISTERS
VAULT OF THE AGES

POUL ANDERSON

THE EARTH BOOK OF STORMGATE

BERKLEY BOOKS, NEW YORK

THE EARTH BOOK OF STORMGATE

A Berkley Book / published by arrangement with
the author's agent

PRINTING HISTORY
Berkley edition / May 1979
Fifth printing / May 1983

ISBN: 0-425-05933-2

ACKNOWLEDGMENTS

These stories were originally published as follows:

"Wings of Victory," *Analog Science Fiction/Science Fact,* April 1972. Copyright © 1972 by Condé Nast Publications, Inc.

"The Problem of Pain," *The Magazine of Fantasy and Science Fiction,* February 1973. Copyright © 1973 by Mercury Press, Inc.

"How to Be Ethnic in One Easy Lesson" (as "How to Be Ethnic"), *Future Quest,* ed. Roger Elwood, Avon Books, 1974. Copyright © 1974 by Roger Elwood.

"Margin of Profit" (in a different form), *Astounding Science Fiction,* September 1956. Copyright © 1956 by Street and Smith Publications, Inc.

"Esau" (as "Birthright"), *Analog Science Fiction/Science Fact,* February 1970. Copyright © 1970 by Condé Nast Publications, Inc.

"The Season of Forgiveness," *Boys' Life,* December 1973. Copyright © 1973 by The Boy Scouts of America.

"The Man Who Counts," *Astounding Science Fiction,* February-April 1958. Copyright © 1958 by Street and Smith Publications, Inc.

"A Little Knowledge," *Analog Science Fiction/Science Fact,* August 1971. Copyright © 1971 by Condé Nast Publications, Inc.

"Day of Burning" (as "Supernova"), *Analog Science Fiction/Science Fact,* January 1967. Copyright © 1967 by Condé Nast Publications, Inc.

"Lodestar," in *Astounding: John W. Campbell Memorial Anthology,* ed. Harry Harrison, Random House, 1973. Copyright © 1973 by Random House, Inc.

"Wingless" (as "Wingless on Avalon"), *Children of Infinity,* Roger Elwood, ed., Franklin Watts, 1973. Copyright © 1973 by Franklin Watts, Inc.

"Rescue on Avalon," *Boys' Life,* July 1973. Copyright © 1973 by The Boy Scouts of America.

TO GEOFF KIDD

A CHRONOLOGY OF TECHNIC
CIVILIZATION

Note: Although Poul Anderson was consulted during the preparation of this chart, he is not responsible for its dating nor in any way specifically committed to it. Stories are listed by their most recently published titles.

21st C	century of recovery
22nd C	interstellar exploration, the Breakup, formation of Commonwealth
2150	"Wings of Victory," *Analog Science Fiction* (cited as ASF), April, 1972.
23rd C	establishment of Polesotechnic League
24th C	"The Problem of Pain," *Fantasy and Science Fiction* (cited as F & SF), February, 1973.
2376	Nicholas van Rijn born
2400	Council of Hiawatha
2406	David Falkayn born
2416	"Margin of Profit," ASF, September, 1956. (van Rijn)
	"How to Be Ethnic in One Easy Lesson," in *Future Quest,* ed. Roger Elwood, Avon Books, 1974.
———	"Three-Cornered Wheel," ASF, October, 1963. (Falkayn)
stories overlap around	"A Sun Invisible," ASF, April, 1966. (Falkayn)
2426	*War of the Wing-Men,* Ace Books, 1958 as "The Man Who Counts," ASF, February-April, 1958. (van Rijn) See below: *The Earth Book of Stormgate*
——— 2427	"Birthright," ASF, February, 1970. (van Rijn)

Burning," "A Little Knowledge," "The Season of Forgiveness," "Lodestar," "Wingless on Avalon," "Rescue on Avalon"), G.P. Putnam's/Berkley, 1978.

27th C   the Time of Troubles

"The Star Plunderer," *Planet Stories* (cited as PS), September, 1952.

28th C   foundation of Terran Empire, Principate phase begins

"Sargasso of Lost Starships," PS, January, 1952.

29th C   *The People of the Wind*. New American Library and ASF, February-April, 1973.

30th C   the Covenant of Alfzar

3000   Dominic Flandry born

3019   *Ensign Flandry*. Chilton, 1966. Abridged version in *Amazing* (cited as Amz), October, 1966.

3021   *A Circus of Hells*. New American Library, 1970 (incorporates "The White King's War," *Galaxy* (cited as Gal), October, 1969.

3022   Josip succeeds Georgios as Emperor

3025   *The Rebel Worlds*. New American Library, 1969.

3027   "Outpost of Empire," *Gal*, December, 1967. (non-Flandry)

3028   *The Day of Their Return*, Doubleday, 1973. (non-Flandry)

3032   "Tiger by the Tail," PS, January, 1951.

3033   "Honorable Enemies," *Future Combined with Science Fiction Stories,* May, 1951.

3035   "The Game of Glory," *Venture,* March, 1958.

3037   "A Message in Secret," as *Mayday Orbit*. Ace Books, 1961, from short version, "A Message in Secret," *Fantastic,* December, 1959.

3038   "A Plague of Masters," *Fantastic,* December,

—Original chart by Sandra Miesel

THE EARTH BOOK OF STORMGATE

To those who read, good flight.

It is Hloch of the Stormgate Choth who writes, on the peak of Mount Anrovil in the Weathermother. His Wyvan, Tariat son of Lythran and Blawsa, has asked this. Weak though his grip upon the matter be, bloodpride requires he undertake the task.

Judge, O people. The father of Hloch was Ferannian and the mother was Rennhi. They held the country around Spearhead Lake. He was an engineer who was often in Gray, Centauri, and other towns, dealing with humans. They in their turn came often thither, for travel routes crisscrossed above and there was, too, a copper mine not far off. Hloch's parents were guest-free and would house whoever pleased them for days in line, giving these leave to roam and hunt. Moreover, as you well know, because of its nearness to populous Gray, our choth receives more humans into membership than most. Hence we younglings grew up friendly with many of this race and familiar with no few of the winds that blow on their souls.

Rennhi was a quester into the centuries, remembered for her scholarship and for the flame she kindled in those whom she saw fit to teach. High above all, she is remembered for writing *The Sky Book of Stormgate*. In this, as you well know, she traced and described the whole history of our choth. Of the ancestors upon Ythri; of the founders here upon Avalon; of the descendants and their doings unto her own years; of how past and present and future have forever been intermingled and, in living minds, ever begetting each other—of this does her work pursue the truth, and will as long as thought flies over our world.

God stooped upon her before she could begin the next chronicle. Already she had gathered in much that was needful, aided in small compass by her son Hloch. Then came the Terran War, and when it had passed by, ruined landscapes lay underneath skies gone strange. We are still raising our lives anew from the wreckage left by that hurricane. Hloch, who had served in space, afterward found himself upon Imperial planets, member of a merchant crew, as trade was reborn. Thus maychance he gained some further sight across the human species.

So did the Wyvan Tariat think of late, when Hloch had wearied of the void and returned to the winds. His word: "We have need to grasp the realness of those folk, both those who dwell among us and those who are of the Empire. For this, your mother knew, it is best to fly their ways and see through their eyes—ancestral still more than incarnate, that we may sense what is rising ahead of us in time. Hloch, write the book she did not live to write."

Therefore, behold these annals, from the Discovery and on through the World-Taking. They are garnered from different trees, and few of them will seem at once to grow toward the same sun. Yet they do, they all do. This is the tale, told afresh, of how Avalon came to settlement and thus our choth to being. This is the tale as told, not by Rennhi and those on whom she drew for the *Sky Book,* but by Terrans, who walk the earth. Hloch will seek to explain what is alien: though only by swinging your mind into that same alienness may you hope to seize the knowledge behind.

Then read.

WINGS OF VICTORY

Our part in the Grand Survey had taken us out beyond the
great suns Alpha and Beta Crucis. From Earth we would
have been in the constellation Lupus. But Earth was 278
light-years remote, Sol itself long dwindled to invisibility,
and stars drew strange pictures across the dark.

After three years we were weary and had suffered
losses. Oh, the wonder wasn't gone. How could it ever
go—from world after world after world? But we had seen
so many, and of those we had walked on, some were
beautiful and some were terrible and most were both
(even as Earth is) and none were alike and all were
mysterious. They blurred together in our minds.

It was still a heart-speeding thing to find another
sentient race, actually more than to find another planet
colonizable by man. Now Ali Hamid had perished of a
poisonous bite a year back, and Manuel Gonsalves had
not yet recovered from the skull fracture inflicted by the
club of an excited being at our last stop. This made
Vaughn Webner our chief xenologist, from whom was to
issue trouble.

Not that he, or any of us, wanted it. You learn to gang
warily, in a universe not especially designed for you, or
you die; there is no third choice. We approached this
latest star because every G-type dwarf beckoned us. But

we did not establish orbit around its most terrestroid attendant until neutrino analysis had verified that nobody in the system had developed atomic energy. And we exhausted every potentiality of our instruments before we sent down our first robot probe.

The sun was a G9, golden in hue, luminosity half of Sol's. The world which interested us was close enough in to get about the same irradiation as Earth. It was smaller, surface gravity 0.75, with a thinner and drier atmosphere. However, that air was perfectly breathable by humans, and bodies of water existed which could be called modest oceans. The globe was very lovely where it turned against star-crowded night, blue, tawny, rusty-brown, white-clouded. Two little moons skipped in escort.

Biological samples proved that its life was chemically similar to ours. None of the microorganisms we cultured posed any threat that normal precautions and medications could not handle. Pictures taken at low altitude and on the ground showed woods, lakes, wide plains rolling toward mountains. We were afire to set foot there.

But the natives—

You must remember how new the hyperdrive is, and how immense the cosmos. The organizers of the Grand Survey were too wise to believe that the few neighbor systems we'd learned something about gave knowledge adequate for devising doctrine. Our service had one law, which was its proud motto: "We come as friends." Otherwise each crew was free to work out its own procedures. After five years the survivors would meet and compare experiences.

For us aboard the *Olga,* Captain Gray had decided that, whenever possible, sophonts should not be disturbed by preliminary sightings of our machines. We would try to set the probes in uninhabited regions. When we ourselves landed, we would come openly. After all, the shape of a body counts for much less than the shape of the mind within. Thus went our belief.

Naturally, we took in every datum we could from orbit and upper-atmospheric overflights. While not extremely informative under such conditions, our pictures did reveal a few small towns on two continents—clusters of buildings, at least, lacking defensive walls or regular streets—hard by primitive mines. They seemed insignificant against immense and almost unpopulated landscapes. We guessed we could identify a variety of cultures, from Stone Age through Iron. Yet invariably, aside from those petty communities, settlements consisted of one or a few houses standing alone. We found none less than ten kilometers apart; most were more isolated.

"Carnivores, I expect," Webner said. "The primitive economies are hunting-fishing-gathering, the advanced economies pastoral. Large areas which look cultivated are probably just to provide fodder; they don't have the layout of proper farms." He tugged his chin. "I confess to being puzzled as to how the civilized—well, let's say the 'metallurgic' people, at this stage—how they manage it. You need trade, communication, quick exchange of ideas, for that level of technology. And if I read the pictures aright, roads are virtually nonexistent, a few dirt tracks between towns and mines, or to the occasional dock for barges or ships—Confound it, water transportation is insufficient."

"Pack animals, maybe?" I suggested.

"Too slow," he said. "You don't get progressive cultures when months must pass before the few individuals capable of originality can hear from each other. The chances are they never will."

For a moment the pedantry dropped from his manner. "Well," he said, "we'll see," which is the grandest sentence that any language can own.

We always made initial contact with three, the minimum who could do the job, lest we lose them. This time they were Webner, xenologist; Aram Turekian, pilot; and Yukiko Sachansky, gunner. It was Gray's idea to give women that last assignment. He felt they were better than men at watching and waiting, less likely to open fire in doubtful situations.

The site chosen was in the metallurgic domain, though not a town. Why complicate matters unnecessarily? It was on a rugged upland, thick forest for many kilometers around. Northward the mountainside rose steeply until, above timberline, its crags were crowned by a glacier. Southward it toppled to a great plateau, open country where herds grazed on a reddish analogue of grass or shrubs. Maybe they were domesticated, maybe not. In either case, probably the dwellers did a lot of hunting.

"Would that account for their being so scattered?" Yukiko wondered. "A big range needed to support each individual?"

"Then they must have a strong territoriality," Webner said. "Stand sharp by the guns."

We were not forbidden to defend ourselves from attack, whether or not blunders of ours had provoked it. Nevertheless the girl winced. Turekian glanced over his shoulder and saw. That, and Webner's tone, made him flush. "Blow down, Vaughn," he growled.

Webner's long, gaunt frame stiffened in his seat. Light gleamed off the scalp under his thin hair as he thrust his head toward the pilot. "What did you say?"

"Stay in your own shop and run it, if you can."

"Mind your manners. This may be my first time in charge, but I *am*—"

"On the ground. We're aloft yet."

"Please." Yukiko reached from her turret and laid a hand on either man's shoulder. "Please don't quarrel . . . when we're about to meet a whole new history."

They couldn't refuse her wish. Tool-burdened coverall or no, she remained in her Eurasian petiteness the most desired woman aboard the *Olga*; and still the rest of the girls liked her. Gonsalves' word for her was *simpático*.

The men only quieted on the surface. They were an ill-assorted pair, not enemies—you don't sign on a person who'll allow himself hatred—but unfriends. Webner was the academic type, professor of xenology at the University of Oceania. In youth he'd done excellent field work, especially in the trade-route cultures of Cynthia, and he'd been satisfactory under his superiors. At heart, though, he was a theorist, whom middle age had made dogmatic.

Turekian was the opposite: young, burly, black-bearded, boisterous and roisterous, born in a sealtent on

Mars to a life of banging around the available universe. If half his brags were true, he was mankind's boldest adventurer, toughest fighter, and mightiest lover; but I'd found to my profit that he wasn't the poker player he claimed. Withal he was able, affable, helpful, popular—which may have kindled envy in poor self-chilled Webner.

"Okay, sure," Turekian laughed. "For you, Yu." He tossed a kiss in her direction.

Webner unbent less easily. "What did you mean by running my own shop if I can?" he demanded.

"Nothing, nothing," the girl almost begged.

"Ah, a bit more than nothing," Turekian said. "A tiny bit. I just wish you were less convinced your science has the last word on all the possibilities. Things I've seen—"

"I've heard your song before," Webner scoffed. "In a jungle on some exotic world you met animals with wheels."

"Never said that. Hm-m-m...make a good yarn, wouldn't it?"

"No. Because it's an absurdity. Simply ask yourself how nourishment would pass from the axle bone to the cells of the disc. In like manner—"

"Yeh, yeh. Quiet, now, please. I've got to conn us down."

The target waxed fast in the bow screen. A booming of air came faint through the hull plates and vibration shivered flesh. Turekian hated dawdling. Besides, a slow descent might give the autochthons time to become hysterical, with perhaps tragic consequences.

Peering, the humans saw a house on the rim of a canyon at whose bottom a river rushed gray-green. The structure was stone, massive and tile-roofed. Three more buildings joined to define a flagged courtyard. Those were of timber, long and low, topped by blossoming sod. A corral outside the quadrangle held four-footed beasts, and nearby stood a row of what Turekian, pointing, called overgrown birdhouses. A meadow surrounded the ensemble. Elsewhere the woods crowded close.

There was abundant bird or, rather, ornithoid life, flocks strewn across the sky. A pair of especially large creatures hovered above the steading. They veered as the boat descended.

Abruptly, wings exploded from the house. Out of its windows flyers came, a score or better, all sizes from tiny ones which clung to adult backs, up to those which dwarfed the huge extinct condors of Earth. In a gleam of bronze feathers, a storm of wingbeats which pounded through the hull, they rose, and fled, and were lost among the treetops.

The humans landed in a place gone empty.

Hands near sidearms, Webner and Turekian trod forth, looked about, let the planet enter them.

You always undergo that shock of first encounter. Not only does space separate the newfound world from yours; time does, five billion years at least. Often you need minutes before you can truly see the shapes around, they are that alien. Before, the eye has registered them but not the brain.

This was more like home. Yet the strangenesses were uncountable.

Weight: three-fourths of what the ship maintained. An ease, a bounciness in the stride . . . and a subtle kinesthetic adjustment required, sensory more than muscular.

Air: like Earth's at about two kilometers' altitude. (Gravity gradient being less, the density dropoff above sea level went slower.) Crystalline vision, cool flow and murmur of breezes, soughing in the branches and river clangorous down in the canyon. Every odor different, no hint of sun-baked resin or duff, instead a medley of smokinesses and pungencies.

Light: warm gold, making colors richer and shadows deeper than you were really evolved for; a midmorning sun which displayed almost half again the apparent diameter of Earth's, in a sky which was deep blue and had only thin streaks of cloud.

Life: wild flocks, wheeling and crying high overhead; lowings and cacklings from the corral; rufous carpet underfoot, springy, suggestive more of moss than grass though not very much of either, starred with exquisite flowers; trees whose leaves were green (from silvery to murky), whose bark (if it was bark) might be black or gray or brown or white, whose forms were little more odd to you than were pine or gingko if you came from oak and beech country, but which were no trees of anywhere on Earth. A swarm of midgelike entomoids went by, and a big coppery-winged "moth" leisurely feeding on them.

Scenery: superb. Above the forest, peaks shouldered into heaven, the glacier shimmered blue. To the right, canyon walls plunged roseate, ocher-banded, and cragged. But your attention was directed ahead.

The house was of astonishing size. "A flinking castle," Turekian exclaimed. An approximate twenty-meter cube, it rose sheer to the peaked roof, built from well-dressed blocks of granite. Windows indicated six stories. They were large openings, equipped with wooden shutters and wrought-iron balconies. The sole door, on ground level, was ponderous. Horns, skulls, and sculptured weapons of the chase—knife, spear, shortsword, blowgun, bow and arrow—ornamented the façade.

The attendant buildings were doubtless barns or sheds. Trophies hung on them too. The beasts in the corral looked, and probably weren't, mammalian. Two species were vaguely reminiscent of horses and oxen, a third of sheep. They were not many, could not be the whole support of the dwellers here. The "dovecotes" held ornithoids as big as turkeys, which were not penned but were prevented from leaving the area by three hawklike guardians. "Watchdogs," Turekian said of those. "No, watchfalcons." They swooped about, perturbed at the invasion.

Yukiko's voice came wistful from a receiver behind his ear: "Can I join you?"

"Stand by the guns," Webner answered. "We have yet to meet the owners of this place."

"Huh?" Turekian said. "Why, they're gone. Skedaddled when they saw us coming."

"Timid?" Yukiko asked. "That doesn't fit with their being eager hunters."

"On the contrary, I imagine they're pretty scrappy,"

Turekian said. "They jumped to the conclusion we must be hostile, because they wouldn't enter somebody else's land uninvited unless they felt that way. Our powers being unknown, and they having wives and kiddies to worry about, they prudently took off. I expect the fighting males—or whatever they've got—will be back soon."

"What are you talking about?" Webner inquired.

"Why,... the locals." Turekian blinked at him. "You saw them."

"Those giant ornithoids? Nonsense."

"Hoy? They came right out of the house there!"

"Domestic animals." Webner's hatchet features drew tight. "I don't deny we confront a puzzle here."

"We always do," Yukiko put in softly.

Webner nodded. "True. However, facts and logic solve puzzles. Let's not complicate our task with pseudo-problems. Whatever they are, the flyers we saw leave cannot be the sophonts. On a planet as Earthlike as this, aviform intelligence is impossible."

He straightened. "I suspect the inhabitants have barricaded themselves," he finished. "We'll go closer and make pacific gestures."

"Which could be misunderstood," Turekian said dubiously. "An arrow or javelin can kill you just as dead as a blaster."

"Cover us, Yukiko," Webner ordered. "Follow me, Aram. If you have the nerve."

He stalked forward, under the eyes of the girl. Turekian cursed and joined him in haste.

They were near the door when a shadow fell over them. They whirled and stared upward. Yukiko's indrawn breath hissed from their receivers.

Aloft hovered one of the great ornithoids. Sunlight struck through its outermost pinions, turning them golden. Otherwise it showed stormcloud-dark. Down the wind stooped a second.

The sight was terrifying. Only later did the humans realize it was magnificent. Those wings spanned six meters. A muzzle full of sharp white fangs gaped before them. Two legs the length and well-nigh the thickness of a man's arms reached crooked talons between them. At their angles grew claws. In thrust after thrust, they hurled the creature at torpedo speed. Air whistled and thundered.

Their guns leaped into the men's hands. "Don't shoot!" Yukiko's cry came as if from very far away.

The splendid monster was almost upon them. Fire speared from Webner's weapon. At the same instant, the animal braked—a turning of quills, a crack and gust in their faces—and rushed back upward, two meters short of impact.

Turekian's gaze stamped a picture on his brain which he would study over and over and over. The unknown was feathered, surely warm-blooded, but no bird. A keelbone like a ship's prow jutted beneath a strong neck. The head was blunt-nosed, lacked external ears; fantastically, Turekian saw that the predator mouth had lips. Tongue and palate were purple. Two big golden eyes stabbed at him, burned at him. A crest of black-tipped white plumage rose stiffly above, a control surface and protection for the backward-bulging skull. The fan-shaped tail bore the same colors. The body was mahogany, the naked legs and claws yellow.

Webner's shot hit amidst the left-side quills. Smoke streamed after the flameburst. The creature uttered a high-pitched yell, lurched, and threshed in retreat. The damage wasn't permanent, had likely caused no pain, but now that wing was only half-useful.

Turekian thus had time to see three slits in parallel on the body. He had time to think there must be three more on the other side. They weirdly resembled gills. As the wings lifted, he saw them drawn wide, a triple yawn; as the downstroke began, he glimpsed them being forced shut.

Then he had cast himself against Webner. "Drop that, you clotbrain!" he yelled. He seized the xenologist's gun wrist. They wrestled. He forced the fingers apart. Meanwhile the wounded ornithoid struggled back to its companion. They flapped off.

"What're you doing?" Webner grabbed at Turekian.

The pilot pushed him away, brutally hard. He fell. Turekian snatched forth his magnifier.

Treetops cut off his view. He let the instrument drop. "Too late," he groaned. "Thanks to you."

Webner climbed erect, pale and shaken by rage. "Have you gone heisenberg?" he gasped. "I'm your commander!"

"You're maybe fit to command plastic ducks in a bathtub," Turekian said. "Firing on a native!"

Webner was too taken aback to reply.

"And you capped it by spoiling my chance for a good look at Number Two. I think I spotted a harness on him, holding what might be a weapon, but I'm not sure." Turekian spat.

"Aram, Vaughn," Yukiko pleaded from the boat.

An instant longer, the men bristled and glared. Then Webner drew breath, shrugged, and said in a crackly voice: "I suppose it's incumbent on me to put things on a reasonable basis, if you're incapable of that." He paused. "Behave yourself and I'll excuse your conduct as being due to excitement. Else I'll have to recommend you be relieved from further initial-contact duty."

"*I* be relieved—?" Turekian barely checked his fist, and kept it balled. His breath rasped.

"Hadn't you better check the house?" Yukiko asked.

The knowledge that something, anything, might lurk behind yonder walls restored them to a measure of coolness.

Save for livestock, the steading was deserted.

Rather than offend the dwellers by blasting down their barred door, the searchers went through a window on grav units. They found just one or two rooms on each story. Evidently the people valued ample floor space and high ceilings above privacy. Connection up and down was by circular staircases whose short steps seemed at variance with this. Decoration was austere and nonrepresentational. Furniture consisted mainly of benches and tables. Nothing like a bed or an *o-futon* was found.

Did the indigenes sleep, if they did, sitting or standing? Quite possibly. Many species can lock the joints of their limbs at will.

Stored food bore out the idea of carnivorousness. Tools, weapons, utensils, fabrics were abundant, well made, neatly put away. They confirmed an Iron Age technology, more or less equivalent to that of Earth's Classical civilization. Exceptions occurred: for example, a few books, seemingly printed from hand-set type. How avidly those pages were ransacked! But the only illustrations were diagrams suitable to a geometry text in one case and a stonemason's manual in another. Did this culture taboo pictures of its members, or had the boat merely chanced on a home which possessed none?

The layout and contents of the house, and of the sheds when these were examined, gave scant clues. Nobody had expected better. Imagine yourself a nonhuman xenologist, visiting Earth before man went into space. What could you deduce from the residences and a few household items belonging to, say, a European, an Eskimo, a Congo pygmy, and a Japanese peasant? You might have wondered if the owners were of the same genus.

In time you could learn more. Turekian doubted that time would be given. He set Webner in a cold fury by his nagging to finish the survey and get back to the boat. At length the chief gave in. "Not that I don't plan a detailed study, mind you," he said. Scornfully: "Still, I suppose we can hold a conference, and I'll try to calm your fears."

After you had been out, the air in the craft smelled dead and the view in the screens looked dull. Turekian took a pipe from his pocket. "No," Webner told him.

"What?" The pilot was bemused.

"I won't have that foul thing in this crowded cabin."

"I don't mind," Yukiko said.

"I do," Webner replied, "and while we're down, I'm your captain."

Turekian reddened and obeyed. Discipline in space is steel hard, a matter of survival. A good leader gives it a soft sheath. Yukiko's eyes reproached Webner; her fingers dropped to rest on the pilot's arm. The xenologist saw. His mouth twitched sideways before he pinched it together.

"We're in trouble," Turekian said. "The sooner we haul mass out of here, the happier our insurance carriers will be."

"Nonsense," Webner snapped. "If anything, our problem is that we've terrified the dwellers. They may take days to send even a scout."

"They've already sent two. You had to shoot at them."

"I shot at a dangerous animal. Didn't you see those talons, those fangs? And a buffet from a wing that big— ignoring the claws on it—could break your neck."

Webner's gaze sought Yukiko's. He mainly addressed her: "Granted, they must be domesticated. I suspect they're used in the hunt, flown at game like hawks though working in packs like hounds. Conceivably the pair we encountered were, ah, sicced onto us from afar. But that they themselves are sophonts—out of the question."

Her murmur was uneven. "How can you be sure?"

Webner leaned back, bridged his fingers, and grew calmer while he lectured: "You realize the basic principle. All organisms make biological sense in their particular environments, or they become extinct. Reasoners are no exception—and are, furthermore, descended from nonreasoners which adapted to environments that had never been artificially modified.

"On nonterrestroid worlds, they can be quite outré by our standards, since they developed under unearthly conditions. On an essentially terrestroid planet, evolution basically parallels our own because it must. True, you get considerable variation. Like, say, hexapodal vertebrates liberating the forelimbs to grow hands and becoming centauroids, as on Woden. That's because the ancestral chordates were hexapods. On this world, you can see for yourself the higher animals are four-limbed.

"A brain capable of designing artifacts such as we observe here is useless without some equivalent of hands. Nature would never produce it. Therefore the inhabitants are bound to be bipeds, however different from us in detail. A foot which must double as a hand, and vice versa, would be too grossly inefficient in either function. Natural selection would weed out any mutants of that tendency, fast, long before intelligence could evolve.

"What do those ornithoids have in the way of hands?" He smiled his tight little smile.

"The claws on their wings?" Yukiko asked shyly.

"'Fraid not," Turekian said. "I got a fair look. They can grasp, sort of, but aren't built for manipulation."

"You saw how the fledgling uses them to cling to the parent," Webner stated. "Perhaps it climbs trees also. Earth has a bird with similar structures, the hoactzin. It loses them in adulthood. Here they may become extra weapons for the mature animal."

"The feet." Turekian scowled. "Two opposable digits flanking three straight ones. Could serve as hands."

"Then how does the creature get about on the ground?" Webner retorted. "Can't forge a tool in midair, you know, let alone dig ore and erect stone houses."

He wagged a finger. "Another, more fundamental point," he went on. "Flyers are too limited in mass. True, the gravity's weaker than on Earth, but air pressure's lower. Thus admissible wing loadings are about the same. The biggest birds that ever lumbered into Terrestrial skies weighed some fifteen kilos. Nothing larger could get aloft. Metabolism simply can't supply the power required. We established aboard ship, from specimens, that local biochemistry is close kin to our type. Hence it is not possible for those ornithoids to outweigh a maximal vulture. They're big, yes, and formidable. Nevertheless, that size has to be mostly feathers, hollow bones—spidery, kitelike skeletons anchoring thin flesh.

"Aram, you hefted several items today, such as a stone pot. Or consider one of the buckets, presumably used to bring water up from the river. What would you say the greatest weight is?"

Turekian scratched in his beard. "Maybe twenty kilos," he answered reluctantly.

"There! No flyer could lift that. It was always

superstition about eagles stealing lambs or babies. They weren't able to. The ornithoids are similarly handicapped. Who'd make utensils he can't carry?"

"M-m-m," Turekian growled rather than hummed. Webner pressed the attack:

"The mass of any flyer on a terrestroid planet is insufficient to include a big enough brain for true intelligence. The purely animal functions require virtually all those cells. Birds have at least lightened their burden, permitting a little more brain, by changing jaws to beaks. So have those ornithoids you called 'watchfalcons.' The big fellows have not."

He hesitated. "In fact," he said slowly, "I doubt if they can even be considered bright animals. They're likely stupid . . . and vicious. If we're set on again, we need have no compunctions about destroying them."

"Were you going to?" Yukiko whispered. "Couldn't he, she, it simply have been coming down for a quick, close look at you—unarmed as a peace gesture?"

"If intelligent, yes," Webner said. "If not, as I've proven to be the case, positively no. I saved us some nasty wounds. Perhaps I saved a life."

"The dwellers might object if we shoot at their property," Turekian said.

"They need only call off their, ah, dogs. In fact, the attack on us may not have been commanded, may have been brute reaction after panic broke the order of the pack." Webner rose. "Are you satisfied? We'll make thorough studies till nightfall, then leave gifts, withdraw, hope for a better reception when we see the indigenes have returned." A television pickup was customary among diplomatic presents of that kind.

Turekian shook his head. "Your logic's all right, I suppose. But it don't smell right somehow."

Webner started for the airlock.

"Me too?" Yukiko requested. "Please?"

"No," Turekian said. "I'd hate for you to be harmed."

"We're in no danger," she argued. "Our sidearms can handle any flyers that may arrive feeling mean. If we plant sensors around, no walking native can come within bowshot before we know. I feel caged." She aimed her smile at Webner.

The xenologist thawed. "Why not?" he said. "I can use a level-headed assistant." To Turekian: "Man the boat guns yourself if you wish."

"Like blazes," the pilot grumbled, and followed them.

He had to admit the leader knew his business. The former cursory search became a shrewd, efficient examination of object after object, measuring, photographing, commenting continuously into a minirecorder. Yukiko helped. On Survey, everybody must have some knowledge of everybody else's specialty. But Webner needed just one extra person.

"What can I do?" Turekian asked.

"Move an occasional heavy load," the other man said. "Keep watch on the forest. Stay out of my way."

Yukiko was too fascinated by the work to chide him. Turekian rumbled in his throat, stuffed his pipe, and slouched around the grounds alone, blowing furious clouds.

At the corral he gripped a rail and glowered. "You want feeding," he decided, went into a barn—unlike the house, its door was not secured—and found a haymow and pitchforks which, despite every strangeness of detail, reminded him of a backwoods colony on Hermes that he'd visited once, temporarily primitive because shipping space was taken by items more urgent than modern agromachines. The farmer had had a daughter.... He consoled himself with memories while he took out a mess of cinnamon-scented red herbage.

"You!"

Webner leaned from an upstairs window. "What're you about?" he called.

"Those critters are hungry," Turekian replied. "Listen to 'em."

"How do you know what their requirements are? Or the owners'? We're not here to play God, for your information. We're here to learn and, maybe, help. Take that stuff back where you got it."

Turekian swallowed rage—that Yukiko should have heard his humiliation—and complied. Webner was his captain till he regained the blessed sky.

Sky... birds.... He observed the "cotes." The pseudo-hawks fluttered about, indignant but too small to tackle him. Were the giant ornithoids kept partly as protection against large ground predators? Turekian studied the flock. Its members dozed, waddled, scratched the dirt, fat and placid, obviously long bred to tameness. Both types lacked the gill-like slits he had noticed....

A shadow. Turekian glanced aloft, snatched for his magnifier. Half a dozen giants were back. The noon sun flamed on their feathers. They were too high for him to see details.

He flipped the controls on his grav unit and made for the house. Webner and Yukiko were on the fifth floor. Turekian arced through a window. He had no eye, now, for the Spartan grace of the room. "They've arrived," he panted. "We better get in the boat quick."

Webner stepped onto the balcony. "No need," he said. "I hardly think they'll attack. If they do, we're safer here than crossing the yard."

"Might be smart to close the shutters," the girl said.

"And the door to this chamber," Webner agreed. "That'll stop them. They'll soon lose patience and wander off—if they attempt anything. Or if they do besiege us, we can shoot our way through them, or at worst relay a call for help via the boat, once *Olga*'s again over our horizon."

He had re-entered. Turekian took his place on the balcony and squinted upward. More winged shapes had joined the first several; and more came into view each second. They dipped, soared, circled through the wind, which made surf noises in the forest.

Unease crawled along the pilot's spine. "I don't like this half a bit," he said. "They don't act like plain beasts."

"Conceivably the dwellers plan to use them in an assault," Webner said. "If so, we may have to teach the dwellers about the cost of unreasoning hostility." His tone was less cool than the words, and sweat beaded his countenance.

Sparks in the magnifier field hurt Turekian's eyes. "I swear they're carrying metal," he said. "Listen, if they are intelligent—and out to get us, after you nearly killed one of 'em—the house is no place for us. Let's scramble. We may not have many more minutes."

"Yes, I believe we'd better, Vaughn," Yukiko urged. "We can't risk...being forced to burn down conscious beings...on their own land."

Maybe his irritation with the pilot spoke for Webner: "How often must I explain there is no such risk, yet? Instead, here's a chance to learn. What happens next could give us invaluable clues to understanding the whole ethos. We stay." To Turekian: "Forget about that alleged metal. Could be protective collars, I suppose. But take the supercharger off your imagination."

The other man froze where he stood.

"Aram." Yukiko seized his arm. He stared beyond her. "What's wrong?"

He shook himself. "Supercharger," he mumbled. "By God, yes."

Abruptly, in a bellow: "We're leaving! This second! They *are* the dwellers, and they've gathered the whole countryside against us!"

"Hold your tongue," Webner said, "or I'll charge insubordination."

Laughter rattled in Turekian's breast. "Uh-uh. Mutiny."

He crouched and lunged. His fist rocketed before him. Yukiko's cry joined the thick smack as knuckles hit—not the chin, which is too hazardous, the solar plexus. Air whoofed from Webner. His eyes glazed. He folded over, partly conscious but unable to stand while his diaphragm spasmed. Turekian gathered him in his arms. "To the boat!" the pilot shouted. "Hurry, girl!"

His grav unit wouldn't carry two, simply gentled his fall when he leaped from the balcony. He dared not stop to adjust the controls on Webner's. Bearing his chief, he pounded across the flagstones. Yukiko came above. "Go ahead!" Turekian bawled. "Get into shelter, for God's sake!"

"Not till you can," she answered. "I'll cover you." He was helpless to prevent her.

The scores above had formed themselves into a vast revolving wheel. It tilted. The first flyers peeled off and roared downward. The rest came after.

Arrows whistled ahead of them. A trumpet sounded. Turekian dodged, zigzag over the meadow. Yukiko's gun clapped. She shot to miss, but belike the flashes put those archers—and, now, spearthrowers—off their aim. Shafts sang wickedly around. One edge grazed Webner's neck. He screamed.

Yukiko darted to open the boat's airlock. While she did, Turekian dropped Webner and straddled him, blaster drawn. The leading flyer hurtled close. Talons of the right foot, which was not a foot at all but a hand, gripped a sword curved like a scimitar. For an instant, Turekian looked squarely into the golden eyes, knew a brave male defending his home, and also shot to miss.

In a brawl of air, the native sheered off. The valve swung wide. Yukiko flitted through. Turekian dragged Webner, then stood in the lock chamber till the entry was shut.

Missiles clanged on the hull. None would pierce. Turekian let himself join Webner for a moment of shuddering in each other's embrace, before he went forward to Yukiko and the raising of his vessel.

When you know what to expect, a little, you can lay plans. We next sought the folk of Ythri, as the planet is called by its most advanced culture, a thousand kilometers from the triumph which surely prevailed in the mountains. Approached with patience, caution, and symbolisms appropriate to their psyches, they welcomed us rapturously. Before we left, they'd thought of sufficient inducements to trade that I'm sure they'll have spacecraft of their own in a few generations.

Still, they are as fundamentally territorial as man is fundamentally sexual, and we'd better bear that in mind.

The reason lies in their evolution. It does for every drive in every animal everywhere. The Ythrian is carnivorous, aside from various sweet fruits. Carnivores require larger regions per individual than herbivores or omnivores do, in spite of the fact that meat has more calories per kilo than most vegetable matter. Consider how each antelope needs a certain amount of space, and how many antelope are needed to maintain a pride of lions. Xenologists have written thousands of papers on the correlations between diet and genotypical personality in sophonts.

I have my doubts about the value of those papers. At least, they missed the possibility of a race like the Ythrians, whose extreme territoriality and individualism—with the consequences to governments, mores, arts, faiths, and souls—come from the extreme appetite of the body.

They mass as high as thirty kilos; yet they can lift an equal weight into the air or, unhampered, fly like demons. Hence they maintain civilization without the need to crowd together in cities. Their townspeople are mostly wing-clipped criminals and slaves. Today their wiser heads hope robots will end the need for that.

Hands? The original talons, modified for manipulating. Feet? Those claws on the wings, a juvenile feature which persisted and developed, just as man's large head and sparse hair derive from the juvenile or fetal ape. The forepart of the wing skeleton consists of humerus, radius, and ulnar, much as in true birds. These lock together in flight. Aground, when the wing is folded downward, they produce a "knee" joint. Bones grow from their base to make the claw-foot. Three fused digits, immensely lengthened, sweep backward to be the alatan which braces the rest of that tremendous wing and can, when desired, give additional support on the surface. To rise, the Ythrians usually do a handstand during the initial upstroke. It takes less than a second.

Oh, yes, they are slow and awkward afoot. They manage, though. Big and beweaponed, instantly ready to mount the wind, they need fear no beast of prey.

You ask where the power comes from to swing this hugeness through the sky. The oxidation of food, what else? Hence the demand of each household for a great hunting or ranching demesne. The limiting factor is the oxygen supply. A molecule in the blood can carry more than hemoglobin does, but the gas must be furnished. Turekian first realized how that happens. The Ythrian has lungs, a passive system resembling ours. In addition he has his supercharger, evolved from the gills of an amphibianlike ancestor. Worked in bellows fashion by the flight muscles, connecting directly with the bloodstream, those air-intake organs let him burn his fuel as fast as necessary.

I wonder how it feels to be so alive.

I remember how Yukiko Sachansky stood in the curve of Aram Turekian's arm, under a dawn heaven, and watched the farewell dance the Ythrians gave for us, and cried through tears: "To fly like that! To fly like that!"

This happened early in the course of starflight. The tale is in *Far Adventure* by Maeve Downey, the autobiography of a planetologist. Aside from scientific reports which the same expedition rendered, it appears to be the first outside account of us.

You well know how the Discovery gale-seized those peoples who had the learning to see what it meant, so that erelong all Ythri could never again speak in full understanding, through books and songs and art, with the ancestors. The dealings with Terrans as these returned, first for study and later for trade; the quest and strife which slowly won for us our own modern technics; the passion of history through life after life: these are in many writings. What is less known than it should be is how the Terrans themselves were faring meanwhile.

Their Commonwealth had been formed out of numerous *nations*. A few more came into being and membership afterward. To explain the concept "nation" is stiffly upwind. As a snatching at the task—Within a sharply defined territory dwell a large number of humans who, in a subtle sense which goes beyond private property or shared range, identify their souls with this land and with each other. Law and mutual obligation are maintained less by usage and pride than by physical violence or the threat thereof on the part of that institution called the government. It is as if a single group could permanently cry Oherran against the entire rest of society, bring death and devastation wherever it chose, and claimed this as an exclusive right. Compliance and assistance are said to be honorable, resistance dishonorable, especially when one nation is at war with another—for each of these entities has powers which are limited not by justice, decency, or prudence, but only by its own strength.

You well know how most humans on Avalon still maintain a modified form of government. However, this is of sharply limited force, both in practice and in law. It is merely their way. You cannot mind-grasp the modern Terran Empire without knowing what a nation truly is.

To curb these inordinate prerogatives of a few, whose quarrels and mismanagement threatened to lay waste their native planet, the Commonwealth was finally established, as a nation of nations. This did not happen quickly, easily, or rationally. The story of it is long and terrible. Nevertheless, it happened: and, for a time, the Commonwealth was on the whole a benign influence. Under its protection, both prosperity and freedom from demands flourished ever more greatly.

Meanwhile exploration exploded throughout this part of the galaxy. Human-habitable worlds which had no intelligent life of their own began to be settled. Our species, in slow youngling wise, began to venture from its nest, at first usually in a flock with Terrans.

The same expedition which made the Discovery of Ythri had chanced upon Avalon. Though rich prey for colonists, at the time it lay too far from Sol and remained nameless. The season came at last for taking real knowledge of it. Because Ythrians were also a-wing in this, there happened an incident which is worth the telling here. Rennhi found the account, transcribed from a recording made on Terra, in the archives of the University of Fleurville upon the planet Esperance. It was originally part of a private correspondence between two humans, preserved by the heirs of the recipient after his death; a visiting historian obtained a copy but never published it. God hunted down all persons concerned so long ago that no pride will be touched by planting the story here.

The value of it lies in the human look upon us, a look which tried to reach down into the spirit and thereby, maychance, now opens for us a glimpse into theirs.

THE PROBLEM OF PAIN

Maybe only a Christian can understand this story. In that case I don't qualify. But I do take an interest in religion, as part of being an amateur psychologist, and—for the grandeur of its language if nothing else—a Bible is among the reels that accompany me wherever I go. This was one reason Peter Berg told me what had happened in his past. He desperately needed to make sense of it, and no priest he'd talked to had quite laid his questions to rest. There was an outside chance that an outside viewpoint like mine would see what a man within the faith couldn't.

His other reason was simple loneliness. We were on Lucifer, as part of a study corporation. That world is well named. It will never be a real colony for any beings whose ancestors evolved amidst clean greenery. But it might be marginally habitable, and if so, its mineral wealth would be worth exploiting. Our job was to determine whether that was true. The gentlest-looking environment holds a thousand death traps until you have learned what the difficulties are and how to grip them. (Earth is no exception.) Sometimes you find problems which can't be solved economically, or can't be solved at all. Then you write off the area or the entire planet, and look for another.

We'd contracted to work three standard years on

Lucifer. The pay was munificent, but presently we realized that no bank account could buy back one day we might have spent beneath a kindlier sun. It was a knowledge we carefully avoided discussing with team-mates.

About midway through, Peter Berg and I were assigned to do an in-depth investigation of a unique cycle in the ecology of the northern middle latitudes. This meant that we settled down for weeks—which ran into months—in a sample region, well away from everybody else to minimize human disturbances. An occasional supply flitter gave us our only real contact; electronics were no proper substitute, especially when that hell-violent star was forever disrupting them.

Under such circumstances, you come to know your partner maybe better than you know yourself. Pete and I got along well. He's a big, sandy-haired, freckle-faced young man, altogether dependable, with enough kind-liness, courtesy, and dignity that he need not make a show of them. Soft-spoken, he's a bit short in the humor department. Otherwise I recommend him as a compan-ion. He has a lot to tell from his own wanderings, yet he'll listen with genuine interest to your memories and brags; he's well read too, and a good cook when his turn comes; he plays chess at just about my level of skill.

I already knew he wasn't from Earth, had in fact never been there, but from Aeneas, nearly 200 light-years distant, more than 300 from Lucifer. And, while he'd gotten an education at the new little university in Nova Roma, he was raised in the outback. Besides, that town is only a faroff colonial capital. It helped explain his utter commitment to belief in a God who became flesh and died for love of man. Not that I scoff. When he said his prayers, night and morning in our one-room shelterdome, trustingly as a child, I didn't rag him nor he reproach me. Of course, over the weeks, we came more and more to talk about such matters.

At last he told me of that which haunted him.

We'd been out through the whole of one of Lucifer's long, long days; we'd toiled, we'd sweated, we'd itched and stunk and gotten grimy and staggered from weariness, we'd come near death once: and we'd found the uranium-concentrating root which was the key to the whole weirdness around us. We came back to base as day's fury was dying in the usual twilight gale; we washed, ate something, went to sleep with the hiss of storm-blown dust for a lullaby. Ten or twelve hours later we awoke and saw, through the vitryl panels, stars cold and crystalline beyond this thin air, auroras aflame, landscape hoar, and the twisted things we called trees all sheathed in glittering ice.

"Nothing we can do now till dawn," I said, "and we've earned a celebration." So we prepared a large meal, elaborate as possible—breakfast or supper, what relevance had that here? We drank wine in the course of it, and afterward much brandy while we sat, side by side in our loungers, watching the march of constellations which Earth or Aeneas never saw. And we talked. Finally we talked of God.

"—maybe you can give me an idea," Pete said. In the dim light, his face bore a struggle. He stared before him and knotted his fingers.

"M-m, I dunno," I said carefully. "To be honest, no offense meant, theological conundrums strike me as silly."

He gave me a direct blue look. His tone was soft: "That is, you feel the paradoxes don't arise if we don't insist on believing?"

"Yes. I respect your faith, Pete, but it's not mine. And if I did suppose a, well, a spiritual principle or something is behind the universe—" I gestured at the high and terrible sky— "in the name of reason, can we confine, can we understand whatever made *that,* in the bounds of one little dogma?"

"No. Agreed. How could finite minds grasp the infinite? We can see parts of it, though, that've been revealed to us." He drew breath. "'Way back before space travel, the Church decided Jesus had come only to Earth, to man. If other intelligent races need salvation—and obviously a lot of them do!—God will have made His suitable arrangements for them. Sure. However, this does not mean Christianity is not true, or that certain different beliefs are not false."

"Like, say, polytheism, wherever you find it?"

"I think so. Besides, religions evolve. The primitive faiths see God, or the gods, as power; the higher ones see Him as justice; the highest see Him as love." Abruptly he fell silent. I saw his fist clench, until he grabbed up his glass and drained it and refilled it in nearly a single savage motion.

"I must believe that," he whispered.

I waited a few seconds, in Lucifer's crackling night stillness, before saying: "An experience made you wonder?"

"Made me . . . disturbed. Mind if I tell you?"

"Certainly not." I saw he was about to open himself; and I may be an unbeliever, but I know what is sacred.

"Happened about five years ago. I was on my first real job. So was the—" his voice stumbled the least bit— "the wife I had then. We were fresh out of school and apprenticeship, fresh into marriage." In an effort at detachment: "Our employers weren't human. They were Ythrians. Ever heard of them?"

I sought through my head. The worlds, races, beings are unknowably many, in this tiny corner of this one dust-mote galaxy which we have begun to explore a little. "Ythrians, Ythrians . . . wait. Do they fly?"

"Yes. Surely one of the most glorious sights in creation. Your Ythrian isn't as heavy as a man, of course; adults mass around twenty-five or thirty kilos—but his wingspan goes up to six meters, and when he soars with those feathers shining gold-brown in the light, or stoops in a crack of thunder and whistle of wind—"

"Hold on," I said. "I take it Ythri's a terrestroid planet?"

"Pretty much. Somewhat smaller and drier than Earth, somewhat thinner atmosphere—about like Aeneas, in fact, which it's not too far from as interstellar spaces go. You can live there without special protection. The biochemistry's quite similar to ours."

"Then how the devil can those creatures be that size? The wing loading's impossible, when you have only cell tissue to oxidize for power. They'd never get off the ground."

"Ah, but they have antlibranchs as well." Pete smiled, though it didn't go deep. "Those look like three gills, sort of, on either side, below the wings. They're actually more like bellows, pumped by the wing muscles. Extra oxygen is forced directly into the bloodstream during flight. A biological supercharger system."

"Well, I'll be a ... never mind what." I considered, in delight, this new facet of nature's inventiveness, "Um-mm ... if they spend energy at that rate, they've got to have appetites to match."

"Right. They're carnivores. A number of them are still hunters. The advanced societies are based on ranching. In either case, obviously, it takes a lot of meat animals, a lot of square kilometers, to support one Ythrian. So they're fiercely territorial. They live in small groups—single families or extended households—which attack, with intent to kill, any uninvited outsider who doesn't obey an order to leave."

"And still they're civilized enough to hire humans for space exploration?"

"Uh-huh. Remember, being flyers, they've never needed to huddle in cities in order to have ready communication. They do keep a few towns, mining or manufacturing centers, but those are inhabited mostly by wing-clipped slaves. I'm glad to say that institution's dying out as they get modern machinery."

"By trade?" I guessed.

"Yes," Pete replied. "When the first Grand Survey discovered them, their most advanced culture was at an Iron Age level of technology; no industrial revolution, but plenty of sophisticated minds around, and subtle philosophies." He paused. "That's important to my question—that the Ythrians, at least of the Planha-speaking *choths,* are not barbarians and have not been for many centuries. They've had their equivalents of

Socrates, Aristotle, Confucius, Galileo, yes, and their prophets and seers."

After another mute moment: "They realized early what the visitors from Earth implied, and set about attracting traders and teachers. Once they had some funds, they sent their promising young folk off-planet to study. I met several at my own university, which is why I got my job offer. By now they have a few spacecraft and native crews. But you'll understand, their technical people are spread thin, and in several branches of knowledge they have no experts. So they employ humans."

He went on to describe the typical Ythrian: warm-blooded, feathered like a golden eagle (though more intricately) save for a crest on the head, and yet not a bird. Instead of a beak, a blunt muzzle full of fangs juts before two great eyes. The female bears her young alive. While she does not nurse them, they have lips to suck the juices of meat and fruits, wherefore their speech is not hopelessly unlike man's. What were formerly the legs have evolved into arms bearing three taloned fingers, flanked by two thumbs, on each hand. Aground, the huge wings fold downward and, with the help of claws at the angles, give locomotion. That is slow and awkward—but aloft, ah!

"They become more alive, flying, than we ever do," Pete murmured. His gaze had lost itself in the shuddering auroras overhead. "They must: the metabolic rate they have then, and the space around them, speed, sky, a hundred winds to ride on and be kissed by. . . . That's what made me think Enherrian, in particular, believed more keenly than I could hope to. I saw him and others dancing, high, high in the air, swoops, glides, hoverings, sunshine molten on their plumes; I asked what they did, and was told they were honoring God."

He sighed. "Or that's how I translated the Planha phrase, rightly or wrongly," he went on. "Olga and I had taken a cram course, and our Ythrian teammates all knew Anglic; but nobody's command of the foreign tongue was perfect. It couldn't be. Multiple billion years of separate existence, evolution, history—what a miracle that we could think as alike as we did!

"However, you could call Enherrian religious, same as you could call me that, and not be too grotesquely off the mark. The rest varied, just like humans. Some were also devout, some less, some agnostics or atheists; two were pagans, following the bloody rites of what was called the Old Faith. For that matter, my Olga—" the knuckles stood forth where he grasped his tumbler of brandy— "had tried, for my sake, to believe as I did, and couldn't.

"Well. The New Faith interested me more. It was new only by comparison—at least half as ancient as mine. I hoped for a chance to study it, to ask questions and compare ideas. I really knew nothing except that it was monotheistic, had sacraments and a theology though no official priesthood, upheld a high ethical and moral standard—for Ythrians, I mean. You can't expect a race which can only live by killing animals, and has an oestrous cycle, and is incapable by instinct of maintaining what we'd recognize as a true nation or government, and on and on—you can't expect them to resemble Christians much. God has given them a different message. I wished to know what. Surely we could learn from it." Again he paused. "After all . . . being a faith with a long tradition . . . and not static but a seeking, a history of prophets and saints and believers . . . I thought it must know God is love. Now what form would God's love take to an Ythrian?"

He drank. I did too, before asking cautiously: "Uh, where was this expedition?"

Pete stirred in his lounger. "To a system about eighty light-years from Ythri's," he answered. "The original Survey crew had discovered a terrestroid planet there. They didn't bother to name it. Prospective colonists would choose their own name anyway. Those could be human or Ythrian, conceivably both—if the environment proved out.

"Offhand, the world—our group called it, unofficially, Gray, after that old captain—the world looked brilliantly promising. It's intermediate in size between Earth and

Ythri, surface gravity 0.8 terrestrial; slightly more irradiation, from a somewhat yellower sun, than Earth gets, which simply makes it a little warmer; axial tilt, therefore seasonal variations, a bit less than terrestrial; length of year about three-quarters of ours, length of day a bit under half; one small, close-in, bright moon; biochemistry similar to ours—we could eat most native things, though we'd require imported crops and livestock to supplement the diet. All in all, seemingly well-nigh perfect."

"Rather remote to attract Earthlings at this early date," I remarked. "And from your description, the Ythrians won't be able to settle it for quite a while either."

"They think ahead," Pete responded. "Besides, they have scientific curiosity and, yes, in them perhaps even more than in the humans who went along, a spirit of adventure. Oh, it was a wonderful thing to be young in that band!"

He had not yet reached thirty, but somehow his cry was not funny.

He shook himself. "Well, we had to make sure," he said. "Besides planetology, ecology, chemistry, oceanography, meteorology, a million and a million mysteries to unravel for their own sakes—we must scout out the death traps, whatever those might be.

"At first everything went like Mary's smile on Christmas morning. The spaceship set us off—it couldn't be spared to linger in orbit—and we established base on the largest continent. Soon our hundred-odd dispersed across the globe, investigating this or that. Olga and I made part of a group on the southern shore, where a great gulf swarmed with life. A strong current ran eastward from there, eventually striking an archipelago which deflected it north. Flying over those waters, we spied immense, I mean immense, patches—no, floating islands—of vegetation, densely interwoven, grazed on by monstrous marine creatures, no doubt supporting any number of lesser plant and animal species.

"We wanted a close look. Our camp's sole aircraft wasn't good for that. Anyhow, it was already in demand for a dozen jobs. We had boats, though, and launched one. Our crew was Enherrian, his wife Whell, their grown children Rusa and Arrach, my beautiful new bride Olga, and me. We'd take three or four Gray days to reach the nearest atlantis weed, as Olga dubbed it. Then we'd be at least a week exploring before we turned back—a vacation, a lark, a joy."

He tossed off his drink and reached for the bottle. "You ran into grief," I prompted.

"No." He bent his lips upward, stiffly. "It ran into us. A hurricane. Unpredicted; we knew very little about that planet. Given the higher solar energy input and, especially, the rapid rotation, the storm was more violent than would've been possible on Earth. We could only run before it and pray.

"At least, I prayed, and imagined that Enherrian did."

Wind shrieked, hooted, yammered, hit flesh with fists and cold knives. Waves rumbled in that driven air, black and green and fang-white, fading from view as the sun sank behind the cloud-roil which hid it. Often a monster among them loomed castlelike over the gunwale. The boat slipped by, spilled into the troughs, rocked onto the crests and down again. Spindrift, icy, stinging, bitter on lips and tongue, made a fog across her length.

"We'll live if we can keep sea room," Enherrian had said when the fury first broke. "She's well-found. The engine capacitors have ample kilowatt-hours in them. Keep her bow on and we'll live."

But the currents had them now, where the mighty gulfstream met the outermost islands and its waters churned, recoiled, spun about and fought. Minute by minute, the riptides grew wilder. They made her yaw till she was broadside on and surges roared over her deck; they shocked her onto her beam ends, and the hull became a toning bell.

Pete, Olga, and Whell were in the cabin, trying to rest before their next watch. That was no longer possible. The Ythrian female locked hands and wing-claws around the net-covered framework wherein she had slept, hung on, and uttered nothing. In the wan glow of a single overhead fluoro, among thick restless shadows, her eyes gleamed topaz. They did not seem to look at the crampedness around—at what, then?

The humans had secured themselves by a line onto a lower bunk. They embraced, helping each other fight the leaps and swings which tried to smash them against the sides. Her fair hair on his shoulder was the last brightness in his cosmos. "I love you," she said, over and over, through hammerblows and groans. "Whatever happens, I love you, Pete, I thank you for what you've given me."

"And you," he would answer. *And You,* he would think. *Though You won't take her, not yet, will You? Me, yes, if that's Your will. But not Olga. It'd leave Your creation too dark.*

A wing smote the cabin door. Barely to be heard through the storm, an Ythrian voice—high, whistly, but reasonant out of full lungs—shouted: "Come topside!"

Whell obeyed at once, the Bergs as fast as they could slip on life jackets. Having taken no personal grav units along, they couldn't fly free if they went overboard. Dusk raved around them. Pete could just see Rusa and Arrach in the stern, fighting the tiller. Enherrian stood before him and pointed forward. "Look," the captain said. Pete, who had no nictitating membranes, must shield eyes with fingers to peer athwart the hurricane. He saw a deeper darkness hump up from a wall of white; he heard surf crash.

"We can't pull free," Enherrian told him. "Between wind and current—too little power. We'll likely be wrecked. Make ready."

Olga's hand went briefly to her mouth. She huddled against Pete and might have whispered, "Oh, no." Then she straightened, swung back down into the cabin, braced herself as best she could and started assembling the most vital things stored there. He saw that he loved her still more than he had known.

The same calm descended on him. Nobody had time to be afraid. He got busy too. The Ythrians could carry a limited weight of equipment and supplies, but sharply limited under these conditions. The humans, buoyed by their jackets, must carry most. They strapped it to their bodies.

When they re-emerged, the boat was in the shoals. Enherrian ordered them to take the rudder. His wife, son, and daughter stood around—on hands which clutched the rails with prey-snatching strength—and spread their wings to give a bit of shelter. The captain clung to the cabin top as lookout. His yelled commands reached the Bergs dim, tattered.

"Hard right!" Upward cataracts burst on a skerry to port. It glided past, was lost in murk. "Two points starboard—steady!" The hull slipped between a pair of rocks. Ahead was a narrow opening in the island's sheer black face. To a lagoon, to safety? Surf raged on either side of that gate, and everywhere else.

The passage was impossible. The boat struck, threw Olga off her feet and Arrach off her perch. Full reverse engine could not break loose. The deck canted. A billow and a billow smashed across.

Pete was in the water. It grabbed him, pulled him under, dragged him over a sharp bottom. He thought: *Into Your hands, God. Spare Olga, please, please*—and the sea spewed him back up for one gulp of air.

Wallowing in blindness, he tried to gauge how the breakers were acting, what he should do. If he could somehow belly-surf in, he might make it, he barely might.... He was on the neck of a rushing giant, it climbed and climbed, it shoved him forward at what he knew was lunatic speed. He saw the reef on which it was about to smash him and knew he was dead.

Talons closed on his jacket. Air brawled beneath wings. The Ythrian could not raise him, but could draw him aside ... the bare distance needed, and Pete went past the rock whereon his bones were to have been crushed, down into the smother and chaos beyond. The Ythrian didn't get free in time. He glimpsed the plumes go under, as he himself did. They never rose.

He beat on, and on, without end.

He floated in water merely choppy, swart palisades to

right and left, a slope of beach ahead. He peered into the clamorous dark and found nothing. "Olga," he croaked. "Olga. Olga."

Wings shadowed him among the shadows. "Get ashore before an undertow eats you!" Enherrian whooped, and beat his way off in search.

Pete crawled to gritty sand, fell, and let annihilation have him. He wasn't unconscious long. When he revived, Rusa and Whell were beside him. Enherrian was further inland. The captain hauled on a line he had snubbed around a tree. Olga floated at the other end. She had no strength left, but he had passed a bight beneath her arms and she was alive.

At wolf-gray dawn the wind had fallen to gale force or maybe less, and the cliffs shielded lagoon and strand from it. Overhead it shrilled, and outside the breakers cannonaded, their rage aquiver through the island. Pete and Olga huddled together, a shared cloak across their shoulders. Enherrian busied himself checking the salvaged material. Whell sat on the hindbones of her wings and stared seaward. Moisture gleamed on her grizzled feathers like tears.

Rusa flew in from the reefs and landed. "No trace," he said. His voice was emptied by exhaustion. "Neither the boat nor Arrach." Through the rust in his own brain, Pete noticed the order of those words.

Nevertheless—He leaned toward the parents and brother of Arrach, who had been beautiful and merry and had sung to them by moonlight. "How can we say—?" he began, realized he didn't have Planha words, and tried in Anglic: "How can we say how sorry we both are?"

"No necessity," Rusa answered.

"She died saving me!"

"And what you were carrying, which we needed badly." Some energy returned to Rusa. He lifted his head and its crest. "She had deathpride, our lass."

Afterward Pete, in his search for meaning, would learn about that Ythrian concept. "Courage" is too simple and weak a translation. Certain Old Japanese words come closer, though they don't really bear the same value either.

Whell turned her hawk gaze full upon him. "Did you see anything of what happened in the water?" she asked. He was too unfamiliar with her folk to interpret the tone: today he thinks it was loving. He did know that, being creatures of seasonal rut, Ythrians are less sexually motivated than man is, but probably treasure their young even more. The strongest bond between male and female is children, who are what life is all about.

"No, I ... I fear not," he stammered.

Enherrian reached out to lay claws, very gently and briefly, on his wife's back. "Be sure she fought well," he said. "She gave God honor." (Glory? Praise? Adoration? His due?)

Does he mean she prayed, made her confession, while she drowned? The question dragged itself through Pete's weariness and caused him to murmur: "She's in heaven now." Again he was forced to use Anglic words.

Enherrian gave him a look which he could have sworn was startled. "What do you say? Arrach is dead."

"Why, her ... her spirit—"

"Will be remembered in pride." Enherrian resumed his work.

Olga said it for Pete: "So you don't believe the spirit outlives the body?"

"How could it?" Enherrian snapped. "Why should it?" His motions, his posture, the set of his plumage added: Leave me alone.

Pete thought: *Well, many faiths, including high ones, including some sects which call themselves Christian, deny immortality. How sorry I feel for these my friends, who don't know they will meet their beloved afresh!*

They will, regardless. It makes no sense that God, Who created what is because in His goodness he wished to share existence, would shape a soul only to break it and throw it away.

Never mind. The job on hand is to keep Olga alive, in her dear body. "Can I help?"

"Yes, check our medical kit," Enherrian said.

It had come through undamaged in its box. The items

for human use—stimulants, sedatives, anesthetics, antitoxins, antibiotics, coagulants, healing promoters, et standard cetera—naturally outnumbered those for Ythrians. There hasn't been time to develop a large scientific pharmacopoeia for the latter species. True, certain materials work on both, as does the surgical and monitoring equipment. Pete distributed pills which took the pain out of bruises and scrapes, the heaviness out of muscles. Meanwhile Rusa collected wood, Whell started and tended a fire, Olga made breakfast. They had considerable food, mostly freeze-dried, gear to cook it, tools like knives and a hatchet, cord, cloth, flashbeams, two blasters and abundant recharges: what they required for survival.

"It may be insufficient," Enherrian said. "The portable radio transceiver went down with Arrach. The boat's transmitter couldn't punch a call through that storm, and now the boat's on the bottom—nothing to see from the air, scant metal to register on a detector."

"Oh, they'll check on us when the weather slacks off," Olga said. She caught Pete's hand in hers. He felt the warmth.

"If their flitter survived the hurricane, which I doubt," Enherrian stated. "I'm convinced the camp was also struck. We had built no shelter for the flitter, our people will have been too busy saving themselves to secure it, and I think that this thin shell was tumbled about and broken. If I'm right, they'll have to call for an aircraft from elsewhere, which may not be available at once. In either case, we could be anywhere in a huge territory; and the expedition has no time or personnel for an indefinite search. They will seek us, aye; however, if we are not found before an arbitrary date—" A ripple passed over the feathers of face and neck; a human would have shrugged.

"What . . . can we do?" the girl asked.

"Clear a sizeable area in a plainly artificial pattern, or heap fuel for beacon fires should a flitter pass within sight—whichever is practicable. If nothing comes of that, we should consider building a raft or the like."

"Or modify a life jacket for me," Rusa suggested, "and I can try to fly to the mainland."

Enherrian nodded. "We must investigate the possibilities. First let's get a real rest."

The Ythrians were quickly asleep, squatted on their locked wing joints like idols of a forgotten people. Pete and Olga felt more excited and wandered a distance off, hand in hand.

Above the crag-enclosed beach, the island rose toward a crest which he estimated as three kilometers away. If it was in the middle, this was no large piece of real estate. Nor did he see adequate shelter. A mat of mossy, intensely green plants squeezed out any possibility of forest. A few trees stood isolated. Their branches tossed in the wind. He noticed particularly one atop a great outcrop nearby, gaunt brown trunk and thin leaf-fringed boughs that whipped insanely about. Blossoms, torn from vines, blew past, and they were gorgeous; but there would be naught to live on here, and he wasn't hopeful about learning, in time, how to catch Gray's equivalent of fish.

"Strange about them, isn't it?" Olga murmured.

"Eh?" He came, startled, out of his preoccupations.

She gestured at the Ythrians. "Them. The way they took poor Arrach's death."

"Well, you can't judge them by our standards. Maybe they feel grief less than we would, or maybe their culture demands stoicism." He looked at her and did not look away again. "To be frank, darling, I can't really mourn either. I'm too happy to have you back."

"And I you—oh, Pete, Pete, my only—"

They found a secret spot and made love. He saw nothing wrong in that. Do you ever in this life come closer to the wonder which is God?

Afterward they returned to their companions. Thus the clash of wings awoke them, hours later. They scrambled from their bedrolls and saw the Ythrians swing aloft.

The wind was strong and loud as yet, though easing off in fickleness, flaws, downdrafts, whirls, and eddies. Clouds were mostly gone. Those which remained raced gold and hot orange before a sun low in the west, across blue serenity. The lagoon glittered purple, the greensward lay aglow. It had warmed up till rich odors of growth, of flowers, blent with the sea-salt.

And splendid in the sky danced Enherrian, Whell, and Rusa. They wheeled, soared, pounced, and rushed back into light which ran molten off their pinions. They chanted, and fragments blew down to the humans: *"High flew your spirit on many winds. . . . be always remembered. . . ."*

"What *is* that?" Olga breathed.

"Why, they—they—" The knowledge broke upon Pete. "They're holding a service for Arrach."

He knelt and said a prayer for her soul's repose. But he wondered if she, who had belonged to the air, would truly want rest. And his eyes could not leave her kindred.

Enherrian screamed a hunter's challenge and rushed down at the earth. He flung himself meteoric past the stone outcrop Pete had seen; for an instant the man gasped, believing he would be shattered; then he rose, triumphant.

He passed by the lean tree of thin branches. Gusts flailed them about. A nearly razor edge took off his left wing. Blood spurted; Ythrian blood is royal purple. Somehow Enherrian slewed around and made a crash landing on the bluff top, just beyond range of what has since been named the surgeon tree.

Pete yanked the medikit to him and ran. Olga wailed, briefly, and followed. When they reached the scene, they found that Whell and Rusa had pulled feathers from their breasts to try staunching the wound.

Evening, night, day, evening, night.

Enherrian sat before a campfire. Its light wavered, picked him red out of shadow and let him half-vanish again, save for the unblinking yellow eyes. His wife and son supported him. Stim, cell-freeze, and plasma surrogate had done their work, and he could speak in a weak roughness. The bandages on his stump were a nearly glaring white.

Around crowded shrubs which, by day, showed low and russet-leaved. They filled a hollow on the far side of the island, to which Enherrian had been carried on an improvised litter. Their odor was rank, in an atmosphere once more subtropically hot, and they clutched at feet with raking twigs. But this was the most sheltered spot his companions could find, and he might die in a new storm on the open beach.

He looked through smoke, at the Bergs, who sat as close together as they were able. He said—the surf growled faintly beneath his words, while never a leaf rustled in the breathless dark—"I have read that your people can make a lost part grow forth afresh."

Pete couldn't answer. He tried but couldn't. It was Olga who had the courage to say, "We can do it for ourselves. None except ourselves." She laid her head on her man's breast and wept.

Well, you need a lot of research to unravel a genetic code, a lot of development to make the molecules of heredity repeat what they did in the womb. Science hasn't had time yet for other races. It never will for all. They are too many.

"As I thought," Enherrian said. "Nor can a proper prosthesis be engineered in my lifetime. I have few years left; an Ythrian who cannot fly soon becomes sickly."

"Grav units—" Pete faltered.

The scorn in those eyes was like a blow. Dead metal to raise you, who have had wings?

Fierce and haughty though the Ythrian is, his quill-clipped slaves have never rebelled: for they are only half-alive. Imagine yourself, human male, castrated. Enherrian might flap his remaining wing and the stump to fill his blood with air; but he would have nothing he could do with that extra energy, it would turn inward and corrode his body, perhaps at last his mind.

For a second, Whell laid an arm around him.

"You will devise a signal tomorrow," Enherrian said, "and start work on it. Too much time has already been wasted."

Before they slept, Pete managed to draw Whell aside. "He needs constant care, you know," he whispered to her in the acrid booming gloom. "The drugs got him over the shock, but he can't tolerate more and he'll be very weak."

True, she said with feathers rather than voice. Aloud: "Olga shall nurse him. She cannot get around as easily as Rusa or me, and lacks your physical strength. Besides, she can prepare meals and the like for us."

Pete nodded absently. He had a dread to explain. "Uh . . . uh . . . do you think—well, I mean in your ethic, in the New Faith—might Enherrian put an end to himself?" And he wondered if God would really blame the captain.

Her wings and tail spread, her crest erected, she glared. "You say that of him?" she shrilled. Seeing his concern, she eased, even made a *krrr* noise which might answer to a chuckle. "No, no, he has his deathpride. He would never rob God of honor."

After survey and experiment, the decision was to hack a giant cross in the island turf. That growth couldn't be ignited, and what wood was burnable—deadfall—was too scant and stingy of smoke for a beacon.

The party had no spades; the vegetable mat was thick and tough; the toil became brutal. Pete, like Whell and Rusa, would return to camp and topple into sleep. He wouldn't rouse till morning, to gulp his food and plod off to labor. He grew gaunt, bearded, filthy, numb-brained, sore in every cell.

Thus he did not notice how Olga was waning. Enherrian was mending, somewhat, under her care. She did her jobs, which were comparatively light, and would have been ashamed to complain of headaches, giddiness, diarrhea, and nausea. Doubtless she imagined she suffered merely from reaction to disaster, plus a sketchy and ill-balanced diet, plus heat and brilliant sun and— She'd cope.

The days were too short for work, the nights too short for sleep. Pete's terror was that he would see a flitter pass and vanish over the horizon before the Ythrians could hail it. Then they might try sending Rusa for help. But that was a long, tricky flight; and the gulf coast camp was due to be struck rather soon anyway.

Sometimes he wondered dimly how he and Olga might

do if marooned on Gray. He kept enough wits to dismiss his fantasy for what it was. Take the simple fact that native life appeared to lack certain vitamins—

Then one darkness, perhaps a terrestrial week after the shipwreck, he was roused by her crying his name. He struggled to wakefulness. She lay beside him. Gray's moon was up, nearly full, swifter and brighter than Luna. Its glow drowned most of the stars, frosted the encroaching bushes, fell without pity to show him her fallen cheeks and rolling eyes. She shuddered in his arms; he heard her teeth clapping. "I'm cold, darling, I'm cold," she said in the subtropical summer night. She vomited over him, and presently she was delirious.

The Ythrians gave what help they could, he what medicines he could. By sunrise (an outrageousness of rose and gold and silver-blue, crossed by the jubilant wings of waterfowl) he knew she was dying.

He examined his own physical state, using a robot he discovered he had in his skull: yes, his wretchedness was due to more than overwork, he saw that now; he too had had the upset stomach and the occasional shivers, nothing like the disintegration which possessed Olga, nevertheless the same kind of thing. Yet the Ythrians stayed healthy. Did a local germ attack humans while finding the other race undevourable?

The rescuers, who came on the island two Gray days later, already had the answer. That genus of bushes is widespread on the planet. A party elsewhere, after getting sick and getting into safety suits, analyzed its vapors. They are a cumulative poison to man; they scarcely harm an Ythrian. The analysts named it the hell shrub.

Unfortunately, their report wasn't broadcast until after the boat left. Meanwhile Pete had been out in the field every day, while Olga spent her whole time in the hollow, over which the sun regularly created an inversion layer.

Whell and Rusa went grimly back to work. Pete had to get away. He wasn't sure of the reason, but he had to be alone when he screamed at heaven, "Why did You do this to her, why did You do it?" Enherrian could look after

Olga, who had brought him back to a life he no longer wanted. Pete had stopped her babblings, writhings, and sawtoothed sounds of pain with a shot. She ought to sleep peacefully into that death which the monitor instruments said was, in the absence of hospital facilities, ineluctable.

He stumbled off to the heights. The sea reached calm, in a thousand hues of azure and green, around the living island, beneath the gentle sky. He knelt in all that emptiness and put his question.

After an hour he could say, "Your will be done" and return to camp.

Olga lay awake. "Pete, Pete!" she cried. Anguish distorted her voice till he couldn't recognize it; nor could he really see her in the yellowed sweating skin and lank hair drawn over a skeleton, or find her in the stench and the nails which flayed him as they clutched. "Where were you, hold me close, it hurts, how it hurts—"

He gave her a second injection, to small effect.

He knelt again, beside her. He has not told me what he said, or how. At last she grew quiet, gripped him hard and waited for the pain to end.

When she died, he says, it was like seeing a light blown out.

He laid her down, closed eyes and jaw, folded her hands. On mechanical feet he went to the pup tent which had been rigged for Enherrian. The cripple calmly awaited him. "She is fallen?" he asked.

Pete nodded.

"That is well," Enherrian said.

"It is not," Pete heard himself reply, harsh and remote. "She shouldn't have aroused. The drug should've—Did you give her a stim shot? Did you bring her back to suffer?"

"What else?" said Enherrian, though he was unarmed and a blaster lay nearby for Pete to seize. *Not that I'll ease him out of his fate!* went through the man in a spasm. "I saw that you, distraught, had misgauged. You were gone and I unable to follow you. She might well die before your return."

Out of his void, Pete gaped into those eyes. "You

mean," rattled from him, "you mean . . . she . . . mustn't?"

Enherrian crawled forth—he could only crawl, on his single wing—to take Pete's hands. "My friend," he said, his tone immeasurably compassionate, "I honored you both too much to deny her her deathpride."

Pete's chief awareness was of the cool sharp talons.

"Have I misunderstood?" asked Enherrian anxiously. "Did you not wish her to give-God a battle?"

Even on Lucifer, the nights finally end. Dawn blazed on the tors when Pete finished his story.

I emptied the last few cc. into our glasses. We'd get no work done today. "Yeh," I said. "Cross-cultural semantics. Given the best will in the universe, two beings from different planets—or just different countries, often—take for granted they think alike; and the outcome can be tragic."

"I assumed that at first," Pete said. "I didn't need to forgive Enherrian—how could he know? For his part, he was puzzled when I buried my darling. On Ythri they cast them from a great height into wilderness. But neither race wants to watch the rotting of what was loved, so he did his lame best to help me."

He drank, looked as near the cruel bluish sun as he was able, and mumbled: "What I couldn't do was forgive God."

"The problem of evil," I said.

"Oh, no. I've studied these matters, these past years: read theology, argued with priests, the whole route. Why does God, if He is a loving and personal God, allow evil? Well, there's a perfectly good Christian answer to that. Man—intelligence everywhere—must have free will. Otherwise we're puppets and have no reason to exist. Free will necessarily includes the capability of doing wrong. We're here, in this cosmos during our lives, to learn how to be good of our unforced choice."

"I spoke illiterately," I apologized. "All that brandy. No, sure, your logic is right, regardless of whether I accept your premises or not. What I meant was: the problem of pain. Why does a merciful God permit undeserved agony? If He's omnipotent, He isn't compelled to.

"I'm not talking about the sensation which warns you to take your hand from the fire, anything useful like that. No, the random accident which wipes out a life...or a mind—" I drank. "What happened to Arrach, yes, and to Enherrian, and Olga, and you, and Whell. What happens when a disease hits, or those catastrophes we label acts of God. Or the slow decay of us if we grow very old. Every such horror. Never mind if science has licked some of them; we have enough left, and then there were our ancestors who endured them all.

"Why? What possible end is served? It's not adequate to declare we'll receive an unbounded reward after we die and therefore it makes no difference whether a life was gusty or grisly. That's no explanation.

"Is this the problem you're grappling with, Pete?"

"In a way." He nodded, cautiously, as if he were already his father's age. "At least, it's the start of the problem.

"You see, there I was, isolated among Ythrians. My fellow humans sympathized, but they had nothing to say that I didn't know already. The New Faith, however .... Mind you, I wasn't about to convert. What I did hope for was an insight, a freshness, that'd help me make Christian sense of our losses. Enherrian was so sure, so learned, in his beliefs—

"We talked, and talked, and talked, while I was regaining my strength. He was as caught as me. Not that he couldn't fit our troubles into his scheme of things. That was easy. But it turned out that the New Faith has no satisfactory answer to the problem of *evil*. It says God allows wickedness so we may win honor by fighting for the right. Really, when you stop to think, that's weak, especially in carnivore Ythrian terms. Don't you agree?"

"You know them, I don't," I sighed. "You imply they have a better answer to the riddle of pain than your own religion does."

"It seems better." Desperation edged his slightly blurred tone:

"They're hunters, or were until lately. They see God like that, as the Hunter. Not the Torturer—you absolutely must understand this point—no, He rejoices in our happiness the way we might rejoice to see a game animal gamboling. Yet at last He comes after us. Our noblest moment is when we, knowing He is irresistible, give Him a good chase, a good fight.

"Then He wins honor. And some infinite end is furthered. (The same one as when my God is given praise? How can I tell?) We're dead, struck down, lingering at most a few years in the memories of those who escaped this time. And that's what we're here for. That's why God created the universe."

"And this belief is old," I said. "It doesn't belong just to a few cranks. No, it's been held for centuries by millions of sensitive, intelligent, educated beings. You can live by it, you can die by it. If it doesn't solve every paradox, it solves some that your faith won't, quite. This is your dilemma, true?"

He nodded again. "The priests have told me to deny a false creed and to acknowledge a mystery. Neither instruction feels right. Or am I asking too much?"

"I'm sorry, Pete," I said, altogether honestly. It hurt. "But how should I know? I looked into the abyss once, and saw nothing, and haven't looked since. You keep looking. Which of us is the braver?

"Maybe you can find a text in Job. I don't know, I tell you, I don't know."

The sun lifted higher above the burning horizon.

What Rennhi, her flightmates in the endeavor, and more lately Hloch were able to seek out has been limited and in great measure chance-blown. No scholar from Avalon has yet prevailed over the time or the means to ransack data banks on Terra itself. Yonder must abide records more full by a cloud-height than those which have reached the suns where Domain of Ythri and Terran Empire come together.

It may be just as well. They would surely overwhelm the writer of this book, whose aim is at no more than an account of certain human events which helped bring about the founding of the Stormgate Choth. Even the fragmentary original material he has is more than he can directly use. He rides among whatever winds blow, choosing first one, then another, hoping that in this wise he may find the overall set of the airstream.

Here is a story of no large import, save that it gives a picture from within of Terran society when the Polesotechnic League was in its glory—and, incidentally, makes the first mention known to Hloch of a being who was to take a significant part in later history. The source is a running set of reminiscences written down through much of his life by James Ching, a spaceman who eventually settled on Catawrayannis. His descendants kept the notebooks and courteously made them available to Rennhi after she had heard of their existence. To screen a glossary of obscure terms, punch Library Central 254-0691.

HOW TO BE ETHNIC
IN ONE EASY LESSON

Adzel talks a lot about blessings in disguise, but this disguise was impenetrable. In fact, what Simon Snyder handed me was an exploding bomb.

I was hard at study when my phone warbled. That alone jerked me half out of my lounger. I'd set that instrument to pass calls from no more than a dozen people, to all of whom I'd explained that they shouldn't bother me about anything much less urgent than a rogue planet on a collision course.

You see, my preliminary tests for the Academy were coming up soon. Not the actual entrance exams—I'd face those a year hence—but the tests as to whether I should be allowed to apply for admission. You can't blame that policy on the Brotherhood. Not many regular spaceman's berths become available annually, and a hundred young Earthlings clamor for each of them. The ninety-nine who don't make it . . . well, mostly they try to get work with some company which will maybe someday assign them to a post somewhere outsystem; or they set their teeth and save their money till at last they can go as shepherded tourists.

At night, out above the ocean in my car, away from city glow, I'd look upward and be ripped apart by longing. As for the occasional trips to Luna—last time, several months before, I'd found my eyes running over at sight of that sky, when the flit was my sixteenth-birthday present.

And now tensor calculus was giving me trouble. No doubt the Education Central computer would have gotten monumentally bored, projecting the same stuff over and over on my screen, if it had been built to feel emotions. Is that why is hasn't been?

The phone announced: "Freeman Snyder."

You don't refuse your principal counselor. His or her word has too much to do with the evaluation of you as a potential student by places like the Academy. "Accept," I gulped. As his lean features flashed on: "Greeting, sir."

"Greeting, Jim," he said. "How are you?"

"Busy," I hinted.

"Indeed. You are a rather intense type, eh? The indices show you're apt to work yourself into the ground. A change of pace is downright necessary."

Why are we saddled with specialists who arbite our lives on the basis of a psychoprofile and a theory? If I'd been apprenticed to a Master Merchant of the Polesotechnic League instead, he wouldn't have given two snorts in vacuum about my "optimum developmental strategy." He'd have told me, "Ching, do this or learn that"; and if I didn't cut it satisfactorily, I'd be fired—or dead, because we'd be on strange worlds, out among the stars, the stars.

No use daydreaming. League apprenticeships are scarcer than hair on a neutron, and mostly filled by relatives. (That's less nepotism for its own sake than a belief that kin of survivor types are more likely to be the same than chance-met groundhugger kids.) I was an ordinary student bucking for an Academy appointment, from which I'd graduate to service on regular runs and maybe, at last, a captaincy.

"To be frank," Simon Snyder went on, "I've worried about your indifference to extracurricular activities. It doesn't make for an outgoing personality, you know. I've thought of an undertaking which should be right in your orbit. In addition, it'll be a real service, it'll bring real credit, to—" he smiled afresh to pretend he was joking while he intoned— "the educational complex of San Francisco Integrate."

"I haven't time!" I wailed.

"Certainly you do. You can't study twenty-four hours a day, even if a medic would prescribe the stim. Brains go stale. All work and no play, remember. Besides, Jim, this matter has its serious aspect. I'd like to feel I could endorse your altruism as well as your technological abilities."

I eased my muscles, let the lounger mold itself around me, and said in what was supposed to be a hurrah voice: "Please tell me, Freeman Snyder."

He beamed. "I knew I could count on you. You've heard of the upcoming Festival of Man."

"Haven't I?" Realizing how sour my tone was, I tried again. "I have."

He gave me a pretty narrow look. "You don't sound too enthusiastic."

"Oh, I'll tune in ceremonies and such, catch a bit of music and drama and whatnot, if and when the chance comes. But I've got to get these transformations in hyperdrive theory straight, or—"

"I'm afraid you don't quite appreciate the importance of the Festival, Jim. It's more than a set of shows. It's an affirmation."

Yes, I'd heard that often enough before—too dismally often. Doubtless you remember the line of argument the promoters used: "Humankind, gaining the stars, is in grave danger of losing its soul. Our extraterrestrial colonies are fragmenting into new nations, whole new cultures, to which Earth is scarcely a memory. Our traders, our explorers push ever outward, ever further away; and no missionary spirit drives them, nothing but lust for profit and adventure. Meanwhile the Solar Commonwealth is deluged with alien—nonhuman—influence, not only diplomats, entrepreneurs, students, and visitors, but the false glamour of ideas never born on man's true home.—We grant we have learned much of value from these outsiders. But much else has been unassimilable or has had a disastrously distorting effect, especially in the arts. Besides, they are learning far more from us. Let us proudly affirm that fact. Let us hark back to our own origins, our own variousness. Let us strike new roots in the soil from which our forebears sprang."

A year-long display of Earth's past—well, it'd be colorful, if rather fakey most of the time. I couldn't take it more seriously than that. Space was where the future lay, I thought. At least, it was where I dreamed my personal future would lie. What were dead bones to me, no matter how fancy the costumes you put on them? Not that I scorned the past; even then, I wasn't so foolish. I just believed that what was worth saving would save itself, and the rest had better be let fade away quietly.

I tried to explain to my counselor: "Sure, I've been told about 'cultural pseudomorphosis' and the rest. Really, though, Freeman Snyder, don't you think the shoe is on the other foot? Like, well, I've got this friend from Woden, name of Adzel, here to learn planetology. That's a science we developed; his folk are primitive hunters, newly discovered by us. He talks human languages too— he's quick at languages—and lately he was converted to Buddhism and—Shouldn't the Wodenites worry about being turned into imitation Earthlings?"

My example wasn't the best, because you can only humanize a four-and-a-half-meter-long dragon to a limited extent. Whether he knew that or not (who can know all the races, all the worlds we've already found in our small corner of this wonderful cosmos?) Snyder wasn't impressed. He snapped, "The sheer variety of extraterrestrial influence is demoralizing. Now I want our complex to make a decent showing during the Festival. Every department, office, club, church, institution in the Integrate will take part. I want its schools to have a leading role."

"Don't they, sir? I mean, aren't projects under way?"

"Yes, yes, to a degree." He waved an impatient hand. "Far less than I'd expect from our youth. Too many of you are spacestruck—" He checked himself, donned his smile again, and leaned forward till his image seemed ready to fall out of the screen. "I've been thinking about what my own students might do. In your case, I have a first-class idea. You will represent San Francisco's Chinese community among us."

"What?" I yelped. "Bu—but—"

"A very old, almost unique tradition," he said. "Your people have been in this area for five or six hundred years."

"*My* people?" The room wobbled around me. "I mean . . . well, sure, my name's Ching and I'm proud of it. And maybe the, uh, the chromosome recombinations do make me look like those ancestors. But . . . half a thousand years, sir! If I haven't got blood in me of every breed of human being that ever lived, why, then I'm a statistical monstrosity!"

"True. However, the accident which makes you a throwback to your Mongoloid forebears is helpful. Few of my students are identifiably anything. I try to find roles for them, on the basis of surnames, but it isn't easy."

Yeh, I thought bitterly. *By your reasoning, everybody named Marcantonio should dress in a toga for the occasion, and everybody named Smith should paint himself blue.*

"There is a local ad hoc committee on Chinese-American activities," Snyder went on. "I suggest you contact them and ask for ideas and information. What can you present on behalf of our educational system? And then, of course, there's Library Central. It can supply more historical material than you could read in a lifetime. Do you good to learn a few subjects besides math, physics, xenology—" His grimace passed by. I gave him marks for sincerity: "Perhaps you can devise something, a float or the like, something which will call on your engineering ingenuity and knowledge. That would please them too, when you apply at the Academy."

Sure, I thought, *if it hasn't eaten so much of my time that I flunk these prelims.*

"Remember," Snyder said, "the Festival opens in barely three months. I'll expect progress reports from you. Feel free to call on me for help or advice at any time. That's what I'm here for, you know: to guide you in developing your whole self."

More of the same followed. I haven't the stomach to record it.

• • •

I called Betty Riefenstahl, but just to find out if I could come see her. Though holovids are fine for image and sound, you can't hold hands with one or catch a whiff of perfume and girl.

Her phone told me she wasn't available till evening. That gave me ample chance to gnaw my nerves raw. I couldn't flat-out refuse Snyder's pet notion. The right was mine, of course, and he wouldn't consciously hold a grudge; but neither would he speak as well as he might of my energy and team spirit. On the other hand, what did I know about Chinese civilization? I'd seen the standard sights; I'd read a classic or two in literature courses; and that was that. What persons I'd met over there were as modern-oriented as myself. (No pun, I hope!) And as for Chinese-Americans—

Vaguely remembering that San Francisco had once had special ethnic sections, I did ask Library Central. It screened a fleet of stuff about a district known as Chinatown. Probably contemporaries found that area picturesque. (Oh, treetop highways under the golden-red sun of Cynthia! Four-armed drummers who sound the mating call of Gorzun's twin moons! Wild wings above Ythri!) The inhabitants had celebrated a Lunar New Year with fireworks and a parade. I couldn't make out details—the photographs had been time-blurred when their information was recorded—and was too disheartened to plow through the accompanying text.

For me, dinner was a refueling stop. I mumbled something to my parents, who mean well but can't understand why I must leave the nice safe Commonwealth, and flitted off to the Riefenstahl place.

The trip calmed me a little. I was reminded that, to outworlders like Adzel, the miracle was here. Light glimmered in a million earthbound stars across the hills, far out over the great sheen of Bay and ocean; often it fountained upward in a many-armed tower, often gave way to the sweet darkness of a park or ecocenter. A murmur of machines beat endlessly through cool, slightly foggy air. Traffic Control passed me so near a bus that I looked in its canopy and saw the passengers were from the whole globe and beyond—a dandified Lunarian, a stocky blueskin of Alfzar, a spacehand identified by his Brotherhood badge, a journeyman merchant of the Polesotechnic League who didn't bother with any identification except the skin weathered beneath strange suns, the go-to-hell independence in his face, which turned me sick with envy.

The Riefenstahls' apartment overlooked the Golden Gate. I saw lights twinkle and flare, heard distant clangor and hissing, where crews worked around the clock to replicate an ancient bridge. Betty met me at the door. She's slim and blonde and usually cheerful. Tonight she looked so tired and troubled that I myself paid scant attention to the briefness of her tunic.

"Sh!" she cautioned. "Let's don't say hello to Dad right now. He's in his study, and it's very brown." I knew that her mother was away from home, helping develop the tape of a modern musical composition. Her father conducted the San Francisco Opera.

She led me to the living room, sat me down, and punched for coffee. A full-wall transparency framed her where she continued standing, in city glitter and shimmer, a sickle moon with a couple of pinpoint cities visible on its dark side, a few of the brightest stars. "I'm glad you came, Jimmy," she said. "I need a shoulder to cry on."

"Like me," I answered. "You first, however."

"Well, it's Dad. He's ghastly worried. This stupid Festival—"

"Huh?" I searched my mind and found nothing except the obvious. "Won't he be putting on a, uh, Terrestrial piece?"

"He's expected to. He's been researching till every hour of the mornings, poor dear. I've been helping him go through playbacks—hundreds and hundreds of years' worth—and prepare synopses and excerpts to show the directors. We only finished yesterday, and I *had* to catch up on sleep. That's why I couldn't let you come earlier."

"But what's the problem?" I asked. "Okay, you've been forced to scan those tapes. But once you've picked your show, you just project it, don't you? At most, you may need to update the language. And you've got your mother to handle reprogramming."

Betty sighed. "It's not that simple. You see, they—his board of directors, plus the officials in charge of San Francisco's participation—they insist on a live performance."

Partly I knew what she was talking about, partly she explained further. Freeman Riefenstahl had pioneered the revival of in-the-flesh opera. Yes, he said, we have holographic records of the greatest artists; yes, we can use computers to generate original works and productions which no mortal being could possibly match. Yet neither approach will bring forth new artists with new concepts of a part, nor do they give individual brains a chance to create—and, when a million fresh ideas are flowing in to us from the galaxy, natural-born genius must create or else revolt.

"Let us by all means use technical tricks where they are indicated, as for special effects," Freeman Riefenstahl said. "But let us never forget that music is only alive in a living performer." While I don't claim to be very esthetic, I tuned in his shows whenever I could. They did have an excitement which no tape and no calculated stimulus interplay—no matter how excellent—can duplicate.

"His case is like yours," Betty told me near the start of our acquaintance. "We could send robots to space. Nevertheless men go, at whatever risk." That was when I stopped thinking of her as merely pretty.

Tonight, her voice gone bleak, she said: "Dad succeeded too well. He's been doing contemporary things, you know, letting the archives handle the archaic. Now they insist he won't be showing sufficient respect, as a representative of the Integrate, for the Human Ethos—unless he puts on a historic item, live, as the Opera Company's share of the Festival."

"Well, can't he?" I asked. "Sure, it's kind of short notice, same as for me. Still, given modern training methods for his cast—"

"Of course, of course," she said irritably. "But don't

you see, a routine performance isn't good enough either? People today are conditioned to visual spectacles. At least, the directors claim so. And—Jimmy, the Festival is important, if only because of the publicity. If Dad's part in it falls flat, his contract may not be renewed. Certainly his effort would be hurt, to educate the public back to real music." Her tone and her head drooped. "And that'd hurt him."

She drew a breath, straightened, even coaxed a smile into existence. "Well, we've made our précis of suggestions," she said. "We're waiting to hear what the board decides, which may take days. Meanwhile, you need to tell me your woes." Sitting down opposite me: "Do."

I obeyed. At the end I grinned on one side of my face and remarked: "Ironic, huh? Here your father has to stage an ultraethnic production—I'll bet they'll turn handsprings for him if he can make it German, given a name like his—only he's not supposed to use technology for much except backdrops. And here I have to do likewise, in Chinese style, the flashier the better, only I really haven't time to apply the technology for making a firework fountain or whatever. Maybe he and I should pool our efforts."

"How?"

"I dunno." I shifted in the chair. "Let's get out of here, go someplace where we can forget this mess."

What I had in mind was a flit over the ocean or down to the swimmably warm waters off Baja, followed maybe by a snack in a restaurant featuring outsystem food. Betty gave me no chance. She nodded and said quickly, "Yes, I've been wanting to. A serene environment—Do you think Adzel might be at home?"

The League scholarship he'd wangled back on his planet didn't reach far on Earth, especially when he had about a ton of warm-blooded mass to keep fed. He couldn't afford special quarters, or anything near the Clement Institute of Planetology. Instead, he paid exorbitant rent for a shack 'way down in the San Jose district. The sole public transportation he could fit into was a rickety old twice-a-day gyrotrain, which meant he lost hours commuting to his laboratory and live-lecture classes, waiting for them to begin and waiting around after they were finished. Also, I strongly suspected he was undernourished. I'd fretted about him ever since we met, in the course of a course in micrometrics.

He always dismissed my fears: "Once, Jimmy, I might well have chafed, when I was a prairie-galloping hunter. Now, having gained a minute measure of enlightenment, I see that these annoyances of the flesh are no more significant than we allow them to be. Indeed, we can turn them to good use. Austerities are valuable. As for long delays, why, they are opportunities for study or, better yet, meditation. I have even learned to ignore spectators, and am grateful for the discipline which that forced me to acquire."

We may be used to extraterrestrials these days. Nevertheless, he was the one Wodenite on this planet. And you take a being like that: four hoofed legs supporting a spike-backed, green-scaled, golden-bellied body and tail; torso, with arms in proportion, rising two meters to a crocodilian face, fangs, rubbery lips, bony ears, wistful brown eyes—you take that fellow and set him on a campus, in his equivalent of the lotus position, droning "*Om mani padme hum*" in a rich basso profundo, and see if you don't draw a crowd.

Serious though he was, Adzel never became a prig. He enjoyed good food and drink when he could get them, being especially fond of rye whiskey consumed out of beer tankards. He played murderous chess and poker. He sang, and sang well, everything from his native chants through human folk ballads on to the very latest spinnies. (A few things, such as *Eskimo Nell,* he refused to render in Betty's presence. From his avid reading of human history, he'd picked up anachronistic inhibitions.) I imagine his jokes often escaped me by being too subtle.

All in all, I was tremendously fond of him, hated the thought of his poverty, and had failed to hit on any way of helping him out.

I set my car down on the strip before his hut. A

moldering conurb, black against feverish reflections off thickening fog, cast it into deep and sulfurous shadow. Unmuffled industrial traffic brawled around. I took a stun pistol from a drawer before escorting Betty outside.

Adzel's doorplate was kaput, but he opened at our knock. "Do come in, do come in," he greeted. Fluorolight shimmered gorgeous along his scales and scutes. Incense puffed outward. He noticed my gun. "Why are you armed, Jimmy?"

"The night's dark here," I said. "In a crime area like this—"

"Is it?" He was surprised. "Why, I have never been molested."

We entered. He waved us to mats on the floor. Those, and a couple of cheap tables, and bookshelves cobbled together from scrap and crammed with codexes as well as reels, were his furniture. An Old Japanese screen—repro, of course—hid that end of the single room which contained a miniature cooker and some complicated specially installed plumbing. Two scrolls hung on the walls, one showing a landscape and one the Compassionate Buddha.

Adzel bustled about, making tea for us. He hadn't quite been able to adjust to these narrow surroundings. Twice I had to duck fast before his tail clonked me. (I said nothing, lest he spend the next half-hour in apologies.) "I am delighted to see you," he boomed. "I gathered, however, from your call, that the occasion is not altogether happy."

"We hoped you'd help us relax," Betty replied. I myself felt a bit disgruntled. Sure, Adzel was fine people; but couldn't Betty and I relax in each other's company? I had seen too little of her these past weeks.

He served us. His pot held five liters, but—thanks maybe to that course in micrometrics—he could handle the tiniest cups and put on an expert tea ceremony. Appropriate silence passed. I fumed. Charming the custom might be; still, hadn't Oriental traditions caused me ample woe?

At last he dialled for *pipa* music, settled down before us

on hocks and front knees, and invited: "Share your troubles, dear friends."

"Oh, we've been over them and over them," Betty said. "I came here for peace."

"Why, certainly," Adzel answered. "I am glad to try to oblige. Would you like to join me in a spot of transcendental meditation?"

That tore my patience apart. "No!" I yelled. They both stared at me. "I'm sorry," I mumbled. "But . . . chaos, everything's gone bad and—"

A gigantic four-digited hand squeezed my shoulder, gently as my mother might have done. "Tell, Jimmy," Adzel said low.

It flooded from me, the whole sad, ludicrous situation. "Freeman Snyder can't understand," I finished. "He thinks I can learn those equations, those facts, in a few days at most."

"Can't you? Operant conditioning, for example—"

"You know better. I can learn to parrot, sure. But I won't get the knowledge down in my bones where it belongs. And they'll set me problems which require original thinking. They must. How else can they tell if I'll be able to handle an emergency in space?"

"Or on a new planet." The long head nodded. "Yes-s-s."

"That's not for me," I said flatly. "I'll never be tagged by the merchant adventurers." Betty squeezed my hand. "Even freighters can run into grief, though."

He regarded me for a while, most steadily, until at last he rumbled: "A word to the right men—that does appear to be how your Technic civilization operates, no? *Zothkh.* Have you prospects for a quick performance of this task, that will allow you to get back soon to your proper work?"

"No. Freeman Snyder mentioned a float or display. Well, I'll have to soak up cultural background, and develop a scheme, and clear it with a local committee, and design the thing—which had better be spectacular as well as ethnic—and build it, and test it, and find the bugs in the design, and rebuild it, and—And I'm no artist anyhow. No matter how clever a machine I make, it won't look like much."

Suddenly Betty exclaimed: "Adzel, you know more about Old Oriental things than he does! Can't you make a suggestion?"

"Perhaps. Perhaps." The Wodenite rubbed his jaw, a sandpaper noise. "The motifs—Let me see." He hooked a book off a shelf and started leafing through it. "They are generally of pagan origin in Buddhistic, or for that matter Christian art.... *Gr-r-rrr'm*.... Betty, my sweet, while I search, won't you unburden yourself too?"

She twisted her fingers and gazed at the floor. I figured she'd rather not be distracted. Rising from my mat, I went to look over his shoulder—no, his elbow.

"My problem is my father's, actually," she began. "And maybe he and I already have solved it. That depends on whether or not one of the possibilities we've found is acceptable. If not—how much further can we research? Time's getting so short. He needs time to assemble a cast, rehearse, handle the physical details—" She noticed Adzel's puzzlement and managed a sort of chuckle. "Excuse me. I got ahead of my story. We—"

"Hoy!" I interrupted. My hand slapped down on a page. "What's that?...Uh, sorry, Betty."

Her smile forgave me. "Have you found something?" She sprang to her feet.

"I don't know," I stammered, "b-b-but, Adzel, that thing in this picture could almost be you. What is it?"

He squinted at the ideograms. "The *lung*," he said.

"A dragon?"

"Western writers miscalled it thus." Adzel settled happily down to lecture us. "The dragon proper was a creature of European and Near Eastern mythology, almost always a destructive monster. In Chinese and related societies, contrariwise, these herpetoids represented beneficent powers. The *lung* inhabited the sky, the *li* the ocean, the *chiao* the marshes and mountains. Various other entities are named elsewhere. The *lung* was the principal type, the one which was mimed on ceremonial occasions—"

The phone warbled. "Would you please take that, Betty?" Adzel asked, reluctant to break off. "I daresay it's a notification I am expecting of a change in class schedules. Now, Jimmy, observe the claws on hind and forefeet. Their exact number is a distinguishing characteristic of—"

"Dad!" Betty cried. Glancing sideways, I saw John Riefenstahl's mild features in the screen, altogether woebegone.

"I was hoping I'd find you, dear," he said wearily. I knew that these days she seldom left the place without recording a list of numbers where she could probably be reached.

"I've just finished a three-hour conference with the board chairman," her father's voice plodded. "They've vetoed every one of our proposals."

"Already?" she whispered. "In God's name, why?"

"Various reasons. They feel *Carmen* is too parochial in time and space; hardly anybody today would understand what motivates the characters. *Alpha of the Centaur* is about space travel, which is precisely what we're supposed to get away from. *La Traviata* isn't visual enough. *Götterdämmerung*, they agree, has the Mythic Significance they want, but it's *too* visual. A modern audience wouldn't accept it unless we supply a realism of effects which would draw attention away from the live performers on whom it ought to center in a production that emphasizes Man. Et cetera, et cetera."

"They're full of nonsense!"

"They're also full of power, dear. Can you bear to run through more tapes?"

"I'd better."

"I beg your pardon, Freeman Riefenstahl," Adzel put in. "We haven't met but I have long admired your work. May I ask if you have considered Chinese opera?"

"The Chinese themselves will be doing that, Freeman—er—" The conductor hesitated.

"Adzel." My friend moved into scanner range. His teeth gleamed alarmingly sharp. "Honored to make your acquaintance, sir . . . ah . . . sir?"

John Riefenstahl, who had gasped and gone bloodless, wiped his forehead. "Eh-eh-excuse me," he stuttered. "I didn't realize you—That is, here I had Wagner on my mind, and then Fafner himself confronted me—"

I didn't know those names, but the context was obvious. All at once Betty and I met each other's eyes and let out a yell.

Knowing how Simon Snyder would react, I insisted on a live interview. He sat behind his desk, surrounded by his computers, communicators, and information retrievers, and gave me a tight smile.

"Well," he said. "You have an idea, Jim? Overnight seems a small time for a matter this important."

"It was plenty," I answered. "We've contacted the head of the Chinese-American committee, and he likes our notion. But since it's on behalf of the schools, he wants your okay."

"'We'?" My counselor frowned. "You have a partner?"

"Chaos, sir, he *is* my project. What's a Chinese parade without a dragon? And what fake dragon can possibly be as good as a live one? Now we take this Wodenite, and just give him a wig and false whiskers, claws over his hoofs, lacquer on his scales—"

"A nonhuman?" The frown turned into a scowl. "Jim, you disappoint me. You disappoint me sorely. I expected better from you, some dedication, some application of your talents. In a festival devoted to your race, you want to feature an alien! No, I'm afraid I cannot agree—"

"Sir, please wait till you've met Adzel." I jumped from my chair, palmed the hall door, and called: "C'mon in."

He did, meter after meter of him, till the office was full of scales, tail, spikes, and fangs. He seized Snyder's hand in a gentle but engulfing grip, beamed straight into Snyder's face, and thundered: "How joyful I am at this opportunity, sir! What a way to express my admiration for terrestrial culture, and thus help glorify your remarkable species!"

"Um, well, that is," the man said feebly.

I had told Adzel that there was no reason to mention his being a pacifist. He continued: "I do hope you will approve Jimmy's brilliant idea, sir. To be quite frank, my motives are not unmixed. If I perform, I understand that the local restaurateurs' association will feed me during rehearsals. My stipend is exiguous and—" he licked his lips, two centimeters from Snyder's nose— "sometimes I get *so* hungry."

He would tell only the strict, if not always the whole truth. I, having fewer compunctions, whispered in my counselor's ear: "He is kind of excitable, but he's perfectly safe if nobody frustrates him."

"Well." Snyder coughed, backed away till he ran into a computer, and coughed again. "Well. Ah . . . yes. Yes, Jim, your concept is undeniably original. There is a—" he winced but got the words out—"a certain quality to it which suggests that you—" he strangled for a moment— "will go far in life."

"You plan to record that opinion, do you not?" Adzel asked. "In Jimmy's permanent file? At once?"

I hurried them both through the remaining motions. My friend, my girl, and her father had an appointment with the chairman of the board of the San Francisco Opera Company.

The parade went off like rockets. Our delighted local merchants decided to revive permanently the ancient custom of celebrating the Lunar New Year. Adzel will star in that as long as he remains on Earth. In exchange—since he brings in more tourist credits than it costs—he has an unlimited meal ticket at the Silver Dragon Chinese Food and Chop Suey Palace.

More significant was the production of Richard Wagner's *Siegfried*. At least, in his speech at the farewell performance, the governor of the Integrate said it was significant. "Besides the bringing back of a musical masterpiece too many centuries neglected," he pomped, "the genius of John Riefenstahl has, by his choice of cast, given the Festival of Man an added dimension. He has reminded us that, in seeking our roots and pride, we must never grow chauvinistic. We must always remember to reach forth the hand of friendship to our brother beings throughout God's universe," who might otherwise be less anxious to come spend their money on Earth.

The point does have its idealistic appeal, though. Besides, the show was a sensation in its own right. For years to come, probably, the complete Ring cycle will be presented here and there around the Commonwealth; and Freeman Riefenstahl can be guest conductor, and Adzel can sing Fafner, at top salary, any time they wish.

I won't see the end of that, because I won't be around. When everything had been settled, Adzel, Betty, and I threw ourselves a giant feast in his new apartment. After his fifth magnum of champagne, he gazed a trifle blurrily across the table and said to me:

"Jimmy, my affection for you, my earnest wish to make a fractional return of your kindness, has hitherto been baffled."

"Aw, nothing to mention," I mumbled while he stopped a volcanic hiccough.

"At any rate." Adzel wagged a huge finger. "He would be a poor friend who gave a dangerous gift." He popped another cork and refilled our glasses and his stein. "That is, Jimmy, I was aware of your ambition to get into deep space, and not as a plyer of routine routes but as a discoverer, a pioneer. The question remained, could you cope with unpredictable environments?"

I gaped at him. The heart banged in my breast. Betty caught my hand.

"You have convinced me you can," Adzel said. "True, Freeman Snyder may not give you his most ardent recommendation to the Academy. No matter. The cleverness and, yes, toughness with which you handled this problem—those convinced me, Jimmy, you are a true survivor type."

He knocked back half a liter before tying the star-spangled bow knot on his package: "Being here on a League scholarship, I have League connections. I have been in correspondence. A certain Master Merchant I know will soon be in the market for another apprentice and accepts what I have told him about you. Are you interested?"

I collapsed into Betty's arms. She says she'll find a way to follow me.

Too many of us unthinkingly think of David Falkayn as if he flashed into being upon Avalon like a lightning bolt. The Polesotechnic League we know of only in its decadence and downfall. Yet for long and long it was wing and talon of that Technic civilization which humans begot and from which many other races—Ythrians too, Ythrians too—drew fresh blood that still flows within them.

Remote from the centers of Technic might, unaccustomed to the idea that alien sophonts are alien in more than body, our ancestors in the first lifetimes after the Discovery were little aware of anything behind the occasional merchant vessels, scientists, hired teachers and consultants, that came to their planet. The complexity of roots, trunks, boughs, which upbore the leaf-crown they saw, lay beyond their ken. Even the visits of a few to Terra brought scant enlightenment.

Later ancestors, moving vigorously into space on their own, were better informed. Paradoxically, though, they had less to do with the League. By then they required no imports to continue development. Furthermore, being close to the stars in this sector, they competed so successfully for trade that League members largely withdrew from a region which had never been highly profitable for them. The main point of contact was the planet Esperance and it, being as yet thinly settled, was not a market which drew great flocks from either side.

Thus the ordinary Ythrian, up to this very year, has had only a footgrip upon reality where the League is concerned. He/she/youngling must strengthen this if the origins of the Avalonian colony are to be made clear. What winds did Falkayn ride, what storms blew him hitherward at last?

His biographies tell how he became a protégé of Nicholas van Rijn, but say little about that merchant lord. You may well be surprised to learn that on numerous other worlds, it is the latter who lives in folk memory, whether as hero or rogue. He did truthfully fly in the front echelon of events when several things happened whose thunders would echo through centuries. With him as our archetype, we can approach knowledge.

Though hardly ever read or played anymore upon this globe, a good many accounts of him exist in Library Central, straightforward, semifictional, or romantic. Maychance the best introduction is the story which follows, from *Tales of the Great Frontier* by A. A. Craig.

MARGIN OF PROFIT

It was an anachronism to have a human receptionist in this hall of lucent plastic, among machines that winked and talked between jade columns soaring up into vaulted dimness—but a remarkably pleasant one when she was as long-legged and redheaded a stunblast as the girl behind the desk. Captain Torres drew to a crisp halt and identified himself. Traveling down sumptuous curves, his glance was jarred by the needle gun at her waist.

"Good day, sir," she smiled. "I'll see if Freeman van Rijn is ready for you." She switched on an intercom. A three-megavolt oath bounced out. "No, he's still in conference on the audivid. Won't you be seated?"

Before she turned the intercom off, Torres caught a few words: "—he'll give us the exclusive franchise or we embargo, *ja,* and maybe arrange a little blockade too. Who in Satan's squatpot do these emperors on a single planet think they are? Hokay, he has a million soldiers under arms. You go tell him to take those soldiers, with hobnailed boots and rifles at port, and stuff them—" *Click*.

Torres wrapped cape around tunic and sat down, laying one polished boot across the other knee of his white culottes. He felt awkward, simultaneously overdressed and naked. The formal garb of a Lodgemaster in the

70

Federated Brotherhood of Spacefarers was a far remove from the coverall he wore in his ship or the loungers of groundside leave. And the guards in the lobby, a kilometer below, had not only checked his credentials and retinal patterns, they had made him deposit his sidearm.

Damn Nicholas van Rijn and the whole Polesotechnic League! Good saints, drop him on Pluto with no underwear!

Of course, a merchant prince did have to be wary of kidnappers and assassins, though van Rijn himself was said to be murderously fast with a handgun. Nevertheless, arming your receptionist was not a polite thing to do.

Torres wondered, a trifle wistfully, if she was among the old devil's mistresses. Perhaps not. However, given the present friction between the Company—by extension, the entire League—and the Brotherhood, she'd have no time for him; her contract doubtless had a personal fealty clause. His gaze went to the League emblem on the wall behind her, a golden sunburst afire with jewels, surrounding an ancient rocketship, and the motto: *All the traffic will bear*. That could be taken two ways, he reflected sourly. Beneath it was the trademark of this outfit, the Solar Spice & Liquors Company.

The girl turned the intercom back on and heard only a steady rumble of obscenities. "You may go in now, please," she said, and to the speaker: "Lodgemaster Captain Torres, sir, here for his appointment."

The spaceman rose and passed through the inner door. His lean dark features were taut. This would be a new experience, meeting his ultimate boss. It was ten years since he had had to call anybody "sir" or "madam."

The office was big, an entire side transparent, overlooking a precipitous vista of Djakarta's towers, green landscape hot with tropical gardens, and the molten glitter of the Java Sea. The other walls were lined with the biggest datacom Torres had ever seen, with shelves of extraterrestrial curios, and, astonishingly, a thousand or more codex-type books whose fine leather bindings showed signs of wear. Despite its expanse, the desktop was littered, close to maximum entropy. The most noticeable object on it was a small image of St. Dismas, carved from Martian sandroot. Ventilators could not quite dismiss a haze and reek of tobacco smoke.

The newcomer snapped a salute. "Lodgemaster Captain Rafael Torres speaking for the Brotherhood. Good day, sir."

Van Rijn grunted. He was a huge man, two meters in height and more than broad enough to match. A triple chin and swag belly did not make him appear soft. Rings glittered on hairy fingers and bracelets on brawny wrists, under snuff-soiled lace. Small black eyes, set close to a great hook nose under a sloping forehead, peered with laser intensity. He continued filling his pipe and said nothing until he had a good head of steam up.

"So," he growled then, basso profundo, in an accent as thick as himself. "You speak for the whole unspeakable union, I hope. Women members too? I have never understood why they want to say they belong to a brotherhood." Waxed mustaches and long goatee waggled above a gorgeously embroidered waistcoat. Beneath it was only a sarong, which gave way to columnar ankles and bare splay feet.

Torres checked his temper. "Yes, sir. Privately, informally, of course...thus far. I have the honor to represent all locals in the Commonwealth, and lodges outside the Solar System have expressed solidarity. We assume you will be a spokesman for the master merchants of the League."

"In a subliminary way. I will shovel your demands along at my associates, what of them as don't hide too good in their offices and harems. Sit."

Torres gave the chair no opportunity to mold itself to him. Perched on the edge, he proceeded harshly: "The issue is very simple. The votes are now in, and the result can't surprise you. We are not calling a strike, you realize. But contracts or no, we will not take any more ships through the Kossaluth of Borthu until that menace has been ended. Any owner who tries to hold us to the articles and send us there will be struck. The idea of our meeting today, Freeman van Rijn, is to make that clear and get the

League's agreement, without a lot of public noise that might bring on a real fight."

"By damn, you cut your own throats like with a butterknife, slow and outscruciating." The merchant's tone was surprisingly mild. "Not alone the loss of pay and commissions. No, but if Sector Antares is not kept steady supplied, it loses taste maybe for cinnamon and London dry gin. Nor can other companies be phlegmatic about what they hawk. Like if Jo-Boy Technical Services bring in no more engineers and scientists, the colonies will train up their own. Hell's poxy belles! In a few years, no more market on any planet in those parts. You lose, I lose, we all lose."

"The answer is obvious, sir. We detour around the Kossaluth. I know that'll take us through more hazardous regions, astronomically speaking, unless we go very far aside indeed. However, the brothers and sisters will accept either choice."

"What?" Somehow van Rijn managed a bass scream. "Is you developed feedback of the bowels? Double or quadruple the length of the voyage! Boost heaven-high the salaries, capital goods losses, survivors' compensation, insurance! Halve or quarter the deliveries per year! We are ruined! Better we give up Antares at once!"

The route was already expensive, Torres knew. He wasn't sure whether or not the companies could afford the extra cost; their books were their own secret. Having waited out the dramatics, he said patiently:

"The Borthudian press gangs have been operating for two years now, you know. Nothing that's been tried has stopped them. We have not panicked. If it had been up to the siblings at large, we'd have voted right at the start to bypass that horrorhole. But the Lodgemasters held back, hoping something could be worked out. Apparently that isn't possible."

"See here," van Rijn urged. "I don't like this no better than you. Worse, maybe. The losses my company alone has took could make me weep snot. We can afford it, though. Naked-barely, but we can. Figure it. About fifteen percent of our ships altogether gets captured. We would lose more, traveling through the Gamma Mist or the Stonefields. And those crews would not be prisoners that we are still working to have released. No, they would be kind of dead. As for making a still bigger roundabout through nice clear vacuum, well, that would be safe, but means an absolute loss on each run. Even if your brotherhood will take a big cut in the exorbital wages you draw, still, consider the tieup of bottom on voyages so long. We do have trade elsewheres to carry on."

Torres' temper snapped across. "Go flush your dirty financial calculations! Try thinking about human beings for once. We'll face meteoroid swarms, infrasuns, rogue planets, black holes, radiation bursts, hostile natives—but have you *met* one of those impressed men? I have. That's what decided me, and made me take a lead in getting the Brotherhood to act. I'm not going to risk it happening to me, nor to any lodge sibling of mine. Why don't you and your fellow moneymen conn the ships personally?"

"Ho-o-o," murmured van Rijn. He showed no offense, but leaned across the desk on his forearms. "You tell me, ha?"

Torres must force the story out. "Met him on Arkan III—on the fringe of the Kossaluth, autonomous planet, you recall. We'd put in with a consignment of tea. A ship of theirs was in too, and you can bet your brain we went around in armed parties, ready to shoot any Borthudian who might look like a crimp. Or any Borthudian at all; but they kept to themselves. Instead, I saw him, this man they'd snatched, going on some errand. I spoke to him. My friends and I even tried to capture him, so we could bring him back to Earth and get reversed what that electronic hell-machine had done to him—He fought us and got away. God! He'd've been more free if he were in chains. And still I could feel how he wanted out, he was screaming inside, but he couldn't break the conditioning *and he couldn't go crazy either*—"

Torres grew aware that van Rijn had come around the desk and was thrusting a bottle into his hand. "Here, you drink some from this," the merchant said. The liquor burned the whole way down. "I have seen a conditioned man myself once, long ago when I was a rough-and-tumbler. A petty native prince had got it done to him, to keep him for a technical expert when he wanted to go home. We did catch him that time, and took him back for treatment." He returned to his chair and rekindled his pipe. "First, though, we got together with the ship's engineer and made us a little firecracker what we blew off at the royal palace." He chuckled. "The yield was about five kilotons."

"If you want to outfit a punitive expedition, sir," Torres rasped, "I guarantee you can get full crews."

"No." Curled, shoulder-length black locks swished greasily as van Rijn shook his head. "You know the League does not have much of a combat fleet. The trouble with capital ships is, they tie up capital. It is one thing to use a tiny bit of force on a planetbound lordling what has got unreasonable. It is another thing to take on somebody what can take you right on back. Simple tooling up for a war with Borthu, let alone fighting one, would bring many member companies close to bankrupture."

"But what about the precedent, if you tamely let these outrages go on? Who'll be next to make prey of you?"

"*Ja*, there is that. But there is also the Commonwealth government. We try any big-size action, we traders, even though it is far outside the Solar System, and right away we get gibberings about our 'imperialism.' We could get lots of trouble made for us, right here in the heart of civilization. Maybe we get called pirates, because we is not a government ourselves with politicians and bureaucrats telling people what to do. Maybe Sol would actual-like intervene against us on behalf of the Kossaluth, what is 'only exercising sovereignty within its legitimate sphere.' You know how diplomats from Earth has not made any hard effort for getting Borthu to stop. In fact, I tell you, a lot of politicians feel quite chortlesome when they see us wicked profiteers receiving some shaftcraft."

Torres stirred in his seat. "Yes, of course, I'm as disgusted as you with the official reaction, or lack of reaction. But what about the League? I mean, its leaders must have been trying measures short of war. I take it those have come to naught."

"You take that, boy, and keep it for yourself, because I for sure don't want it. *Ja.* Correct. Threats the Borthudians grin at, knowing how hard pinched we is and where. Not good trade offers nor economic sanctions has worked; they is not interested in trade with us. Rathermore, they do expect we will soon shun their territory, like you now want us to. That suits their masters well, not having foreign influentials. . . . Bribes? How do you bribe a being what ranks big in his own civilization and species, both those alien to you? Assassins? *Ach,* I am afraid we squandered several good assassins for no philanthropic result." Van Rijn cursed for two straight minutes without repeating himself. "And there they sit, fat and greedy-gut, across the route to Antares and all stars beyond! It is not to be stood for! No, it is to be jumped on!"

Presently he finished in a calmer tone: "This ultimatum of yours brings matters to a head. Speaking of heads, it is getting time for a tall cold beer. I will soon throw a little brainbooting session with a few fellows and see what oozes out. Maybe we can invent something. You go tell the crewmen they should sit bottom-tight for a while yet, *nie?* Now, would you like to join me in the bar?—No? Then good day to you, Captain, if possible."

It is a truism that the structure of a society is basically determined by its technology. Not in an absolute sense—there may be totally different cultures using identical tools—but the tools settle the possibilities; you can't have interstellar trade without spaceships. A race limited to a single planet, possessing a high knowledge of mechanics but with its basic machines of industry and war requiring a large capital investment, will inevitably tend toward collectivism under one name or another. Free enterprise needs elbow room.

Automation and the mineral wealth of the Solar System made the manufacture of most goods cheap. The cost of energy nosedived when small, clean, simple fusion units became available. Gravitics led to the hyperdrive, which opened a galaxy to exploitation. This also provided a safety valve. A citizen who found his government oppressive could often emigrate elsewhere, an exodus— the Breakup, as it came to be called—that planted liberty on a number of worlds. Their influence in turn loosened bonds upon the mother planet.

Interstellar distances being what they are, and intelligent races having their separate ideas of culture, there was no political union of them. Nor was there much armed conflict; besides the risk of destruction, few had anything to fight about. A race rarely gets to be intelligent without an undue share of built-in ruthlessness, so all was not sweetness and fraternity. However, the various balances of power remained fairly stable. Meanwhile the demand for cargoes grew huge. Not only did colonies want the luxuries of home, and home want colonial products, but the older civilizations had much to swap. It was usually cheaper to import such things than to create the industry needed to make synthetics and substitutes.

Under such conditions, an exuberant capitalism was bound to arise. It was also bound to find mutual interests, form alliances, and negotiate spheres of influence. The powerful companies might be in competition, but their magnates had the wit to see that, overriding this, they shared a need to cooperate in many activities, arbitrate disputes among themselves, and present a united front to the demands of the state—any state.

Governments were limited to a few planetary systems at most; they could do little to control their cosmopolitan merchants. One by one, through bribery, coercion, or sheer despair, they gave up the struggle.

Selfishness is a potent force. Governments, officially dedicated to altruism, remained divided. The Polesotechnic League became a loose kind of supergovernment, sprawling from Canopus to Deneb, drawing its membership and employees from perhaps a thousand species. It was a horizontal society, cutting across political and cultural boundaries. It set its own policies, made its own treaties, established its own bases, fought its own battles... and for a time, in the course of milking the Milky Way, did more to spread a truly universal civilization and enforce a solid *Pax* than all the diplomats in known history.

Nevertheless, it had its troubles.

A mansion among those belonging to Nicholas van Rijn lay on the peak of Kilimanjaro, up among the undying snows. It was an easy spot to defend, just in case, and a favorite for conferences.

His car slanted down through a night of needle-sharp stars, toward high turrets and glowing lights. Looking through the canopy, he picked out Scorpio. Antares flashed a red promise. He shook his fist at the fainter, unseen suns between him and it. "So!" he muttered. "Monkey business with van Rijn. The whole Sagittarius direction waiting to be opened, and you in the way. By damn, this will cost you money, gut and kipper me if it don't."

He thought back to days when he had ridden ships through yonder spaces, bargaining in strange cities or stranger wildernesses, or beneath unblue skies and in poisonous winds, for treasures Earth had not yet imagined. For a moment, wistfulness tugged at him. A long time now since he had been any further than the Moon... poor, aging fat man, chained to a single planet and cursed whenever he turned an honest credit. The Antares route was more important than he cared to admit aloud. If he lost it, he lost his chance at the pioneering that went on beyond, to corporations with offices on the other side of the Kossaluth. You went on expanding or you went under, and being a conspicuous member of the League wouldn't save you. Of course, he could retire, but then what would there be to engage his energies?

The car landed itself. Household staff, liveried and beweaponed, sprang to flank him as he emerged. He wheezed thin chill air into sooty lungs, drew his cloak of phosphorescent onthar skin tightly around him, and scrunched up a graveled garden path to the house. A new maid stood at the door, pert and pretty. He tossed his plumed cap at her and considered making a proposition, but the butler said that the invited persons were already here. Seating himself, more for show than because of weariness, he told the chair, "Conference room" and rolled along corridors paneled in the woods of a dozen planets. A sweet smell of attar of janie and a softly played Mozart quintet enlivened the air.

Four colleagues were poised around a table when he entered, a datacom terminal before each. Kraaknach of the Martian Transport Company was glowing his yellow eyes at a Frans Hals on the wall. Firmage of North American Engineering registered impatience with a puffed cigar. Mjambo, who owned Jo-Boy Technical Services, was talking into his wristphone, but stopped when his host entered. Gornas-Kiew happened to be on Earth and was authorized to speak for the Centaurian conglomerate; "he" sat hunched into "his" shell, naught moving save the delicate antennae.

Van Rijn plumped his mass into an armchair at the head of the table. Waiters appeared with trays of drinks, snacks, and smokes catered for the individuals present. He took a large bite from a limburger-and-onion sandwich and looked inquiringly at the rest.

Kraaknach's face, owlish within the air helmet, turned to him. "Well, Freeman who receives us," he trilled and croaked, "I understand we are met on account of this Borthudian *hrokna*. Did the spacemen make their expected demand?"

"*Ja.*" Van Rijn chose a cigar and rolled it between his fingers. "The situation is changed from desperate to serious. They will not take ships through the Kossaluth, except to fight, while this shanghai business goes on."

"I suppose it is quite unfeasible to deliver a few gigatons' worth of warhead at the Borthudian home planet?" asked Mjambo.

Van Rijn tugged his goatee. "Death and damnation!" He checked his temper. After all, he had invited these specific sophonts here precisely because they had not yet been much concerned with the problem. It had affected their enterprises in varying degrees, of course, but interests elsewhere had been tying up their direct attention. This tiny, outlying corner of the galaxy which Technic civilization has slightly explored is that big and various. Van Rijn was hoping for a fresh viewpoint.

Having repeated the objections he had given Torres, he added: "I must got to admit, also, supposing we could, slaughtering several billion sentients because their leaders make trouble for us is not nice. I do not think the League would long survive being so guilty. Besides, it is wasteful. They should better be made customers of ours."

"Limited action, whittling down their naval strength till they see reason?" wondered Firmage.

"I have had more such programs run through the computers than there is politicians in hell," van Rijn answered. "They every one give the same grismal answer. Allowing for minimal losses, compensations, salaries, risk bonuses, construction, maintenance, replacement, ammunition, depreciation, loss of business due to lack of supervision elsewhere, legal action brought by the Solar Commonwealth and maybe other governments, bribes, loss of profit if the money was invested where it ought to be, et bloody-bestonkered cetera... in a nutshell, we cannot afford it." Reminded, he told the butler, "Simmons, you gluefoot, a bowl of mixed-up nuts, chop-chop, only you don't chop them, understand?"

"You will pardon my ignorance, good sirs," clicked Gornas-Kiew's vocalizer. "I have been quite marginally aware of this unpleasantness. Why are the Borthudians impressing human crews?"

Firmage and Mjambo stared. They had known Centaurians are apt to be single-minded—but this much? Van Rijn simply cracked a Brazil nut between his teeth, awing everybody present except for Gornas-Kiew, and reached for a snifter of brandy. "The gruntbrains have not enough of their own," he said.

"Perhaps I can make it clear," said Kraaknach. Like many Martians of the Sirruch Horde—the latest wave of immigrants to Earth's once desolate neighbor—he was a natural-hatched lecturer. He ran a clawed hand across gray feathers, stuck a rinn tube through the intake sphincter on his helmet, and lit it.

"Borthu is a backward planet, terrestroid to eight points, with autochthons describable as humanoid," he began. "They were at an early industrial, nuclear-power stage when explorers visited them, and their reaction to the presence of a superior culture was paranoid. At least, it was in the largest nation, which shortly proceeded to conquer the rest. It had modernized technologically with extreme rapidity, aided by certain irresponsible elements of this civilization who helped it for high pay. United, the Borthudians set out to acquire an interstellar empire. Today they dominate a space about forty light-years across, though they actually occupy just a few Solar-type systems within it. By and large, they want nothing to do with the outside universe: doubtless because the rulers fear that such contact will be dangerous to the stability of their régime. Certainly they are quite able to supply their needs within the boundaries of their dominion—with the sole exception of efficient spacemen. If we ourselves, with all our capabilities in the field of robotics, have not yet been able to produce totally automated spacecraft which are reliable, how much worse must the Borthudians feel the lack of enough crews."

"Hm," said Firmage. "I've already thought about subversion. I can't believe their whole populace is happy. If we could get only a few regularly scheduled freighters in there...double agents...the Kossalu and his whole filthy government overthrown from within—"

"Of course we will follow that course in due course, if we can," van Rijn interrupted. "But at best it takes much time. Meanwhile, competitors sew up the Sagittarius frontier. We need a *quick* way to get back our routes through that space."

Kraaknach puffed oily smoke. "To continue," he said, "the Borthudians can build as many ships as they wish, which is a great many since their economy is expanding. In fact, that economy requires constant expansion if the whole empire is not to collapse, inasmuch as the race-mystique of its masters has promoted a population explosion. But they cannot produce trained spacehands at the needful rate. Pride, and a not unjustified fear of ideological contamination, prevents them from sending students to Technic planets, or hiring from among us; and they have only one understaffed astronautical academy of their own."

"I know," said Mjambo. "It'd be a whopping good market for me if we could change their minds for them."

"Accordingly," Kraaknach proceeded, "they have in the past two years taken to waylaying our vessels. Doubtless they expect to be shunned eventually, as the Brotherhood has now voted to do. But then they can afford to let much of their population die back, while using what manned ships they have to maintain the rest. Without fear of direct or indirect interference from outside, the masters can 'remold' Borthudian society at leisure. It is a pattern not unknown to Terrestrial history, I believe.

"At present, their actions are obviously in defiance of what has been considered interstellar law. However, only the Commonwealth, among governments, has the potential of doing anything about it—and there is such popular revulsion on Earth at the thought of war that the Commonwealth has confined itself to a few feeble protests. Indeed, a strong faction in it is not displeased to see the arrogant Polesotechnic League discomfited. Certain spokesmen are even arguing that territorial sovereignty should be formally recognized as extending through interstellar space. A vicious principle if ever there was one, *hru*?"

He extracted the rinn tube and dropped it down an ashtaker. "In any event," he finished, "they capture the men, brain-channel them, and assign them to their own transport fleet. It takes years to train an astronaut. We are losing a major asset in this alone."

"Can't we improve our evasive action?" inquired Firmage. "Any astronomical distance is so *damn* big. Why can't we avoid their patrols altogether?"

"Eighty-five percent of our ships do precisely that," van Rijn reminded him. "It is not enough. The unlucky minority—"

—who were detected by sensitive instruments within the maximum range of about a light-year, by the instantaneous pseudogravitational pulses of hyperdrive; on whom the Borthudians then closed in, using naval vessels which were faster and more maneuverable than merchantmen—

"—they is gotten to be too many by now. The Brotherhood will accept no more. Confidential amongst the we of us, I would not either. And, *ja,* plenty different escape tactics is been tried, as well as cutting engines and lying low. None of them work very good."

"Well, then, how about convoying our ships through?" Firmage persisted.

"At what cost? I have been with the figures. It also would mean operating the Antares run at a loss—quite apart from those extra warcraft we would have to build. It would make Sagittarian trade out of the damned question."

"Why can't we arm the merchantmen themselves?"

"Bah! Wasn't you listening to Freeman Kraaknach? Robotics is never yet got to where live brains can be altogether replaced, except in bureaucrats." Deliberately irritating, which might pique forth ideas, van Rijn added what was everybody's knowledge:

"A frigate-class ship needs twenty men for the weapons and instruments. An unarmed freighter needs only four. Consider the wages paid to spacefolk; we would really get folked. Also, sixteen extra on every ship would mean cutting down operations elsewhere, for lack of crews. Not to mention the cost of the outfitting. We cannot afford all this; we would lose money in big fat globs. What is worse, the Kossalu knows we would. He need only wait, holding back his fig-plucking patrols, till we is too broke to continue. Then he would maybe be tempted to start conquering some more, around Antares."

Firmage tapped the table with a restless finger. "Everything we've thought of seems to be ruled out," he said. "Suggestions, anybody?"

Silence grew, under the radiant ceiling.

Gornas-Kiew broke it: "Precisely how are captures made? It is impossible to exchange shots while in hyperdrive."

"Statistically impossible," amended Kraaknach. "Energy beams are out of the question. Material missiles have to be hypered themselves, or they would revert to true, sublight velocity and be left behind as soon as they emerged from the drive field. Furthermore, to make a hit, they must be precisely in phase with the target. A good pilot can phase in on another ship, but the operation involves too many variables for any cybernet of useful size."

"I tell you how," snarled van Rijn. "The pest-bedamned Borthudians detect the vibration-wake from afar. They compute an intercept course. Coming close, they phase in and slap on a tractor beam. Then they haul themselves up alongside, burn through the hull or an airlock, and board."

"Why, the answer looks simple enough," said Mjambo. "Equip our craft with pressor beams. Keep the enemy ships at arm's length."

"You forget, esteemed colleague, that beams of either positive or negative sign are powered from the engine," said Kraaknach. "A naval vessel has much stronger engines than a merchantman."

"Give our crews small arms. Let them blast down the boarding parties."

"The illegitimate - offspring - of - interspecies - crosses Borthudians already have arms, also hands what hold weapons," snorted van Rijn. "Phosphor and farts! Do you think four men can stand off twenty?"

"M-m-m . . . yes, I see your point." Firmage nodded. "But look here, we can't do anything about this without laying out *some* cash. I'm not sure what the mean profit is—"

"On the average, for everybody's combined Antarean voyages, about thirty percent on each run," said van Rijn promptly.

Mjambo started. "How the devil do you get the figures for my company?" he exclaimed.

Van Rijn grinned and drew on his cigar.

"That gives us a margin to use," said Gornas-Kiew. "We can invest in military equipment to such an extent that our profit is less—though I agree there must still be a final result in the black—for the duration of this emergency."

"It'd be worth it," said Mjambo. "In fact, I'd take a fair-sized loss just to teach those bastards a lesson."

"No, no." Van Rijn lifted a hand which, after years in offices, was still the broad muscular paw of a working spaceman. "Revenge and destruction are un-Christian thoughts. Also, I have told you, they do not pay very well, since it is hard to sell anything to a corpse. The problem is to find some means inside our resources what will make it unprofitable for Borthu to raid us. Not being stupid heads, they will then stop raiding and we can maybe later do business."

"You're a cold-blooded one," said Mjambo.

"Not always," replied van Rijn blandly. "Like a sensible man, I set my thermostat according to what is called for. In this case, what we need is a scientifical approach with elegant mathematics—"

Abruptly he dropped his glance and covered a shiver by pouring himself another glassful. He had gotten an idea.

When the others had argued for a fruitless hour, he said: "Freemen, this gets us nowhere, *nie?* Perhaps we are not stimulated enough to think clear."

"What do you propose?" sighed Mjambo.

"Oh . . . an agreement. A pool, or prize, or reward for whoever solves this problem. For example, ten percent of everybody else's Antarean profits for the next ten years."

"Hoy, there!" burst from Firmage. "If I know you, you robber, you've come up with an answer."

"No, no, no. By my honor I swear it. I have some beginning thoughts, maybe, but I am only a poor rough old space walloper without the fine education you beings have had. I could too easy be wrong."

"What is your notion?"

"Best I not say yet, until it is more fermented. But please to note, he who tries something active will take on the risk and expense. If he succeeds, he saves profits for all. Does not a tiny return on his investment sound fair and proper?"

There was more argument. Van Rijn smiled with

infinite benevolence. He settled at last for a compact, recorded on ciphertape, whose details would be computed later.

Beaming, he clapped his hands. "Freemen," he said, "we have worked hard tonight and soon comes much harder work. By damn, I think we deserve a little celebration. Simmons, prepare an orgy."

Rafael Torres had considered himself unshockable by any mere words. He was wrong. "Are you serious?" he gasped.

"In confidentials, of course," van Rijn answered. "The crew must be good men like you. Can you recommend more?"

"No—"

"We will not be stingy with the bonuses."

Torres shook his head violently. "Out of the question, sir. The Brotherhood's refusal to enter the Kossaluth on anything except a punitive expedition is absolute. This one you propose is not, as you describe it. We can't lift the ban without another vote, which would necessarily be a public matter."

"You can publicly vote again after we see if the idea works," van Rijn pressed him. "The first trip will have to be secret."

"Then the first trip will have to do without a crew."

"Bile on a boomerang!" Van Rijn's fist crashed against his desk. He surged to his feet. "What sort of putzing cowards do I deal with? In my day we were men! And we had ideals, I can tell you. We would have boosted through hell's open gates if you paid us enough."

Torres sucked hard on his cigarette. "The ban must stand. None but a Lodgemaster can—Well, all right, I'll say it." Anger was a cold flaring in him. "You want men to take an untried ship into enemy sky and invite attack. If they lose, they're condemned to a lifetime of praying, with what's left of their free wills, for death. If they succeed, they win a few measly kilocredits. In either case, you sit back here plump and safe. God damn it, no!"

Van Rijn stood quiet for a while. This was something he had not quite foreseen.

His gaze wandered forth, out the transparency, to the narrow sea. A yacht was passing by, lovely in white sails and slender hull. Really, he ought to spend more time on his own. Money wasn't that important. Was it? This was not such a bad world, this Earth, even when one was being invaded by age and fat. It was full of blossoms and burgundy, clean winds and lovely women, Mozart melodies and fine books. Doubtless his memories of earlier days in space were colored by nostalgia. . . .

He reached a decision and turned around to face his visitor. "A Lodgemaster can come on such a trip without telling peoples," he said. "The union rules give you discretion. You think you can raise two more like yourself, hah?"

"I told you, Freeman, I won't so much as consider it."

"Even if I myself am the skipper?"

The *Mercury* did not, outwardly, look different after the engineers were finished with her. Her cargo was the same as usual, too: cinnamon, ginger, pepper, cloves, tea, whisky, gin. If he was going to Antares, van Rijn did not intend to waste the voyage. He did omit wines, doubting their quality could stand as rough a trip as this one would be.

The alterations were internal, extra hull bracing and a new and monstrously powerful engine. The actuarial computers estimated the cost of such an outfitting as three times the total profit from all her journeys during an average service life. Van Rijn had winced, but put a shipyard to work.

In truth, his margin was slim, and he was gambling more on it than he could afford to lose. However, if the Kossalu of Borthu had statisticians of his own—always assuming that the idea proved out—

Well, if it didn't, Nicholas van Rijn would die in battle, or be liquidated as too old for usefulness, or become a brain-channeled slave, or be held for a ruinous ransom. The possibilities looked about equally bad.

He installed himself, dark-haired and multiply curved Dorcas Gherardini, and a stout supply of brandy, tobacco, and ripe cheese, in the captain's cabin. One might as well be comfortable. Torres was his mate, Captains Petrovich and Seiichi his engineers. The *Mercury* lifted from Quito Spaceport without fanfare, waited unpretentiously in orbit for clearance, then accelerated on negagrav away from Sol. At the required distance, she went on hyperdrive and outpaced light.

Van Rijn sat back on the bridge and lit his churchwarden pipe. "Now is a month's going to Antares," he said piously. "Good St. Dismas, watch over us."

"I'll stick by St. Nicholas, patron of travelers," replied Torres. "In spite of his being your namesake."

Van Rijn looked hurt. "By damn, do you not respect my morals?"

Torres shrugged. "Well, I admire your courage— nobody can say you lack guts—" van Rijn gave him a hard look—"and if anybody can pull this off, you can. Set a pirate to catch a pirate."

"You younger generations got a loud mouth and no manners." The merchant blew malodorous clouds. "In my day, we said 'sir' to the captain even when we mutinied."

"I'm still worried about a particular detail," admitted Torres. He had had much more to occupy mind and body than the working out of strategies, mainly the accumulation of as many enjoyable memories as possible. "I suppose it's a fairly safe bet that the enemy hasn't yet heard about our travel ban. Still, the recent absence of ships must have made him think. Besides, our course brings us so near a known Borthudian base that we're certain to be detected. Suppose he gets suspicious and dispatches half a dozen vessels to jump us?"

"The likelihood of that is quite low, because he keeps his bloody-be-damned patrol craft cruising far apart, to maximize their chances of spotting a catch. If he feels wary of us, he will simply not attack; but this also I doubt, for a prize is valuable." Van Rijn heaved his bulk onto his feet. One good thing about spacefaring, you could set the gravity-field generator low and feel almost lissome again. "What you at your cockamamie age do not quite understand, my friend, is that there are hardly any certainties in life. Always we must go on probabilities.

The secret of success is to make the odds favor you. Then in the long run you are sure to come out ahead. It is your watch now, and I recommend you project a book on statistical theory to pass the time. The data bank has an excellent library. As for me, I will be in conference with Freelady Gherardini."

"I wish to blazes I could run commands of mine the way you run this of yours," said Torres mournfully.

Van Rijn waved an expansive hand. "Why not, my boy, why not? So long as you make money and no trouble for the Company, the Company does not peek over your shoulder. The trouble with you young snapperwhippers is you lack initiative. When you are a poor old feeble fat man like me, you will look back and regret your lost opportunities."

Low-gee or no, the deck thumped beneath his feet as he departed.

Heaven was darkness filled with a glory of suns. Viewscreens framed the spilling silver of the Milky Way, ruby spark of Antares, curling edge of a nebula limned by the glare of an enmeshed star. Brightest in vision stood Borthu's, yellow as minted gold.

The ship drove on as she had done for a pair of weeks, pulsing in and out of four-space at thousands of times per second, loaded with a tension that neared the detonation point.

On a wardroom bench, Dorcas posed slim legs and high prow with a care so practiced as to be unconscious. She could not pull her eyes from the screen. "It's beautiful," she said in a small voice. "Somehow that doubles the horror."

Van Rijn sprawled beside her, his majestic nose aimed aloft. "What is horrible, my little sinusoid?" he asked.

"Them . . . waiting to pounce on us and—In God's name, why did I come along?"

"I believe there was mention of a tygron coat and flamedrop earrings."

"But suppose they do capture us." Cold, her fingers clutched at his arm. "What will happen to me?"

"I told you I have set up a ransom fund for you. I told

you also, maybe they will not bother to collect it, or maybe we get broken to bits in the fight. Satan's horns and the devil who gave them to him! Be still, will you?"

The audio intercom came to life with Torres' urgent words: "Wake of high-powered ship detected, approaching to intercept."

"All hands to stations!" roared van Rijn.

Dorcas screamed. He tucked her under one arm, carried her down the passageway—collecting a few scratches en route—to his cabin, where he tossed her on the bed and told her she'd better strap in. Puffing, he arrived on the bridge. The visuals showed Petrovich and Seiichi in the engine room, armored, their faces a-glisten with sweat. Torres sat gnawing his lip, fingers unsteady as he tuned instruments.

"Hokay," said van Rijn, "here is the thing we have come for. I hope you each remember what you have to do, because this is not another rehearsal where I can gently correct your thumb-brained mistakes." He whacked his great bottom into the main control chair and secured the safety harness. When his fingers tickled the console, giving computers and efferent circuits their orders, he felt the sensitive response of that entire organism which was the ship. Thus far *Mercury* had been under normal power, the energy generator half-idle. It was good to know how many wild horses he could call up.

The strange vessel drew in communication range, where the two drive fields measurably impinged on each other. As customary, both pilots felt their way toward the same phase and frequency of oscillation, until a radio wave could pass between them and be received. On the bridge of the human craft, the outercom chimed. Torres pressed the accept button and the screen came to life.

A Borthudian officer looked out. His garments clung dead black to a cat-lithe frame. The face was semihuman, though hairless and tinged with blue; yellow eyes smoldered under a narrow forehead. Behind him could be seen his own bridge, a companion who sat before a fire-control terminal, and the usual six-armed basalt idol.

"Terrestrial ship ahoy!" He ripped out fluent Anglic,

harshly accented by the shapes of larynx and mouth. "This is Captain Rentharik of the Kossalu's frigate *Gantok*. By the law, most sacred, of the Kossaluth of Borthu, you are guilty of trespass on the domains of His Mightiness. Stand by to be boarded."

"Why, you out-from-under-wet-logs-crawling cocky-pop!" Van Rijn made himself flush turkey red. "Not bad enough you hijack my men and transports, with their good expensive cargoes, but you have the copperbound nerve to call it legal!"

Rentharik fingered a small ceremonial dagger hung about his neck. "Old man, the writ of the Kossalu runs through this entire volume of space. You can save yourself added punishment—nerve-pulsing—by submitting peacefully to judgment."

"It is understood by *civilized* races that interstellar space is free for every innocent passage."

Rentharik smiled, revealing bright-green teeth of nonhuman shape. "We enforce our own laws here, Captain."

"Ja, but by damn, this time you are trying to use force on van Rijn. They are going to be surprised back on that dingleberry you call your home planet."

Rentharik spoke at a recorder in his native language. "I have just made a note recommending you be assigned to the Ilyan run after conditioning. Organic compounds in the atmosphere there produce painful allergic reactions in your species, yet not so disabling that we consider it worthwhile to issue airsuits. Let the rest of your crew pay heed."

Van Rijn's face lit up. "Listen, if you would hire spacemen honest instead of enslaving them, we got plenty of antiallergenic treatments and medicines. I would be glad to supply you them, at quite a reasonable commission."

"No more chatter. You are to be grappled and boarded. Captured personnel receive nerve-pulsing in proportion to the degree of their resistance."

Rentharik's image blanked.

Torres licked sandy lips. Turning up the magnification

in a viewscreen, he picked out the Borthudian frigate. She was a darkling shark-form, only half the tonnage of the dumpy merchantman but with gun turrets etched against remote star-clouds. She came riding in along a smooth curve, matched hypervelocities with practiced grace, and flew parallel to her prey, a few kilometers off.

The intercom gave forth a scream. Van Rijn swore as the visual showed him Dorcas, out of her harness and raving around his cabin in utter hysterics. Why, she might spill all his remaining liquor, and Antares still eleven days off!

A small, pulsing jar went through hull and bones. *Gantok* had reached forth a tractor beam and laid hold of *Mercury*.

"Torres," said van Rijn. "You stand by, boy, and take over if somewhat happens to me. I maybe want your help anyway, if the game gets too gamy. Petrovich, Seiichi, you got to maintain our own beams and hold them tight, no matter what. Hokay? We go!"

Gantok was pulling herself closer. Petrovich kicked in full power. For a moment, safety arcs blazed blue, ozone spat forth a smell of thunder, a roar filled the air. Then equilibrium was reached, with only a low droning to bespeak unthinkable energies at work.

A pressor beam lashed out, an invisible hammerblow of repulsion, five times the strength of the enemy tractor. Van Rijn heard *Mercury*'s ribs groan with the stress. *Gantok* shot away, turning end over end, until she was lost to vision among the stars.

"Ha, ha!" bellowed van Rijn. "We spill their apples, eh? By damn! Next we show them real fun!"

The Borthudian hove back in sight. She clamped on again, full-strength attraction. Despite the pressor, *Mercury* was yanked toward her. Seiichi cursed and gave back his full thrust.

For a moment van Rijn thought his ship would burst open. He saw a deckplate buckle under his feet and heard metal elsewhere shear. But *Gantok* was batted away as if by a troll's fist.

"Not so hard! Not so hard, you dumbhead! Let me

control the beams." Van Rijn's hands danced over the console. "We want to keep him for a souvenir, remember?"

He used a spurt of drive to overhaul the foe. His right hand steered *Mercury* while his left wielded the tractor and the pressor, seeking a balance. The engine noise rose to a sound like heavy surf. The interior gee-field could not compensate for all the violence of accelerations now going on; harness creaked as his weight was hurled against it. Torres, Petrovich, and Seiichi made themselves part of the machinery, additions to the computer systems which implemented the commands his fingers gave.

The Borthudian's image vanished out of viewscreens as he slipped *Mercury* into a different phase. Ordinarily this would have sundered every contact between the vessels. However, the gravitic forces which he had locked onto his opponent paid no heed to how she was oscillating between relativistic and nonrelativistic quantum states; her mass remained the same. He had simply made her weapons useless against him, unless her pilot matched his travel pattern again. To prevent that, he ordered a program of random variations, within feasible limits. Given time to collect data, perform stochastic analysis, and exercise the intuition of a skilled living brain, the enemy pilot could still have matched; such a program could not be random in an absolute sense. Van Rijn did not propose to give him time.

Now thoroughly scared, the Borthudian opened full drive and tried to break away. Van Rijn equalized positive and negative forces in a heterodyning interplay which, in effect, welded him fast. Laughing, he threw his own superpowered engine into reverse. *Gantok* shuddered to a halt and went backwards with him. The fury of that made *Mercury* cry out in every member. He could not keep the linkage rigid without danger of being broken apart; he must vary it, flexibly, yet always shortening the gap between hulls.

"Ha, like a fish we play him! Good St. Peter the Fisherman, help us not let him get away!"

Through the racket around him, van Rijn heard

something snap, and felt a rushing of air. Petrovich cried it for him: "Burst plate—section four. If it isn't welded back soon, we'll take worse damage."

The merchant leaned toward Torres. "Can you take this rod and reel?" he asked. "I need a break from it, I feel my judgment getting less quick, and as for the repair, we must often make such in my primitive old days."

Torres nodded, grim-faced. "You ought to enjoy this, you know," van Rijn reproved him, and undid his harness.

Rising, he crossed a deck which pitched beneath his feet almost as if he were in a watercraft. *Gantok* was still making full-powered spurts of drive, trying to stress *Mercury* into ruin. She might succeed yet. The hole in the side had sealed itself, but remained a point of weakness from which further destruction could spread.

At the lockers, van Rijn clambered into his outsize spacesuit. Hadn't worn armor in a long time . . . forgotten how quickly sweat made it stink. . . . The equipment he would need was racked nearby. He loaded it onto his back and cycled through the airlock. Emerging on the hull, he was surrounded by a darkness-whitening starblaze.

Any of those shocks that rolled and yawed the ship underfoot could prove too much for the grip of his bootsoles upon her. Pitched out beyond the hyperdrive fields and reverting to normal state, he would be forever lost in a microsecond as the craft flashed by at translight hyperspeed. Infinity was a long ways to fall.

Electric discharges wavered blue around him. Occasionally he saw a flash in the direction of *Gantok,* when phasings happened momentarily to coincide. She must be shooting wildly, on the one-in-a-billion chance that some missile would be in exactly the right state when it passed through *Mercury* . . . or through van Rijn's stomach . . . no, through the volume of space where these things coexisted with different frequencies . . . must be precise. . . .

There was the fit-for-perdition hull plate. Clamp on the jack, bend the thing back toward some rough semblance of its proper shape . . . ah, heave ho . . . electric-powered hydraulics or not, it still took strength to do this; maybe some muscle remained under the blubber...lay out the reinforcing bars, secure them temporarily, unlimber your torch, slap down your glare filter...handle a flame and recall past years when he went hell-roaring in his own person...whoops, that lunge nearly tossed him off into God's great icebox!

He finished his job, reflected that the next ship of this model would need still heavier bracing, and crept back to the airlock, trying to ignore the aches that throbbed in his entire body. As he came inside, the rolling and plunging and racketing stopped. For an instant he wondered if he had been stricken deaf.

Torres' face, wet and haggard, popped into an intercom screen. Hoarsely, he said: "They've quit. They must realize their own boat will most likely go to pieces before ours—"

Van Rijn, who had heard him through a sonic pickup in his space helmet, straightened his bruised back and whooped. "Excellent! Now pull us up quick according to plan, you butterbrain!"

He felt the twisting sensation of reversion to normal state, and the hyperdrive thrum died away. Almost he lost his footing as *Mercury* flew off sidewise.

It had been Rentharik's last, desperate move, killing his oscillations, dropping solidly back into the ordinary condition of things where no speed can be greater than that of light. Had his opponent not done likewise, had the ships drawn apart at such an unnatural rate, stresses along the force-beams linking them would promptly have destroyed both, and he would have had that much vengeance. The Terran craft was, however, equipped with a detector coupled to an automatic cutoff, for just this possibility.

Torres barely averted a collision. At once he shifted *Mercury* around until her beams, unbreakably strong, held her within a few meters of *Gantok,* at a point where the weapons of the latter could not be brought to bear. If the Borthudian crew should be wild enough to suit up and try to cross the intervening small distance, to cut a way in and board, it would be no trick to flick them off into the deeps with a small auxiliary pressor.

Van Rijn bellowed mirth, hastened to discard his gear, and sought the bridge for a heart-to-heart talk with Rentharik. "—You is now enveloped in our hyperfield any time we switch it on, and it is strong enough to drag you along no matter what you do with your engines, understand? We is got several times your power. You better relax and let us take you with us peaceful, because if we get any suspicions about you, we will use our beams to pluck your vessel in small bits. Like they say on Earth, what is sauce for the stews is sauce for the pander.... Do not use bad language, please; my receiver is blushing." To his men: "Hokay, full speed ahead with this little minnow what thought it was a shark!"

A laser call as they entered the Antarean System brought a League cruiser out to meet them. The colony was worth that much protection against bandits, political agitators, and other imaginable nuisances. Though every planet here was barren, the innermost long since engulfed by the expansion of the great dying sun, sufficient mineral wealth existed on the outer worlds—together with a convenient location as a trade center for this entire sector—to support a human population equal to that of Luna. Van Rijn turned his prize over to the warcraft and let Torres bring the battered *Mercury* in. Himself, he slept a great deal, while Dorcas kept her ears covered. Though the Borthudians had, sanely, stayed passive, the strain of keeping alert for some further attempt of theirs had been considerable.

Torres had wanted to communicate with the prisoners, but van Rijn would not allow it. "No, no, my boy, we unmoralize them worse by refusing the light of our eyes. I want the good Captain Rentharik's fingernails chewed down to the elbow when I see him again."

Having landed, he invited himself to stay at the governor's mansion in Redsun City and make free use of wine cellar and concubines. Between banquets, he found time to check on local prices and raise the tag on pepper a millicredit per gram. The settlers would grumble, but they could afford it. Besides, were it not for him, their meals would be drab affairs, or else they'd have to synthesize their condiments at twice the cost, so didn't he deserve an honest profit?

After three days of this, he decided it was time to summon Rentharik. He lounged on the governor's throne in the high-pillared reception hall, pipe in right fist, bottle in left, small bells braided into his ringlets but merely a dirty bathrobe across his belly. One girl played on a shiverharp, one fanned him with peacock feathers, and one sat on an arm of the seat, giggling and dropping chilled grapes into his mouth. For the time being, he approved of the universe.

Gaunt and bitter between two League guardsmen, Rentharik advanced across the gleaming floor, halted before his captor, and waited.

"Ah, so. Greetings and salubrications," van Rijn boomed. "I trust you have had a pleasant stay? The local jails are much recommended, I am told."

"For your race, perhaps," the Borthudian said in dull anger. "My crew and I have been wretched."

"Dear me. My nose bleeds for you."

Pride spat: "More will bleed erelong, you pirate. His Mightiness will take measures."

"Your maggoty kinglet will take no measurements except of how far his crest is fallen," declared van Rijn. "If the civilized planets did not dare fight when he was playing buccaneer, he will not when the foot is in the other shoe. No, he will accept the facts and learn to love them."

"What are your immediate intentions?" Rentharik asked stoically.

Van Rijn stroked his goatee. "Well, now, it may be we can collect a little ransom, perhaps, eh? If not, the local mines are always short of labor, because conditions is kind of hard. Criminals get assigned to them. However, out of my sugar-sweet goodness, I let you choose one person, not yourself, what may go home freely and report what has happened. I will supply a boat what can make the trip. After that we negotiate, starting with rental on the boat."

Rentharik narrowed his eyes. "See here. I know how

your vile mercantile society works. You do nothing that
has no money return. You are not capable of it. And to
equip a vessel like yours—able to seize a warship—must
cost more than the vessel can ever hope to earn."

"Oh, very quite. It costs about three times as much. Of
course, we gain some of that back from auctioning off our
prizes, but I fear they is too specialized to raise high bids."

"So. We will strangle your Antares route. Do not
imagine we will stop patrolling our sovereign realm. If
you wish a struggle of attrition, we can outlast you."

"Ah, ah." Van Rijn waggled his pipestem. "That is
what you cannot do, my friend. You can reduce our gains
considerably, but you cannot eliminate them. Therefore
we can continue our traffic so long as we choose. You see,
each voyage nets an average thirty percent profit."

"But it costs three hundred percent of that profit to
outfit a ship—"

"Indeed. But we are only special-equipping every
fourth ship. That means we operate on a small margin,
yes, but a little arithmetic should show you we can still
scrape by in the black ink."

"Every fourth?" Rentharik shook his head, frankly
puzzled. "What is your advantage? Out of every four
encounters, we will win three."

"True. And by those three victories, you capture twelve
slaves. The fourth time, we rope in twenty Borthudian
spacemen. The loss of ships we can absorb, because it will
not go on too long and will be repaid us. You see, you will
never know beforehand which craft is going to be the one
that can fight back. You will either have to disband your
press gangs or quickly get them whittled away." Van Rijn
swigged from his bottle. "Understand? You are up against
loaded dice which will prong you edgewise unless you
drop out of the game fast."

Rentharik crouched, as if to leap, and raged: "I
learned, here, that your spacefolk will no longer travel
through the Kossaluth. Do you think reducing the
number of impressments by a quarter will change that
resolution?"

Van Rijn demonstrated what it is to grin fatly. "If I

know my spacefolk . . . why, of course. Because if you do continue to raid us, you will soon reduce yourselves to such few crews as you are helpless. Then you will *have* to deal with us, or else the League comes in and overthrows your whole silly hermit-kingdom system. That would be so quick and easy an operation, there would be no chance for the politicians at home to interfere.

"Our terms will include freeing of all slaves and big fat indemnities. Great big fat indemnities. They do right now, naturally, so the more prisoners you take in future, the worse it will cost you. Any man or woman worth salt can stand a couple years' service on your nasty rustbuckets, if this means afterward getting paid enough to retire on in luxuriance. Our main trouble will be fighting off the excessive volunteers."

He cleared his throat, buttered his tone, and went on: "Is you therefore not wise for making agreement right away? We will be very lenient if you do. Since you are then short of crews, you can send students to our academies at not much more than the usual fees. Otherwise we will just want a few minor trade concessions—"

"And in a hundred years, you will own us," Rentharik half-snarled, half-groaned.

"If you do not agree, by damn, we will own you in much less time than that. You can try impressing more of our people and bleed yourselves to death; then we come in and free them and take what is left of everything you had. Or you can leave our ships alone on their voyages—but then your subjects will soon know, and your jelly-built empire will break up nearly as quick, because how you going to keep us from delivering subversionists and weapons for rebels along the way? Or you can return your slaves right off, and make the kind of bargain with us what I have been pumping at you. In that case, you at least arrange that your ruling class loses power only, in an orderly way, and not their lives. Take your choice. You is well enough hooked that it makes no big matter to me."

The merchant shrugged. "You, personal," he continued, "you pick your delegate and we will let him go report to your chief swine. You might maybe pass on the word how Nicholas van Rijn of the Polesotechnic League does nothing without good reason, nor says anything what is not calm and sensible. Why, just the name of my ship could have warned you."

Rentharik seemed to shrivel. "How?" he whispered.

"Mercury," the man explained, "was the old Roman god of commerce, gambling . . . and, *ja,* thieves."

The following tale is here because it shows a little more of the philosophy and practice which once animated the Polesotechnic League. Grip well: already these were becoming somewhat archaic, if not obsolete. Nevertheless, the person concerned appears to have soared high for long years afterward. Children of his moved to Avalon with Falkayn. This story was written in her later years by one of them, Judith, drawing upon her father's reminiscences when she was young and on a good knowledge of conditions as they had been in his own youth. It appeared in a periodical of the time called *Morgana*.

ESAU

The cab obtained clearance from certain machines and landed on the roof of the Winged Cross. Emil Dalmady paid and stepped out. When it took off, he felt suddenly very alone. The garden was fragrant around him in a warm deep-blue summer's dusk; at this height, the sounds of Chicago Integrate were a murmur as of a distant ocean; the other towers and the skyways between them were an elven forest through which flitted will-o'-the-wisp aircars and beneath which—as if Earth had gone transparent—a fantastic galaxy of many-colored lights was blinking awake farther than eye could reach. But the penthouse bulking ahead might have been a hill where a grizzly bear had its den.

The man squared his shoulders. *Haul in,* he told himself. *He won't eat you.* Anger lifted afresh. *I might just eat him.* He strode forward: a stocky, muscular figure in a blue zipskin, features broad, high of cheekbones, snubnosed, eyes green and slightly tilted, hair reddish black.

But despite stiffened will, the fact remained that he had not expected a personal interview with any merchant prince of the Polesotechnic League, and in one of the latter's own homes. When a live butler had admitted him, and he had crossed an improbably long stretch of trollcat rug to the VieWall end of a luxury-cluttered living room, and was confronting Nicholas van Rijn, his throat tightened and his palms grew wet.

"Good evening," the host rumbled. "Welcome." His corpulent corpus did not rise from the lounger. Dalmady didn't mind. Not only bulk but height would have dwarfed him. Van Rijn waved a hand at a facing seat; the other gripped a liter tankard of beer. "Sit. Relax. You look quivery like a blanc-mange before a firing squad. What you drink, smoke, chew, sniff, or elsewise make amusements with?"

Dalmady lowered himself to an edge. Van Rijn's great hook-beaked, multichinned, mustached and goateed visage, framed in black shoulder-length ringlets, crinkled with a grin. Beneath the sloping brow, small jet eyes glittered at the newcomer. "Relax," he urged again. "Give the form-fitting a chance. Not so fun-making an embrace like a pretty girl, but less extracting, ha? I think maybe a little glass Genever and bitters over dry ice is a tranquilizator for you." He clapped.

"Sir," Dalmady said, harshly in his tension, "I don't want to seem ungracious, but—"

"But you came to Earth breathing flame and brimrocks, and went through six echelons of the toughest no-saying secretaries and officers what the Solar Spice and Liquors Company has got, like a bulldozer chasing a cowdozer, demanding to see whoever the crockhead was what fired you after what you done yonderways. Nobody had a chance to explain. Trouble was, they assumptioned you knew things what they take for granted. So natural, what they said sounded to you like a flushoff and you hurricaned your way from them to somebody else."

Van Rijn offered a cigar out of a gold humidor whose workmanship Dalmady couldn't identify except that it was nonhuman. The young man shook his head. The merchant selected one himself, bit off the end and spat that expertly into a receptor, and inhaled the tobacco to ignition. "Well," he continued, "somebody would have got through into you at last, only then I learned about you and ordered this meeting. I would have wanted to talk at you anyhows. Now I shall clarify everything like Hindu butter."

His geniality was well nigh as overwhelming as his wrath would have been, assuming the legends about him were true. *And he could be setting me up for a thunderbolt,* Dalmady thought, and clung to his indignation as he answered:

"Sir, if your outfit is dissatisfied with my conduct on Suleiman, it might at least have told me why, rather than sending a curt message that I was being replaced and should report to HQ. Unless you can prove to me that I bungled, I will not accept demotion. It's a question of personal honor more than professional standing. They think that way where I come from. I'll quit. And ... there are plenty of other companies in the League that will be glad to hire me."

"Ture, true, in spite of every candle I burn to St. Dismas." Van Rijn sighed through his cigar, engulfing Dalmady in smoke. "Always they try to pirate my executives what have not yet sworn fealty, like the thieves they are. And I, poor old lonely fat man, trying to run this enterprise personal what stretches across so many whole worlds, even with modern computer technology I get melted down from overwork, and too few men for helpers what is not total gruntbrains, and some of them got to be occupied just luring good executives away from elsewhere." He took a noisy gulp of beer. "Well."

"I suppose you've read my report, sir," was Dalmady's gambit.

"Today. So much information flowing from across the light-years, how can this weary old noggle hold it without data flowing back out like ear wax? Let me review to make sure I got it tesseract. Which means—ho, ho!— straight in four dimensions."

Van Rijn wallowed deeper into his lounger, bridged hairy fingers, and closed his eyes. The butler appeared with a coldly steaming and hissing goblet. *If this is his idea of a small drink—!* Dalmady thought. Grimly, he forced himself to sit at ease and sip.

"Now." The cigar waggled in time to the words. "This star what its discoverer called Osman is out past Antares, on the far edge of present-day regular-basis League activities. One planet is inhabited, called by humans Suleiman. Subjovian; life based on hydrogen, ammonia, methane; primitive natives, but friendly. Turned out, on the biggest continent grows a plant we call...um-m-m ...bluejack, what the natives use for a spice and tonic. Analysis showed a complicated blend of chemicals, answering sort of to hormonal stuffs for us, with synergistic effects. No good to oxygen breathers, but maybe we can sell to hydrogen breathers elsewhere.

"Well, we found very few markets, at least what had anythings to offer we wanted. You need a special biochemistry for bluejack to be beneficient. So synthesis would cost us more, counting investment and freight charges from chemical-lab centers, than direct harvesting by natives on Suleiman, paid for in trade goods. Given that, we could show a wee profit. Quite teensy—whole operation is near-as-damn marginal—but as long as things stayed peaceful, well, why not turn a few honest credits?

"And things was peaceful, too, for years. Natives cooperated fine, bringing in bluejack to warehouses. Outshipping was one of those milk runs where we don't knot up capital in our own vessels, we contract with a freighter line to make regular calls. Oh, *ja,* contretemps kept on countertiming—bad seasons, bandits raiding caravans, kings getting too greedy about taxes—usual stuffing, what any competent factor should could handle on the spot, so no reports about it ever come to pester me.

"And then—Ahmed, more beer!—real trouble. Best market for bluejack is on a planet we call Babur. Its star, Mogul, lies in the same general region, about thirty light-years from Osman. Its top country been dealing with Technic civilization off and on for decades. Trying to modernize, they was mainly interested in robotics for some reason; but at last they did pile together enough outplanet exchange for they could commission a few hyperdrive ships built and crews trained. So now the

Solar Commonwealth and other powers got to treat them with a little more respect; blast cannon and nuclear missiles sure improve manners, by damn! They is still small tomatoes, but ambitious. And to them, with the big domestic demand, bluejack is not an incidental thing."

Van Rijn leaned forward, wrinkling the embroidered robe that circled his paunch. "You wonder why I tell you what you know, ha?" he said. "When I need direct reports on a situation, especial from a world as scarcely known as Suleiman, I can't study each report from decades. Data retrieval got to make me an abstract. I check with you now, who was spotted there, whether the machine give me all what is significant to our talking. Has I been correct so far?"

"Yes," Dalmady said. "But—"

*   *   *   *   *

Yvonne Vaillancourt looked up from a console as the factor passed the open door of her collation lab. "What's wrong, Emil?" she asked. "I heard you clattering the whole way down the hall."

Dalmady stopped for a look. Clothing was usually at a minimum in the Earth-conditioned compound, but, while he had grown familiar with the skins of its inhabitants, he never tired of hers. Perhaps, he had thought, her blonde shapeliness impressed him the more because he had been born and raised on Altai. The colonists of that chill planet went heavily dressed of necessity. The same need to survive forced austere habits on them; and, isolated in a largely unexplored frontier section, they received scant news about developments in the core civilization.

When you were half a dozen humans on a world whose very air was death to you—when you didn't even have visitors of your own species, because the ship that regularly called belonged to a Cynthian carrier—you had no choice but to live in free and easy style. Dalmady had had that explained to him while he was being trained for this post, and recognized it and went along with it. But he wondered if he would ever become accustomed to the *casualness* of the sophisticates whom he bossed.

"I don't know," he answered the girl. "The Thalasso-crat wants me at the palace."

"Why, he knows perfectly well how to make a visi call."

"Yes, but a nomad's brought word of something nasty in the Uplands, and won't come near the set. Afraid it'll imprison his soul, I imagine."

"M-m-m, I think not. We're still trying to chart the basic Suleimanite psychology, you know, with only inadequate data from three or four cultures to go on ... but they don't seem to have animistic tendencies like man's. Ceremony, yes, in abundance, but nothing we can properly identify as magic or religion."

Dalmady barked a nervous laugh. "Sometimes I think my whole staff considers our commerce an infernal nuisance that keeps getting in the way of their precious science."

"Sometimes you'd be right," Yvonne purred. "What'd hold us here except the chance to do research?"

"And how long would your research last if the company closed down this base?" he flared. "Which it will if we start losing money. My job's to see that we don't. I could use cooperation."

She slipped from her stool, came to him, and kissed him lightly. Her hair smelled like remembered steppe grass warmed by an orange sun, rippling under the rings of Altai. "Don't we help?" she murmured. "I'm sorry, dear."

He bit his lip and stared past her, down the length of gaudy murals whose painting had beguiled much idle time over the years. "No, I'm sorry," he said with the stiff honesty of his folk. "Of course you're all loyal and— It's me. Here I am, the youngest among you, a half-barbarian herdboy, supposed to make a go of things ... in one of the easiest, most routinized outposts in this sector ... and after a bare fifteen months—"

If I fail, he thought, *well, I can return home, no doubt, and dismiss the sacrifices my parents made to send me to managerial school offplanet, scorn the luck that Solar Spice and Liquors had an opening here and no more experienced employee to fill it, forget every dream about walking in times to come on new and unknown worlds that really call forth every resource a man has to give. Oh, yes, failure isn't fatal, except in subtler ways than I have words for.*

"You fret too much." Yvonne patted his cheek. "Probably this is just another tempest in a chickenhouse. You'll bribe somebody, or arm somebody, or whatever's needful, and that will once again be that."

"I hope so. But the Thalassocrat acted—well, not being committed to xenological scholarly precision, I'd say he acted worried too." Dalmady stood a few seconds longer, scowling, before: "All right, I'd better be on my way." He gave her a hug. "Thanks, Yvonne."

She watched him till he was out of sight, then returned to her work. Officially she was the trade post's secretary-treasurer, but such duties seldom came to her except when a freighter had landed. Otherwise she used the computers to try to find patterns in what fragments of knowledge her colleagues could wrest from a world—an entire, infinitely varied world—and hoped that a few scientists elsewhere might eventually scan a report on Suleiman (one among thousands of planets) and be interested.

Airsuit donned, Dalmady left the compound by its main personnel lock. Wanting time to compose himself, he went afoot through the city to the palace.

If they were city and palace.

He didn't know. Books, tapes, lectures, and neuroinductors had crammed him with information about this part of this continent; but those were the everyday facts and skills needed to manage operations. Long talks with his subordinates here had added a little insight, but only a little. Direct experience with the autochthons was occasionally enlightening, but just as apt to be confusing. No wonder that, once a satisfactory arrangement was made with Coast and Upland tribes (?), his predecessors had not attempted expansion or improvement. When you don't understand a machine but it seems to be running reasonably smoothly, you don't tinker much.

Outside the compound's forcefield, local gravity dragged at him with forty percent greater pull than

Earth's. Though his suit was light and his muscles hard, the air recycler necessarily included the extra mass of a unit for dealing with the hydrogen that seeped through any material. Soon he was sweating. Nevertheless it was as if the chill struck past all thermostatic coils, into his heavy bones.

High overhead stood Osman, a furious white spark, twice as luminous as Sol but, at its distance, casting a bare sixteenth of what Earth gets. Clouds, tinged red by organic compounds, drifted on slow winds through a murky sky where one of the three moons was dimly visible. That atmosphere bore thrice a terrestrial standard pressure. It was mostly hydrogen and helium, with vapors of methane and ammonia and traces of other gas. Greenhouse effect did not extend to unfreezing water.

Indeed, the planetary core was overlaid by a shell of ice, mixed with rock, penetrated by tilted metal-poor strata. The land glittered amidst its grayness and scrunched beneath Dalmady's boots. It sloped down to a dark, choppy sea of liquid ammonia whose horizon was too remote—given a 17,000-kilometer radius—for him to make out through the red-misted air.

Ice also were the buildings that rose blocky around him. They shimmered glasslike where doorways or obscure carved symbols did not break their smoothness. There were no streets in the usual sense, but aerial observation had disclosed an elaborate pattern in the layout of structures, about which the dwellers could not or would not speak. Wind moved ponderously between them. The air turned its sound, every sound, shrill.

Traffic surged. It was mainly pedestrian, natives on their business, carrying the oddly shaped tools and containers of a fireless neolithic nonhuman culture. A few wagons lumbered in with produce from the hinterland; their draught animals suggested miniature dinosaurs modeled by someone who had heard vague rumors of such creatures. A related, more slender species was ridden. Coracles bobbed across the sea; you might as well say the crews were fishing, though a true fish could live here unprotected no longer than a man.

Nothing reached Dalmady's earphones except the wind, the distant wave-rumble, the clop of feet and creak of wagons. Suleimanites did not talk casually. They did communicate, however, and without pause: by gesture, by ripple across erectile fur, by delicate exchanges between scent glands. They avoided coming near the human, but simply because his suit was hot to their touch. He gave and received many signals of greeting. After two years—twenty-five of Earth's—Coast and Uplands alike were becoming dependent on metal and plastic and energy-cell trade goods. Local labor had been eagerly available to help build a spaceport on the mesa overlooking town, and still did most of the work. That saved installing automatic machinery—one reason for the modest profit earned by this station.

Dalmady leaned into his uphill walk. After ten minutes he was at the palace.

The half-score natives posted outside the big, turreted building were not guards. While wars and robberies occurred on Suleiman, the slaying of a "king" seemed to be literally unthinkable. (An effect of pheromones? In every community the xenologists had observed thus far, the leader ate special foods which his followers insisted would poison anyone else; and maybe the followers were right.) The drums, plumed canes, and less identifiable gear which these beings carried were for ceremonial use.

Dalmady controlled his impatience and watched with a trace of pleasure the ritual of opening doors and conducting him to the royal presence. The Suleimanites were a graceful and handsome species. They were plantigrade bipeds, rather like men although the body was thicker and the average only came to his shoulder. The hands each bore two fingers between two thumbs, and were supplemented by a prehensile tail. The head was round, with a parrotlike beak, tympani for hearing, one large golden-hued eye in the middle and two smaller, less developed ones for binocular and peripheral vision. Clothing was generally confined to a kind of sporran, elaborately patterned with symbols, to leave glands and mahogany fur available for signals. The fact that

Suleimanite languages had so large a nonvocal compo-
nent handicapped human efforts at understanding as
much as anything else did.

The Thalassocrat addressed Dalmady by voice alone,
in the blue-glimmering ice cavern of his audience room.
Earphones reduced the upper frequencies to some the
man could hear. Nonetheless, that squeak and gibber
always rather spoiled the otherwise impressive effect of
flower crown and carven staff. So did the dwarfs,
hunchbacks, and cripples who squatted on rugs and skin-
draped benches. It was not known why household
servants were always recruited among the handicapped.
Suleimanites had tried to explain when asked, but their
meaning never came through.

"Fortune, power, and wisdom to you, Factor." They
didn't use personal names on this world, and seemed
unable to grasp the idea of an identification which was not
a scent-symbol.

"May they continue to abide with you, Thalassocrat."
The vocalizer on his back transformed Dalmady's version
of local speech into sounds that his lips could not bring
forth.

"We have here a Master of caravaneers," the monarch
said.

Dalmady went through polite ritual with the Upland-
er, who was tall and rangy for a Suleimanite, armed with
a stoneheaded tomahawk and a trade rifle designed for his
planet, his barbarianism showing in gaudy jewels and
bracelets. They were okay, however, those hill-country
nomads. Once a bargain had been struck, they held to it
with more literal-mindedness than humans could have
managed.

"And what is the trouble for which I am summoned,
Master? Has your caravan met bandits on its way to the
Coast? I will be glad to equip a force for their
suppression."

Not being used to talking with men, the chief went into
full Suleimanite language—his own dialect, at that—and
became incomprehensible. One of the midgets stumped
forward. Dalmady recognized him. A bright mind dwelt

in that poor little body, drank deep of whatever knowledge about the universe was offered, and in return had frequently helped with counsel or knowledge. "Let me ask him out, Factor and Thalassocrat," he suggested.

"If you will, Advisor," his overlord agreed.

"I will be in your debt, Translator," Dalmady said, with his best imitation of the prancing thanks-gesture.

Beneath the courtesies, his mind whirred and he found himself holding his breath while he waited. Surely the news couldn't be really catastrophic!

He reviewed the facts, as if hoping for some hitherto unnoticed salvation in them. With little axial tilt, Suleiman lacked seasons. Bluejack needed the cool, dry climate of the Uplands, but there it grew the year around. Primitive natives, hunters and gatherers, picked it in the course of their wanderings. Every several months, terrestrial, such a tribe would make rendezvous with one of the more advanced nomadic herding communities, who bartered for the parched leaves and fruits. A caravan would then form and make the long trip to this city, where Solar's folk would acquire the bales in exchange for Technic merchandise. You could count on a load arriving about twice a month. Four times in an Earth-side year, the Cynthian vessel took away the contents of Solar's warehouse . . . and left a far more precious cargo of letters, tapes, journals, books, news from the stars that were so rarely seen in these gloomy heavens.

It wasn't the most efficient system imaginable, but it was the cheapest, once you calculated what the cost would be—in capital investment and civilized-labor salaries—of starting plantations. And costs must be kept low or the enterprise would change from a minor asset to a liability, which would soon be liquidated. As matters were, Suleiman was a typical outpost of its kind: to the scientists, a fascinating study and a chance to win reputation in their fields; to the factors, a comparatively easy job, a first step on a ladder at the top of which waited the big, glamorous, gorgeously paid managerial assignments.

Or thus it had been until now.

The Translator turned to Dalmady. "The Master says this," he piped. "Lately in the Uplands have come what he calls—no, I do not believe that can be said in words alone—It is clear to me, they are machines that move about harvesting the bluejack."

"What?" The man realized he had exclaimed in Anglic. Through suddenly loud pulses, he heard the Translator go on:

"The wild folk were terrified and fled those parts. The machines came and took what they had stored against their next rendezvous. That angered this Master's nomads, who deal there. They rode to protest. From afar they saw a vessel, like the great flying vessel that lands here, and a structure a-building. Those who oversaw that work were...low, with many legs and claws for hands...long noses....A gathering robot came and shot lightning past the nomads. They saw they too must flee, lest its warning shot become deadly. The Master himself took a string of remounts and posted hither as swiftly as might be. In words, I cannot say more of what he has to tell."

Dalmady gasped into the frigid blueness that enclosed him. His mouth felt dry, his knees weak, his stomach in upheaval. "Baburites," he mumbled. "Got to be. But why're they doing this to us?"

Brush, herbage, leaves on the infrequent trees, were many shades of black. Here and there a patch of red or brown or blue flowering relieved it, or an ammonia river cataracting down the hills. Further off, a range of ice mountains flashed blindingly; Suleiman's twelve-hour day was drawing to a close, and Osman's rays struck level through a break in roiling ruddy cloud cover. Elsewhere a storm lifted like a dark wall on which lightning scribbled. The dense air brought its thunder-noise to Dalmady as a high drumroll. He paid scant attention. The gusts that hooted around his car, the air pockets into which it lurched, made piloting a fulltime job. A cybernated vehicle would have been too expensive for this niggardly rewarding planet.

"There!" cried the Master. He squatted with the Translator in an after compartment, which was left under native conditions and possessed an observation dome. In deference to his superstitions, or whatever they were, only the audio part of the intercom was turned on.

"Indeed," the Translator said more calmly. "I descry it now. Somewhat to our right, Factor—in a valley by a lake—do you see?"

"A moment." Dalmady locked the altitude controls. The car would bounce around till his teeth rattled, but the grav field wouldn't let it crash. He leaned forward in his harness, tried to ignore the brutal pull on him, and adjusted the scanner screen. His race had not evolved to see at those wavelengths which penetrated this atmosphere best; and the distance was considerable, as distances tend to be on a subjovian.

Converting light frequencies, amplifying, magnifying, the screen flung a picture at him. Tall above shrubs and turbulent ammonia stood a spaceship. He identified it as a Holbert-X freighter, a type commonly sold to hydrogen breathers. There had doubtless been some modifications to suit its particular home world, but he saw none except a gun turret and a couple of missile tube housings.

A prefabricated steel and ferrocrete building was being assembled nearby. The construction robots must be working fast, without pause; the cube was already more than half-finished. Dalmady glimpsed flares of energy torches, like tiny blue novas. He couldn't make out individual shapes, and didn't want to risk coming near enough.

"You see?" he asked the image of Peter Thorson, and transmitted the picture to another screen.

Back at the base, his engineer's massive head nodded. Behind could be seen the four remaining humans. They looked as strained and anxious as Dalmady felt, Yvonne perhaps more so.

"Yeh. Not much we can do about it," Thorson declared. "They pack bigger weapons than us. And see, in the corners of the barn, those bays? That's for blast cannon, I swear. Add a heavy-duty forcefield generator for passive defense, and it's a nut we can't hope to crack."

"The home office—"

"Yeh, they *might* elect to resent the invasion and dispatch a regular warcraft or three. But I don't believe it. Wouldn't pay, in economic terms. And it'd make every kind of hooraw, because remember, SSL hasn't got any legal monopoly here." Thorson shrugged. "My guess is, Old Nick'll simply close down on Suleiman, probably wangling a deal with the Baburites that'll cut his losses and figuring to diddle them good at a later date." He was a veteran mercantile professional, accustomed to occasional setbacks, indifferent to the scientific puzzles around him.

Yvonne, who was not, cried softly, "Oh, no! We can't! The insights we're gaining—"

And Dalmady, who could not afford a defeat this early in his career, clenched one fist and snapped, "We can at least talk to those bastards, can't we? I'll try to raise them. Stand by." He switched the outercom to a universal band and set the Come In going. The last thing he had seen from the compound was her stricken eyes.

The Translator inquired from aft: "Do you know who the strangers are and what they intend, Factor?"

"I have no doubt they come from Babur, as we call it," the man replied absently. "That is a world"—the more enlightened Coast dwellers had acquired some knowledge of astronomy—"akin to yours. It is larger and warmer, with heavier air. Its folk could not endure this one for long without becoming sick. But they can move about unarmored for a while. They buy most of our bluejack. Evidently they have decided to go to the source."

"But why, Factor?"

"For profit, I suppose, Translator." *Maybe just in their nonhuman cost accounting. That's a giant investment they're making in a medicinal product. But they don't operate under capitalism, under anything that human history ever saw, or so I've heard. Therefore they may consider it an investment in . . . empire? No doubt they can expand their foothold here, once we're out of the way—*

The screen came to life.

The being that peered from it stood about waist-high to a man in its erect torso. The rest of the body stretched behind in a vaguely caterpillar shape, on eight stumpy legs. Along that glabrous form was a row of opercula protecting tracheae which, in a dense hydrogen atmosphere, aerated the organism quite efficiently. Two arms ended in claws reminiscent of a lobster's; from the wrists below sprouted short, tough finger-tendrils. The head was dominated by a spongy snout. A Baburite had no mouth. It—individuals changed sex from time to time—chewed food with the claws and put it in a digestive pouch to be dissolved before the snout sucked it up. The eyes were four, and tiny. Speech was by diaphragms on either side of the skull, hearing and smell were associated with the tracheae. The skin was banded orange, blue, white, and black. Most of it was hidden by a gauzy robe.

The creature would have been an absurdity, a biological impossibility, on an Earth-type world. In its own ship, in strong gravity and thick cold air and murk through which shadowy forms moved, it had dignity and power.

It thrummed noises which a vocalizer rendered into fairly good League Latin: "We expected you. Do not approach closer."

Dalmady moistened his lips. He felt cruelly young and helpless. "G-g-greeting. I am the factor."

The Baburite made no comment.

After a while, Dalmady plowed on: "We have been told that you ... well, you are seizing the bluejack territory. I cannot believe that is correct."

"It is not, precisely," said the flat mechanical tone. "For the nonce, the natives may use these lands as heretofore, except that they will not find much bluejack to harvest. Our robots are too effective. Observe."

The screen flashed over to a view of a squat, cylindrical machine. Propelled by a simple grav drive, it floated several centimeters off the ground. Its eight arms terminated in sensors, pluckers, trimmers, brush cutters. On its back was welded a large basket. On its top was a maser transceiver and a swivel-mounted blaster.

"It runs off accumulators," the unseen Baburite stated. "These need only be recharged once in thirty-odd hours, at the fusion generator we are installing, unless a special energy expenditure occurs . . . like a battle, for instance. High-hovering relay units keep the robots in constant touch with each other and with a central computer, currently in the ship, later to be in the blockhouse. It controls them all simultaneously, greatly reducing the cost per unit." With no trace of sardonicism: "You will understand that such a beamcasting system cannot feasibly be jammed. The computer will be provided with missiles as well as guns and defensive fields. It is programmed to strike back at any attempt to hamper its operations."

The robot's image disappeared, the being's returned. Dalmady felt faint. "But that would . . . would be . . . an act of war!" he stuttered.

"No. It would be self-protection, legitimate under the rules of the Polesotechnic League. You may credit us with the intelligence to investigate the social as well as physical state of things before we acted and, indeed, to become an associate member of the League. No one will suffer except your company. That will not displease its competitors. They have assured our representatives that they can muster enough Council votes to prevent sanctions. It is not as if the loss were very great. Let us recommend to you personally that you seek employment elsewhere."

Uh-huh . . . after I dropped a planet . . . I might maybe get a job cleaning latrines someplace, went through the back of Dalmady's head. "No," he protested, "what about the autochthons? They're hurting already."

"When the land has been cleared, bluejack plantations will be established," the Baburite said. "Doubtless work can be found for some of the displaced savages, if they are sufficiently docile. Doubtless other resources, ignored by you oxygen breathers, await exploitation. We may in the end breed colonists adapted to Suleiman. But that will be of no concern to the League. We have investigated the practical effect of its prohibition on imperialism by members. Where no one else is interested in a case, a treaty with a native government is considered sufficient, and native governments with helpful attitudes are not hard to set up. Suleiman is such a case. A written-off operation that was never much more than marginal, out on an extreme frontier, is not worth the League's worrying about."

"The principle—"

"True. We would not provoke war, nor even our own expulsion and a boycott. However, recall that you are not being ordered off this planet. You have simply met a superior competitor, superior by virtue of living closer to the scene, being better suited to the environment, and far more interested in succeeding here. We have the same right to launch ventures as you."

"What do you mean, 'we'?" Dalmady whispered. "Who are you? What are you? A private company, or—"

"Nominally, we are so organized, though like many other League associates we make no secret of this being *pro forma*," the Baburite told him. "Actually, the terms on which our society must deal with the Technic aggregate have little relevance to the terms of its interior structure. Considering the differences—sociological, psychological, biological—between us and you and your close allies, our desire to be free of your civilization poses no real threat to the latter and hence will never provoke any real reaction. At the same time, we will never win the freedom of the stars without the resources of modern technology.

"To industrialize with minimum delay, we must obtain the initial capacity through purchases from the Technic worlds. This requires Technic currency. Thus, while we spend what appears to be a disproportionate amount of effort and goods on this bluejack project, it will result in saving outplanet exchange for more important things.

"We tell you what we tell you in order to make clear, not only our harmlessness to the League as a whole, but our determination. We trust you have taped this discussion. It may prevent your employer from wasting our determination. We trust you have taped this discussion. It may prevent your employer from wasting Suleiman, observe well. When you go back, report faithfully."

The screen blanked. Dalmady tried for minutes to make the connection again, but got no answer.

● ● ●

Thirty days later, which would have been fifteen of Earth's, a conference met in the compound. Around a table, in a room hazed and acrid with smoke, sat the humans. In a full-size screen were the images of the Thalassocrat and the Translator, a three-dimensional realism that seemed to breathe out the cold of the ice chamber where they crouched.

Dalmady ran a hand through his hair. "I'll summarize," he told them wearily. The Translator's fur began to move, his voice to make low whistles, as he rendered from the Anglic for his king. "The reports of our native scouts were waiting for me, recorded by Yvonne, when I returned from my own latest flit a couple of hours ago. Every datum confirms every other.

"We'd hoped, you recall, that the computer would be inadequate to cope with us, once the Baburite ship had left."

"Why should the live crew depart?" Sanjuro Nakamura asked.

"That's obvious," Thorson said. "They may not run their domestic economy the way we run ours, but that doesn't exempt them from the laws of economics. A planet like Babur—actually, a single dominant country on it, or whatever they have—still backward, still poor, has limits on what it can afford. They may enjoy shorter lines of communication than we do, but we, at home, enjoy a lot more productivity. At their present stage, they can't spend what it takes to create and maintain a permanent, live-staffed base like ours. Suleiman isn't too healthy for them, either, you know; and they lack even our small background of accumulated experience. So they've got to automate at first, and just send somebody once in a while to check up and collect the harvest."

"Besides," Alice Bergen pointed out, "the nomads are sworn to us. They wouldn't make a deal with another party. Not that the Baburites could use them profitably anyway. We're sitting in the only suitable depot area, the only one whose people have a culture that makes it easy to train them in service jobs for us. So the Baburites have to operate right on the spot where the bluejack grows. The nomads resent having their caravan trade ended, and would stage guerrilla attacks on live workers."

"Whew!" Nakamura said, with an attempted grin. "I assure you, my question was only rhetorical. I simply wanted to point out that the opposition would not have left everything in charge of a computer if they weren't confident the setup would function, including holding us at bay. I begin to see why their planners concentrated on developing robotics at the beginning of modernization. No doubt they intend to use machines in quite a few larcenous little undertakings."

"Have you found out yet how many robots there are?" Isabel da Fonseca asked.

"We estimate a hundred," Dalmady told her, "though we can't get an accurate count. They operate fast, you see, covering a huge territory—in fact, the entire territory where bluejack grows thickly enough to be worth gathering—and they're identical in appearance except for the relay hoverers."

"That must be some computer, to juggle so many at once, over such varying conditions," Alice remarked. Cybernetics was not her field.

Yvonne shook her head; the gold tresses swirled. "Nothing extraordinary. We have long-range telephotos, taken during its installation. It's a standard multichannel design, only the electronics modified for ambient conditions. Rudimentary awareness: more isn't required, and would be uneconomic to provide, when its task is basically simple."

"Can't we outwit it, then?" Alice asked.

Dalmady grimaced. "What do you think my native helpers and I have been trying to do thereabouts, this past week? It's open country; the relayers detect you coming a huge ways off, and the computer dispatches robots. Not many are needed. If you come too close to the blockhouse, they fire warning blasts. That's terrified the natives. Few of them will approach anywhere near, and in fact the savages are starting to evacuate, which'll present us with a nice bunch of hungry refugees. Not that I blame them. A low-temperature organism cooks easier than you or me. I did push ahead, and was fired on for real. I ran away before my armor should be pierced."

"What about airborne attack?" Isabel wondered.

Thorson snorted. "In three rattly cars, with handguns? Those robots fly too, remember. Besides, the centrum has forcefields, blast cannon, missiles. A naval vessel would have trouble reducing it."

"Furthermore," interjected the Thalassocrat, "I am told of a threat to destroy this town by airborne weapons, should a serious assault be made on yonder place. That cannot be risked. Sooner would I order you to depart for aye, and strike what bargain I was able with your enemies."

He can make that stick, Dalmady thought, *by the simple process of telling our native workers to quit.*

Not that that would necessarily make any difference. He recalled the last statement of a nomad Master, as the retreat from a reconnaisance took place, Suleimanites on their animals, man on a gravscooter. "We have abided by our alliance with you, but you not by yours with us. Your predecessors swore we should have protection from skyborne invaders. If you fail to drive off these, how shall we trust you?" Dalmady had pleaded for time and had grudgingly been granted it, since the caravaneers did value their trade with him. *But if we don't solve this problem soon, I doubt the system can ever be renewed.*

"We shall not imperil you," he promised the Thalassocrat.

"How real is the threat?" Nakamura asked. "The League wouldn't take kindly to slaughter of harmless autochthons."

"But the League would not necessarily do more than complain," Thorson said, "especially if the Baburites argue that we forced them into it. They're banking on its indifference, and I suspect their judgment is shrewd."

"Right or wrong," Alice said, "their assessment of the psychopolitics will condition what they themselves do. And what assessment have they made? What do we know about their ways of thinking?"

"More than you might suppose," Yvonne replied. "After all, they've been in contact for generations, and you don't negotiate commercial agreements without having done some studies in depth first. The reason you've not seen much of me, these past days, is that I've buried myself in our files. We possess, right here, a bucketful of information about Babur."

Dalmady straightened in his chair. His pulse picked up the least bit. It was no surprise that a large and varied xenological library existed in this insignificant outback base. Microtapes were cheaply reproduced, and you never knew who might chance by or what might happen, so you were routinely supplied with references for your entire sector. "What do we have?" he barked.

Yvonne smiled wryly. "Nothing spectacular, I'm afraid. The usual: three or four of the principal languages, sketches of history and important contemporary cultures, state-of-technology analyses, statistics on stuff like population and productivity—besides the planetology, biology, psychoprofiling, et cetera. I tried and tried to find a weak point, but couldn't. Oh, I can show that this operation must be straining their resources, and will have to be abandoned if it doesn't quickly pay off. But that's been just as true of us."

Thorson fumed on his pipe. "If we could fix a gadget— We have a reasonably well-equipped workshop. That's where I've been sweating, myself."

"What had you in mind?" Dalmady inquired. The dullness of the engineer's voice was echoed in his own.

"Well, at first I wondered about a robot to go out and hunt theirs down. I could build one, a single one, more heavily armed and armored." Thorson's hand flopped empty, palm up, on the table. "But the computer has a hundred; and it's more sophisticated by orders of magnitude than any brain I could cobble together from spare cybernetic parts; and as the Thalassocrat says, we can't risk a missile dropped on our spaceport in retaliation, because it'd take out most of the city.

"Afterward I thought about jamming, or about somehow lousing the computer itself, but that's totally hopeless. It'd never let you get near."

He sighed. "My friends, let's admit that we've had the course, and plan how to leave with minimum loss."

The Thalassocrat stayed imperturbable, as became a monarch. But the Translator's main eye filmed over, his tiny body shrank into itself, and he cried: "We had hoped—one year our descendants, learning from you, joining you among the uncounted suns— Is there instead to be endless rule by aliens?"

Dalmady and Yvonne exchanged looks. Their hands clasped. He believed the same thought must be twisting in her: *We, being of the League, cannot pretend to altruism. But we are not monsters either. Some cold accountant in an office on Earth may order our departure. But can we who have been here, who like these people and were trusted by them, can we abandon them and continue to live with ourselves? Would we not forever feel that any blessings given us were stolen?*

And the old, old legend crashed into his awareness.

He sat for a minute or two, unconscious of the talk that growled and groaned around him. Yvonne first noticed the blankness in his gaze. "Emil," she murmured, "are you well?"

Dalmady sprang to his feet with a whoop.

"What in space?" Nakamura said.

The Factor controlled himself. He trembled, and small chills ran back and forth along his nerves; but his words came steady. "I have an idea."

* * * * *

Above the robes that billowed around him in the wind, the Translator carried an inconspicuous miniature audiovisual two-way. Dalmady in the car which he had landed behind a hill some distance off, Thorson in the car which hovered to relay, Yvonne and Alice and Isabel and Nakamura and the Thalassocrat in the city, observed a bobbing, swaying landscape on their tuned-in screens. Black leaves streamed, long and ragged, on bushes whose twigs clicked an answer to the whining air; boulders and ice chunks hunched among them; an ammonia fall boomed on the right, casting spray across the field of view. The men in the cars could likewise feel the planet's traction and the shudder of hulls under that slow, thick wind.

"I still think we should've waited for outside help," Thorson declared on a separate screen. "That rig's a godawful lash-up."

"And I still say," Dalmady retorted, "your job's made you needlessly fussy in this particular case. Besides, the natives couldn't've been stalled much longer." *Furthermore, if we can rout the Baburites with nothing but what was on hand, that ought to shine in my record. I'd like to think that's less important to me, but I can't deny it's real.*

One way or another, the decision had to be mine. I am the Factor.

It's a lonesome feeling. I wish Yvonne were here beside me.

"Quiet," he ordered. "Something's about to happen."

The Translator had crossed a ridge and was gravscooting down the opposite slope. He required no help at that; a few days of instruction had made him a very fair driver, even in costume. He was entering the robot-held area, and already a skyborne unit slanted to intercept him. In the keen Osmanlight, against ocherous clouds, it gleamed like fire.

Dalmady crouched in his seat. He was airsuited. If his friend got into trouble, he'd slap down his faceplate, open the cockpit, and swoop to an attempted rescue. A blaster lay knobby in his lap. The thought he might come too late made a taste of sickness in his mouth.

The robot paused at hover, arms extended, weapon pointed. The Translator continued to glide at a steady rate. When near collision, the two-way spoke for him: "Stand aside. We are instituting a change of program."

Spoke, to the listening computer, in the principal language of Babur.

Yvonne had worked out the plausible phrases, and spent patient hours with vocalizer and recorder until they seemed right. Engineer Thorson, xenologists Nakamura and Alice Bergen, artistically inclined biologist Isabel da Fonseca, Dalmady himself and several Suleimanite advisors who had spied on the Baburites, had created the disguise. Largely muffled in cloth, it didn't have to be too elaborate—a torso shaven and painted; a simple mechanical caterpillar body behind, steered by the hidden tail, automatically pacing its six legs with the wearer's two; a flexible mask with piezoelectric controls guided by the facial muscles beneath; claws and tendrils built over the natural arms, fake feet over the pair of real ones.

A human or an ordinary Suleimanite could not successfully have worn such an outfit. If nothing else, they were too big. But presumably it had not occurred to the Baburites to allow for midgets existing on this planet. The disguise was far from perfect; but presumably the computer was not programmed to check for any such contingency; furthermore, an intelligent, well-rehearsed actor, adapting his role moment by moment as no robot ever can, creates a gestalt transcending any minor errors of detail.

And . . . logically, the computer *must* be programmed to allow Baburites into its presence, to service it and collect the bluejack stored nearby.

Nonetheless, Dalmady's jaws ached from the tension on them.

The robot shifted out of the viewfield. In the receiving screens, ground continued to glide away underneath the scooter.

Dalmady switched off audio transmission from base. Though none save Yvonne, alone in a special room, was now sending to the Translator, and she via a bone conduction receiver—still, the cheers that had filled the car struck him as premature.

But the kilometers passed and passed. And the blockhouse hove in view, dark, cubical, bristling with sensors and antennae, cornered with the sinister shapes of gun emplacements and missile silos. No forcefield went up. Yvonne said through the Translator's unit: "Open; do not close again until told," and the idiot-savant computer directed a massive gate to swing wide.

What happened beyond was likewise Yvonne's job. She scanned through the portal by the two-way, summoned what she had learned of Baburite automation technology, and directed the Translator. Afterward she said it hadn't been difficult except for poor visibility; the builders had used standard layouts and programming languages. But to the Factor it was an hour of sweating, cursing, pushing fingers and belly muscles against each other, staring and staring at the image of enigmatic units which loomed between blank walls, under bluish light that was at once harsh and wan.

When the Translator emerged and the gate closed behind him, Dalmady almost collapsed.

Afterward, though—well, League people were pretty good at throwing a celebration!

* * * * *

"Yes," Dalmady said. "But—"

"Butter me no buts," van Rijn said. "Fact is, you reset that expensive computer so it should make those expensive robots stand idle. Why not leastwise use them for Solar?"

"That would have ruined relations with the natives, sir. Primitives don't take blandly to the notion of technological unemployment. So scientific studies would have become impossible. How then would you attract personnel?"

"What personnel would we need?"

"Some on the spot, constantly. Otherwise the Baburites, close as they are, could come back and, for example, organize and arm justly disgruntled Suleiman-ites against us. Robots or no, we'd soon find the bluejack costing us more than it earned us.... Besides, machines wear out and it costs to replace them. Live native help will reproduce for nothing."

"Well, you got that much sense, anyhows," van Rijn rumbled. "But why did you tell the computer it and its robots should attack *any* kind of machine, like a car or spacecraft, what comes near, and anybody of any shape what tells it to let him in? Supposing situations change, our people can't do nothings with it now neither."

"I told you, they don't need to," Dalmady rasped. "We get along—not dazzlingly, but we get along, we show a profit—with our traditional arrangements. As long as we maintain those, we exclude the Baburites from them. If we ourselves had access to the computer, we'd have to mount an expensive guard over it. Otherwise the Baburites could probably pull a similar trick on us, right? As is, the system interdicts any attempt to modernize operations in the bluejack area. Which is to say, it protects our monopoly—free—and will protect it for years to come."

He started to rise. "Sir," he continued bitterly, "the whole thing strikes me as involving the most elementary economic calculations. Maybe you have something subtler in mind, but if you do—"

"Whoa!" van Rijn boomed. "Squat yourself. Reel in some more of your drink, boy, and listen at me. Old and fat I am, but lungs and tongue I got. Also in working order is two other organs, one what don't concern you but one which is my brain, and my brain wants I should get information from you and stuff it."

Dalmady found he had obeyed.

"You need to see past a narrow specialism," van Rijn said. "Sometimes a man is too stupid good at his one job. He booms it, no matter the consequentials to everything else, and makes trouble for the whole organization he is supposed to serve. Like, you considered how Babur would react?"

"Of course. Freelady Vaillancourt—" *When will I be with her again?*—"and Drs. Bergen and Nakamura in particular, did an exhaustive analysis of materials on hand. As a result, we gave the computer an additional directive: that it warn any approaching vehicle before opening fire. The conversation I had later, with the spaceship captain or whatever he was, bore out our prediction."

(A quivering snout. A bleak gleam in four minikin eyes. But the voice, strained through a machine, emotionless: "Under the rules your civilization has devised, you have not given us cause for war; and the

League always responds to what it considers unprovoked attack. Accordingly, we shall not bombard.")

"No doubt they feel their equivalent of fury," Dalmady said. "But what can they do? They're realists. Unless they think of some new stunt, they'll write Suleiman off and try elsewhere."

"And they buy our bluejack yet?"

"Yes."

"We should maybe lift the price, like teaching them a lesson they shouldn't make fumblydiddles with us?"

"You can do that, if you want to make them decide they'd rather synthesize the stuff. My report recommends against it."

This time Dalmady did rise. "Sir," he declared in anger, "I may be a yokel, my professional training may have been in a jerkwater college, but I'm not a congenital idiot who's mislaid his pills and I do take my pride seriously. I made the best decision I was able on Suleiman. You haven't tried to show me where I went wrong, you've simply had me dismissed from my post, and tonight you drone about issues that anybody would understand who's graduated from diapers. Let's not waste more of our time. Good evening."

Van Rijn avalanched upward to his own feet. "Ho, ho!" he bawled. "Spirit, too! I like, I like!"

Dumfounded, Dalmady could only gape.

Van Rijn clapped him on the shoulder, nearly felling him. "Boy," the merchant said, "I didn't mean to rub your nose in nothings except sweet violets. I did have to know, did you stumble onto your answer, which is beautiful, or can you think original? Because you take my saying, maybe everybody understands like you what is not wearing diapers no more; but if that is true, why, ninety-nine point nine nine percent of every sophont race is wearing diapers, at least on their brains, and it leaks out of their mouths. I find you is in the oh point oh one percent, and I want you. Hoo-ha, how I want you!"

He thrust the gin-filled goblet back into Dalmady's hand. His tankard clanked against it. "Drink!"

Dalmady took a sip. Van Rijn began to prowl.

"You is from a frontier planet and so is naive," the

merchant said, "but that can be outlived like pimples. See, when my underlings at HQ learned you had pulled our nuts from the fire on Suleiman, they sent you a standard message, not realizing an Altaian like you would not know that in such cases the proceeding is SOP," which he pronounced "sop." He waved a gorilla arm, splashing beer on the floor. "Like I say, we had to check if you was lucky only. If so, we would promote you to be manager someplace better and forget about you. But if you was, actual, extra smart and tough, we don't want you for a manager. You is too rare and precious for that. Would be like using a Hokusai print in a catbox."

Dalmady raised goblet to mouth, unsteadily. "What do you mean?" he croaked.

"Entrepreneur! You will keep title of factor, because we can't make jealousies, but what you do is what the old Americans would have called a horse of a different dollar.

"Look." Van Rijn reclaimed his cigar from the disposal rim, took a puff, and made forensic gestures with it and tankard alike while he continued his earthquake pacing. "Suleiman was supposed to be a nice routine post, but you told me how little we know on it and how sudden the devil himself came to lunch. Well, what about the real new, real hairy—and real fortune-making—places? Ha?

"You don't want a manager for them, not till they been whipped into shape. A good manager is a very high-powered man, and we need a lot of him. But in his bottom, he is a routineer; his aim is to make things go smooth. No, for the wild places you need an innovator in charge, a man what likes to take risks, a heterodoxy if she is female—somebody what can meet wholly new problems in unholy new ways—you see?

"Only such is rare, I tell you. They command high prices: high as they can earn for themselves. Natural, I want them earning for me too. So I don't put that kind of factor on salary and dangle a promotion ladder in front of him. No, the entrepreneur kind, first I get his John Bullcock on a ten-year oath of fealty. Next I turn him loose with a stake and my backup, to do what he wants, on straight commission of ninety percent.

"Too bad nobody typed you before you went in

managerial school. Now you must have a while in an entrepreneurial school I got tucked away where nobody notices. Not dull for you; I hear they throw fine orgies; but mainly I think you will enjoy your classes, if you don't mind working till brain-sweat runs out your nose. Afterward you go get rich, if you survive, and have a big ball of fun even if you don't. Hokay?"

Dalmady thought for an instant of Yvonne; and then he thought, *What the deuce, if nothing better develops, in a few years I can set any hiring policies I feel like;* and: "Hokay!" he exclaimed, and tossed off his drink in a single gulp.

The following story was also written by Judith Dalmady/
Lundgren for the periodical *Morgana*. She based it upon
an incident whereof her father had told her, he having
gotten the tale from one of the persons directly concerned
when he was an entrepreneur in those parts. Hloch
includes it, first, because it shows more than the usual
biographies do of a planet on which Falkayn had, earlier,
had a significant adventure. Second, it gives yet another
glimpse into a major human faith, alive unto this year and
surely of influence upon him and his contemporaries.

THE SEASON OF
FORGIVENESS

It was a strange and lonely place for a Christmas celebration—the chill planet of a red dwarf star, away off in the Pleiades region, where half a dozen humans laired in the ruins of a city which had been great five thousand years ago, and everywhere else reached wilderness.

"No!" said Master Trader Thomas Overbeck. "We've got too much work on our hands to go wasting man-hours on a piece of frivolity."

"It isn't, sir," answered his apprentice, Juan Hernández. "On Earth it's important. You have spent your life on the frontier, so perhaps you don't realize this."

Overbeck, a large blond man, reddened. "Seven months here, straight out of school, and you're telling me how to run my shop? If you've learned all the practical technique I have to teach you, why, you may as well go back on the next ship."

Juan hung his head. "I'm sorry, sir. I meant no disrespect."

Standing there, in front of the battered desk, against a window which framed the stark, sullenly lit landscape and a snag of ancient wall, he seemed younger than his sixteen Terrestrial years, slight, dark-haired, big-eyed. The company-issue coverall didn't fit him especially well. But he was quick-witted, Overbeck realized; he had to be, to graduate from the Academy that soon. And he was hard-working, afire with eagerness. The merchants of the League operated over so vast and diverse a territory that promising recruits were always in short supply.

That practical consideration, as well as a touch of sympathy, made the chief growl in a milder tone: "Oh, of course I've no objection to any small religious observance you or the others may want to hold. But as for doing more—" He waved his cigar at the scene outside. "What does it mean, anyway? A date on a chronopiece. A chronopiece adjusted for Earth! Ivanhoe's year is only two-thirds as long; but the globe takes sixty hours to spin around once; and to top it off, this is local summer, even if you don't dare leave the dome unless you're bundled to the ears. You see, Juan, I've got the same right as you to repeat the obvious."

His laughter boomed loud. While the team kept their living quarters heated, they found it easiest to maintain ambient air pressure, a fourth again as high as Terrestrial standard. Sound carried strongly. "Believe it or not," he finished, "I do know something about Christmas traditions, including the very old ones. You want to decorate the place and sing 'Jingle Bells'? That's how to make 'em ridiculous!"

"Please, no, sir," Juan said. "Also on Earth, in the southern hemisphere the feast comes at summer. And nobody is sure what time of year the Nativity really happened." He knotted his fists before he plunged on. "I thought not of myself so much, though I do remember how it is in my home. But that ship will come soon. I'm told small children are aboard. Here will be a new environment for them, perhaps frightening at first. Would we not help them feel easy if we welcomed them with a party like this?"

"Hm." Overbeck sat still a minute, puffing smoke and tugging his chin. His apprentice had a point, he admitted.

Not that he expected the little ones to be anything but a nuisance as far as he himself was concerned. He'd be delighted to leave them behind in a few more months, when his group had ended its task. But part of that task was to set up conditions which would fit the needs of their successors. The sooner those kids adjusted to life here, the sooner the parents could concentrate on their proper business.

And that was vital. Until lately, Ivanhoe had had no more than a supply depot for possible distressed spacecraft. Then a scientific investigator found the *adir* herb in the deserts of another continent. It wouldn't grow outside its own ecology; and it secreted materials which would be valuable starting points for several new organic syntheses. In short, there was money to be gotten. Overbeck's team was assigned to establish a base, make friends with the natives, learn their ways and the ways of their country, and persuade them to harvest the plant in exchange for trade goods.

That seemed fairly well in order now, as nearly as a man could judge amidst foreignness and mystery. The time looked ripe for putting the trade on a regular basis. Humans would not sign a contract to remain for a long stretch unless they could bring their families. Nor would they stay if the families grew unhappy.

And Tom Overbeck wouldn't collect his big, fat bonus until the post had operated successfully for five standard years.

Wherefore the Master Trader shrugged and said, "Well, okay. If it doesn't interfere too much with work, go ahead."

He was surprised at how enthusiastically Ram Gupta, Nikolai Sarychev, Mamoru Noguchi, and Philip Feinberg joined Juan's project. They were likewise young, but not boys; and they had no common faith. Yet together they laughed a lot as they made ready. The rooms and passageways of the dome filled with ornaments cut from foil or sheet metal, twisted together from color-coded wire, assembled from painted paper. Smells of baking cookies filled the air. Men went about whistling immemorial tunes.

Overbeck didn't mind that they were cheerful. That was a boost to efficiency, in these grim surroundings. He argued a while when they wanted to decorate outdoors as well, but presently gave in.

After all, he had a great deal else to think about.

A couple of Ivanhoan days after their talk, he was standing in the open when Juan approached him. The apprentice stopped, waited, and listened, for his chief was in conversation with Raffak.

The dome and sheds of the human base looked oddly bright, totally out of place. Behind them, the gray walls of Dahia lifted sheer, ten meters to the parapets, overtopped by bulbous-battlemented watchtowers. They were less crumbled than the buildings within. Today's dwindled population huddled in what parts of the old stone mansions and temples had not collapsed into rubble. A few lords maintained small castles for themselves, a few priests carried on rites behind porticos whose columns were idols, along twisting dusty streets. Near the middle of town rose the former Imperial palace. Quarried for centuries, its remnants were a colossal shapelessness.

The city dwellers were more quiet than humans. Not even vendors in their flimsy booths cried their wares. Most males were clad in leather kilts and weapons, females in zigzag-patterned robes. The wealthy and the military officers rode on beasts which resembled narrow-snouted, feathery-furred horses. The emblems of provinces long lost fluttered from the lances they carried. Wind, shrill in the lanes, bore sounds of feet, hoofs, groaning cartwheels, an occasional call or the whine of a bone flute.

A human found it cold. His breath smoked into the dry air. Smells were harsh in his nostrils. The sky above was deep purple, the sun a dull ruddy disc. Shadows lay thick; and nothing, in that wan light, had the same color as it did on Earth.

The deep tones of his language rolled from Raffak's mouth. "We have made you welcome, we have given you a place, we have aided you by our labor and counsel," declared the speaker of the City Elders.

"You have...for a generous payment," Overbeck answered.

"You shall not, in return, exclude Dahia from a full share in the wealth the *adir* will bring." A four-fingered hand, thumb set oppositely to a man's, gestured outward. Through a cyclopean gateway showed a reach of dusky-green bush, part of the agricultural hinterland. "It is more than a wish to better our lot. You have promised us that. But Dahia was the crown of an empire reaching from sea to sea. Though it lies in wreck, we who live here preserve the memories of our mighty ancestors, and faithfully serve their gods. Shall desert-prowling savages wax rich and strong, while we descendants of their overlords remain weak—until they become able to stamp out this final spark of glory? Never!"

"The nomads claim the wild country," Overbeck said. "No one has disputed that for many centuries."

"Dahia disputes it at last. I came to tell you that we have sent forth emissaries to the Black Tents. They bore our demand that Dahia must share in the *adir* harvest."

Overbeck, and a shocked Juan, regarded the Ivanhoan closely. He seemed bigger, more lionlike than was right. His powerful, long-limbed body would have loomed a full two meters tall did it not slant forward. A tufted tail whipped the bent legs. Mahogany fur turned into a mane around the flat face. That face lacked a nose—breathing was through slits beneath the jaws—but the eyes glowed green and enormous, ears stood erect, teeth gleamed sharp.

The human leader braced himself, as if against the drag of a gravity slightly stronger than Earth's, and stated: "You were foolish. Relations between Dahia and the nomads are touchy at best, violent at worst. Let war break out, and there will be no *adir* trade. Then Dahia too will lose."

"Lose material goods, maybe," Raffak said. "Not honor."

"You have already lost some honor by your action. You knew my people had reached agreement with the nomads. Now you Elders seek to change that agreement before consulting us." Overbeck made a chopping gesture which signified anger and determination. "I insist on meeting with your council."

After an argument, Raffak agreed to this for the next day, and stalked off. Hands jammed into pockets, Overbeck stared after him. "Well, Juan," he sighed, "there's a concrete example for you, of how tricky this business of ours can get."

"Might the tribes really make trouble, sir?" wondered the boy.

"I hope not." Overbeck shook his head. "Though how much do we know, we Earthlings, as short a while as we've been here? Two whole societies, each with its own history, beliefs, laws, customs, desires—in a species that isn't human!"

"What do you suppose will happen?"

"Oh, I'd guess the nomads will refuse flat-out to let the Dahians send gathering parties into their territory. Then I'll have to persuade the Dahians all over again, to let nomads bring the stuff here. That's what happens when you try to make hereditary rivals cooperate."

"Couldn't we base ourselves in the desert?" Juan asked.

"It's better to have a large labor force we can hire at need, one that stays put," Overbeck explained. "Besides, well—" He looked almost embarrassed. "We're after a profit, yes, but not to exploit these poor beings. An *adir* trade would benefit Dahia too, both from the taxes levied on it and from developing friendlier relations with the tribesfolk. In time, they could start rebuilding their civilization here. It was great once, before its civil wars and the barbarian invasions that followed." He paused. "Don't ever quote me to them."

"Why not, sir? I should think—"

"*You* should. I doubt they would. Both factions are proud and fierce. They might decide they were being patronized, and resent it in a murderous fashion. Or they might get afraid we intend to undermine their martial virtues, or their religions, or something." Overbeck smiled rather grimly. "No, I've worked hard to keep matters simple, on a level where nobody can misunderstand. In native eyes, we Earthlings are tough but fair. We've come to build a trade that will pay off for us, and for no other reason. It's up to them to keep us interested in remaining, which we won't unless they behave. That attitude, that image is clear enough, I hope, for the most alien mind to grasp. They may not love us, but they don't hate us either, and they're willing to do business."

Juan swallowed and found no words.

"What'd you want of me?" Overbeck inquired.

"Permission to go into the hills, sir," the apprentice said. "You know those crystals along Wola Ridge? They'd be beautiful on the Christmas tree." Ardently: "I've finished all my jobs for the time being. It will only take some hours, if I can borrow a flitter."

Overbeck frowned. "When a fight may be brewing? The Black Tents are somewhere that way, last I heard."

"You said, sir, you don't look for violence. Besides, none of the Ivanhoans have a grudge against us. And they respect our power. Don't they? Please!"

"I aim to preserve that state of affairs." Overbeck pondered. "Well, shouldn't be any risk. And, hm-m-m, a human going out alone might be a pretty good demonstration of confidence.... Okay," he decided. "Pack a blaster. If a situation turns ugly, don't hesitate to use it. Not that I believe you'll get in any scrape, or I wouldn't let you go. But—" He shrugged. "There's no such thing as an absolutely safe bet."

Three hundred kilometers north of Dahia, the wilderness was harsh mountainsides, deep-gashed canyons, umber crags, thinly scattered thorn-shrubs and wind-gnarled trees with ragged leaves. Searching for the mineral which cropped here and there out of the sandy ground, Juan soon lost sight of his flitter. He couldn't get lost from it himself. The aircraft was giving off a radio signal, and the transceiver in his pocket included a directional meter for homing on it. Thus he wandered further than he realized before he had collected a bagful.

However slowly Ivanhoe rotates, its days must end. Juan grew aware of how low the dim red sun was, how long and heavy the shadows. Chilliness had turned to a cold which bit at his bare face. Evening breezes snickered in the brush. Somewhere an animal howled. When he passed a rivulet, he saw that it had begun to freeze.

I'm in no trouble, he thought, *but I am hungry, and late*

for supper, and the boss will be annoyed. Even now, it was
getting hard for him to see. His vision was meant for
bright, yellow-white Sol. He stumbled on rocks. Had his
radio compass not been luminous-dialed, he would have
needed a flashbeam to read it.

Nevertheless he was happy. The very weirdness of this
environment made it fascinating; and he could hope to go
on to many other worlds. Meanwhile, the Christmas
celebration would be a circle of warmth and cheer, a
memory of home—his parents, his brother and two
sisters, Tío Pepe and Tía Carmen, the dear small Mexican
town and the laughter as children struck at a *piñata*—

"*Raielli, Erratan!*"

Halt, Earthling! Juan jarred to a stop.

He was near the bottom of a ravine, which he was
crossing as the most direct way to the flitter. The sun lay
hidden behind one wall of it, and dusk filled the heavens.
He could just make out boulders and bushes, vague in the
gloom.

Then metal caught what light there was in a faint
glimmer. He saw spearheads and a single breastplate. The
rest of the warriors had only leather harness. They were
blurs around him, save where their huge eyes gleamed like
their steel.

Juan's heart knocked. *These are friends!* he told
himself. *The People of the Black Tents are anxious to deal
with us—Then why did they wait here for me? Why have a
score of them risen out of hiding to ring me in?*

His mouth felt suddenly parched. He forced it to form
words, as well as it could imitate the voice of an Ivanhoan.
City and wilderness dwellers spoke essentially the same
language. "G-greeting." He remembered the desert form
of salutation. "I am Juan Sancho's-child, called Hernández, pledged follower of the merchant Thomas William's-
child, called Overbeck, and am come in peace."

"I am Tokonnen Undassa's-child, chief of the Elassi
Clan," said the lion-being in the cuirass. His tone was a
snarl. "We may no longer believe that any Earthling
comes in peace."

"What?" cried Juan. Horror smote him. "But we do!
How—"

"You camp among the City folk. Now the City demands the right to encroach on our land.... Hold! I know what you carry."

Juan had gripped his blaster. The natives growled. Spears drew back, ready to throw. Tokonnen confronted the boy and continued:

"I have heard tell about weapons like yours. A fire-beam, fiercer than the sun, springs forth, and rock turns molten where it strikes. Do you think a male of Elassi fears that?" Scornfully: "Draw it if you wish."

Juan did, hardly thinking. He let the energy gun dangle downward in his fingers and exclaimed, "I only came to gather a few crystals—"

"If you slay me," Tokonnen warned, "that will prove otherwise. And you cannot kill more than two or three of us before the spears of the rest have pierced you. We know how feebly your breed sees in the least of shadows."

"But what do you *want*?"

"When we saw you descend, afar off, we knew what we wanted—you, to hold among us until your fellows abandon Dahia."

Half of Juan realized that being kept hostage was most likely a death sentence for him. He couldn't eat Ivanhoan food; it was loaded with proteins poisonous to his kind of life. In fact, without a steady supply of antiallergen, he might not keep breathing. How convince a barbarian herder of that?

The other half pleaded, "You are being wild. What matter if a few City dwellers come out after *adir?* Or... you can tell them 'no.' Can't you? We, we Earthlings—we had nothing to do with the embassy they sent."

"We dare not suppose you speak truth, you who have come here for gain," Tokonnen replied. "What is our freedom to you, if the enemy offers you a fatter bargain? And we remember, yes, across a hundred generations we remember the Empire. So do they in Dahia. They would restore it, cage us within their rule or drive us into the badlands. Their harvesters would be their spies, the first agents of their conquest. This country is ours. It is strong with the bones of our fathers and rich with the flesh of our mothers. It is too holy for an Imperial foot to tread. You would not understand this, merchant."

"We mean you well," Juan stammered. "We'll give you things—"

Tokonnen's mane lifted haughtily against darkling cliff, twilit sky. From his face, unseen in murk, the words rang: "Do you imagine things matter more to us than our liberty or our land?" Softer: "Yield me your weapon and come along. Tomorrow we will bring a message to your chief."

The warriors trod closer.

There went a flash through Juan. He knew what he could do, must do. Raising the blaster, he fired straight upward.

Cloven air boomed. Ozone stung with a smell of thunderstorms. Blue-white and dazzling, the energy beam lanced toward the earliest stars.

The Ivanhoans yelled. By the radiance, Juan saw them lurch back, drop their spears, clap hands to eyes. He himself could not easily look at that lightning bolt. They were the brood of a dark world. Such brilliance blinded them.

Juan gulped a breath and ran.

Up the slope! Talus rattled underfoot. Across the hills beyond! Screams of wrath pursued him.

The sun was now altogether down, and night came on apace. It was less black than Earth's, for the giant stars of the Pleiades cluster bloomed everywhere aloft, and the nebula which enveloped them glowed lacy across heaven. Yet often Juan fell across an unseen obstacle. His pulse roared, his lungs were aflame.

It seemed forever before he glimpsed his vehicle. Casting a glance behind, he saw what he had feared, the warriors in pursuit. His shot had not permanently damaged their sight. And surely they tracked him with peripheral vision, ready to look entirely away if he tried another flash.

Longer-legged, born to the planet's gravity, they overhauled him, meter after frantic meter. To him they were barely visible, bounding blacknesses which often disappeared into the deeper gloom around. He could not have hoped to pick them all off before one of them got to range, flung a spear from cover, and struck him.

Somehow, through every terror, he marveled at their bravery.

Run, run.

He had barely enough of a head start. He reeled into the hull, dogged the door shut, and heard missiles clatter on metal. Then for a while he knew nothing.

When awareness came back, he spent a minute giving thanks. Afterward he dragged himself to the pilot chair. *What a scene!* passed across his mind. And, a crazy chuckle: *The old definition of adventure. Somebody else having a hard time a long ways off.*

He slumped into the seat. The vitryl port showed him a sky turned wonderful, a land of dim slopes and sharp ridges—He gasped and sat upright. The Ivanhoans were still outside.

They stood leaning on their useless spears or clinging to the hilts of their useless swords, and waited for whatever he would do. Shakily, he switched on the sound amplifier and bullhorn. His voice boomed over them: "What do you want?"

Tokonnen's answer remained prideful. "We wish to know your desire, Earthling. For in you we have met a thing most strange."

Bewildered, Juan could merely respond with, "How so?"

"You rendered us helpless," Tokonnen said. "Why did you not at once kill us? Instead, you chose to flee. You must have known we would recover and come after you. Why did you take the unneeded risk?"

"You *were* helpless," Juan blurted. "I couldn't have...hurt you...especially at this time of year."

Tokonnen showed astonishment. "Time of year? What has that to do with it?"

"Christmas—" Juan paused. Strength and clarity of mind were returning to him. "You don't know about that. It's a season which, well, commemorates one who came to us Earthlings, ages ago, and spoke of peace as well as much else. For us, this is a holy time." He laid hands on controls. "No matter. I only ask you believe that we don't mean you any harm. Stand aside. I am about to raise this wagon."

"No," Tokonnen said. "Wait. I ask you, wait." He was silent for a while, and his warriors with him. "What you have told us—We must hear further. Talk to us, Earthling."

Once he had radioed that he was safe, they stopped worrying about Juan at the base. For the next several hours, the men continued their jobs. It was impossible for them to function on a sixty-hour day, and nobody tried. Midnight had not come when they knocked off. Recreation followed. For four of them, this meant preparing their Christmas welcome to the ship.

As they worked outdoors, more and more Dahians gathered, fascinated, to stand silently around the plaza and watch. Overbeck stepped forth to observe the natives in his turn. Nothing like this had ever happened before.

A tree had been erected on the flagstones. Its sparse branches and stiff foliage did not suggest an evergreen; but no matter, it glittered with homemade ornaments and lights improvised from electronic parts. Before it stood a manger scene that Juan had constructed. A risen moon, the mighty Pleiades, and the luminous nebular veil cast frost-cold brilliance. The beings who encompassed the square, beneath lean houses and fortress towers, formed a shadow-mass wherein eyes glimmered.

Feinberg and Gupta decorated. Noguchi and Sary-chev, who had the best voices, rehearsed. Breath from their song puffed white.

"O little town of Bethlehem,
How still we see thee lie—"

A muted "A-a-ahhh!" rose from the Dahians, and Juan landed his flitter.

He bounded forth. Behind him came a native in a steel breastplate. Overbeck had awaited this since the boy's last call. He gestured to Raffak, speaker of the Elders.

Together, human and Ivanhoan advanced to greet human and Ivanhoan.

Tokonnen said, "It may be we misjudged your intent, City folk. The Earthling tells me we did."

"And his lord tells me we of Dahia pushed forward too strongly," Raffak answered. "That may likewise be."

Tokonnen touched sword-hilt and warned, "We shall yield nothing which is sacred to us."

"Nor we," said Raffak. "But surely our two people can reach an agreement. The Earthlings can help us make terms."

"They should have special wisdom, now in the season of their Prince of Peace."

"Aye. My fellows and I have begun some hard thinking about that."

"How do you know of it?"

"We were curious as to why the Earthlings were making beauty, here where we can see it away from the dreadful heat," Raffak said. "We asked. In the course of this, they told us somewhat of happenings in the desert, which the far-speaker had informed them of."

"It is indeed something to think about," Tokonnen nodded. "They, who believe in peace, are more powerful than us."

"And it was war which destroyed the Empire. But come," Raffak invited. "Tonight be my guest. Tomorrow we will talk."

They departed. Meanwhile the men clustered around Juan. Overbeck shook his hand again and again. "You're a genius," he said. "I ought to take lessons from you."

"No, please, sir," his apprentice protested. "The thing simply happened."

"It wouldn't have, if I'd been the one who got caught."

Sarychev was puzzled. "I don't quite see what did go on," he confessed. "It was good of Juan to run away from those nomads, instead of cutting them down when he had the chance. However, that by itself can't have turned them meek and mild."

"Oh, no." Overbeck chuckled. His cigar end waxed and waned like a variable star. "They're as ornery as ever—

same as humans." Soberly: "The difference is, they've become willing to listen to us. They can take our ideas seriously, and believe we'll be honest brokers, who can mediate their quarrels."

"Why could they not before?"

"My fault, I'm afraid. I wasn't allowing for a certain part of Ivanhoan nature. I should have seen. After all, it's part of human nature too."

"What is?" Gupta asked.

"The need for—" Overbeck broke off. "You tell him, Juan. You were the one who did see the truth."

The boy drew breath. "Not at first," he said. "I only found I could not bring myself to kill. Is Christmas not when we should be quickest to forgive our enemies? I told them so. Then...when suddenly their whole attitude changed...I guessed what the reason must be." He searched for words. "They knew—both Dahians and nomads knew—we are strong; we have powers they can't hope to match. That doesn't frighten them. They have to be fearless, to survive in as bleak a country as this.

"Also, they have to be dedicated. To keep going through endless hardship, they must believe in something greater than themselves, like the Imperial dream of Dahia or the freedom of the desert. They're ready to die for those ideals.

"We came, we Earthlings. We offered them a fair, profitable bargain. But nothing else. We seemed to have no other motive than material gain. They could not understand this. It made us too peculiar. They could never really trust us.

"Now that they know we have our own sacrednesses, well, they see we are not so different from them, and they'll heed our advice."

Juan uttered an unsteady laugh. "What a long lecture, no?" he ended. "I'm very tired and hungry. Please, may I go get something to eat and afterward to bed?"

As he crossed the square, the carol followed him:

*"—The hopes and fears of all the years
Are met in thee tonight."*

A full sky-dance portaying Nicholas van Rijn needs the space of a small book. Several historical novels wherein he figures exist, and maychance you will wish to screen them. For the purpose which his Wyvan gave him, Hloch chooses the following. This is partly because van Rijn is more central in it than in others; partly because the consequences had some importance to Falkayn's home world; and partly because winged sophonts have a special interest for us, rare as they are. In addition, Diomedes, freak among planets, helps remind of the awesome unforeseeability of the universe, a fact before which starfaring races must humble their very deathpride.

While this tale appears to be reasonably factual, its source is uncertain. Original publication was either on Terra or Hermes; separate authors and dates are given on those two worlds, and Rennhi did not feel the matter was worth pursuing further.

THE MAN WHO COUNTS

I

Grand Admiral Syranax hyr Urnan, hereditary Commander-in-Chief of the Fleet of Drak'ho, Fisher of the Western Seas, Leader in Sacrifice, and Oracle of the Lodestar, spread his wings and brought them together again in an astonished thunderclap. For a moment, it snowed papers from his desk.

"No!" he said. "Impossible! There's some mistake."

"As my Admiral wills it." Chief Executive Officer Delp hyr Orikan bowed sarcastically. "The scouts saw nothing."

Anger crossed the face of Captain T'heonax hyr Urnan, son of the Grand Admiral and therefore heir apparent. His upper lip rose until the canine tushes showed, a white flash against the dark muzzle.

"We have no time to waste on your insolence, Executive Delp," he said coldly. "I would advise my father to dispense with an officer who has no more respect."

Under the embroidered cross-belts of office, Delp's big frame tautened. Captain T'heonax glided one step toward him. Tails curled back and wings spread, instinctive readiness for battle, until the room was full of their bodies and their hate. With a calculation which made it seem accidental, T'heonax dropped a hand to the obsidian rake at his waist. Delp's yellow eyes blazed and his fingers clamped on his own tomahawk.

Admiral Syranax's tail struck the floor. It was like a fire-bomb going off. The two young nobles jerked, remembered where they were, and slowly, muscle by muscle laying itself back to rest under the sleek brown fur, they relaxed.

"Enough!" snapped Syranax. "Delp, your tongue will flap you into trouble yet. Theonax, I've grown bored with your spite. You'll have your chance to deal with personal enemies, when I am fish food. Meanwhile, spare me my few able officers!"

It was a firmer speech than anyone had heard from him for a long time. His son and his subordinate recalled that this grizzled, dim-eyed, rheumatic creature had once been the conqueror of the Maion Navy—a thousand wings of enemy leaders had rattled grisly from the mastheads—and was still their chief in the war against the Flock. They assumed the all-fours crouch of respect and waited for him to continue.

"Don't take me so literally, Delp," said the admiral in a milder tone. He reached to the rack above his desk and got down a long-stemmed pipe and began stuffing it with flakes of dried sea driss from the pouch at his waist. Meanwhile, his stiff old body fitted itself more comfortably into the wood-and-leather seat. "I was quite surprised, of course, but I assume that our scouts still know how to use a telescope. Describe to me again exactly what happened."

"A patrol was on routine reconnaissance about thirty obdisai north-north-west of here," said Delp with care. "That would be in the general area of the island called . . . I can't pronounce that heathenish local name, sir; it means Banners Flew."

"Yes, yes," nodded Syranax. "I have looked at a map now and then, you know."

Theonax grinned. Delp was no courtier. That was Delp's trouble. His grandfather had been a mere Sailmaker, his father never advanced beyond the captaincy of a single raft. That was after the family had been ennobled for heroic service at the Battle of Xarit'ha, of course—but they had still been very minor peers, a tarry-handed lot barely one cut above their own crewfolk.

Syranax, the Fleet's embodied response to these grim days of hunger and uprooting, had chosen officers on a basis of demonstrated ability, and nothing else. Thus it was that simple Delp hyr Orikan had been catapulted in a few years to the second highest post in Drak'ho. Which had not taken the rough edges off his education, or taught him how to deal with *real* nobles.

If Delp was popular with the common sailors, he was all the more disliked by many aristocrats—a parvenu, a boor, with the nerve to wed a sa Axollon! Once the old admiral's protecting wings were folded in death—

T'heonax savored in advance what would happen to Delp hyr Orikan. It would be easy enough to find some nominal charge.

The executive gulped. "Sorry, sir," he mumbled. "I didn't mean . . . we're still so new to this whole sea . . . well. The scouts saw this drifting object. It was like nothing ever heard of before. A pair of 'em flew back to report and ask for advice. I went to look for myself. Sir, it's true!"

"A floating object—six times as long as our longest canoe—like ice, and yet not like ice—" The admiral shook his gray-furred head. Slowly, he put dry tinder in the bottom of his firemaker. But it was with needless violence that he drove the piston down into the little hardwood cylinder. Removing the rod again, he tilted fire out into the bowl of his pipe, and drew deeply.

"The most highly polished rock crystal might look a bit like that stuff, sir," offered Delp. "But not so bright. Not with such a *shimmer*."

"And there are animals scurrying about on it?"

"Three of them, sir. About our size, or a little bigger, but wingless and tailless. Yet not just animals either . . . I think . . . they seem to wear clothes and—I don't think the shining thing was ever intended as a boat, though. It rides abominably, and appears to be settling."

"If it's not a boat, and not a log washed off some beach," said T'heonax, "then where, pray tell, is it from? The Deeps?"

"Hardly, captain," said Delp irritably. "If that were so, the creatures on it would be fish or sea mammals or—well, adapted for swimming, anyway. They're not. They look like typical flightless land forms, except for having only four limbs."

"So they fell from the sky, I presume?" sneered T'heonax.

"I wouldn't be at all surprised," said Delp in a very low voice. "There isn't any other direction left."

T'heonax sat up on his haunches, mouth falling open. His father only nodded.

"Very good," murmered Syranax. "I'm pleased to see a little imagination around here."

"But where did they fly *from*?" exploded T'heonax.

"Perhaps our enemies of Lannach would have some account of it," said the admiral. "They cover a great deal more of the world every year than we do in many generations; they meet a hundred other barbarian flocks down in the tropics and exchange news."

"And females," said T'heonax. He spoke in that mixture of primly disapproving voice and lickerish overtones with which the entire Fleet regarded the habits of the migrators.

"Never mind that," snapped Delp.

T'heonax bristled. "You deck-swabber's whelp, do you dare—"

"Shut up!" roared Syranax.

After a pause, he went on: "I'll have inquiries made among our prisoners. Meanwhile, we had better send a fast canoe to pick up these beings before that object they're on founders."

"They may be dangerous," warned T'heonax.

"Exactly," said his father. "If so, they're better in our hands than if, say, the Lannach'honai should find them and make an alliance. Delp, take the *Nemnis*, with a reliable crew, and crowd sail on her. And bring along that fellow we captured from Lannach, what's his name, the professional linguist—"

"Tolk?" The executive stumbled over the unfamiliar pronunciation.

"Yes. Maybe he can talk to them. Send scouts back to report to me, but stand well off the main Fleet until you're sure that the creatures are harmless to us. Also till I've allayed whatever superstitious fears about sea demons there are in the lower classes. Be polite if you can, get rough if you must. We can always apologize later... or toss the bodies overboard. Now, jump!"

Delp jumped.

II

Desolation walled him in.

Even from this low, on the rolling, pitching hull of the murdered skycruiser, Eric Wace could see an immensity of horizon. He thought that the sheer size of that ring, where frost-pale heaven met the gray which was cloud and storm-scud and great marching waves, was enough to terrify a man. The likelihood of death had been faced before, on Earth, by many of his forebears; but Earth's horizon was not so remote.

Never mind that he was a hundred-odd light-years from his own sun. Such distances were too big to be understood: they became mere numbers, and did not frighten one who reckoned the pseudo-speed of a secondary-drive spaceship in parsecs per week.

Even the ten thousand kilometers of open ocean to this world's lone human settlement, the trading post, was only another number. Later, if he lived, Wace would spend an agonized time wondering how to get a message across that emptiness. But at present he was too occupied with keeping alive.

But the breadth of the planet was something he could see. It had not struck him before, in his eighteen-month stay; but then he had been insulated, psychologically as well as physically, by an unconquerable machine technology. Now he stood alone on a sinking vessel, and it was twice as far to look across chill waves to the world's rim as it had been on Earth.

The skycruiser rolled under a savage impact. Wace lost his footing and slipped across curved metal plates. Frantic, he clawed for the light cable which lashed cases of food to the navigation turret. If he went over the side, his boots and clothes would pull him under like a stone. He caught it in time and strained to a halt. The disappointed wave slapped his face, a wet salt hand.

Shaking with cold, Wace finished tucking the last box into place and crawled back toward the entry hatch. It was a miserable little emergency door, but the glazed promenade deck, on which his passengers had strolled while the cruiser's gravbeams bore her through the sky, was awash, its ornate bronze portal submerged.

Water had filled the smashed engine compartment when they ditched. Since then it had been seeping around twisted bulkheads and strained hull plates, until the whole thing was about ready for a last long dive to the sea bottom.

Wind passed gaunt fingers through his drenched hair and tried to hold open the hatch when he wanted to close it after him. He had a struggle against the gale... Gale? Hell, no! It had only the velocity of a stiffish breeze—but with six times the atmospheric pressure of Earth behind it, that breeze struck like a Terrestrial storm. Damn PLC 2987165 II! Damn the PL itself, and damn Nicholas van Rijn, and most particularly damn Eric Wace for being fool enough to work for the Company!

Briefly, while he fought the hatch, Wace looked out over the coaming as if to find rescue. He glimpsed only a reddish sun, and great cloud-banks dirty with storm in the north, and a few specks which were probably natives.

Satan fry those natives on a slow griddle, that they did not come to help! Or at least go decently away while the humans drowned, instead of hanging up there in the sky to gloat!

●   ●   ●

"Is all in order?"

Wace closed the hatch, dogged it fast, and came down the ladder. At its foot, he had to brace himself against the heavy rolling. He could still hear waves beat on the hull, and the wind-yowl.

"Yes, my lady," he said. "As much as it'll ever be."

"Which isn't much, not?" Lady Sandra Tamarin played her flashlight over him. Behind it, she was only another shadow in the darkness of the dead vessel. "But you look a saturated rat, my friend. Come, we have at least fresh clothes for you."

Wace nodded and shrugged out of his wet jacket and kicked off the squelching boots. He would have frozen up there without them—it couldn't be over five degrees C.— but they seemed to have blotted up half the ocean. His teeth clapped in his head as he followed her down the corridor.

He was a tall young man of North American stock, ruddy-haired, blue-eyed, with bluntly squared-off features above a well-muscled body. He had begun as a warehouse apprentice at the age of twelve, back on Earth, and now he was the Solar Spice & Liquors Company's factor for the entire planet known as Diomedes. It wasn't exactly a meteoric rise—van Rijn's policy was to promote according to results, which meant that a quick mind, a quick gun, and an eye firmly held to the main chance were favored. But it had been a good solid career, with a future of posts on less isolated and unpleasant worlds, ultimately an executive position back Home and—and what was the use, if alien waters were to eat him in a few hours more?

At the end of the hall, where the navigation turret poked up, there was again the angry copper sunlight, low in the wan smoky-clouded sky, south of west as day declined. Lady Sandra snapped off her torch and pointed to a coverall laid out on the desk. Beside it were the outer garments, quilted, hooded, and gloved, he would need before venturing out again into the pre-equinoctial springtime. "Put on everything," she said. "Once the boat starts going down, we will have to leave in a most horrible hurry."

"Where's Freeman van Rijn?" asked Wace.

"Making some last-minute work on the raft. That one is a handy man with the tools, not? But then, he was once a common spacehand."

Wace shrugged and waited for her to leave.

"Change, I told you," she said.

"But—"

"Oh." A thin smile crossed her face. "I thought not there was a nudity taboo on Earth."

"Well . . . not exactly, I guess, my lady . . . but after all, you're a noble born, and I'm only a trader—"

"From republican planets like Earth come the worst snobs of all," she said. "Here we are all human beings. Quickly, now, change. I shall turn my back if you desire so."

Wace scrambled into the outfit as fast as possible. Her mirth was an unexpected comfort to him. He considered what luck always appeared to befall that pot-bellied old goat van Rijn.

It wasn't right!

The colonists of Hermes had been, mostly, a big fair stock, and their descendants had bred true: especially the aristocrats, after Hermes set up as an autonomous grand duchy during the Breakup. Lady Sandra Tamarin was nearly as tall as he, and shapeless winter clothing did not entirely hide the lithe full femaleness of her. She had a face too strong to be pretty—wide forehead, wide mouth, snub nose, high cheekbones—but the large smoky-lashed green eyes, under heavy dark brows, were the most beautiful Wace had ever seen. Her hair was long, straight, ash-blond, pulled into a knot at the moment but he had seen it floating free under a coronet by candlelight—

"Are you quite through, Freeman Wace?"

"Oh . . . I'm sorry, my lady. I got to thinking. Just a moment!" He pulled on the padded tunic, but left it unzipped. There was still some human warmth lingering in the hull. "Yes. I beg your pardon."

"It is nothing." She turned about. In the little space available, their forms brushed together. Her gaze went out to the sky. "Those natives, are they up there yet?"

"I imagine so, my lady. Too high for me to be sure, but

they can go up several kilometers with no trouble at all."

"I have wondered, Trader, but got no chance to ask. I thought not there could be a flying animal the size of a man, and yet these Diomedeans have a six-meter span of bat wings. How?"

"At a time like *this* you ask?"

She smiled. "We only wait now for Freeman van Rijn. What else shall we do but talk of curious things?"

"We . . . help him . . . finish that raft soon or we'll all go under!"

"He told me he has just batteries enough for one cutting torch, so anyone else is only in the way. Please continue talking. The highborn of Hermes have their customs and taboos, also for the correct way to die. What else is man, if not a set of customs and taboos?" Her husky voice was light, she smiled a little, but he wondered how much of it was an act.

He wanted to say: We're down in the ocean of a planet whose life is poison to us. There is an island a few score kilometers hence, but we only know its direction vaguely. We may or may not complete a raft in time, patched together out of old fuel drums, and we may or may not get our human-type rations loaded on it in time, and it may or may not weather the storm brewing yonder in the north. Those were natives who swooped low above us a few hours ago, but since then they have ignored us . . . or watched us . . . anything except offer help.

Someone hates you or old van Rijn, he wanted to say. Not me, I'm not important enough to hate. But van Rijn is the Solar Spice & Liquors Company, which is a great power in the Polesotechnic League, which is *the* great power in the known galaxy. And you are the Lady Sandra Tamarin, heiress to the throne of an entire planet, if you live; and you have turned down many offers of marriage from its decaying, inbred aristocracy, publicly preferring to look elsewhere for a father for your children, that the next Grand Duke of Hermes may be a man and not a giggling clothes horse; so no few courtiers must dread your accession.

Oh, yes, he wanted to say, there are plenty of people

who would gain if either Nicholas van Rijn or Sandra Tamarin failed to come back. It was a calculated gallantry for him to offer you a lift in his private ship, from Antares where you met, back to Earth, with stopovers at interesting points along the way. At the very least, he can look for trade concessions in the Duchy. At best... no, hardly a formal alliance; he has too much hell in him; even you—most strong and fair and innocent—would never let him plant himself on the High Seat of your fathers.

But I wander from the subject, my dear, he wanted to say; and the subject is, that someone in the spaceship's crew was bribed. The scheme was well-hatched; the someone watched his chance. It came when you landed on Diomedes, to see what a really new raw planet is like, a planet where even the main continental outlines have scarcely been mapped, in the mere five years that a spoonful of men have been here. The chance came when I was told to ferry you and my evil old boss to those sheer mountains, halfway around this world, which have been noted as spectacular scenery. A bomb in the main generator... a slain crew, engineers and stewards gone in the blast, my co-pilot's skull broken when we ditched in the sea, the radio shattered... and the last wreckage is going to sink long before they begin to worry at Thursday Landing and come in search of us... and assuming we survive, is there the slightest noticeable chance that a few skyboats, cruising a nearly unmapped world twice the size of Earth, will happen to see three human flyspecks on it?

Therefore, he wanted to say, since all our schemings and posturings have brought us merely to this, it would be well to forget them in what small time remains, and kiss me instead.

But his throat clogged up on him, and he said none of it.

"So?" A note of impatience entered her voice. "You are very silent, Freeman Wace."

"I'm sorry, my lady," he mumbled. "I'm afraid I'm no good at making conversation under... uh, these circumstances."

"I regret I have not qualifications to offer to you the

consolations of religion," she said with a hurtful scorn.

A long gray-bearded comber went over the deck outside and climbed the turret. They felt steel and plastic tremble under the blow. For a moment, as water sheeted, they stood in a blind roaring dark.

Then, as it cleared, and Wace saw how much farther down the wreck had burrowed, and wondered if they would even be able to get van Rijn's raft out through the submerged cargo hatch, there was a whiteness that snatched at his eye.

First he didn't believe it, and then he wouldn't believe because he dared not, and then he could no longer deny it.

"Lady Sandra." He spoke with immense care; he *must* not scream his news at her like any low-born Terrestrial.

"Yes?" She did not look away from her smoldering contemplation of the northern horizon, empty of all but clouds and lightning.

"There, my lady. Roughly southeast, I'd guess . . . sails, beating upwind."

"What?" It was a shriek from her. Somehow, that made Wace laugh aloud.

"A boat of some kind," he pointed. "Coming this way."

"I didn't know the natives were sailors," she said, very softly.

"They aren't, my lady—around Thursday Landing," he replied. "But this is a big planet. Roughly four times the surface area of Earth, and we only know a small part of one continent."

"Then you know not what they are like, these sailors?"

"My lady, I have no idea."

III

Nicholas van Rijn came puffing up the companionway at their shout. "Death and damnation!" he roared. "A boat, do you say, *ja*? Better for you it is a shark, if you are mistaken. By damn!" He stumped into the turret and glared out through salt-encrusted plastic. The light was dimming as the sun went lower and the approaching storm clouds swept across its ruddy face. "So! Where is it, this pestilential boat?"

"There, sir," said Wace. "That schooner—"

"Schooner! Schnork! Powder and balls, you cement head, that is a yawl rig ... no, wait, by damn, there is a furled square sail on the mainmast too, and yes, an outrigger—*Ja*, the way she handles, she must have a regular rudder—Good saints help us! A bloody-be-damned-to-blazes dugout!"

"What else do you expect, on a planet without metals?" said Wace. His nerves were worn too thin for him to remember the deference due a merchant prince.

"Hm-m-m ... coracles, maybe so, or rafts or catamarans—Quick, dry clothes! Too cold it is for brass monkeys!"

Wace grew aware that van Rijn was standing in a puddle, and that bitter sea water streamed from his waist and legs. The storeroom where he had been at work must have been awash for—for hours!

"I know where they are, Nicholas." Sandra loped off down the corridor. It slanted more ominously every minute, as the sea pushed in through a ruined stern.

Wace helped his chief off with the sopping coverall. Naked, van Rijn suggested ... what was that extinct ape? ... a gorilla, two meters tall, hairy and huge-bellied, with shoulders like a brick warehouse, loudly bawling his indignation at the cold and the damp and the slowness of assistants. But rings flashed on the thick fingers and bracelets on the wrists, and a little St. Dismas medal swung from his neck. Unlike Wace, who found a crew cut and a clean shave more practical, van Rijn let his oily black locks hang curled and perfumed in an archaic mode, flaunted a goatee on his triple chin and intimidating waxed mustaches beneath the great hook nose.

He rummaged in the navigator's cabinet, wheezing, till he found a bottle of rum. "Ahhh! I knew I had the devil-begotten thing stowed somewhere." He put it to his frog-mouth and tossed off several shots at a gulp. "Good! Fine! Now maybe we can begin to be like self-respectful humans once more, *nie*?"

He turned about, majestic and globular as a planet, when Sandra came back. The only clothes she could find to fit him were his own, a peacock outfit of lace-trimmed shirt, embroidered waistcoat, shimmersilk culottes and stockings, gilt shoes, plumed hat, and holstered blaster. "Thank you," he said curtly. "Now, Wace, while I dress, in the lounge you will find a box of Perfectos and one small bottle applejack. Please to fetch them, then we go outside and meet our hosts."

"Holy St. Peter!" cried Wace. "The lounge is under water!"

"Ah?" Van Rijn sighed, woebegone. "Then you need only get the applejack. Quick, now!" He snapped his fingers.

Wace said hastily: "No time, sir. I still have to round up the last of our ammunition. Those natives could be hostile."

"If they have heard of us, possible so," agreed van Rijn. He began donning his natural-silk underwear. "*Brrrr!* Five thousand candles I would give to be back in my office in Jakarta!"

"To what saint do you make the offer?" asked Lady Sandra.

"St. Nicholas, natural—my namesake, patron of wanderers and—"

"St. Nicholas had best get it in writing," she said.

Van Rijn purpled; but one does not talk back to the heiress apparent of a nation with important trade concessions to offer. He took it out by screaming abuse after the departing Wace.

It was some time before they were outside. Van Rijn got stuck in the emergency hatch and required pushing, while his anguished basso obscenities drowned the nearing thunder. Diomedes' period of rotation was only twelve and a half hours, and this latitude, thirty degrees north, was still on the winter side of equinox; so the sun was toppling seaward with dreadful speed. They clung to the lashings and let the wind claw them and the waves burst over them. There was nothing else they could do.

"It is no place for a poor old fat man," snuffled van Rijn. The gale ripped the words from him and flung them tattered over the rising seas. His shoulder-length curls flapped like forlorn pennons. "Better I should have stayed at home in Java where it is warm, not lost my last few pitiful years out here."

Wace strained his eyes into the gloom. The dugout had come near. Even a landlubber like himself could appreciate the skill of its crew, and van Rijn was loud in his praises. "I nominate him for the Sunda Yacht Club, by damn, yes, and enter him in the next regatta and make bets!"

It was a big craft, more than thirty meters long, with an elaborate stempost, but dwarfed by the reckless spread of its blue-dyed sails. Outrigger or no, Wace expected it to capsize any moment. Of course, a flying species had less to worry about if that should happen than—

"The Diomedeans." Sandra's tone was quiet in his ear, under shrill wind and booming waters. "You have dealt with them for a year and a half, not? What can we await for from them?"

Wace shrugged. "What could we expect from any random tribe of humans, back in the Stone Age? They might be poets, or cannibals, or both. All I know is the Tyrlanian Flock, who are migratory hunters. They always stick by the letter of their law—not quite so scrupulous about its spirit, of course, but on the whole a decent tribe."

"You speak their language?"

"As well as my human palate and Techno-Terrestrial culture permit me to, my lady. I don't pretend to understand all their concepts, but we get along—" The broken hull lurched. He heard some abused wall rend, and the inward pouring of still more sea, and felt the sluggishness grow beneath his feet. Sandra stumbled against him. He saw that the spray was freezing in her brows.

"That does not mean I'll understand the local language," he finished. "We're farther from Tyrlan than Europe from China."

The canoe was almost on them now. None too soon:

the wreck was due to dive any minute. It came about, the sails rattled down, a sea anchor was thrown and brawny arms dug paddles into the water. Swiftly, then, a Diomedean flapped over with a rope. Two others hovered close, obviously as guards. The first one landed and stared at the humans.

Tyrlan being farther north, its inhabitants had not yet returned from the tropics and this was the first Diomedean Sandra had encountered. She was too wet, cold, and weary to enjoy the unhuman grace of his movements, but she looked very close. She might have to dwell with this race a long time, if they did not murder her.

He was the size of a smallish man, plus a thick meter-long tail ending in a fleshy rudder and the tremendous chiropteral wings folded along his back. His arms were set below the wings, near the middle of a sleek otterlike body, and looked startlingly human, down to the muscular five-fingered hands. The legs were less familiar, bending backward from four-taloned feet which might almost have belonged to some bird of prey. The head, at the end of a neck that would have been twice too long on a human, was round, with a high forehead, yellow eyes with nictitating membranes under heavy brow ridges, a blunt-muzzled black-nosed face with short cat-whiskers, a big mouth and the bearlike teeth of a flesh-eater turned omnivore. There were no external ears, but a crest of muscle on the head helped control flight. Short, soft brown fur covered him; he was plainly a male mammal.

He wore two belts looped around his "shoulders," a third about his waist, and a pair of bulging leather pouches. An obsidian knife, a slender flint-headed ax, and a set of bolas were hung in plain view. Through the thickening dusk, it was hard to make out what his wheeling comrades bore for weapons—something long and thin, but surely not a rifle, on this planet without copper or iron. . . .

Wace leaned forward and forced his tongue around the grunting syllables of Tyrlanian: "We are friends. Do you understand me?"

A string of totally foreign words snapped at him. He

shrugged, ruefully, and spread his hands. The Diomedean moved across the hull—bipedal, body slanted forward to balance wings and tail—and found the stud to which the humans' lashings were anchored. Quickly, he knotted his own rope to the same place.

"A bowline," said van Rijn, almost quietly. "It makes me homesick."

At the other end of the line, they began to haul the canoe closer. The Diomedean turned to Wace and pointed at his vessel. Wace nodded, realized that the gesture was probably meaningless here, and took a precarious step in that direction. The Diomedean caught another rope flung to him. He pointed at it, and at the humans, and made gestures.

"I understand," said van Rijn. "Nearer than this they dare not come. Too easy their boat gets smashed against us. We get this cord tied around our bodies, and they haul us across. Good St. Christopher, what a thing to do to a poor creaky-boned old man!"

"There's our food, though," said Wace.

The skycruiser jerked and settled deeper. The Diomedean jittered nervously.

"No, no!" shouted van Rijn. He seemed under the impression that if he only bellowed loudly enough, he could penetrate the linguistic barrier. His arms windmilled. "*Nie!* Never! Do you not understand, you oatmeal brains? Better to guggle down in your pest-begotten ocean than try eating your food. We die! Bellyache! Suicide!" He pointed at his mouth, slapped his abdomen, and waved at the rations.

Wace reflected grimly that evolution was too flexible. Here you had a planet with oxygen, nitrogen, hydrogen, carbon, sulfur . . . a protein biochemistry forming genes, chromosomes, cells, tissues . . . protoplasm by any reasonable definition . . . and the human who tried to eat a fruit or steak from Diomedes would be dead ten minutes later of about fifty lethal allergic reactions. These just weren't the *right* proteins. In fact, only immunization shots prevented men from getting chronic hay fever, asthma, and hives, merely from the air they breathed or the water they drank.

He had spent many cold hours today piling the cruiser's food supplies out here, for transference to the raft. This luxury atmospheric vessel had been carried in van Rijn's spaceship, ready-stocked for extended picnic orgies when the mood struck him. There was enough rye bread, sweet butter, Edam cheese, lox, smoked turkey, dill pickles, fruit preserves, chocolate, plum pudding, beer, wine, and God knew what else, to keep three people going for a few months.

The Diomedean spread his wings, flapping them to maintain his footing. In the wan stormy light, the thumbs-turned-claws on their leading edge seemed to whicker past van Rijn's beaky face like a mowing machine operated by some modernistic Death. The merchant waited stolidly, now and then aiming a finger at the stacked cases. Finally the Diomedean got the idea, or simply gave in. There was scant time left. He whistled across to the canoe. A swarm of his fellows came over, undid the lashings and began transporting boxes. Wace helped Sandra fasten the rope about her. "I'm afraid it will be a wet haul, my lady," he tried to smile.

She sneezed. "So this is the brave pioneering between the stars! I will have a word or two for my court poets when I get home... if I do."

When she was across, and the rope had been flown back, van Rijn waved Wace ahead. He himself was arguing with the Diomedean chief. How it was done without a word of real language between them, Wace did not know, but they had reached the stage of screaming indignation at each other. Just as Wace set his teeth and went overboard, van Rijn sat mutinously down.

And when the younger man made his drowned-rat arrival on board the canoe, the merchant had evidently won his point. A Diomedean could air-lift about fifty kilos for short distances. Three of them improvised a rope sling and carried van Rijn over, above the water.

He had not yet reached the canoe when the skycruiser sank.

IV

The dugout held about a hundred natives, all armed, some wearing helmets and breastplates of hard laminated leather. A catapult, just visible through the dark, was mounted at the bows; the stern held a cabin, made from sapling trunks chinked with sea weed, that towered up almost like the rear end of a medieval caravel. On its roof, two helmsmen strained at the long tiller.

"Plain to see, we have found a navy ship," grunted van Rijn. "Not so good, that. With a trader, I can talk. With some pest-and-pox officer with gold braids on his brain, him I can only shout." He raised small, close-set eyes to a night heaven where lightning ramped. "I am a poor old sinner," he shouted, "but this I have not deserved! Do you hear me?"

After a while the humans were prodded between lithe devil-bodies, toward the cabin. The dugout had begun to run before the gale, on two reef points and a jib. The roll and pitch, clamor of waves and wind and thunder, had receded into the back of Wace's consciousness. He wanted only to find some place that was dry, take off his clothes and crawl into bed and sleep for a hundred years.

The cabin was small. Three humans and two Diomedeans left barely room to sit down. But it was warm, and a stone lamp hung from the ceiling threw a dim light full of grotesquely moving shadows.

The native who had first met them was present. His volcanic-glass dagger lay unsheathed in one hand, and he held a wary lion-crouch; but half his attention seemed aimed at the other one, who was leaner and older, with flecks of gray in the fur, and who was tied to a corner post by a rawhide leash.

Sandra's eyes narrowed. The blaster which van Rijn had lent her slid quietly to her lap as she sat down. The Diomedean with the knife flicked his gaze across it, and van Rijn swore. "You little all-thumbs brain, do you let him see what is a weapon?"

The first autochthon said something to the leashed one. The latter made a reply with a growl in it, then turned to the humans. When he spoke, it did not sound like the same language.

"So! An interpreter!" said van Rijn. "You speakee Angly, ha? Haw, haw, haw!" He slapped his thigh.

"No, wait. It's worth trying." Wace dropped into Tyrlanian: "Do you understand me? This is the only speech we could possibly have in common."

The captive raised his head-crest and sat up on his hands and haunches. What he answered was *almost* familiar. "Speak slowly, if you will," said Wace, and felt sleepiness drain out of him.

Meaning came through, thickly: "You do not use a version (?) of the Carnoi that I have heard before."

"Carnoi—" Wait, yes, one of the Tyrlanians had mentioned a confederation of tribes far to the south, bearing some such name. "I am using the tongue of the folk of Tyrlan."

"I know not that race (?). They do not winter in our grounds. Nor do any Carnoi as a regular (?) thing, but now and then when all are in the tropics (?) one of them happens by, so—" It faded into unintelligibility.

The Diomedean with the knife said something, impatiently, and got a curt answer. The interpreter said to Wace:

"I am Tolk, a *mochra* of the Lannachska—"

"A what of the what?" said Wace.

It is not easy even for two humans to converse, when it must be in different patois of a language foreign to both. The dense accents imposed by human vocal cords and Diomedean ears—they heard farther into the subsonic, but did not go quite so high in pitch, and the curve of maximum response was different—made it a slow and painful process indeed. Wace took an hour to get a few sentences' worth of information.

Tolk was a linguistic specialist of the Great Flock of Lannach; it was his function to learn every language that came to his tribe's attention, which were many. His title might, perhaps, be rendered Herald, for his duties included a good deal of ceremonial announcements and he presided over a corps of messengers. The Flock was at war with the Drak'honai, and Tolk had been captured in a recent skirmish. The other Diomedean present was named Delp, and was a high-ranking officer of the Drak'honai.

Wace postponed saying much about himself, less from a wish to be secretive than from a realization of how appalling a task it would be. He did ask Tolk to warn Delp that the food from the cruiser, while essential to Earthlings, would kill a Diomedean.

"And why should I tell him that?" asked Tolk, with a grin that was quite humanly unpleasant.

"If you don't," said Wace, "it may go hard with you when he learns that you did not."

"True." Tolk spoke to Delp. The officer made a quick response.

"He says you will not be harmed unless you yourselves make it necessary," explained Tolk. "He says you are to learn his language so he can talk with you himself."

"What was it now?" interrupted van Rijn.

Wace told him. Van Rijn exploded. "What? What does he say? Stay here till—Death and wet liver! I tell that filthy toad—" He half-rose to his feet. Delp's wings rattled together. His teeth showed. The door was flung open and a pair of guards looked in. One of them carried a tomahawk, another had a wooden rake set with chips of flint.

Van Rijn clapped a hand to his gun. Delp's voice crackled out. Tolk translated: "He says to be calm."

After more parley, and with considerable effort and guesswork on Wace's part: "He wishes you no harm, but he must think of his own people. You are something new. Perhaps you can help him, or perhaps you are so harmful that he dare not let you go. He must have time to find out. You will remove all your garments and implements, and leave them in his charge. You will be provided other clothing, since it appears you have no fur."

When Wace had interpreted for van Rijn, the

merchant said, surprisingly at ease: "I think we have no choice just now. We can burn down many of them, *ja*. Maybe we can take the whole boat. But we cannot sail it all the way home by ourselves. If nothing else, we would starve en route, *nie?* Were I younger, yes, by good St. George, I would fight on general principles. Single-handed I would take him apart and play a xylophone on his ribs, and try to bluster his whole nation into helping me. But now I am too old and fat and tired. It is hard to be old, my boy—"

He wrinkled his sloping forehead and nodded in a wise fashion. "But, where there are enemies to bid against each other, that is where an honest trader has a chance to make a little bit profit!"

V

"First," said Wace, "you must understand that the world is shaped like a ball."

"Our philosophers have known it for a long time," said Delp complacently. "Even barbarians like the Lannach-'honai have an idea of the truth. After all, they cover thousands of obdisai every year, migrating. We're not so mobile, but we had to work out an astronomy before we could navigate very far."

Wace doubted that the Drak'honai could locate themselves with great precision. It was astonishing what their neolithic technology had achieved, not only in stone but in glass and ceramics; they even molded a few synthetic resins. They had telescopes, a sort of astrolabe, and navigational tables based on sun, stars, and the two small moons. However, compass and chronometer require iron, which simply did not exist in any noticeable quantity on Diomedes.

Automatically, he noted a rich potential market. The primitive Tyrlanians were avid for simple tools and weapons of metal, paying exorbitantly in the furs, gems, and pharmaceutically useful juices which made this planet worth the attention of the Polesotechnic League.

The Drak'honai could use more sophisticated amenities, from clocks and slide rules to Diesel engines—and were able to meet proportionately higher prices.

He recollected where he was: the raft *Gerunis*, headquarters of the Chief Executive Officer of the Fleet; and that the amiable creature who sat on the upper deck and talked with him was actually his jailer.

How long had it been since the crash—fifteen Diomedean days? That would be more than a week, Terrestrial reckoning. Several per cent of the Earthside food was already eaten.

He had lashed himself into learning the Drak'ho tongue from his fellow-prisoner Tolk. It was fortunate that the League had, of necessity, long ago developed the principles by which instruction could be given in minimal time. When properly focused, a trained mind need only be told something once. Tolk himself used an almost identical system; he might never have seen metal, but the Herald was semantically sophisticated.

"Well, then," said Wace, still haltingly and with gaps in his vocabulary, but adequately for his purposes, "do you know that this world-ball goes around the sun?"

"Quite a few of the philosophers believe that," said Delp. "I'm a practical (?) one myself, and never cared much one way or another."

"The motion of your world is unusual. In fact, in many ways this is a freak place. Your sun is cooler and redder than ours, so your home is colder. This sun has a *mass* . . . what do you say? . . . not much less than that of our own; and it is about the same distance. Therefore Diomedes, as we call your world, has a year only somewhat longer than our Earth's. Seven hundred eighty-two Diomedean days, isn't it? Diomedes has more than twice the diameter of Earth, but lacks the heavy materials found in most worlds. Therefore its *gravity*—hell!—therefore I only weigh about one-tenth more here than I would at home."

"I don't understand," said Delp.

"Oh, never mind," said Wace gloomily.

The planetographers were still puzzling about Dio-medes. It didn't fall into either of the standard types, the small hard ball like Earth or Mars, or the gas giant with a collapsed core like Jupiter or 61 Cygni C. It was intermediate, with a mass of 4.75 Earths; but its overall density was only half as much. This was due to the nearly total absence of all elements beyond calcium.

There was one sister freak, uninhabitable; the remaining planets were more or less normal giants, the sun a G8 dwarf not very different from other stars of that size and temperature. It was theorized that because of some improbable turbulence, or possibly an odd magnetic effect—a chance-created cosmic mass spectrograph—no heavy elements had occurred in the local section of the primordial gas cloud... But why hadn't thee at least been a density-increasing molecular collapse at the center of Diomedes? Sheer mass-pressure ought to have produced degeneracy. The most plausible answer to that was, the minerals in the body of this world were not normal ones, being formed in the absence of such elements as chromium, manganese, iron, and nickel. Their crystal structure was apparently more stable than, say, olivine, the most important of the Earth materials condensed by pressure—

The devil with it!

"Never mind that weight stuff," said Delp. "What's so unusual about the motion of Ikt'hanis?" It was his name for this planet, and did not mean "earth" but—in a language where nouns were compared—could be trans-lated "Oceanest," and was feminine.

Wace needed time to reply; the technicalities outran his vocabulary.

It was merely that the axial tilt of Diomedes was almost ninety degrees, so that the poles were virtually in the ecliptic plane. But that fact, coupled with the cool ultra-violet-poor sun, had set the pattern of life.

At either pole, nearly half the year was spent in total night. The endless daylight of the other half did not really compensate; there were polar species, but they were unimpressive hibernators. Even at forty-five degrees latitude, a fourth of the year was darkness, in a winter grimmer than Earth had ever seen. That was as far north or south as any intelligent Diomedeans could live; the annual migration used up too much of their time and energy, and they fell into a stagnant struggle for existence on the paleolithic level.

Here, at thirty degrees north, the Absolute Winter lasted one-sixth of the year—a shade over two Terrestrial months—and it was only (!) a few weeks' flight to the equatorial breeding grounds and back during that time. Therefore the Lannachska were a fairly cultivated people. The Drak'honai were originally from even farther south—,

But you could only do so much without metals. Of course, Diomedes had abundant magnesium, beryllium, and aluminum, but what use was that unless you first developed electrolytic technology, which required copper or silver.

Delp cocked his head. "You mean it's always equinox on your Eart'?"

"Well, not quite. But by your standards, very nearly!"

"So that's why you haven't got wings. The Lodestar didn't give you any, because you don't need them."

"Uh...perhaps. They'd have been no use to us, anyway. Earth's air is too thin for a creature the size of you or me to fly under its own power."

"What do you mean, thin? Air is...is air."

"Oh, never mind. Take my word for it."

How did you explain gravitational potential to a nonhuman whose mathematics was about on Euclid's level? You could say: "Look, if you go sixty-three hundred kilometers upward from the surface of Earth, the attraction has dropped off to one-fourth; but you must go thirteen thousand kilometers upward from Diomedes to diminish its pull on you correspondingly. Therefore Diomedes can hold a great deal more air. The weaker solar radiation helps, to be sure, especially the relatively less ultraviolet. But on the whole, gravitational potential is the secret.

"In fact, so dense is this air that if it held proportionate amounts of oxygen, or even of nitrogen, it would poison me. Luckily, the Diomedean atmosphere is a full seventy-nine per cent neon. Oxygen and nitrogen are lesser constituents: their partial pressures do not amount to very much more than on Earth. Likewise carbon dioxide and water vapor."

But Wace said only: "Let's talk about ourselves. Do you understand that the stars are other suns, like yours, but immensely farther away; and that Earth is a world of such a star?"

"Yes. I've heard the philosophers wonder—I'll believe you."

"Do you realize what our powers are, to cross the space between the stars? Do you know how we can reward you for your help in getting us home, and how our friends can punish you if you keep us here?"

For just a moment, Delp spread his wings, the fur bristled along his back and his eyes became flat yellow chips. He belonged to a proud folk.

Then he slumped. Across all gulfs of race, the human could sense how troubled he was:

"You told me yourself, Eart'ho, that you crossed The Ocean from the west, and in thousands of obdisai you didn't see so much as an island. It bears our own explorings out. We couldn't possibly fly that far, carrying you or just a message to your friends, without some place to stop and rest between times."

Wace nodded, slowly and carefully. "I see. And you couldn't take us back in a fast canoe before our food runs out."

"I'm afraid not. Even with favoring winds all the way, a boat is so much slower than wings. It'd take us half a year or more to sail the distance you speak of."

"But there must be *some* way—"

"Perhaps. But we're fighting a hard war, remember. We can't spare much effort or many workers for your sake."

"I don't think the Admiralty even intends to try."

VI

To the south was Lannach, an island the size of Britain. From it Homenach, an archipelago, curved northward for some hundreds of kilometers, into regions still wintry. Thus the islands acted as boundary and shield: defining the Sea of Achan, protecting it from the great cold currents of The Ocean.

Here the Drak'honai lay.

Nicholas van Rijn stood on the main deck of the *Gerunis*, glaring eastward to the Fleet's main body. The roughly woven, roughly fitted coat and trousers which a Sailmaker had thrown together for him irritated a skin long used to more expensive fabrics. He was tired of sugar-cured ham and brandied peaches—though when such fare gave out, he would begin starving to death. The thought of being a captured chattel whose wishes nobody need consult was pure anguish. The reflection on how much money the company must be losing for lack of his personal supervision was almost as bad.

"Bah!" he rumbled. "If they would make it a goal of their policy to get us home, it could be done."

Sandra gave him a weary look. "And what shall the Lannachs be doing while the Drak'honai bend all their efforts to return us?" she answered. "It is still a close thing, this war of theirs. Drak'ho could lose it yet."

"Satan's hoof-and-mouth disease!" He waved a hairy fist in the air. "While they squabble about their stupid little territories, the Solar Spice & Liquors is losing a million credits a day!"

"The war happens to be a life-and-death matter for both sides," she said.

"Also for us. *Nie?*" He fumbled after a pipe, remembered that his meerschaums were on the sea bottom, and groaned. "When I find who it was stuck that bomb in my cruiser—" It did not occur to him to offer excuses for getting her into this. But then, perhaps it was she who had indirectly caused the trouble. "Well," he finished on a calmer note, "it is true we must settle matters here, I think. End the war for them so they can do important business like getting me home."

Sandra frowned across the bright sun-blink of waters. "Do you mean help the Drak'honai? I do not care for that so much. They are the aggressors. But then, they saw the wives and little ones hungry—" She sighed. "It is hard to unravel. Let such be so, then."

"Oh, no!" Van Rijn combed his goatee. "We help the other side. The Lannachska."

"What!" She stood back from the rail and dropped her jaw at him. "But ... but—"

"You see," explained van Rijn, "I know a little something about politics. It is needful for an honest businessman seeking to make him a little hard-earned profit, else some louse-bound politician comes and taxes it from him for some idiot school or old-age pension. The politics here is not so different from what we do out in the galaxy. It is a culture of powerful aristocrats, this Fleet, but the balance of power lies with the throne—the Admiralty. Now the admiral is old, and his son the crown prince has more to say than is rightful. I waggle my ears at gossip—they forget how much better we hear than they, in this pea-soup-with-sausages atmosphere. I know. He is a hard-cooked one, him that T'heonax.

"So we help the Drak'honai win over the Flock. So what? They are already winning. The Flock is only making guerrilla now, in the wild parts of Lannach. They are still powerful, but the Fleet has the upper hand, and need only maintain *status quo* to win. Anyhow, what can we, who the good God did not offer wings, do at guerrillas? We show T'heonax how to use a blaster, well, how do we show him how to find somebodies to use it on?"

"Hm-m-m ... yes." She nodded, stiffly. "You mean that we have nothing to offer the Drak'honai, except trade and treaty later on, if they get us home."

"Just so. And what hurry is there for them to meet the League? They are natural wary of unknowns like us from Earth. They like better to consolidate themselves in their new conquest before taking on powerful strangers, *nie?* I hear the scuttled butt, I tell you; I know the trend of thought about us. Maybe T'heonax lets us starve, or cuts our throats. Maybe he throws our stuff overboard and says later he never heard of us. Or maybe, when a League boat finds him at last, he says *ja*, we pulled some humans from the sea, and we was good to them, but we could not get them home in time."

"But could they—actually? I mean, Freeman van Rijn, how would *you* get us home, with any kind of Diomedean help?"

"Bah! Details! I am not an engineer. Engineers I hire. My job is not to do what is impossible, it is to make others do it for me. Only how can I organize things when I am only a more-than-half prisoner of a king who is not interested in meeting my peoples? Hah?"

"Whereas the Lannach tribe is hard pressed and will let you, what they say, write your own ticket. Yes." Sandra laughed, with a touch of genuine humor. "Very good, my friend! Only one question now, how do we get to the Lannachs?"

She waved a hand at their surroundings. It was not an encouraging view.

The *Gerunis* was a typical raft: a big structure, of light tough balsalike logs lashed together with enough open space and flexibility to yield before the sea. A wall of uprights, pegged to the transverse logs, defined a capacious hold and supported a main deck of painfully trimmed planks. Poop and forecastle rose at either end, their flat decks bearing artillery and, in the former case, the outsize tiller. Between them were seaweed-thatched cabins for storage, workshops, and living quarters. The overall dimensions were about sixty meters by fifteen, tapering toward a false bow which provided a catapult platform and some streamlining. A foremast and mainmast each carried three big square sails, a lateen-rigged mizzen stood just forward of the poop. Given a favoring wind—remembering the force of most winds on this planet—the seemingly awkward craft could make several knots, and even in a dead calm it could be rowed.

It held about a hundred Diomedeans plus wives and children. Of those, ten couples were aristocrats, with private apartments in the poop; twenty were ranking sailors, with special skills, entitled to one room per family in the main-deck cabins; the rest were common deckhands, barracked into the forecastle.

Not far away floated the rest of this squadron. There were rafts of various types, some primarily dwelling units like the *Gerunis*, some triple-decked for cargo, some bearing the long sheds in which fish and seaweed were processed. Often several at a time were linked together to form a little temporary island. Moored to them, or patrolling between, were the outrigger canoes. Wings beat in the sky, where aerial detachments kept watch for an enemy: full-time professional warriors, the core of Drak'ho's military strength.

Beyond this outlying squadron, the other divisions of the Fleet darkened the water as far as a man's eyes would reach. Most of them were fishing. It was brutally hard work, where long nets were trolled by muscle power. Nearly all a Drak'ho's life seemed to go to back-bending labor. But out of these fluid fields they were dragging a harvest which leaped and flashed.

"Like fiends they must drive themselves," observed van Rijn. He slapped the stout rail. "This is tough wood, even when green, and they chew it smooth with stone and glass tools! Some of these fellows I would like to hire, if the union busybodies can be kept away from them."

Sandra stamped her foot. She had not complained at danger of death, cold and discomfort and the drudgery of Tolk's language lessons filtered through Wace. But there are limits. "Either you talk sense, Freeman, or I go somewhere else! I asked you how we get away from here."

"We get rescued by the Lannachska, of course," said van Rijn. "Or, rather, they come steal us. Yes, so-fashion will be better. Then, if they fail, friend Delp cannot say it is our fault we are so desired by all parties."

Her tall form grew rigid. "What do you mean? How are they to know we are even here?"

"Maybe Tolk will tell them."

"But Tolk is even more a prisoner than we, not?"

"So. However—" van Rijn rubbed his hands. "We have a little plan made. He is a good head, him. Almost as good as me."

Sandra glared. "And will you deign to tell me how you plotted with Tolk, under enemy surveillance, when you cannot even speak Drak'ho?"

"Oh, I speak Drak'ho pretty good," said van Rijn blandly. "Did you not just hear me admit how I eavesdrop on all the palaver aboard? You think just because I make so much trouble, and still sit hours every day taking special instruction from Tolk, it is because I am a dumb old bell who cannot learn so easy? Horse maneuvers! Half the time we mumble together, he is teaching me his own Lannach lingo. Nobody on this raft knows it, so when they hear us say funny noises they think maybe Tolk tries words of Earth language out, ha? They think he despairs of teaching me through Wace and tries himself to pound some Drak'ho in me. Ho, ho, they are bamboozles, by damn! Why, yesterday I told Tolk a dirty joke in Lannachamael. He looked very disgusted. There is proof that poor old van Rijn is not fat between the ears. We say nothing of the rest of his anatomy."

Sandra stood quiet for a bit, trying to understand what it meant to learn two nonhuman languages simultaneously, one of them forbidden.

"I do not see why Tolk looks disgusted," mused van Rijn. "It was a good joke. Listen: there was a salesman who traveled on one of the colonial planets, and—"

"I can guess why," interrupted Sandra hastily. "I mean...why Tolk did not think it was a funny tale. Er...Freeman Wace was explaining it to me the other day. Here on Diomedes they have not the trait of, um, constant sexuality. They breed once each year only, in the tropics. No families in our sense. They would not think our"—she blushed—"our all-year-around interest in these questions was very normal or very polite."

Van Rijn nodded. "All this I know. But Tolk has seen somewhat of the Fleet, and in the Fleet they do have marriage, and get born at any time of year, same like humans."

"I got that impression," she answered slowly, "and it puzzles me. Freeman Wace said the breeding cycle was in their, their heredity. Instinct, or glands, or what it now is called. How *could* the Fleet live differently from what their glands dictate?"

"Well, they do." Van Rijn shrugged massive shoulders. "Maybe we let some scientist worry about it for a thesis later on, hah?"

Suddenly she gripped his arm so he winced. Her eyes were a green blaze. "But you have not said . . . what is to happen? How is Tolk to get word about us to Lannach? What do we do?"

"I have no idea," he told her cheerily. "I play with the ear."

He cocked a beady eye at the pale reddish overcast. Several kilometers away, enormously timbered, bearing what was almost a wooden castle, floated the flagship of all Drak'ho. A swirl of bat wings was lifting from it and streaming toward the *Gerunis*. Faintly down the sky was borne the screech of a blown sea shell.

"But I think maybe we find out quick," finished van Rijn, "because his rheumatic majesty comes here now to decide about us."

VII

The admiral's household troops, a hundred full-time warriors, landed with beautiful exactness and snapped their weapons to position. Polished stone and oiled leather caught the dull light like sea-blink; the wind of their wings roared across the deck. A purple banner trimmed with scarlet shook loose, and the *Gerunis* crew, respectfully crowded into the rigging and on the forecastle roof, let out a hoarse ritual cheer.

Delp hyr Orikan advanced from the poop and crouched before his lord. His wife, the beautiful Rodonis sa Axollon, and his two young children came behind him, bellies to the deck and wings over eyes. All wore the scarlet sashes and jeweled arm-bands which were formal dress.

The three humans stood beside Delp. Van Rijn had vetoed any suggestion that they crouch, too. "It is not right for a member of the Polesotechnic League, he should get down on knees and elbows. Anyway I am not built for it."

Tolk of Lannach sat haughty next to van Rijn. His wings were tucked into a net and the leash on his neck was held by a husky sailor. His eyes were as bleak and steady on the admiral as a snake's.

And the armed young males who formed a rough honor guard for Delp their captain had something of the same chill in their manner—not toward Syranax, but toward his son, the heir apparent on whom the admiral leaned. Their spears, rakes, tomahawks, and wood-bayoneted blowguns were held in a gesture of total respect: nevertheless, the weapons were held.

Wace thought that van Rijn's out-size nose must have an abnormal keenness for discord. Only now did he himself sense the tension on which his boss had obviously been counting.

Syranax cleared his throat, blinked, and pointed his muzzle at the humans. "Which one of you is captain?" he asked. It was still a deep voice, but it no longer came from the bottom of the lungs, and there was a mucous rattle in it.

Wace stepped forward. His answer was the one van Rijn had, hastily and without bothering to explain, commanded that he give: "The other male is our leader, sir. But he does not speak your language very well as yet. I myself still have trouble with it, so we must use this Lannach'ho prisoner to interpret."

T'heonax scowled. "How should he know what you want to say to us?"

"He has been teaching us your language," said Wace. "As you know, sir, foreign tongues are his main task in life. Because of this natural ability, as well as his special experience with us, he will often be able to guess what we may be trying to say when we search for a word."

"That sounds reasonable." Syranax's gray head wove about. "Yes."

"I wonder!" T'heonax gave Delp an ugly look. It was returned in spades.

"So! By damn, now I talk." Van Rijn rolled forward. "My good friend...um...er...*pokker*, what is the word?—my admiral, we, ahem, we talk-um like good brothers—good brothers, is that how I say-um, Tolk—?"

Wace winced. Despite what Sandra had whispered to him, as they were being hustled here to receive the visitors, he found it hard to believe that so ludicrous an accent and grammar were faked.

And why?

Syranax stirred impatiently. "It may be best if we talked through your companion," he suggested.

"Bilge and barnacles!" shouted van Rijn. "Him? No, no, me talk-um talky-talk self. Straight, like, um, er, what-is-your-title. We talk-um like brothers, ha?"

Syranax sighed. But it did not occur to him to overrule the human. An alien aristocrat was still an aristocrat; in the eyes of this caste-ridden society, and as such might surely claim the right to speak for himself.

"I would have visited you before," said the admiral, "but you could not have conversed with me, and there was so much else to do. As they grow more desperate, the Lannach'honai become more dangerous in their raids and ambushes. Not a day goes by that we do not have at least a minor battle."

"Hm-m-m?" van Rijn counted off the declension-comparison on his fingers. "*Xammagapai*...let me see, *xammagan, xammagai*...oh, yes. A small fight! I make-um see no fights, old admiral—I mean, honored admiral."

T'heonax bristled. "Watch your tongue, Eart'ho!" he clipped. He had been over frequently to stare at the prisoners, and their sequestered possessions were in his keeping. Little awe remained—but then, Wace decided, T'heonax was not capable of admitting that a being could possibly exist in any way superior to T'heonax.

"And yours, son," murmured Syranax. To van Rijn: "Oh, they would scarcely venture this far out. I mean our positions on the mainland are constantly harassed."

"Yes," nodded the Terrestrial, rather blankly.

Syranax lay down on the deck in an easy lion-pose. T'heonax remained standing, taut in Delp's presence. "I have, of course, been getting reports about you," went on the admiral. "They are, ah, remarkable. Yes, remarkable. It's alleged you came from the stars."

"Stars, yes!" van Rijn's head bobbed with imbecilic eagerness. "We from stars. Far far away."

"Is it true also that your people have established an outpost on the other shore of The Ocean?"

Van Rijn went into a huddle with Tolk. The Lannacha put the question into childish words. After several explanations, van Rijn beamed. "Yes, yes, we from across Ocean. Far far away."

"Will your friends not come in search of you?"

"They look-um, yes, they look-um plenty hard. By Joe! Look-um all over. You treat-um us good or our friends find out and—" Van Rijn broke off, looking dismayed, and conferred again with Tolk.

"I believe the Eart'ho wishes to apologize for tactlessness," explained the Herald dryly.

"It may be a truthful kind of tactlessness," observed Syranax. "If his friends can, indeed, locate him while he is still alive, much will depend on what kind of treatment he received from us. Eh? The problem is, can they find him that soon? What say, Eart'ho?" He pushed the last question out like a spear.

Van Rijn retreated, lifting his hands as if to ward off a blow. "Help!" he whined. "You help-um us, take us home, old admiral . . . honored admiral . . . we go home and pay-um many many fish."

T'heonax murmured in his father's ear: "The truth comes out—not that I haven't suspected as much already. His friends have no measurable chance of finding him before he starves. If they did, he wouldn't be begging us for help. He'd be demanding whatever struck his fancy."

"*I* would have done that in all events," said the admiral.

"Our friend isn't very experienced in these matters, eh? Well, it's good to know how easily truth can be squeezed out of him."

"So," said T'heonax contemptuously, not bothering to whisper, "the only problem is, to get some value out of the beasts before they die."

Sandra's breath sucked sharply in. Wace grasped her arm, opened his mouth, and caught van Rijn's hurried Anglic murmur: "Shut up! Not a word, you bucket head!" Whereupon the merchant resumed his timid smile and attitude of straining puzzlement.

"It isn't right!" exploded Delp. "By the Lodestar, sir, these are guests—not enemies—we can't just *use* them!"

"What else would you do?" shrugged T'heonax.

His father blinked and mumbled, as if weighing the arguments for both sides. Something like a spark jumped between Delp and T'heonax. It ran along the ranked lines of *Gerunis* crew-folk and household troopers as an imperceptible tautening, the barest ripple of muscle and forward slant of weapons.

Van Rijn seemed to get the drift all at once. He recoiled operatically, covered his eyes, then went to his knees before Delp. "No, no!" he screamed. "You take-um us home! You help-um us, we help-um you! You remember say how you help-um us if we help-um you!"

"What's this?"

It was a wild-animal snarl from T'heonax. He surged forward. "You've been bargaining with them, have you?"

"What do you mean?" The executive's teeth clashed together, centimeters from T'heonax's nose. His wing-spurs lifted like knives.

"What sort of help were these creatures going to give you?"

"What do you think?" Delp flung the gage into the winds, and crouched waiting.

T'heonax did not quite pick it up. "Some might guess you had ideas of getting rid of certain rivals within the Fleet," he purred.

In the silence which fell across the raft, Wace could hear how the dragon shapes up in the rigging breathed more swiftly. He could hear the creak of timbers and cables, the slap of waves and the low damp mumble of wind. Almost, he heard obsidian daggers being loosened in their sheaths.

If an unpopular prince finds an excuse to arrest a subordinate whom the commoners trust, there are likely going to be men who will fight. It was not otherwise here on Diomedes.

Syranax broke the explosive quiet. "There's some kind of misunderstanding," he said loudly. "Nobody is going to charge anyone with anything on the basis of this wingless creature's gabble. What's the fuss about? What could he possibly do for any of us, anyway?"

"That remains to be seen," answered T'heonax. "But a race which can fly across The Ocean in less than an equinoctial day must know some handy arts."

He whirled on a quivering van Rijn. With the relish of the inquisitor whose suspect has broken, he said curtly: "Maybe we can get you home somehow if you help us. We are not sure how to get you home. Maybe your stuff can help us get you home. You show us how to use your stuff."

"Oh, yes!" said van Rijn. He clasped his hands and waggled his head. "Oh, yes, good sir, I do you want-um."

T'heonax clipped an order. A Drak'ho slithered across the deck with a large box. "I've been in charge of these things," explained the heir. "Haven't tried to fool with it, except for a few knives of that shimmery substance—" Momentarily, his eyes glowed with honest enthusiasm. "You've never *seen* such knives, father! They don't hack or grind, they slice! They'll carve seasoned wood!"

He opened the box. The ranking officers forgot dignity and crowded around. T'heonax waved them back. "Give this blubberpot room to demonstrate," he snapped. "Bowmen, blowgunners, cover him from all sides. Be ready to shoot if necessary."

Van Rijn took out a blaster.

"You mean to fight your way clear?" hissed Wace. "You can't!" He tried to step between Sandra and the menace of weapons which suddenly ringed them in. "They'll fill us with arrows before—"

"I know, I know," growled ran Rijn *sotto voce*. "When will you young pridesters learn, just because he is old and lonely, the boss does not yet have teredos in the brain? You keep back, boy, and when trouble breaks loose, hit the deck and dig a hole."

"What? But—"

Van Rijn turned a broad back on him and said in broken Drak'ho, with servile eagerness: "Here a . . . how you call it? . . . thing. It make fire. It burn-um holes, by Joe."

"A portable flame thrower—that small?" For a moment, an edge of terror sharpened T'heonax's voice.

"I told you," said Delp, "we can gain more by dealing honorably with them. By the Lodestar, I think we could get them home, too, if we really tried!"

"You might wait till I'm dead, Delp, before taking the Admiralty," said Syranax. If he meant it as a joke, it fell like a bomb. The nearer sailors, who heard it, gasped. The household warriors touched their bows and blowguns. Rodonis sa Axollon spread her wings over her children and snarled. Deckhand females, jammed into the forecastle, let out a whimper of half-comprehending fear.

Delp himself steadied matters. "Quiet!" he bawled. "Belay there! Calm down! By all the devils in the Rainy Stars, have these creatures driven us crazy?"

"See," chattered van Rijn, "take *blaster* . . . we call-um *blaster* . . . pull-um here—"

The ion beam stabbed out and crashed into the mainmast. Van Rijn yanked it away at once, but it had already made a gouge centimeters deep in that tough wood. Its blue-white flame licked across the deck, whiffed a coiled cable into smoke, and took a section out of the rail, before he released the trigger.

The Drak'honai roared!

It was minutes before they had settled back into the shrouds or onto the decks; curiosity seekers from nearby craft still speckled the sky. However, they were technologically sophisticated in their way. They were excited rather than frightened.

"Let me see that!" T'heonax snatched at the gun.

"Wait. Wait, good sir, wait." Van Rijn snapped open the chamber, in a set of movements screened by his thick hands, and popped out the charge. "Make-um safe first. There."

T'heonax turned it over and over. "What a weapon!" he breathed. "What a *weapon!*"

Standing there in a frosty sweat, waiting for van Rijn to spoon up whatever variety of hell he was cooking, Wace still managed to reflect that the Drak'honai were overestimating. Natural enough, of course. But a gun of this sort would only have a serious effect on ground-fighting tactics—and the old sharper was coolly disarming all the blasters anyway, no uninstructed Diomedean was going to get any value from them—

"I make safe," van Rijn burbled. "One, two, three, four, five I make safe.... Four? Five? Six?" He began turning over the piled-up clothes, blankets, heaters, campstove, and other equipment. "Where other three blasters?"

"What other three?" T'heonax stared at him.

"We have six." Van Rijn counted carefully on his fingers. "*Ja*, six. I give-um all to good sir Delp here."

"WHAT?"

Delp leaped at the human, cursing. "That's a lie! There were only three, and you've got them here!"

"Help!" Van Rijn scuttled behind T'heonax. Delp's body clipped the admiral's son. Both Drak'honai went over in a whirl of wings and tails.

"*He's plotting mutiny!*" screamed T'heonax.

Wace threw Sandra to the deck and himself above her. The air grew dense with missiles.

Van Rijn turned ponderously to grab the sailor in charge of Tolk. But that Drak'ho had already sprung away to Delp's defense. Van Rijn had only to peel off the imprisoning net.

"Now," he said in fluent Lannachamael, "go bring an army to fetch us out of here. Quick, before someone notices!"

The Herald nodded, threshed his wings, and was gone into a sky where battle ran loose.

Van Rijn stooped over Wace and Sandra. "This way," he panted under the racket. A chance tail-buffet, as a sailor fought two troopers, brought a howl from him. "Thunder and lightning! Pest and poison ivy!" He wrestled Sandra to her feet and hustled her toward the comparative shelter of the forecastle.

When they stood inside its door, among terrified females and cubs, looking out at the fight, he said:

"It is a pity that Delp will go under. He has no chance. He is a decent sort; we could maybe have done business."

"All saints in Heaven!" choked Wace. "You touched off a civil war just to get your messenger away?"

"You know perhaps a better method?" asked van Rijn.

VIII

When Commander Krakna fell in battle against the invaders, the Flock's General Council picked one Trolwen to succeed him. They were the elders, and their choice comparatively youthful, but the Lannachska thought it only natural to be led by young males. A commander needed the physical stamina of two, to see them through a hard and dangerous migration every year; he seldom lived to grow feeble. Any rash impulses of his age were curbed by the General Council itself, the clan leaders who had grown too old to fly at the head of their squadron-septs and not yet so old and weak as to be left behind on some winter journey.

Trolwen's mother belonged to the Trekkan group, a distinguished bloodline with rich properties on Lannach; she herself had added to that wealth by shrewd trading. She guessed that his father was Tornak of the Wendru—not that she cared especially, but Trolwen looked noticeably like that fierce warrior. However, it was his own record as a clan-elected officer, in storm and battle and negotiation and everyday routine, which caused the

Council to pick him as leader of all the clans. In the ten-days since, he had been the chief of a losing cause; but possibly his folk were pressed back into the uplands more slowly than would have happened without him.

Now he led a major part of the Flock's fighting strength out against the Fleet itself.

Vernal equinox was barely past, but already the days lengthened with giant strides; each morning the sun rose farther north, and a milder air melted the snows until Lannach's dales were a watery brawling. It took only one hundred thirty days from equinox to Last Sunrise—thereafter, during the endless light of High Summer, there would be nothing but rain or mist to cover an attack.

And if the Drakska were not whipped by autumn, reflected Trolwen grimly, there would be no point in trying further; the Flock would be done.

His wings thrust steadily at the sky, the easy strength-hoarding beat of a wanderer born. Under him reached a broken white mystery of cloud, with the sea far beneath it peering through in a glimmer like polished glass; overhead lay a clear violet-blue roof, the night and the stars. Both moons were up, hasty Flichtan driving from horizon to horizon in a day and a half, Nua so much slower that her phases moved more rapidly than herself. He drew the cold, flowing darkness into his lungs, felt the thrust in muscles and the ripple in fur, but without the sensuous enjoyment of an ordinary flight.

He was thinking too hard about killing.

A commander should not show indecision, but he was young and gray Tolk the Herald would understand. "How shall we know that these beings are on the same raft as when you left?" he asked. He spoke in the measured, breath-conserving rhythm of a route flight. The wind muttered beneath his words.

"We cannot be sure, of course, Flockchief," replied Tolk. "But the fat one considered that possibility, too. He said he would manage, somehow, to be out on deck in plain view every day at sunrise."

"Perhaps, though," worried Trolwen, "the Draka

authorities will have locked him away, suspecting his help in your escape."

"What he did was probably not noticed in the turmoil," said Tolk.

"And perhaps he cannot help us after all." Trolwen shivered. The Council had spoken strongly against this raid: too risky, too many certain casualties. The turbulent clans had roared their own disapproval. He had had difficulty persuading them.

And if it turned out he was throwing away lives on something as grotesque as this, for no good purpose— Trolwen was as patriotic as any young male whose folk have been cruelly attacked; but he was not unconcerned about his own future. It had happened in the past that commanders who failed badly were read forever out of the Flock, like any common thief or murderer.

He flew onward.

A chill thin light had been stealing into the sky for a time. Now the higher clouds began to flush red, and a gleam went over the half-hidden sea. It was crucial to reach the Fleet at just about this moment, enough light to see what to do and not enough to give the enemy ample warning.

A Whistler, with the slim frame and outsize wings of adolescence, emerged from a fog-bank. The shrill notes of his lips carried far and keenly. Tolk, who as Chief Herald guided the education of these messenger-scouts, cocked his head and nodded. "We guessed it very well," he said calmly. "The rafts are only five buaska ahead."

"So I hear." Tension shook Trolwen's voice. "Now—"

He broke off. More of the youths were beating upwind into view, faster than an adult could fly. Their whistles wove into an exuberant battle music. Trolwen read the code like his own speech, clamped jaws together, and waved a hand at his standard bearer. Then he dove.

As he burst through the clouds, he saw the Fleet spread enormous, still far below him but covering the waters, from those islands called The Pups to the rich eastern driss banks. Decks and decks and decks cradled on a purplish-gray calm, masts raked upward like teeth, the dawn-light smote the admiral's floating castle and burned off his banner. There was an explosion skyward from rafts and canoes, as the Drak'honai heard the yells of their own sentries and went to arms.

Trolwen folded his wings and stooped. Behind him, in a wedge of clan-squadrons, roared three thousand Lannacha males. Even as he fell, he glared in search— where was that double-cursed Eart'a monster—*there!* The distance-devouring vision of a flying animal picked out three ugly shapes on a raft's quarterdeck, waving and jumping about.

Trolwen spread his wings to brake. "Here!" he cried. The standard bearer glided to a stop, hovered, and unfurled the red flag of Command. The squadrons changed from wedge to battle formation, peeled off, and dove for the raft.

The Drakska were forming their own ranks with terrifying speed and discipline. "All smoke-snuffing gods!" groaned Trolwen. "If we could just have used a single squadron—a raid, not a full-scale battle—"

"A single squadron could hardly have brought the Eart'ska back alive, Flockchief," said Tolk. "Not from the very core of the enemy. We have to make it seem . . . not worth their while . . . to keep up the engagement, when we retreat."

"They know ghostly well what we've come for," said Trolwen. "Look how they swarm to that raft!"

The Flock troop had now punched through a shaken line of Draka patrols and reached water surface. One detachment attacked the target vessel, landed in a ring around the humans and then struck out to seize the entire craft. The rest stayed airborne to repel the enemy's counter-assault.

It was simple, clumsy ground fighting on deck. Both sides were similarly equipped: weapon technology seems to diffuse faster than any other kind. Wooden swords set with chips of flint, fire-hardened spears, clubs, daggers, tomahawks, struck small wicker shields and leather harness. Tails smacked out, talons ripped, wings buffeted and cut with horny spurs, teeth closed in throats, fists battered on flesh. Hard-pressed, a male would fly upward—there was little attempt to keep ranks, it was a free-for-all. Trolwen had no special interest in that phase of the battle: having landed superior numbers, he knew he could take the raft, if only his aerial squadrons could keep the remaining Draksha off.

He thought—conventionally, in the wake of a thousand bards—how much like a dance a battle in the air was: intricate, beautiful, and terrible. To co-ordinate the efforts of a thousand or more warriors a-wing reached the highest levels of art.

The backbone of such a force was the archers. Each gripped a bow as long as himself in his foot talons, drew the cord with both hands and let fly, plucked a fresh arrow from the belly quiver with his teeth and had it ready to nock before the string snapped taut. Such a corps, trained almost from birth, could lay down a curtain which none might cross alive. But after the whistling death was spent, as it soon was, they must stream back to the bearers for more arrows. That was the most vulnerable aspect of their work, and the rest of the army existed to guard it.

Some cast bolas, some the heavy sharp-edged boomerang, some the weighted net in which a wing-tangled foe could plunge to his death. Blowguns were a recent innovation, observed among foreign tribes in the tropical meeting places. Here the Draksha were ahead: their guns had a bolt-operated repeater mechanism and fire-hardened wooden bayonets. Also, the separate military units in the Fleet were more tightly organized.

On the other hand, they still relied on an awkward set of horn calls to integrate their entire army. Infinitely more flexible, the Whistler corps darted from leader to leader, weaving the Flock into one great wild organism.

Up and down the battle ramped, while the sun rose and the clouds broke apart and the sea grew red-stained. Trolwen clipped his orders: Hunlu to reinforce the upper right flank, Torcha to feint at the admiral's raft while Srygen charged on the opposite wing—

But the Fleet was here, thought Trolwen bleakly, with

all its arsenals: more missiles than his fliers, who were outnumbered anyway, could ever have carried. If this fight wasn't broken off soon—

The raft with the Eart'ska had now been seized. Draka canoes were approaching to win it back. One of them opened up with fire weapons: the dreaded, irresistible burning oil of the Fleet, pumped from a ceramic nozzle; catapults throwing vases of the stuff which exploded in gouts of flame on impact. Those were the weapons which had annihilated the boats owned by the Flock, and taken its coastal towns. Trolwen cursed with a reflex anguish when he saw.

But the Eart'ska were off the raft, six strong porters carrying each one in a specially woven net. By changing bearers often, those burdens could be taken to the Flock's mountain stronghold. The food boxes, hastily dragged up from the hold, were less difficult—one porter to each. A Whistler warbled success.

"Let's go!" Orders rattled from Trolwen, his messengers swooped to the appropriate squadrons. "Hunlu and Srygen, close ranks about the bearers; Dwarn fly above with half his command, the other half guard the left wing. Rearguards—"

The morning was perceptibly further along before he had disengaged. His nightmare had been that the larger Fleet forces would pursue. A running battle all the way home could have snapped the spine of his army. But as soon as he was plainly in retreat, the enemy broke contact and retired to decks.

"As you predicted, Tolk," panted Trolwen.

"Well, Flockchief," said the Herald with his usual calm, "they themselves wouldn't be anxious for such a melee. It would over-extend them, leave their rafts virtually defenseless—for all they know, your whole idea was to lure them into such a move. So they have merely decided that the Eart'ska aren't worth the trouble and risk: an opinion which the Eart'ska themselves must have been busily cultivating in them."

"Let's hope it's not a correct belief. But however the

gods decree, Tolk...you still foresaw this outcome. Maybe you should be Commander."

"Oh, no. Not I. It was the fat Eart'ska who predicted this—in detail."

Trolwen laughed, "Perhaps, then, he should command."

"Perhaps," said Tolk, very thoughtfully, "he will."

IX

The northern coast of Lannach sloped in broad valleys to the Sea of Achan; and here, in game-filled forests and on grassy downs, had arisen those thorps in which the Flock's clans customarily dwelt. Where Sagna Bay made its deep cut into the land, many such hamlets had grown together into larger units. Thus the towns came to be, Ulwen and flinty Mannenach and Yo of the Carpenters.

But their doors were broken down and their roofs burned open; Drak'ho canoes lay on Sagna's beaches, Drak'ho war-bands laired in empty Ulwen and patrolled the Anch Forest and rounded up the hornbeast herds emerging from winter sleep on Duna Brae.

Its boats sunk, its houses taken, and its hunting and fishing grounds cut off, the Flock retired into the uplands. On the quaking lava slopes of Mount Oborch or in the cold canyons of the Misty Mountains, there were a few small settlements where the poorer clans had lived. The females, the very old and the very young could be crowded into these; tents could be pitched and caves occupied. By scouring this gaunt country from Hark Heath to the Ness, and by going often hungry, the whole Flock could stay alive for a while longer.

But the heart of Lannach was the north coast, which the Drak'honai now forbade. Without it, the Flock was nothing, a starveling tribe of savages...until autumn, when Birthtime would leave them altogether helpless.

"It is not well," said Trolwen inadequately.

He strode up a narrow trail, toward the village—what

was its name now? Salmenbrok—which perched on the jagged crest above. Beyond that, dark volcanic rock still streaked with snowfields climbed dizzily upward to a crater hidden in its own vapors. The ground shivered underfoot, just a bit, and van Rijn heard a rumble in the guts of the planet.

Poor isostatic balance... to be expected under these low-density conditions... a geologic history of overly-rapid change, earthquake, eruption, flood, and new lands coughed up from the sea bottom in a mere thousand decades... hence, in spite of all the water, a catastrophically uneven climate—He wrapped the stinking fur blanket they had given him more closely around his rough-coated frame, blew on numbed hands, peered into the damp sky for a glimpse of sun, and swore.

This was no place for a man his age and girth. He should be at home, in his own deeply indented armchair, with a good cigar, a tall drink and the gardens of Jakarta flaming around him. For a moment, the remembrance of Earth was so sharp that he snuffled in self-pity. It was bitter to leave his bones in this nightmare land, when he had thought to pull Earth's soft green turf about his weary body.... Hard and cruel, yes, and every day the company must be getting deeper into the red ink without him there to oversee! That hauled him back to practicalities.

"Let me get this all clear in my head," he requested. He found himself rather more at home in Lannachamael than he had been—even without faking—in the Drak'ho speech. Here, by chance, the grammar and the guttural noises were not too far from his mother tongue. Already he approached fluency.

"You came back from your migration and found the enemy was here waiting for you?" he continued.

Trolwen jerked his head in a harsh and painful gesture. "Yes. Hitherto we had only known vaguely of their existence; their home regions are well to the southeast of ours. We knew they had been forced to leave because suddenly the trech—the fish which are the mainstay of their diet—had altered their own habits, shifting from

Draka waters to Achan. But we had no idea the Fleet was bound for our country."

Van Rijn's long hair swished, lank and greasy-black, the careful curls all gone out of it, as he nodded. "It is like home history. In the Middle Ages on Earth, when the herring changed their ways for some begobbled herring reason, it would change the history of maritime countries. Kings would fall, by damn, and wars would be fought over the new fishing grounds."

"It has never been of great importance to us," said Trolwen. "A few clans in the Sagna region have... had small dugouts and got much of their food with hook and line. None of this beast-labor the Drakska go through, dragging those nets, even if they do pull in more fish! But for our folk generally, it was a minor thing. To be sure, we were pleased, several years ago, when the trech appeared in great numbers in the Sea of Achan. It is large and tasty, its oil and bones have many uses. But it was not such an occasion for rejoicing as if... oh, as if the wild hornbeasts had doubled their herds overnight."

His fingers closed convulsively on the handle of his tomahawk. He was, after all, quite young. "Now I see the gods sent the trech to us in anger and mockery. For the Fleet followed the trech."

Van Rijn paused on the trail, wheezing till he drowned out the distant lava rumbles. "Whoof! Hold it there, you! Not so like a God-forgotten horse race, if you please— Ah. If the fish are not so great for you, why not let the Fleet have the Achan waters?"

It was, he knew, not a true question: only a stimulus. Trolwen delivered himself of several explosive obscenities before answering, "They attacked us the moment we came home this spring. They had already occupied our coastlands! And even had they not done so, would you let a powerful horde of... strangers... whose very habits are alien and evil... would you let them dwell at your windowsill? How long could such an arrangement last?"

Van Rijn nodded again. Just suppose a nation with tyrant government and filthy personal lives were to ask for the Moon, on the grounds that they needed it and it was not of large value to Earth—

Personally, he could afford to be tolerant. In many ways, the Drak'honai were closer to the human norm than the Lannachska. Their master-serf culture was a natural consequence of economics: given only neolithic tools, a raft big enough to support several families represented an enormous capital investment. It was simply not possible for disgruntled individuals to strike out on their own; they were at the mercy of the State. In such cases, power always concentrates in the hands of aristocratic warriors and intellectual priesthoods; among the Drak'honai, those two classes had merged into one.

The Lannachska, on the other hand—more typically Diomedean—were primarily hunters. They had very few highly specialized craftsmen; the individual could survive using tools made by himself. The low calorie/area factor of a hunting economy made them spread out thin over a large region, each small group nearly independent of the rest. They exerted themselves in spasms, during the chase for instance; but they did not have to toil day after day until they nearly dropped, as the common netman or oarsman or deckhand must in the Fleet—hence there was no economic justification on Lannach for a class of bosses and overseers.

Thus, their natural political unit was the little matrilineal clan. Such semiformal blood groups, almost free of government, were rather loosely organized into the Great Flock. And the Flock's *raison d'être*—apart from minor inter-sept business at home—was simply to increase the safety of all when every Diomedean on Lannach flew south for the winter.

Or came home to war!

"It is interesting," murmured van Rijn, half in Anglic. "Among our peoples, like on most planets, only the agriculture folk got civilized. Here they make no farms at all: the big half-wild hornbeast herds is closest thing, *nie?* You hunt, berry-pick, reap wild grain, fish a little—yet some of you know writing and make books; I see you have machines and houses, and weave cloth. Could be, the every-year stimulus of meeting foreigners in the tropics gives you ideas?"

"What?" asked Trolwen vaguely.

"Nothings. I just wondered, me, why—since life here is easy enough so you have time for making civilization—you do not grow so many you eat up all your game and chop down all your woods. That is what we called a successful civilization back on Earth."

"Our numbers do not increase fast," said Trolwen. "About three hundred years ago, a daughter Flock was formed and moved elsewhere, but the increase is very slow. We lost so many on the migrations, you see—storm, exhaustion, sickness, barbarian attack, wild animals, sometimes cold or famine—" He hunched his wings, the Diomedean equivalent of a shrug.

"Ah-ha! Natural selection. Which is all well and good, if nature is obliging to pick you for survival. Otherwise gives awful noises about tragedy." Van Rijn stroked his goatee. The chins beneath it were getting bristly as his last application of antibeard enzyme wore off. "So. It does give one notion of what made your race get brains. Hibernate or migrate! And if you migrate, then be smart enough to meet all kinds trouble, by damn."

He resumed his noisy walk up the trail. "But we got our troubles of now to think about, especially since they are too the troubles belonging with Nicholas van Rijn. Which is not to be stood. Hmpf! Well, now, tell me more. I gather the Fleet scrubbed its decks with you and kicked you up here where the only flat country is the map. You want home to the lowlands again. You also want to get rid of the Fleet."

"We gave them a good fight," said Trolwen stiffly. "We still can—and will, by my grandmother's ghost! There were reasons why we were defeated so badly. We came tired and hungry back from ten-days of flight; one is always weak at the end of the springtime journey home. Our strongholds had already been occupied. The Draka flamethrowers set afire such other defenses as we contrived, and made it impossible for us to fight them on the water, where their real strength lies."

His teeth snapped together in a carnivore reflex. "And we have to overcome them soon! If we don't we are finished. And they know it!"

"I am not clear over this yet," admitted van Rijn. "The hurry is that all your young are born the same time, *nie?*"

"Yes." Trolwen topped the rise and waited beneath the walls of Salmenbrok for his puffing guest.

Like every Lannachska settlement, it was fortified against enemies, animal or intelligent. There was no stockade—that would be pointless here where all the higher life-forms had wings. An average building was roughly in the shape of an ancient Terrestrial blockhouse. The ground floor was doorless and had mere slits for windows; entrance was through an upper story or a trap in the thatched roof. A hamlet was fortified not by outer walls but by being woven together with covered bridges and underground passages.

Up here, above timberline, the houses were of undressed stone mortared in place, rather than the logs more common among the valley clans. But this thorp was solidly made, furnished with a degree of comfort that indicated how bountiful the lowlands must be.

Van Rijn took time to admire such features as wooden locks constructed like Chinese puzzles, a wooden lathe set with a cutting edge of painstakingly fractured diamond, and a wooden saw whose teeth were of renewable volcanic glass. A communal windmill ground nuts and wild grain, as well as powering numerous smaller machines; it included a pump which filled a great stone basin in the overhanging cliff with water, and the water could be let down again to keep the mill turning when there was no wind. He even saw a tiny sail-propelled railroad, with wooden-wheeled basketwork carts running on iron-hard wooden rails. It carried flint and obsidian from the local quarries, timber from the forests, dried fish from the lowlands, handicrafts from all the island. Van Rijn was delighted.

"So!" he said. "Commerce! You are fundamentally capitalists. Ha, by damn, I think soon we do some business!"

Trolwen shrugged. "There is nearly always a strong wind up here. Why should we not let it take our burdens? Actually, all the apparatus you see took many lifetimes to complete—we're not like those Drakska, wearing themselves out with labor."

Salmenbrok's temporary population crowded about the human, with mumbling and twittering and wing-flapping, the cubs twisting around his legs and their mothers shrieking at them to come back. "Ten thousand purple devils!" he choked. "They think maybe I am a politician to kiss their brats, ha?"

"Come this way," said Trolwen. "Toward the Males' Temple—females and young may not follow, they have their own." He led the way along another path, making an elaborate salute to a small idol in a niche on the trail. From its crudity, the thing had been carved centuries ago. The Flock seemed to have only a rather incoherent polytheism for religion, and not to take that very seriously these days; but it was as strict about ritual and tradition as some classic British regiment—which, in many ways, it resembled.

Van Rijn trudged after, casting a glance behind. The females here looked little different from those in the Fleet: a bit smaller and slimmer than the males, their wings larger but without a fully developed spur. In fact, racially the two folk seemed identical.

And yet, if all that the company's agents had learned about Diomedes was not pure gibberish, the Drak'honai represented a biological monstrousness. An impossibility!

Trolwen followed the man's curious gaze, and sighed. "You can notice nearly half our nubile females are expecting their next cub."

"Hm-m-m. *Ja*, there is your problem. Let me see if I understand it right. Your young are all born at the fall equinox—"

"Yes. Within a few days of each other; the exceptions are negligible."

"But it is not so many ten-days thereafter you must leave for the south. Surely a new baby cannot fly?"

"Oh, no. It clings to the mother all the way; it is born

with arms able to grasp hard. There is no cub from the preceding year; a nursing female does not get pregnant. Her two-year-old is strong enough to fly the distance, given rest periods in which it rides on someone's back—though that's the age group where we suffer the most loss. Three-year-olds and above need only be guided and guarded: their wings are quite adequate."

"But this makes much trouble for the mother, not so?"

"She is assisted by the half-grown clan members, or the old who are past childbearing but not yet too old to survive the journey. And the males, of course, do all the hunting, scouting, fighting, and so forth."

"So. You come to the south. I hear told it makes easy to live there, nuts and fruits and fish to scoop from the water. Why do you come back?"

"This is our home," said Trolwen simply.

After a moment: "And, of course, the tropic islands could never support the myriads which gather there each midwinter—twice a year, actually. By the time the migrants are ready to leave, they have eaten that country bare."

"I see. Well, keep on. In the south, at solstice time, is when you rut."

"Yes. The desire comes on us—but you know what I mean."

"Of course," said van Rijn blandly.

"And there are festivals, and trading with the other tribes...frolic or fight—" The Lannacha sighed. "Enough. Soon after solstice, we return, arriving here sometime before equinox, when the large animals on which we chiefly depend have awoken from their winter sleep and put on a little flesh. There you have the pattern of our lives, Eart'ho."

"It sounds like fun, if I was not too old and fat." Van Rijn blew his nose lugubriously. "Do not get old, Trolwen. It is so lonesome. You are lucky, dying on migration when you grow feeble, you do not live wheezy and helpless with nothing but your dear memories, like me."

"I'm not likely to get old as matters stand now," said Trolwen.

"When your young are born, all at once in the fall . . . *ja*," mused van Rijn, "I can see how then is time for nothing much but obstetrics. And if you have not food and shelter and such helps ready, most of the young die—"

"They are replaceable," said Trolwen, with a degree of casualness that showed he was, after all, not just a man winged and tailed. His tone sharpened. "But the females who bear them are more vital to our strength. A recent mother must be properly rested and fed, you understand, or she will never reach the south—and consider what a part of our total numbers are going to become mothers. It's a question of the Flock's survival as a nation! And those filthy Drakska, breeding the year round like . . . like fish . . . *No!*"

"No indeed," said van Rijn. "Best we think of somethings very fast, or I grow very hungry, too."

"I spent lives to rescue you," said Trolwen, "because we all hoped you would think of something yourself."

"Well," said van Rijn, "the problem is to get word to my own people at Thursday Landing. Then they come here quick, by damn, and I will tell them to clean up on the Fleet."

Trolwen smiled. Even allowing for the unhuman shape of his mouth, it was a smile without warmth or humor. "No, no," he said. "Not that easily. I dare not, cannot spare the folk, or the time and effort, in some crazy attempt to cross The Ocean . . . not while Drak'ho has us by the throat. Also—forgive me—how do I know that you will be interested in helping us, once you are able to go home again?"

He looked away from his companion, toward the porticoed cave that was the Males' Temple. Steam rolled from its mouth, there was the hiss of a geyser within.

"I myself might have decided otherwise," he added abruptly, in a very low voice. "But I have only limited powers—any plan of mine—the Council—do you see? The Council is suspicious of three wingless monsters. It thinks . . . we know so little about you . . . our only sure hold on you is your own desperation . . . the Council will allow no help to be brought for you until the war is over."

Van Rijn lifted his shoulders and spread his hands. "Confidential, Trolwen, boy, in their place I would do the same."

X

Now darkness waned. Soon there would be light nights, when the sun hovered just under the sea and the sky was like white blossoms. Already both moons could be seen in full phase after sunset. As Rodonis stepped from her cabin, swift Sk'huanax climbed the horizon and swung up among the many stars toward slow and patient Lykaris. Between them, She Who Waits and He Who Pursues cast a shuddering double bridge over broad waters.

Rodonis was born to the old nobility, and had been taught to smile at Moons worship. Good enough for the common sailors, who would otherwise go back to their primitive bloody sacrifices to Aeak'ha-in-the-Deeps, but really, an educated person knew there was only the Lodestar.... Nevertheless, Rodonis went down on the deck, hooded herself with her wings, and whispered her trouble to bright mother Lykaris.

"A song do I pledge you, a song all for yourself, to be made by the Fleet's finest bards and sung in your honor when next you hold wedding with He Who Pursues you. You will not wed Him again for more than a year, the astrologues tell me; there will be time enough to fashion a song for you which shall live while the Fleet remains afloat, O Lykaris: if but you will spare me my Delp."

She did not address Sk'huanax the Warrior, any more than a male Drak'ho would have dreamed of petitioning the Mother. But she said to Lykaris in her mind, that there could be no harm in calling to his attention the fact that Delp was a brave person who had never omitted the proper offerings.

The moons brightened. A bank of cloud in the west bulked like frosty mountains. Far off stood the ragged loom of an island, and she could hear pack ice cough in the north. It was a big strange seascape, this was not the dear green Southwater whence starvation had driven the Fleet and she wondered if Achan's gods would ever let the Drak'honai call it home.

The *lap-lap* of waves, creaking timbers, cables that sang as the dew tautened them, wind-mumble in shrouds, a slatting sail, the remote plaintiveness of a flute and the nearer homely noises from this raft's own forecastle, snores and cub-whimpers and some couple's satisfied grunt...were a strong steady comfort in this cold emptiness named Achan Sea. She thought of her own young, two small furry shapes in a richly tapestried bed, and it gave her the remaining strength needed. She spread her wings and mounted the air.

From above, the Fleet at night was all clumps of shadow, with the rare twinkle of firepots where some crew worked late. Most were long abed, worn out from a day of dragging nets, manning sweeps and capstans, cleaning and salting and pickling the catch, furling and unfurling the heavy sails of the rafts, harvesting driss and fruitweed, felling trees and shaping timber with stone tools. A common crew member, male or female, had little in life except hard brutal labor. Their recreations were almost as coarse and violent: the dances, the athletic contests, the endless lovemaking, the bawdy songs roared out from full lungs over a barrel of seagrain beer.

For a moment, as such thoughts crossed her mind, Rodonis felt pride in her crewfolk. To the average noble, a commoner was a domestic animal, ill-mannered, unlettered, not quite decent, to be kept in line by whip and hook for his own good. But flying over the great sleeping beast of a Fleet, Rodonis sensed its sheer vigor, coiled like a snake beneath her—these were the lords of the sea, and Drak'ho's haughty banners were raised on the backs of Drak'ho's lusty deckhands.

Perhaps it was simply that her own husband's ancestors had risen from the forecastle not many generations back. She had seen him help his crew often enough, working side by side with them in storm or fish run; she had learned it was no disgrace to swing a quernstone or set up a massive loom for herself.

If labor was pleasing to the Lodestar, as the holy books said, then why should Drak'ho nobles consider it distasteful? There was something bloodless about the old families, something not quite healthy. They died out, to be replaced from below, century after century. It was well-known that deckhands had the most offspring, skilled handicrafters and full-time warriors rather less, hereditary officers fewest of all. Why, Admiral Syranax had in a long life begotten only one son and two daughters. She, Rodonis, had two cubs already, after a mere four years of marriage.

Did this not suggest that the high Lodestar favored the honest person working with honest hands?

But no... those Lannach'honai all had young every other year, like machinery, even though many of the tykes died on migration. And the Lannach'honai did not work: not really: they hunted, herded, fished with their effeminate hooks, they were vigorous enough but they never stuck to a job through hours and days like a Drak'ho sailor... and, of course, their habits were just disgusting. *Animal!* A couple of ten-days a year, down in the twilight of equatorial solstice, indiscriminate lust, and that was all. For the rest of your life, the father of your cub was only another male to you—not that you knew who he was anyway, you hussy!—and at home there was no modesty between the sexes, there wasn't even much distinction in everyday habits, because there was no more desire. Ugh!

Still, those filthy Lannach'honai had flourished, so maybe the Lodestar did not care.... No, it was too cold a thought, here in the night wind under ashen Sk'huanax. Surely the Lodestar had appointed the Fleet an instrument, to destroy those Lannach beasts and take the country they had been defiling.

Rodonis' wings beat a little faster. The flagship was close now, its turrets like mountain peaks in the dark. There were many lamps burning, down on deck or in shuttered rooms. There were warriors cruising endlessly above and around. The admiral's flag was still at the masthead, so he had not yet died; but the death watch thickened hour by hour.

Like carrion birds waiting, thought Rodonis with a shudder.

One of the sentries whistled her to a hover and flapped close. Moonlight glistened on his polished spearhead. "Hold! Who are you?"

She had come prepared for such a halt, but briefly, the tongue clove to her mouth. For she was only a female, and a monster laired beneath her.

A gust of wind rattled the dried things hung from a yardarm: the wings of some offending sailor who now sat leashed to an oar or a millstone, if he still lived. Rodonis thought of Delp's back bearing red stumps, and her anger broke loose in a scream:

"Do you speak in that tone to a sa Axollon?"

The warrior did not know her personally, among the thousands of Fleet citizens, but he knew an officer-class scarf; and it was plain to see that a life's toil had never been allowed to twist this slim-flanked body.

"Down on the deck, scum!" yelled Rodonis. "Cover your eyes when you address me!"

"I . . . my lady," he stammered, "I did not—"

She dove directly at him. He had no choice but to get out of the way. Her voice cracked whip-fashion, trailing her: "Assuming, of course, that your boatswain has first obtained my permission for you to speak to me."

"But . . . but . . . but—" Other fighting males had come now, to wheel as helplessly in the air. Such laws did exist; no one had enforced them to the letter for centuries, but—

An officer on the main deck met the situation when Rodonis landed. "My lady," he said with due deference, "it is not seemly for an unescorted female to be abroad at all, far less to visit this raft of sorrow."

"It is necessary," she told him. "I have a word for Captain T'heonax which will not wait."

"The captain is at his honored father's bunkside, my lady. I dare not—"

"Let it be your teeth he has pulled, then, when he learns that Rodonis sa Axollon could have forestalled another mutiny!"

She flounced across the deck and leaned on the rail, as if brooding her anger above the sea. The officer gasped. It was like a tail-blow to the stomach. "My lady! At once... wait, wait here, only the littlest of moments— Guard! Guard, there! Watch over my lady. See that she lacks not." He scuttled off.

Rodonis waited. Now the real test was coming.

There had been no problem so far. The Fleet was too shaken; no officer, worried ill, would have refused her demand when she spoke of a second uprising.

The first had been bad enough. Such a horror, an actual revolt against the Lodestar's own Oracle, had been unknown for more than a hundred years... and with a war to fight at the same time! The general impulse had been to deny that anything serious had happened at all. A regrettable misunderstanding... Delp's folk misled, fighting their gallant, hopeless fight out of loyalty to their captain... after all, you couldn't expect ordinary sailors to understand the more modern principle, that the Fleet and its admiral transcended any individual raft—

Harshly, her tears at the time only a dry memory, Rodonis rehearsed her interview with Syranax, days ago.

"I am sorry, my lady," he said. "Believe me, I am sorry. Your husband was provoked, and he had more justice on his side than T'heonax. In fact, I know it was just a fight which happened, not planned, only a chance spark touching off old grudges, and my own son mostly to blame."

"Then let your son suffer for it!" she had cried.

The gaunt old skull wove back and forth, implacably. "No. He may not be the finest person in the world, but he is my son. And the heir. I haven't long to live, and wartime is no time to risk a struggle over the succession. For the Fleet's sake, T'heonax must succeed me without argument from anyone; and for this, he must have an officially unstained record."

"But why can't you let Delp go too?"

"By the Lodestar, if I could! But it's not possible. I can give everyone else amnesty, yes, and I will. But there must be one to bear the blame, one on whom to vent the pain of our hurts. Delp has to be accused of engineering a mutiny, and be punished, so that everybody else can say, 'Well, we fought each other, but it was all his fault, so now we can trust each other again.'"

The admiral sighed, a tired breath out of shrunken lungs. "I wish to the Lodestar I didn't have to do this. I wish . . . I'm fond of you too, my lady. I wish we could be friends again."

"We can," she whispered, "if you will set Delp free."

The conqueror of Maion looked bleakly at her and said: "No. And now I have heard enough."

She had left his presence.

And the days passed, and there was the farcical nightmare of Delp's trial, and the nightmare of the sentence passed on him, and the nightmare of waiting for its execution. The Lannach'ho raid had been like a moment's waking from fever-dreams: for it was sharp and real, and your shipmate was no longer your furtive-eyed enemy but a warrior who met the barbarian in the clouds and whipped him home from your cubs!

Three nights afterward, Admiral Syranax lay dying. Had he not fallen sick, Delp would now be a mutilated slave, but in this renewed tension and uncertainty, so controversial a sentence was naturally stayed.

Once T'heonax had the Admiralty, thought Rodonis in a cold corner of her brain, there would be no more delay. Unless—

"Will my lady come this way?"

They were obsequious, the officers who guided her across the deck and into the great gloomy pile of logs. Household servants, pattering up and down windowless corridors by lamplight, stared at her in a kind of terror. Somehow, the most secret things were always known to the forecastle, immediately, as if smelled.

It was dark in here, stuffy, and silent. So silent. The sea is never still. Only now did Rodonis realize that she had not before, in all her life, been shut away from the sound of waves and timber and cordage. Her wings tensed, she wanted to fly up with a scream.

She walked.

They opened a door for her; she went through, and it closed behind her with sound-deadening massiveness. She saw a small, richly furred and carpeted room, where many lamps burned. The air was so thick it made her dizzy. T'heonax lay on a couch watching her, playing with one of the Eart'ho knives. Thee was no one else.

"Sit down," he said.

She squatted on her tail, eyes smoldering into his as if they were equals.

"What did you wish to say?" he asked tonelessly.

"The admiral your father lives?" she countered.

"Not for long, I fear," he said. "Aeak'ha will eat him before noon." His eyes went toward the arras, haunted. "How long the night is!"

Rodonis waited.

"Well?" he said. His head swung back, snakishly. A rawness was in his tone. "You mentioned something about... another mutiny?"

Rodonis sat straight up on her haunches. Her crest grew stiff. "Yes," she replied in a winter voice. "My husband's crew have not forgotten him."

"Perhaps not," snapped T'heonax. "But they've had sufficient loyalty to the Admiralty drubbed into them by now."

"Loyalty to Admiral Syranax, yes," she told him. "But that was never lacking. You know as well as I, what happened was no mutiny... only a riot, by males who were against you. Syranax they have always admired, if not loved.

"The *real* mutiny will be against his murderer."

T'heonax leaped.

"What do you mean?" he shouted. "Who's a murderer?"

"You are." Rodonis pushed it out between her teeth. "You have poisoned your father."

She waited then, through a time which stretched close to breaking. She could not tell if the notoriously violent male she faced would kill her for uttering those words.

Almost, he did. He drew back from her when his knife touched her throat. His jaws clashed shut again, he leaped onto his couch and stood there on all fours with back arched, tail rigid and wings rising.

"Go on," he hissed. "Say your lies. I know well enough how you hate my whole family, because of that worthless husband of yours. All the Fleet knows. Do you expect them to believe your naked word?"

"I never hated your father," said Rodonis, not quite steadily; death had brushed very close. "He condemned Delp, yes. I thought he did wrongly, but he did it for the Fleet, and I ... I am of officer kindred myself. You recall, on the day after the raid I asked him to dine with me, as a token to all that the Drak'honai must close ranks."

"So you did," sneered T'heonax. "A pretty gesture. I remember how hotly spiced the guests said the food was. And the little keepsake you gave him, that shining disk from the Eart'ho possessions. Touching! As if it were yours to give. Everything of theirs belongs to the Admiralty."

"Well, the fat Eart'ho had given it to me himself," said Rodonis. She was deliberately leading the conversation into irrelevant channels, seeking to calm them both. "He had recovered it from his baggage, he said. He called it a *coin* ... an article of trade among his people ... thought I might like it to remember him by. That was just after the ... the riot ... and just before he and his companions were removed from the *Gerunis* to that other raft."

"It was a miser's gift," said T'heonax. "The disk was quite worn out of shape—Bah!" His muscles bunched again. "Come. Accuse me further, if you dare."

"I have not been altogether a fool," said Rodonis. "I have left letters, to be opened by certain friends if I do not return. But consider the facts, T'heonax. You are an ambitious male, and one of whom most persons are willing to think the worst. Your father's death will make you Admiral, the virtual owner of the Fleet—how long you must have chafed, waiting for this! Your father is dying, stricken by a malady unlike any known to our chirurgeons: not even like any known poison, so wildly does it destroy him. Now it is known to many that the raiders did not manage to carry off every bit of the Eart'ho food: three small packets were left behind. The Eart'honai frequently and publicly warned us against eating any of their rations. And *you* have charge of all the Eart'ho things!"

T'heonax gasped.

"It's a lie!" he chattered. "I don't know...I haven't ...I never—Will anyone believe I, anyone, could do such a thing...poison...to his own father?"

"Of you they will believe it," said Rodonis.

"I swear by the Lodestar—!"

"The Lodestar will not give luck to a Fleet commanded by a parricide. There will be mutiny on that account alone, T'heonax."

He glared at her, wild and panting. "What do you want?" he croaked.

Rodonis looked at him with the coldest gaze he had ever met. "I will burn those letters," she said, "and will keep silence forever. I will even join my denials to yours, should the same thoughts occur to someone else. But Delp must have immediate, total amnesty."

T'heonax bristled and snarled at her.

"I could fight you," he growled. "I could have you arrested for treasonable talk, and kill anyone who dared—"

"Perhaps," said Rodonis. "But is it worth it? You might split the Fleet open and leave us all a prey to the Lannach'honai. All I ask is my husband back."

"For that, you would threaten to ruin the Fleet?"

"Yes," she said.

And after a moment: "You do not understand. You males make the nations and wars and songs and science, all the little things. You imagine you are the strong practical sex. But a female goes again and yet again under death's shadow, to bring forth another life. We are the hard ones. We have to be."

T'heonax huddled back, shivering.

"Yes," he whispered at last, "yes, curse you, shrivel

you, yes, you can have him. I'll give you an order now, this instant. Get his rotten feet off my raft before dawn, d'you hear? But I did not poison my father." His wings beat thunderous, until he lifted up under the ceiling and threshed there, trapped and screaming. "I *didn't!*"

Rodonis waited.

Presently she took the written order, and left him, and went to the brig, where they cut the ropes that bound Delp hyr Orikan. He lay in her arms and sobbed. "I will keep my wings, I will keep my wings—"

Rodonis sa Axollon stroked his crest, murmured to him, crooned to him, told him all would be well now, they were going home again, and wept a little because she loved him.

Inwardly she held a chill memory, how old van Rijn had given her the coin but warned her against . . . what had he said? . . . heavy metal poisoning. "To you, iron, copper, tin is unknown stuffs. I am not a chemist, me; chemists I hire when chemicking is needful; but I think better I eat a shovelful arsenic than one of your cubs try teething on this piece money, by damn!"

And she remembered sitting up in the dark, with a stone in her hand, grinding and grinding the coin, until there was seasoning for the unbendable admiral's dinner.

Afterward she recollected that the Eart'ho was not supposed to have such mastery of her language. It occurred to her now, like a shudder, that he could very well have left that deadly food behind on purpose, in hopes it might cause trouble. But how closely had he foreseen the event?

XI

Guntra of the Enklann sept came in through the door. Eric Wace looked wearily up. Behind him, hugely shadowed between rush lights, the mill was a mumble of toiling forms.

"Yes?" he sighed.

Guntra held out a broad shield, two meters long, a light

sturdy construction of wicker on a wooden frame. For many ten-days she had supervised hundreds of females and cubs as they gathered and split and dried the reeds, formed the wood, wove the fabric, assembled the unit. She had not been so tired since homecoming. Nevertheless, a small victory dwelt in her voice: "This is the four thousandth, Councilor." It was not his title, but the Lannacha mind could hardly imagine anyone without definite rank inside the Flock organization. Considering the authority granted the wingless creatures, it fell most naturally to call them Councilors.

"Good." He hefted the object in hands grown calloused. "A strong piece of work. Four thousand are more than enough; your task is done, Guntra."

"Thank you." She looked curiously about the transformed mill. Hard to remember that not so long ago it had existed chiefly to grind food.

Angrek of the Trekkans came up with a block of wood in his grasp. "Councilor," he began, "I—" He stopped. His gaze had fallen on Guntra, who was still in her early middle years and had always been considered handsome.

Her eyes met his. A common smokiness lit them. His wings spread and he took a stiff step toward her.

With a gasp, almost a sob, Guntra turned and fled. Angrek stared after her, then threw his block to the floor and cursed.

"What the devil?" said Wace.

Angrek beat a fist into his palm. "Ghosts," he muttered. "It must be ghosts . . . unrestful spirits of all the evildoers who ever lived . . . possessing the Drakska, and now come to plague us!"

Another pair of bodies darkened the door, which stood open to the short pale night of early summer. Nicholas van Rijn and Tolk the Herald entered.

"How goes it, boy?" boomed van Rijn. He was gnawing a nitro-packed onion; the gauntness which had settled on Wace, even on Sandra, had not touched him. But then, thought Wace bitterly, the old blubberbucket didn't work. All he did was stroll around and talk to the local bosses and complain that things weren't proceeding fast enough.

"Slowly, sir." The younger man bit back words he would rather have said. *You bloated leech, do you expect to be carried home by my labor and my brains, and fob me off with another factor's post on another hell-planet?*

"It will have to be speeded, then," said van Rijn. "We cannot wait so long, you and me."

Tolk glanced keenly at Angrek. The handicrafter was still trembling and whispering charms. "What's wrong?" he asked.

"The... an influence." Angrek covered his eyes. "Herald," he stammered, "Guntra of the Enklann was here just now, and for a moment we... we desired each other."

Tolk looked grave, but spoke without reproof. "It has happened to many. Keep it under control."

"But what *is* it, Herald? A sickness? A judgment? What have I done?"

"These unnatural impulses aren't unknown," said Tolk. "They crop up in most of us, every once in a while. But of course, one doesn't talk about it; one suppresses it, and does his or her best to forget it ever happened." He scowled. "Lately there has been more of such hankering than usual. I don't know why. Go back to your work and avoid females."

Angrek drew a shaky breath, picked up his piece of wood, and nudged Wace. "I wanted your advice; the shape here doesn't seem to me the best for its purpose—"

Tolk looked around. He had just come back from a prolonged journey, cruising over his entire homeland to bear word to scattered clans. "There has been much work done here," he said.

"Ja," nodded van Rijn complacently. "He is a talented engineer, him my young friend. But then, the factor on a new planet had pest-bedamned better be a good engineer."

"I am not so well acquainted with the details of his schemes."

"My schemes," corrected van Rijn, somewhat huffily. "I tell him to make us weapons. All he does then is make them."

"All?" asked Tolk dryly. He inspected a skeletal framework. "What's this?"

"A repeating dart-thrower; a machine gun, I call it. See, this walking beam turns this spurred fly wheel. Darts are fed to the wheel on a belt—s-s-so—and tossed off fast: two or three in an eye-wink, at least. The wheel is swivel-mounted to point in any direction. It is an old idea, really, I think Miller or de Camp or someone first built it long ago. But it is one hard damn thing to face in battle."

"Excellent," approved Tolk. "And that over there?"

"We call it a ballista. It is like the Drak'ho catapults, only more so. This throws large stones, to break down a wall or sink a boat. And here—*ja*." Van Rijn picked up the shield Guntra had brought. "This is not so good advertising copy, maybe, but I think it means a bit more for us than the other machineries. A warrior on the ground wears one on his back."

"Mm-m-m . . . yes, I see where a harness would fit . . . it would stop missiles from above, eh? But our warrior could not fly while he wore it."

"Just so!" roared van Rijn. "Just bloody-be-so! That is the troubles with you folk on Diomedes. Great balls of cheese! How you expect to fight a real war with nothing but air forces, ha? Up here in Salmenbrok, I spend all days hammering into stupid officer heads, it is infantry takes and holds a position, by damn! And then officers have to beat it into the ranks, and practice them—gout of Judas! It is not time enough! In these few ten-days, I have to try make what needs years!"

Tolk nodded, almost casually. Even Trolwen had needed time and argument before he grasped the idea of a combat force whose main body was deliberately restricted to ground operations. It was too alien a concept. But the Herald said only: "Yes. I see your reasoning. It is the strong points which decide who holds Lannach, the fortified towns that dominate a countryside from which the food comes. And to take the town back, we will need to dig our way in."

"You think smartly," approved van Rijn. "In Earth history, it took some peoples a long time to learn there is no victory in air power alone."

"There are still the Drakska fire weapons," said Tolk. "What do you plan to do about them? My whole mission, these past ten-days, has been largely to persuade the outlying septs to join us. I gave them your word that the fire could be faced, that we'd even have flamethrowers and bombs of our own. I'd better have been telling the truth."

He looked about. The mill, converted to a crude factory, was too full of winged laborers for him to see far. Nearby, a primitive lathe, somewhat improved by Wace, was turning out spearshafts and tomahawk handles. Another engine, a whirling grindstone, was new to him: it shaped ax heads and similar parts, not as good as the handmade type but formed in wholesale lots. A drop hammer knocked off flint and obsidian flakes for cutting edges; a circular saw cut wooden members; a rope-twisting machine spun faster than the eye could follow. All of it was belt-powered from the great millwheels—all of it ludicrously haywired and cranky—but it spat forth the stuff of war faster than Lannach could use, filling whole bins with surplus armament.

"It is remarkable," said Tolk. "It frightens me a little."

"I made a new way of life here," said van Rijn expansively. "It is not this machine or that one which has already changed your history beyond changing back. It is the basic idea I have introduced: mass production."

"But the fire—"

"Wace has also begun to make us fire weapons. Sulfur they have gathered from Mount Oborch, and there are oil pools from which we are getting nice arsonish liquids. Distillation, that is another art the Drak'ho have had and you have not. Now we will have some Molotov cocktails for our own selves."

The human scowled. "But there is one thing true, my

friend. We have not time to train your warriors like they should be to use this material. Soon I starve; soon your females get heavy and food must be stored." He heaved a pathetic sigh. "Though I am long dead before you folks have real sufferings."

"Not so," said Tolk grimly. "We have almost half a year left before Birthtime, true. But already we are weakened by hunger, cold, and despair. Already we have failed to perform many ceremonies—"

"Blast your ceremonies!" snapped van Rijn. "I say it is Ulwen town we should take first, where it sits so nice overlooking Duna Brae that all the hornbeasts live at. If we have Ulwen, you have eats enough, also a strong point easy to defend. But no, Trolwen and the Council say we must strike straight for Mannenach, leaving Ulwen enemy-held in our rear, and going down clear to Sagna Bay where their rafts can get at us. For why? So you can hold some blue-befungused rite there!"

"You cannot understand," said Tolk gently. "We are too different. Even I, whose life's work it has been to deal with alien peoples, cannot grasp your attitude. But our life is the cycle of the year. It is not that we take the old gods so seriously any more—but their rituals, the rightness and decency of it all, the *belonging*—" He looked upward, into the shadow-hidden roof, where the wind hooted and rushed about the busy millwheels. "No, I don't believe that ancestral ghosts fly out there of nights. But I do believe that when I welcome High Summer back at the great rite in Mannenach, as my forebears have done for as long as there has been a Flock . . . then I am keeping the Flock itself alive."

"Bah!" Van Rijn extended a dirt-encrusted hand to scratch the matted beard which was engulfing his face. He couldn't shave or wash: even given antiallergen shots, human skin wouldn't tolerate Diomedean soap. "I tell you why you have all this ritual. First, you are a slave to the seasons, more even than any farmer on Earth back in our old days. Second, you must fly so much, and leave your homes empty all the dark time up here, that ritual is your most precious possession. It is the only thing you have not weighing too much to be carried with you everywhere."

"That's as may be," said Tolk. "The fact remains. If there is any chance of greeting the Full Day from Mannenach Standing Stones, we shall take it. The extra lives which are lost because this may not be the soundest strategy, will be offered in gladness."

"If it does not cost us the whole befouled war." Van Rijn snorted. "Devils and dandruff! My own chaplain at home, that pickle face, is not so fussy about what is proper. Why, that poor young fellow there was near making suicide now, just because he got a little bit excited over a wench out of wenching season, *nie?*"

"It isn't done," said Tolk stiffly. He walked from the shop. After a moment, van Rijn followed.

Wace settled the point of discussion with Angrek, checked operations elsewhere, swore at a well-meaning young porter who was storing volatile petroleum fractions beside the hearth, and left. His feet were heavy at the end of his legs. It was too much for one man to do, organizing, designing, supervising, trouble-shooting— Van Rijn seemed to think it was routine to lift neolithic hunters into the machine age in a few weeks. He ought to try it himself! It might sweat some of the lard off the old hog.

Sometimes he wondered if he had ever felt rested ... and clean, and well fed, and comforted in his aloneness.

Morning smoldered on northerly ridges, where a line of volcanoes smeared wrathful black across the sun. Both moons were sinking, each a cold coppery disk twice the apparent size of Earth's Luna. Mount Oborch shivered along giant flanks and spat a few boulders at the pallid sky. The wind came galing, stiff as an iron bar pressed against Wace's suddenly chilled back. Salmenbrok village huddled flinty barren under its loud quick thrust.

He had reached the ladder made for him, so he could reach the tiny loft-room he used, when Sandra Tamarin came from behind the adjoining tower. She paused, one hand stealing to her face. He could not hear what she said, in the blustery air.

He went over to her. Gravel scrunched under the awkward leather boots a Lannacha tailor had made him. "I beg your pardon, my lady?"

"Oh...it was nothing, Freeman Wace." Her green gaze came up to meet his, steadily and proudly, but he saw a redness steal along her cheeks. "I only said...good morning."

"Likewise." He rubbed sandy-lidded eyes. "I haven't seen you for some time, my lady. How are you?"

"Restless," she said. "Unhappy. Will you talk to me for a little, perhaps?"

They left the hamlet behind and followed a dim trail upward, through low harsh bushes breaking into purple bloom. High above them wheeled a few sentries, but those were only impersonal specks against heaven. Wace felt his heartbeat grow hasty.

"What have you been doing?" he asked.

"Nothing of value. What can I do?" She stared down at her hands. "I try, but I have not the skills, not like you the engineer or Freeman van Rijn."

"Him?" Wace shrugged. No doubt the old goat had found plenty of chance to brag himself up, as he lounged superfluous around Salmenbrok. "It—" He stopped, groping after words. "It's enough just to have my lady present."

"Why, Freeman!" She laughed, with genuine half-amused pleasure and no coyness at all. "I never thought you so gallant in the words."

"Never had much chance to be, my lady," he murmured, too tired and strength-emptied to keep up his guard.

"Not?" She gave him a sideways look. The wind laid its fingers in her tightly braided hair and unfurled small argent banners of it. She was not yet starved, but the bones in her face were standing out more sharply; there was a smudge on one cheek and her garments were clumsy baggings hurled together by a tailor who had never seen a human frame before. But somehow, stripped thus of queenliness, she seemed to him more beautiful than erstwhile—perhaps because of being closer? Because her poverty said with frankness that she was only human flesh like himself?

"No," he got out between stiff lips.

"I do not understand," she said.

"Your pardon, my lady. I was thinking out loud. Bad habit. But one does, on these outpost worlds. You see the same few men so often that they stop being company; you avoid them—and, of course, we're always undermanned, so you have to go out by yourself on various jobs, maybe for weeks at a time. Why am I saying all this? I don't know. Dear God, how tired I am!"

They paused on a ridge. At their feet was a cliff tumbling through hundreds of meters down to a foam-white river. Across the canyon were mountains and mountains, their snows tinged bloody by the sun. The wind came streaking up the dales and struck the humans in the face.

"I see. Yes, it clears for me." Sandra regarded him with grave eyes. "You have had to work hard your whole life. There has not been time for the pleasures, the learned manners and culture. Not?"

"No time at all, my lady," he said. "I was born in the slums, one kilometer from the old Triton Docks. Nobody but the very poor would live that close to a spaceport, the traffic and stinks and earthquake noise . . . though you got used to it, till it was a part of you, built into your bones. Half my playmates are now dead or in jail, I imagine, and the other half are scrabbling for the occasional half-skilled hard-and-dirty job no one else wants. Don't pity me, though. I was lucky. I got apprenticed to a fur wholesaler when I was twelve. After two years, I'd made enough contacts to get a hard-and-dirty job myself—only this was on a spaceship, fur-trapping expedition to Rhiannon. I taught myself a little something in odd moments, and bluffed about the rest I was supposed to know, and got a slightly better job. And so on and so on, till they put me in charge of this outpost . . . a very minor enterprise, which may in time become moderately profitable but will never be important. But it's a stepping stone. So here I am, on a mountain top with all Diomedes below me, and what's next?"

He shook his head, violently, wondering why his reserve had broken down. Being so exhausted was like a drunkenness. But more to it than that . . . no, he was *not* fishing for sympathy . . . down underneath, did he want to find out if she would understand? If she could?

"You will get back," she said quietly. "Your kind of man survives."

"Maybe!"

"It is heroic, what you have done already." She looked away from him, toward the driving clouds around Oborch's peak. "I am not certain anything can stop you. Except yourself."

"I?" He was beginning to be embarrassed now, and wanted to talk of other things. He plucked at his bristly red beard.

"Yes. Who else can? You have come so far, so fast. But why not stop? Soon, perhaps here on this mountain, must you not ask yourself how much farther it is worth going?"

"I don't know. As far as possible, I guess."

"Why? Is it necessary to become great? Is it not enough to be free? With your talent and experience, you can make good-enough monies on many settled planets where men are more at home than here. Like Hermes, *exemplia*. In this striving to be rich and powerful, is it not merely that you want to feed and shelter the little boy who once cried himself hungry to sleep back in Triton Docks? But that little boy you can never comfort, my friend. He died long ago."

"Well . . . I don't know . . . I suppose one day I'll have a family. I'd want to give my wife more than just a living; I'd want to leave my children and grandchildren enough resources to go on—to stand off the whole world if they have to—"

"Yes. So. I think maybe—" he saw, before she turned her head from him, how the blood flew up into her face— "the old fighting Dukes of Hermes were like so. It would

be well if we had a breed of men like them again—"
Suddenly she began walking very fast down the path.
"Enough. Best we return, not?"

He followed her, little aware of the ground he trod.

XII

When the Lannachska were ready to fight, they were
called to Salmenbrok by Tolk's Whistlers until the sky
darkened with their wings. Then Trolwen made his way
through a seethe of warriors to van Rijn.

"Surely the gods are weary of us," he said bitterly.
"Near always, at this time of year, there are strong south
winds." He gestured at a breathless heaven. "Do you
know a spell for raising dead breezes?"

The merchant looked up, somewhat annoyed. He was
seated at a table outside the wattle-and-clay hut they had
built for him beyond the village—for he refused to climb
ladders or sleep in a damp cave—dicing with Corps
Captain Srygen for the beryl-like gemstones which were a
local medium of exchange. The number of species in the
galaxy which have independently invented some form of
African golf is beyond estimation.

"Well," he snapped, "and why must you have your tail
fanned?... Ah, seven! No, pox and pills, I remember,
here seven is not a so good number. Well, we try again."
The three cubes clicked in his hand and across the table.
"Hm-m-m, seven again." He scooped up the stakes.
"Double or nothings?"

"The ghost-eaters take it!" Srygen got up. "You've
been winning too motherless often for my taste."

Van Rijn surged to his own feet like a broaching whale.
"By damn, you take that back or—"

"I said nothing challengeable," Srygen told him coldly.

"You implied it. I am insulted, myself!"

"Hold on there," growled Trolwen. "What do you
think this is, a beer feast? Eart'a, all the fighting forces of
Lannach are now gathered on these hills. We cannot feed
them here very long. And yet, with the new weapons

loaded on the railway cars, we cannot stir until we get a south wind. What to do?"

Van Rijn glared at Srygen. "I said I was insulted. I do not think so good when I am insulted."

"I am sure the captain will apologize for any unintended offense," said Trolwen, with a red-shot look at them both.

"Indeed," said Srygen. He spoke it like pulling teeth.

"So." Van Rijn stroked his beard. "Then to prove you make no doubt about my honesties, we throw once more, *nie?* Double or nothings."

Srygen snatched the dice and hurled them. "Ah, a six you have," said van Rijn. "It is not so easy to beat. I am afraid I have already lost. It is not so simple to be a poor tired hungry old man, far away from his home and from the Siamese cats who are all he has to love him for himself, not just his monies. . . . Tum-te-tum-te-tum. . . . Eight! A two, a three, a three! Well, well, well!"

"Transport," said Trolwen, hanging on to his temper by a hair. "The new weapons are too heavy for our porters. They have to go by rail. Without a wind, how do we get them down to Sagna Bay?"

"Simple," said van Rijn, counting his take. "Till you get a good wind, tie ropes to the cars and all these so-husky young fellows pull."

Srygen blew up. "A free clan male, to drag a car like a . . . like a *Draka*?" He mastered himself and choked: "It isn't done."

"Sometimes," said van Rijn, "these things must be done." He scooped up the jewels, dropped them into a purse, and went over to a well. "Surely you have some disciplines in this Flock."

"Oh . . . yes . . . I suppose so—" Trolwen's unhappy gaze went downslope to the brawling, shouting winged tide which had engulfed the village. "But sustained labor like that has always . . . long before the Drakska came . . . always been considered—perverted, in a way—it is not exactly forbidden, but one does not do it without the most compelling necessity. To labor in *public*—No!"

Van Rijn hauled on the windlass. "Why not? The

Drak'honai, them, make all kinds tiresome preachments about the dignity of labor. For them it is needful; in their way of life, one must work hard. But for you? Why must one *not* work hard in Lannach?"

"It isn't right," said Srygen stiffly. "It makes us like some kind of animal."

Van Rijn pulled the bucket to the well coping and took a bottle of Earthside beer from it. "Ahhh, good and cold...hm-m-m, possibly too cold, damn all places without thermostatted coolers—" He opened the bottle on the stone curb and tasted. "It will do. Now, I have made travels, and I find that everywhere the manners and morals of peoples have some good reason at bottom. Maybe the race has forgotten why was a rule made in the first place, but if the rule does not make some sense, it will not last many centuries. Follows then that you do not like prolonged hard work, except to be sure migration, because it is not good for you for some reason. And yet it does not hurt the Drak'honai too much. Paradox!"

"Unlawfulness take your wonderings," snarled Trolwen. "It was your idea that we make all this newfangled apparatus, instead of fighting as our males have always fought. Now, how do we get it down to the lowlands without demoralizing the army?"

"Oh, that!" Van Rijn shrugged. "You have sports—contests—*nie?*"

"Of course."

"Well, you explain these cars must be brought with us and, while it is not necessary we leave at once—"

"But it is! We'll starve if we don't!"

"My good young friend," said van Rijn patiently, "I see plain you have much to learn about politics. You Lannachska do not understand lying, I suppose because you do not get married. You tell the warriors, I say, that we can wait for a south wind all right but you know they are eager to come to grips with the foe and therefore they will be invited to play a small game. Each clan will pull so and so many cars down, and we time how fast it goes and make a prize for the best pullers."

"Well, I'll be accursed," said Srygen.

Trolwen nodded eagerly. "It's just the sort of thing that gets into clan traditions—"

"You see," explained van Rijn, "it is what we call semantics on Earth. I am old and short with breath, so I can look unprejudiced at all these footballs and baseballs and potato races, and I know that a game is hard work you are not required to do."

He belched, opened another bottle, and took a half-eaten salami from his purse. The supplies weren't going to last very much longer.

XIII

When the expedition was halfway down the Misty Mountains, their wind rose behind them. A hundred warriors harnessed to each railway car relaxed and waited for the timers whose hourglasses would determine the winning team.

"But they are not all so dim in the brain, surely," said Sandra.

"Oh, no," answered Wace. "But those who were smart enough to see through Old Nick's scheme were also smart enough to see it was necessary, and keep quiet."

He huddled in a mordant blast that drove down alpine slopes to the distant cloudy green of hills and valleys, and watched the engineers at work. A train consisted of about thirty light little cars roped together, with a "locomotive" at the head and another in the middle. These were somewhat more sturdily built, to support two high masts with square sails. Given wood of almost metallic hardness, plus an oil-drip over the wheels in lieu of ball bearings, plus the hurricane thrust of Diomedean winds, the system became practical. You didn't get up much speed, and you must often wait for a following wind, but this was not a culture bound to hourly schedules.

"It's not too late for you to go back, my lady," said Wace. "I can arrange an escort."

"No." She laid a hand on the bow which had been made for her—no toy, a 25-kilo killing tool such as she had often hunted with in her home forests. Her head lifted, the silver-pale hair caught chill ruddy sunlight and threw back a glow to this dark immensity of cliffs and glaciers. "Here we stand or here we die. It would not be right for a ruler born to stay home."

Van Rijn hawked. "Trouble with aristocrats," he muttered. "Bred for looks and courage, not brains. Now *I* would go back, if not needed here to show I have confidence in my own plans."

"Do you?" asked Wace skeptically.

"Let be with foolishness," snorted van Rijn. "Of course not." He trudged back to the staff car which had been prepared for him: at least it had walls, a roof, and a bunk. The wind shrieked down ringing stony canyons, he leaned against it with his entire weight. Overhead swooped and soared the squadrons of Lannach.

Wace and Sandra each had a private car, but she asked him to ride down with her. "Forgive me if I make dramatics, Eric, but we may be killed and it is lonely to die without a human hand to hold." She laughed, a little breathlessly. "Or at least we can talk."

"I'm afraid—" He cleared a tightened throat. "I'm afraid, my lady, I can't converse as readily as . . . Freeman van Rijn."

"Oh," she grinned, "that was what I meant. I said *we* can talk, not him only."

Nevertheless, when the trains got into motion, she grew quiet as he.

Lacking their watches they could scarcely even guess how long the trip took. High summer had almost come to Lannach; once in twelve and a half hours, the sun scraped the horizon north of west, but there was no more real night. Wace watched the kilometers click away beneath him; he ate, slept, spoke desultorily with Sandra or with young Angrek who served as her aide, and the great land flattened into rolling valleys and forests of low fringe-leaved trees, and the sea came near.

Now and again a hotbox or a contrary wind delayed the caravan. There was restlessness in the ranks: they were used to streaking in a day from the mountains to the coast, not to wheeling above this inchworm of a railway. Drak'honai scouts spied them from afar, inevitably, and a detachment of rafts lumbered into Sagna Bay with powerful reinforcements. Raids probed the flanks of the attackers. And still the trains must crawl.

In point of fact, there were eight Diomedean revolutions between the departure from Salmenbrok and the Battle of Mannenach.

The harbor town lay on the Sagna shore, well in from the open sea and sheltered by surrounding wooded hills. It was a gaunt grim-looking complex of stone towers, tightly knitted together with the usual tunnels and enclosed bridges, talking in the harsh tones of half a dozen big windmills. It overlooked a small pier, which the Drak'honai had been enlarging. Beyond, dark on the choppy brown waters, rocked two score enemy craft.

As his train halted, Wace jumped from Sandra's car. There was nothing to shoot at yet: Mannenach revealed only a few peaked roofs thrusting above the grass ridge before him. Even against the wind, he could hear the thunder of wings as the Drak'honai lifted from the town, twisting upward in a single black mass like some tornado made flesh. But heaven was thick with Lannachska above him, and the enemy made no immediate attack.

His heart thumped, runaway, and his mouth was too dry for him to speak. Almost hazily, he saw Sandra beside him. A Diomedean bodyguard under Angrek closed around in a thornbush of spears.

The girl smiled. "This is a kind of relief," she said. "No more sitting and worrying, only to do what we can, not?"

"Not indeed!" puffed van Rijn, stumping toward them. Like the other humans, he had arranged for an ill-fitting cuirass and helmet of laminated hard leather above the baggy malodorous native clothes. But he wore two sets of armor, one on top of the other, carried a shield on his left arm, had deputed two young warriors to hold another shield over him like a canopy, and bore a tomahawk and a beltful of stone daggers. "Not if I can get out of it, by damn! You go ahead and fight. I will be right behind you—as far behind as the good saints let."

Wace found his tongue and said maliciously: "I've often thought there might be fewer wars among civilized races, if they reverted to this primitive custom that the generals are present at the battles."

"Bah! Ridiculous! Just as many wars, only using generals who have guts more than brains. I think cowards make the best strategists, stands to reason, by damn. Now I stay in my car." Van Rijn stalked off, muttering.

Trolwen's newly-formed field artillery corps were going frantic, unloading their clumsy weapons from the trains and assembling them while squads and patrols skirmished overhead. Wace cursed—here was something he could do!—and hurried to the nearest confusion. "Hoy, there! Back away! What are you trying to do? Here, you, you, you, get up in the car and unlash the main frame . . . that piece *there*, you clothead!" After a while, he almost lost consciousness of the fighting that developed around him.

The Mannenach garrison and its sea-borne reinforcements had begun with cautious probing, a few squadrons at a time swooping to flurry briefly with some of the Lannachska flying troops and then pull away again toward the town. Drak'ho forces here were outnumbered by a fair margin; Trolwen had reasoned correctly that no admiral would dare leave the main Fleet without a strong defense while Lannach was still formidable. In addition, the sailors were puzzled, a little afraid, at the unprecedented attacking formations.

Fully half the Lannachska were ranked on the ground, covered by rooflike shields which would not even permit them to fly! Never in history had such a thing been known!

During an hour, the two hordes came more closely to grips. Much superior in the air, the Drak'honai punched time after time through Trolwen's fliers. But integrated by the Whistler corps, the aerial troops closed again, fluidly. And there was little profit in attacking the Lannachska infantry—those awkward wicker shields trapped edged missiles, sent stones rebounding, an assault from above was almost ignored.

Arrows were falling thickly when Wace had his last fieldpiece assembled. He nodded at a Whistler, who whirled up immediately to bear the word to Trolwen. From the commander's position, where he rode a thermal updraft, came a burst of messengers—banners broke out on the ground, war whoops tore through the wind, it was the word to advance!

Ringed by Angrek's guards, Wace remained all too well aware that he was at the forefront of an army. Sandra went beside him, her lips untense. On either hand stretched spear-jagged lines of walking dragons. It seemed like a long time before they had mounted the ridge.

One by one, Drak'honai officers realized . . . and yelled their bafflement.

These stolid ground troops, unassailable from above, unopposed below, were simply pouring over the hill to Mannenach's walls, trundling their siege tools. When they arrived there, they got to work.

It became a gale of wings and weapons. The Drak'honai plunged, hacked and stabbed at Trolwen's infantry—and were in their turn attacked from above, as his fliers whom they had briefly dispersed resumed formation. Meanwhile, *crunch, crunch, crunch*, rams ate at Mannenach; detachments on foot went around the town and down toward the harbor.

"Over there! Hit 'em again!" Wace heard all at once that he was yelling.

Something broke through the chaos overhead. An arrow-filled body crashed to earth. A live one followed it, a Drak'ho warrior with the air pistol-cracking under his wings. He came low and fast; one of Angrek's lads thrust a sword at him, missed, and had his brains spattered by the sailor's tomahawk.

Without time to know what had happened, Wace saw the creature before him. He struck, wildly, with his own stone ax. A wing-buffet knocked him to the ground. He bounced up, spitting blood, as the Drak'ho came about and dove again. His hands were empty—Suddenly the

Drak'ho screamed and clawed at an arrow in his throat, fluttered down and died.

Sandra nocked a fresh shaft. "I told you I would have some small use today," she said.

"I—" Wace reeled where he stood, looking at her.

"Go on," she said. "Help them break through. I will guard."

Her face was even paler than before, but there was a green in her eyes which burned.

He spun about and went back to directing his sappers. It was plain now that battering rams had been a mistake; they wouldn't get through mortared walls till Matthewsmas. He took everyone off the engines and put them to helping those who dug. With enough wooden shovels—or bare hands—they'd be sure to strike a tunnel soon.

From somewhere near, there lifted a clatter great enough to drown out the struggle around him. Wace jumped up on a ram's framework and looked over the heads of his engineers.

A body of Drak'honai had resorted to the ground themselves. They were not drilled in such tactics; but then, the Lannachska had had only the sketchiest training. By sheer sustained fury the Drak'honai were pushing their opponents back. From Trolwen's airy viewpoint, thought Wace, there must be an ugly dent in the line.

Where the devil were the machine guns?

Yes, here came one, bouncing along on a little cart. Two Lannachska began pumping the flywheel, a third aimed and operated the feed. Darts hosed across the Drak'honai. They broke up, took to the sky again. Wace hugged Sandra and danced her across the field.

Then hell boiled over to the roofs above him. His immediate corps had finally gotten to an underground passage and made it a way of entry. Driving the enemy before them, up to the top floors and out, they seized this one tower in a rush.

"Angrek!" panted Wace. "Get me up there!" Someone lowered a rope. He swarmed up it, with Sandra close behind. Standing on the ridgepole, he looked past stony parapets and turning millwheels, down to the bay. Trolwen's forces had taken the pier without much trouble. But they were getting no farther: a steady hail of fire-streams, oil bombs, and catapult missiles from the anchored rafts staved them off. Their own similar armament was outranged.

Sandra squinted against the wind, shifted north to lash her eyes to weeping, and pointed. "Eric—do you recognize that flag, on the largest of the vessels there?"

"Hm-m-m . . . let me see . . . yes, I do. Isn't that our old chum Delp's personal banner?"

"So it is. I am not sorry he has escaped punishment for the riot we made. But I would rather have someone else to fight, it would be safer."

"Maybe," said Wace. "But there's work to do. We have our toe hold in the city. Now we'll have to beat down doors and push out the enemy—room by room—and you're staying here!"

"I am not!"

Wace jerked his thumb at Angrek. "Detail a squad to take the lady back to the trains," he snapped.

"No!" yelled Sandra.

"You're too late," grinned Wace. "I arranged for this before we ever left Salmenbrok."

She swore at him—then suddenly, softly, she leaned over and murmured beneath the wind and the war-shrieks: "Come back hale, my friend."

He led his troopers into the tower.

Afterward he had no clear memory of the fight. It was a hard and bloody operation, ax and knife, tooth and fist, wing and tail, in narrow tunnels and cavelike rooms. He took blows, and gave them; once, for several seconds, he lay unconscious, and once he led a triumphant break-through into a wide assembly hall. He was not fanged, winged, or caudate himself, but he was heavier than any Diomedean; his blows seldom had to be repeated.

The Lannachska took Mannenach because they had—not training enough to make them good ground fighters—but enough to give them the *concept* of battle with immobilized wings. It was as revolting to Diomede-an instincts as the idea of fighting with teeth alone, hands bound, would be to a human; unprepared for it, the Drak'honai bolted and ran ratlike down the tunnels in search of open sky.

Hours afterward, staggering with exhaustion, Wace climbed to a flat roof at the other end of town. Tolk sat there waiting for him.

"I think . . . we have . . . it all now," gasped the human.

"And yet not enough," said Tolk haggardly. "Look at the bay."

Wace grabbed the parapet to steady himself.

There was no more pier, no more sheds at the waterfront—it all stood in one black smoke. But the rafts and canoes of Drak'ho had edged into the shallows, forming a bridge to shore; and over this the sailors were dragging dismounted catapults and flamethrowers.

"They too good a commander," said Tolk. "He has gotten the idea too fast, that our new methods have their own weaknesses."

"What is . . . Delp . . . going to do?" whispered Wace.

"Stay and see," suggested the Herald. "There is no way for us to help."

The Drak'honai were still superior in the air. Looking up toward a sky low and gloomy, rain clouds driving across angry gunmetal waters, Wace saw them moving to envelop the Lannacha air cover.

"You see," said Tolk, "it is true that their fliers cannot do much against our walkers—but the enemy chief has realized that the converse is also true."

Trolwen was too good a tactician himself to be cut up in such a fashion. Fighting every centimeter, his fliers retreated. After a while there was nothing in the sky but gray wrack.

Down on the ground, covered by arcing bombardment from the rafts, the sailors were setting up their mobile artillery. They had more of it than the Lannachska, and were better shots. A few infantry charges broke up in bloody ruin.

"Our machine guns they do not possess, of course," said Tolk. "But then, we do not have enough to make the difference."

Wace whirled on Angrek, who had joined him. "Don't stand here!" he cried. "Let's get down—rally our folk— seize those—It can be done, I tell you!"

"Theoretically, yes." Tolk nodded his lean head. "I can see where a person on the ground, taking advantage of every bit of cover, might squirm his way up to those catapults and flamethrowers, and tomahawk the operators. But in practice—well, we do not have such skill."

"Then what would you do?" groaned Wace.

"Let us first consider what will assuredly happen," said Tolk. "We have lost our trains; if not captured, they will be fired presently. Thus our supplies are gone. Our forces have been split, the fliers driven off, we groundlings left here. Trolwen cannot fight his way back to us, being outnumbered. We at Mannenach do outnumber our immediate opponents by quite a bit. But we cannot face their artillery.

"Therefore, to continue the fight, we must throw away our big shields and other new-fangled items, and revert to conventional air tactics. But this infantry is not well equipped for normal combat: we have few archers, for instance. Delp need only shelter on the rafts, behind his fire weapons, and for all our greater numbers we'll be unable to touch him. Meanwhile he will have us pinned here, cut off from food and material. The excess war goods your mill produced are valueless lying up in Salmenbrok. And there will certainly be strong reinforcements from the Fleet."

"To hell with that!" shouted Wace. "We have the town, don't we? We can hold it against them till they rot!"

"What can we eat while they are rotting?" said Tolk. "You are a good craftsman, Eart'a, but no student of war. The cold fact is, that Delp managed to split our forces, and therefore he has already won. I propose to cut our losses by retreating now, while we still can."

And then suddenly his manner broke, and he stooped

and covered his eyes with his wings. Wace saw that the Herald was growing old.

XIV

There was dancing on the decks, and jubilant chants rang across Sagna Bay to the enfolding hills. Up and down and around, in and out, the feet and the wings interwove till timbers trembled. High in the rigging, a piper skirled their melody; down below, a great overseer's drum which set the pace of the oars now thuttered their stamping rhythm. In a ring of wing-folded bodies, sweat-gleaming fur and eyes aglisten, a sailor whirled his female while a hundred deep voices roared the song:

> "... A-sailing, a-sailing,
> a-sailing to the Sea of Beer,
> fair lady, spread your sun-bright wings
> and sail with me!"

Delp walked out on the poop and looked down at his folk.

"We'll have many a new soul in the Fleet, sixty tendays hence," he laughed.

Rodonis held his hand, tightly: "I wish—" she began. "Yes?"

"Sometimes... oh, it's nothing—" The dancing pair fluttered upward, and another couple sprang out to beat the deck in their place; planks groaned under one more huge ale barrel, rolled forth to celebrate victory. "Sometimes I wish we could be like them."

"And live in the forecastle?" said Delp dryly.

"Well, no... of course not—"

"There's a price on the apartment, and the servants, and the bright clothes and leisure," said Delp. His eyes grew pale. "I'm about to pay some more of it."

His tail stroked briefly over her back, then he beat wings and lifted into the air. A dozen armed males followed him. So did the eyes of Rodonis.

Under Mannenach's battered walls the Drak'ho rafts lay crowded, the disorder of war not yet cleaned up in the haste to enjoy a hard-bought victory. Only the full-time warriors remained alert, though no one else would need much warning if there should be an attack. It was the boast of the forecastle that a Fleet sailor, drunk and with a female on his knee, could outfight any three foreigners sober.

Delp, flapping across calm waters under a high cloudless day-sky, found himself weighing the morale value of such a pride against the sharp practical fact that a Lannach'ho fought like ten devils. The Drak'honai had won *this* time.

A cluster of swift canoes floated aloof, the admiral's standard drooping from one garlanded masthead. T'heonax had come at Delp's urgent request, instead of making him go out to the main Fleet—which might mean that T'heonax was prepared to bury the old hatred. (Rodonis would tell her husband nothing of what had passed between them, and he did not urge her; but it was perfectly obvious she had forced the pardon from the heir in some way.) Far mòre likely, though, the new admiral had come to keep an eye on this untrusted captain, who had so upset things by turning the holding operation on which he had been contemptuously ordered, into a major victory. It was not unknown for a field commander with such prestige to hoist the rebel flag and try for the Admiralty.

Delp, who had no respect for T'heonax but positive reverence for the office, bitterly resented that imputation.

He landed on the outrigger as prescribed and waited until the Horn of Welcome was blown on board. It took longer than necessary. Swallowing anger, Delp flapped to the canoe and prostrated himself.

"Rise," said T'heonax in an indifferent tone. "Congratulations on your success. Now, you wish to confer with me?" He patted down a yawn. "Please do."

Delp looked around at the faces of officers, warriors,

and crewfolk. "In private, with the admiral's most trusted advisors, if it please him," he said.

"Oh? Do you consider what you have to say is that important?" T'heonax nudged a young aristocrat beside him and winked.

Delp spread his wings, remembered where he was, and nodded. His neck was so stiff it hurt. "Yes, sir, I do," he got out.

"Very well." T'heonax walked leisurely toward his cabin.

It was large enough for four, but only the two of them entered, with the young court favorite, who lay down and closed his eyes in boredom. "Does not the admiral wish advice?" asked Delp.

T'heonax smiled. "So you don't intend to give me advice yourself, captain?"

Delp counted mentally to twenty, unclenched his teeth, and said:

"As the admiral wishes. I've been thinking about our basic strategy, and the battle here has rather alarmed me—"

"I didn't know you were frightened."

"Admiral, I . . . never mind! Look here, sir, the enemy came within two fishhooks of beating us. They had the town. We've captured weapons from them equal or superior to our own, including a few gadgets I've never seen or heard of . . . and in incredible quantities, considering how little time they had to manufacture the stuff. Then too, they had these abominable new tactics, ground fighting—not as an incidental, like when we board an enemy raft, but as the main part of their effort!

"The only reason they lost was insufficient co-ordination between ground and air, and insufficient flexibility. They should have been ready to toss away their shields and take to the air in fully equipped squadrons at an instant's notice.

"And I don't think they'll neglect to remedy that fault, if we give them the chance."

T'heonax buffed his nails on a sleek-furred arm and

regarded them critically. "I don't like defeatists," he said.

"Admiral, I'm trying not to underestimate them. It's pretty clear they got all these new ideas from the Eart'honai. What else do the Eart'honai know?"

"Hm-m-m. Yes." T'heonax raised his head. A moment's uneasiness flickered in his gaze. "True. What do you propose?"

"They're off balance now," said Delp with rising eagerness. "I'm sure the disappointment has demoralized them. And of course, they've lost all that heavy equipment. If we hit them hard, we can end the war. What we must do is inflict a decisive defeat on their entire army. Then they'll have to give up, yield this country to us or die like insects when their birthing time comes."

"Yes." T'heonax smiled in a pleased way. "Like insects. Like dirty, filthy insects. We won't let them emigrate, captain."

"They deserve their chance," protested Delp.

"That's a question of high policy, captain, for me to decide."

"I'm . . . sorry, sir." After a moment: "But will the admiral, then, assign the bulk of our fighting forces to . . . to some reliable officer, with orders to hunt out the Lannach'honai?"

"You don't know just where they are?"

"They could be almost anywhere in the uplands, sir. That is, we have prisoners who can be made to guide us and give some information; Intelligence says their headquarters is a place called Psalmenbrox. But of course they can melt into the land." Delp shuddered. To him, whose world had been lonely islands and flat sea horizon, horror dwelt in the tilted mountains. "It has infinite cover to hide them. This will be no easy campaign."

"How do you propose to wage it at all?" asked T'heonax querulously. He did not like to be reminded, on top of a victory celebration and a good dinner, that there was still much death ahead of him.

"By forcing them to meet us in an all-out encounter, sir. I want to take our main fighting strength, and some native guides compelled to help us, and go from town to town up there, systematically razing whatever we find, burning the woods and slaughtering the game. Give them no chance for the large battues on which they must depend to feed their females and cubs. Sooner or later, and probably sooner, they will have to gather every male and meet us. That's when I'll break them."

"I see." T'heonax nodded. Then, with a grin: "And if they break you?"

"They won't."

"It is written: 'The Lodestar shines for no single nation.'"

"The admiral knows there's always some risk in war. But I'm convinced there's less danger in my plan than in hanging about down here, waiting for the Eart'honai to perfect some new devilment."

T'heonax's forefinger stabbed at Delp. "Ah-hah! Have you forgotten, their food will soon be gone? We can count them out."

"I wonder—"

"Be quiet!" shrilled T'heonax.

After a little time, he went on: "Don't forget, this enormous expeditionary force of yours would leave the Fleet ill defended. And without the Fleet, the rafts, we ourselves are finished."

"Oh, don't be afraid of attack, sir—" began Delp in an eager voice.

"Afraid!" T'heonax puffed himself out. "Captain, it is treason to hint that the admiral is a . . . is not fully competent."

"I didn't mean—"

"I shall not press the matter," said T'heonax smoothly. "However, you may either make full abasement, craving my pardon, or leave my presence."

Delp stood up. His lips peeled back from the fangs; the race memory of animal forebears who had been hunters bade him tear out the other's throat. T'heonax crouched, ready to scream for help.

Very slowly, Delp mastered himself. He half-turned to go. He paused, fists jammed into balls and the membrane of his wings swollen with blood.

"Well?" smiled T'heonax.

Like an ill-designed machine, Delp went down on his belly. "I abase myself," he mumbled. "I eat your offal. I declare that my fathers were the slaves of your fathers. Like a netted fish, I gasp for pardon."

T'heonax enjoyed himself. The fact that Delp had been so cleverly trapped between his pride and his wish to serve the Fleet made it all the sweeter.

"Very good, captain," said the admiral when the ceremony was done. "Be thankful I didn't make you do this publicly. Now let me hear your argument. I believe you were saying something about the protection of our rafts."

"Yes . . . yes, sir. I was saying . . . the rafts need not fear the enemy."

"Indeed? True, they lie well out at sea, but not too far to reach in a few hours. What's to prevent the Flock army from assembling, unknown to you, in the mountains, then attacking the rafts before you can come to our help?"

"I would only hope they do so, sir." Delp recovered a little enthusiasm. "But I'm afraid their leadership isn't that stupid. Since when . . . I mean . . . at no time in naval history, sir, has a flying force, unsupported from the water, been able to overcome a fleet. At best, and at heavy cost, it can capture one or two rafts . . . temporarily, as in the raid when they stole the Eart'honai. Then the other vessels move in and drive it off. You see, sir, flyers can't use the engines of war, catapults and flamethrowers and so on, which alone can reduce a naval organization. Whereas the raft crews can stand under shelters and fire upward, picking the fliers off at leisure."

"Of course." T'heonax nodded. "All this is so obvious as to be a gross waste of my time. But your idea is, I take it, that a small cadre of guards would suffice to hold off a Lannach'ho attack of any size."

"And, if we're lucky, keep the enemy busy out at sea till I could arrive with our main forces. But as I said, sir, they must have brains enough not to try it."

"You assume a great deal, captain," murmured T'heonax. "You assume, not merely that I will let you go into the mountains at all, but that I will put you in command."

Delp bent his head and drooped his wings. "Apology, sir."

"I think ... yes, I think it would be best if you just stayed here at Mannenach with your immediate flotilla."

"As the admiral wishes. Will he consider my plan, though?"

"Aeak'ha eat you!" snarled T'heonax. "I've no love for you, Delp, as well you know; but your scheme is good, and you're the best one to carry it through. I shall appoint you in charge."

Delp stood as if struck with a maul.

"Get out," said T'heonax. "We will have an official conference later."

"I thank my lord admiral—"

"Go, I said!"

When Delp had gone, T'heonax turned to his favorite. "Don't look so worried," he said. "I know what you're thinking. The fellow will win his campaign, and become still more popular, and somewhere along the line he will get ideas about seizing the Admiralty."

"I only wondered how my lord planned to prevent that," said the courtier.

"Simple enough." T'heonax grinned. "I know his type. As long as the war goes on, we've no danger of rebellion from him. So, let him break the Lannach'honai as he wishes. He'll pursue their remnants, to make sure of finishing the job. And in that pursuit—a stray arrow from somewhere—most regrettable—these things are easy to arrange. Yes."

XV

This atmosphere carried the dust particles which are the nuclei of water condensation to a higher, hence colder altitude. Thus Diomedes had more clouds and precipitation of every kind than Earth. On a clear night you saw fewer stars; on a foggy night you did not see at all.

Mist rolled up through stony dales, until the young High Summer became a dripping chill twilight. The hordes lairing about Salmenbrok mumbled in their hunger and hopelessness: now the sun itself had withdrawn from them.

No campfires glowed; the wood of this region had all been burned. And the hinterland had been scoured clean of game, unripe wild grains, the very worms and insects, eaten by these many warriors. Now, in an eerie dank dark, only the wind and the rushing glacial waters lived . . . and Mount Oborch, sullenly prophesying deep in the earth.

Trolwen and Tolk went from the despair of their chieftains, over narrow trails where fog smoked and the high thin houses stood unreal, to the mill where the Eart'ska worked.

Here alone, it seemed, existence remained—fires still burned, stored water came down flumes to turn the wind-abandoned wheels, movement went under flickering tapers as lathes chattered and hammers thumped. Somehow, in some impossible fashion, Nicholas van Rijn had roared down the embittered protests of Angrek's gang, and their factory was at work.

Working for what? thought Trolwen, in a mind as gray as the mist.

Van Rijn himself met them at the door. He folded massive arms on hairy breast and said: "How do you, my friends? Here it goes well, we have soon a many artillery pieces ready."

"And what use will they be?" said Trolwen. "Oh, yes, we have enough to make Salmenbrok well-nigh impregnable. Which means, we could hole up here and let the enemy ring us in till we starve."

"Speak not to me of starving." Van Rijn fished in his pouch, extracted a dry bit of cheese, and regarded it mournfully. "To think, this was not so long ago a rich delicious Swiss. Now, not to rats would I offer it." He stuffed it into his mouth and chewed noisily. "My problem of belly stoking is worse than yours. *Imprimis*, the high boiling point of water here makes this a world of very bad cooks, with no idea about controlled temperatures. *Secundus,* did your porters haul me through the air, that long lumpy way from Mannenach, to let me hunger into death?"

"I could wish we'd left you down there!" flared Trolwen.

"No," said Tolk. "He and his friends have striven, Flockchief."

"Forgive me," said Trolwen contritely. "It was only...I got the news...the Lannachska have just destroyed Eiseldrae."

"An empty town, *nie?*"

"A holy town. And they set afire the woods around it." Trolwen arched his back. "This can't go on! Soon, even if we should somehow win, the land will be too desolated to support us."

"I think still you can spare a few forests," said van Rijn. "This is not an overpopulated country."

"See here," said Trolwen in a harshening tone, "I've borne with you so far. I admit you're essentially right: that to fare out with all our power, for a decisive battle with the massed enemy, is to risk final destruction. But to sit here, doing nothing but make little guerrilla raids on their outposts, while they grind away our nation—that is to make certain we are doomed."

"We needed time," said van Rijn. "Time to modify the extra field pieces, making up for what we lost at Mannenach."

"Why? They're not portable, without trains. And to make matters worse, that motherless Delp has torn up the rails!"

"Oh, yes, they are portable. My young friend Wace has done a little redesigning. Knocked down, with females and cubs to help, everyone carrying a single small piece or two—we can tote a heavy battery of weapons, by damn!"

"I know. You've explained all this before. And I repeat: what will we use them against? If we set them up at some particular spot, the Lannachska need only avoid that spot. And we can't stay very long in any one place, because our numbers eat it barren." Trolwen drew a breath. "I did not come here to argue, Eart'a. I came from the General Council of Lannach, to tell you that Salmenbrok's food is exhausted—and so is the army's patience. We *must* go out and fight!"

"We shall," said van Rijn imperturbably. "Come, I will go talk at these puff-head councilors."

He stuck his head in the door: "Wace, boy, best you start to pack what we have. Soon we transport it."

"I heard you," said the younger man.

"Good. You make the work here, I make the politicking, so it goes along fine, *nie?*" Van Rijn rubbed shaggy fists, beamed, and shuffled off with Trolwen and Tolk.

Wace stared after him, into the blind fog-wall. "Yes," he said. "That's how it has been. We work, and he talks. Very equitable!"

"What do you mean?" Sandra raised her head from the table at which she sat marking gun parts with a small paintbrush. A score of females were working beside her.

"What I said. I wonder why I don't say it to his face. I'm not afraid of that fat parasite, and I don't want his mucking paycheck any more." Wace waved at the mill and its sooty confusion. "Do this, do that, he says, and then strolls off again. When I think how he's eating food which would keep *you* alive—"

"You do not understand?" She stared at him for a moment. "No, I think maybe you have been too busy, all the time here, to stop and think. And before then, you were a small-job man without the art of government, not?"

"What do you mean?" he echoed her. He regarded her with eyes washed-out and bleared by fatigue.

"Maybe later. Now we must hurry. Soon we will leave this town, and everything must be set to go."

This time she had found a place for her hands, in the ten or fifteen Earth-days since Mannenach. Van Rijn had demanded that everything—the excess war matériel, which there had luckily not been room enough to take down to battle—be made portable by air. That involved a certain amount of modification, so that the large wooden members could be cut up into smaller units, for reassembly where needed. Wace had managed that. But it would all be one chaos at journey's end, unless there was a system for identifying each item. Sandra had devised the markings and was painting them on.

Neither she nor Wace had stopped for much sleep. They had not even paused to wonder greatly what use there would be for their labor.

"Old Nick did say something about attacking the Fleet itself," muttered Wace. "Has he gone uncon? Are we supposed to land on the water and assemble our catapults?"

"Perhaps," said Sandra. Her tone was serene. "I do not worry so much any more. Soon it will be decided ... because we have food for just four Earth-weeks or less."

"We can last at least two months without eating at all," he said.

"But we will be weak." She dropped her gaze. "Eric—"

"Yes?" He left his mill-powered obsidian-toothed circular saw, and came over to stand above her. The dull rush light caught drops of fog in her hair, they gleamed like tiny jewels.

"Soon ... it will make no matter what I do ... there will be hard work, needing strength and skill I have not ... maybe fighting, where I am only one more bow, not a very strong bow even." Her fingernails whitened where she gripped her brush. "So when it comes to that, I will eat no more. You and Nicholas take my share."

"Don't be a fool," he said hoarsely.

She sat up straight, turned around and glared at him. Her pale cheeks reddened. "Do you not be the fool, Eric Wace," she snapped. "If I can give you and him just one extra week where you are strong—where your hunger does not keep you from even thinking clearly—then it will be myself I save too, perhaps. And if not, I have only lost one or two worthless weeks. Now get back to your machine!"

He watched her, for some small while, and his heart thuttered. Then he nodded and returned to his own work.

And down the trails to an open place of harsh grass, where the Council sat on a cliff's edge, van Rijn picked his steadily swearing way.

The elders of Lannach lay like sphinxes against a skyline gone formless gray, and waited for him. Trolwen went to the head of the double line, Tolk remained by the human.

"In the name of the All-Wise, we are met," said the commander ritually. "Let sun and moons illumine our minds. Let the ghosts of our grandmothers lend us their guidance. May I not shame those who flew before me, nor those who come after." He relaxed a trifle. "Well, my officers, it's decided we can't stay here. I've brought the Eart'a to advise us. Will you explain the alternatives to him?"

A gaunt, angry-eyed old Lannacha hunched his wings and spat: "First, Flockchief, why is he here at all?"

"By the commander's invitation," said Tolk smoothly.

"I mean... Herald, let's not twist words. You know what I mean. The Mannenach expedition was undertaken at his urging. It cost us the worst defeat in our history. Since then, he has insisted our main body stay here, idle, while the enemy ravages an undefended land. I don't see why we should take his advice."

Trolwen's eyes were troubled. "Are there further challenges?" he asked, in a very low voice.

An indignant mumble went down the lines. *"Yes ...yes... let him answer, if he can."*

Van Rijn turned turkey red and began to swell like a frog.

"The Eart'a has been challenged in Council," said Trolwen. "Does he wish to reply?"

He sat back then, waiting like the others.

Van Rijn exploded.

"Pest and damnation! Four million worms cocooning in hell! How long am I to be saddled with stupid ungratefuls? How many politicians and brass hats have You Up There plagued this universe with?" He waved his fists in the air and screamed. "Satan and sulfur! It is not to be stood! If you are all so hot to make suicides for yourselves, why does poor old van Rijn have to hold on to your coat tails the whole time? *Perbacco*, you stop insulting me or I stuff you down your own throats!" He advanced like a moving mountain, roaring at them. The nearest councilors flinched away.

"Eart'a... sir... officer... please!" whispered Trolwen.

When he had them sufficiently browbeaten, van Rijn said coldly: "All rights. I tell you, by damn. I give you good advices and you stupid them up and blame me—but I am a poor patient old man, not like when I was young and strong no, I suffer it with Christian meekness and keep on giving you good advices.

"I warned you and I warned you, do not hit Mannenach first, I warned you. I told you the rafts could come right up to its walls, and the rafts are the strength of the Fleet. I got down on these two poor old knees, begging and pleading with you first to take the key upland towns, but no, you would not listen to me. And still we *had* Mannenach, but the victory was stupided away... oh, if I had wings like an angel, so I could have led you in person! I would be cock-a-doodle-dooing on the admiral's masthead this moment, by holy Nicolai miter! That is why you take my advices, by damn—no, you take my orders! No more backward talking from you, or I wash my hands with you and make my own way home. From now on, if you want to keep living, when van Rijn says frog, you jump. Understanding?"

He paused. He could hear his own asthmatic wheezes... and the far unhappy mumble of the camp, and the cold wet clinking of water down alien rocks... nothing more in all the world.

Finally Trolwen said in a weak voice: "If... if the challenge is considered answered... we shall resume our business."

No one spoke.

"Will the Eart'a take the word?" asked Tolk at last. He alone appeared self-possessed, in the critical glow of one who appreciates fine acting.

Ja. I will say, I know we cannot remain here any more.

You ask why I kept the army on leash and let Captain Delp have his way." Van Rijn ticked it off on his fingers. "*Imprimis*, to attack him directly is what he wants; he can most likely beat us, since his force is bigger and not so hungry or discouraged. *Secundus*, he will not advance to Salmenbrok while we are all here, since we could bushwhack him; therefore, by staying put the army has gained me a chance to make ready our artillery pieces. *Tertius*, it is my hope that by this delay while I had the mill going, we have won the means of victory."

"What?" It barked from the throat of a councilor who forgot formalities.

"Ah." Van Rijn laid a finger to his imposing nose and winked. "We shall see. Maybe now you think even if I am a pitiful old weak tired man who should be in bed with hot toddies and a good cigar, still a Polesotechnic merchant is not just to sneeze at. So? Well, then. I propose we leave this land and head north."

A hubbub broke loose. He waited patiently for it to subside.

"Order!" shouted Trolwen. "Order!" He slapped the hard earth with his tail. "Quiet, there, officer! . . . Eart'a, there has been some talk of abandoning Lannach altogether—more and more of it, indeed, as our folk lose heart. We could still reach Swampy Kilnu in time to . . . to save most of our females and cubs at Birthtime. But it would be to give up our towns, our fields and forests— everything we have, everything our forebears labored for hundreds of years to create—to sink back into savagery, in a dark fever-haunted jungle, to become nothing—I myself will die in battle before making such a choice."

He drew a breath and hurled out: "But Kilnu is, at least, to the south. North of Achan, there is still ice!"

"Just so," said van Rijn.

"Would you have us starve and freeze on the Dawrnach glaciers? We can't land any further south than Dawrnach; the Fleet's scouts would be certain to spot us anywhere in Holmenach. Unless you want to fight the last fight in the archipelago—?"

"No," said van Rijn. "We should sneak up to this

Dawrnach place. We can pack a lunch—take maybe a ten-days' worth of food and fuel with us, as well as the armament—*nie?*"

"Well...yes...but even so—Are you suggesting we should attack the Fleet itself, the rafts, from the north? It would be an unexpected direction. But it would be just as hopeless."

"Surprise we will need for my plan," said van Rijn. "*Ja.* We cannot tell the army. One of them might be captured in some skirmish and made to tell the Drak'honai. Best maybe I not even tell you."

"Enough!" said Trolwen. "Let me hear your scheme."

Much later: "It won't work. Oh, it might well be technically feasible. But it's a political impossibility."

"Politics!" groaned van Rijn. "What is it this time?"

"The warriors...yes, and the females too, even the cubs, since it would be our whole nation which goes to Dawrnach. They must be told why we do so. Yet the whole scheme, as you admit, will be ruined if one person falls into enemy hands and tells what he knows under torture."

"But he need not know," said van Rijn. "All he need be told is, we spend a little while gathering food and wood to travel with. Then we are to pack up and go some other place, he has not been told where or why."

"We are not Drakska," said Trolwen angrily. "We are a free folk. I have no right to make so important a decision without submitting it to a vote."

"Hm-m-m maybe you could talk to them?" Van Rijn tugged his mustaches. "Orate at them. Persuade them to waive their right to know and help decide. Talk them into following you with no questions."

"No," said Tolk. "I'm a specialist in the arts of persuasion, Eart'a, and I've measured the limits of those arts. We deal less with a Flock now than a mob—cold, hungry, without hope, without faith in its leaders, ready to give up everything—or rush forth to blind battle—they haven't the morale to follow anyone into an unknown venture."

"Morale can be pumped in," said van Rijn. "I will try."

"You!"

"I am not so bad at oratings, myself, when there is need. Let me address them."

"They . . . they—" Tolk stared at him. Then he laughed, a jarringly sarcastic note. "Let it be done, Flockchief. Let's hear what words this Eart'a can find, so much better than our own."

And an hour later, he sat on a bluff, with his people a mass of shadow below him, and he heard van Rijn's bass come through the fog like thunder:

". . . I say only, think what you have here, and what they would take away from you:

> *This royal throne of kings, this sceptr'd isle,*
> *This earth of majesty, this seat of Mars,*
> *This other Eden, demi-paradise,*
> *This fortress built by Nature for herself*
> *Against infection and the hand of war,*
> *This happy breed . . ."*

"I don't comprehend all those words," whispered Tolk.

"Be still!" answered Trolwen. "Let me hear." There were tears in his eyes; he shivered.

". . . This blessed plot, this earth, this realm, this Lannach . . ."

The army beat its wings and screamed.

Van Rijn continued through adaptations of Pericles' funeral speech, "Scots Wha' Hae," and the Gettysburg Address. By the time he had finished discussing St. Crispin's Day, he could have been elected commander if he chose.

XVI

The island called Dawrnach lay well beyond the archipelago's end, several hundred kilometers north of Lannach. However swiftly the Flock flew, with pauses for rest on some bird-shrieking skerry, it was a matter of Earth-days to get there, and a physical nightmare for humans trussed in carrying nets. Afterward Wace's recollections of the trip were dim.

When he stood on the beach at their goal, his legs barely supporting him, it was small comfort.

High Summer had come here also, and this was not too far north; still, the air remained wintry and Tolk said no one had ever tried to live here. The Holmenach islands deflected a cold current out of The Ocean, up into the Iceberg Sea, and those bitter waters flowed around Dawrnach.

Now the Flock, wings and wings and wings dropping down from the sky until they hid its roiling grayness, had reached journey's conclusion: black sands, washed by heavy dark tides and climbing sheer up through permanent glaciers to the inflamed throat of a volcano. Thin straight trees were sprinkled over the lower slopes, between quaking tussocks; there were a few sea birds, to dip above the broken offshore ice-floes; otherwise the hidden sun threw its clotted-blood light on a sterile country.

Sandra shuddered. Wace was shocked to see how thin she had already grown. And now that they were here, in the last phase of their striving—belike of their lives—she intended to eat no more.

She wrapped her stinking coarse jacket more tightly about her. The wind caught snarled pale elflocks of her hair and fluttered them forlorn against black igneous cliffs. Around her crouched, walked, wriggled, and flapped ten thousand angry dragons: whistles and gutturals of unhuman speech, the cannon-crack of leathery wings, overrode the empty wind-whimper. As she rubbed her eyes, pathetically like a child, Wace saw that her once beautiful hands were bleeding where they had clung to the net, and that she shook with weariness.

He felt his heart twisted, and moved toward her. Nicholas van Rijn got there first, fat and greasy, with a roar for comfort: "So, by jolly damn, now we are here and soon I get you home again to a hot bath. Holy St. Dismas, right now I smell you three kilometers upwind!"

Lady Sandra Tamarin, heiress to the Grand Duchy of

Hermes, gave him a ghostly smile. "If I could rest for a little—" she whispered.

"*Ja, ja*, we see." Van Rijn stuck two fingers in his mouth and let out an eardrum-breaking blast. It caught Trolwen's attention. "You there! Find her here a cave or something and tuck her in."

"I?" Trolwen bridled. "I have the Flock to see to!"

"You heard me, pot head." Van Rijn stumped off and buttonholed Wace. "Now, then. You are ready to begin work? Round up your crew, however many you need to start."

"I—" Wace backed away. "Look here, it's been I don't know how many hours since our last stop, and—"

Van Rijn spat. "And how many weeks makes it since *I* had a smoke or even so much a little glass Genever, ha? You have no considerations for other people." He pointed his beak heavenward and screamed: "Do I have to do everything? Why have You Up There filled up the galaxy with no-good loafers? It is not to be stood!"

"Well... well—" Wace saw Trolwen leading Sandra off, to find a place where she could sleep, forgetting cold and pain and loneliness for a few niggard hours. He struck a fist into his palm and said: "All right! But what will you be doing?"

"I must organize things, by damn. First I see Trolwen about a gang to cut trees and make masts and yards and oars. Meanwhiles all this canvas we have brought along has got to somehow be made in sails; and there are the riggings; and also we must fix up for eating and shelter— Bah! These is details. It is not right I should be bothered. Details, I hire ones like you for."

"Is life anything but details?" snapped Wace.

Van Rijn's small gray eyes studied him for a moment. "So," rumbled the merchant, "it gives back talks from you too, ha? You think maybe just because I am old and weak, and do not stand so much the hardships like when I was young... maybe I only leech off your work, *nie*? Now is too small time for beating sense into your head. Maybe you learn for yourself." He snapped his fingers. "Jump!"

• • •

Wace went off, damning himself for not giving the old pig a fist in the stomach. He would, too, come the day! Not now . . . unfortunately, van Rijn had somehow oozed into a position where it was him the Lannachska looked up to . . . instead of Wace, who did the actual work—Was that a paranoid thought? No.

Take this matter of the ships, for instance. Van Rijn had pointed out that an island like Dawrnach, loaded with pack ice and calving glaciers, afforded plenty of building material. Stone chisels would shape a vessel as big as any raft in the Fleet, in a few hours' work. The most primitive kind of blowtorch, an oil lamp with a bellows, would smooth it off. A crude mast and rudder could be planted in holes cut ior the purpose: water, refreezing, would be a strong cement. With most of the Flock, males, females, old, young, made one enormous labor force for the project, a flotilla comparable in numbers to the whole Fleet could be made in a week.

If an engineer figured out all the practical procedure. How deep a hole to step your mast in? Is ballast needed? Just how do you make a nice clean cut in an irregular ice block hundreds of meters long? How about smoothing the bottom to reduce drag? The material was rather friable; it could be strengthened considerably by dashing bucketsful of mixed sawdust and sea water over the finished hull, letting this freeze as a kind of armor—but what proportions?

There was no time to really test these things. Somehow, by God and by guess, with every element against him, Eric Wace was expected to produce.

And van Rijn? What did van Rijn contribute? The basic idea, airily tossed off, apparently on the assumption that Wace was Aladdin's jinni. Oh, it was quite a flash of imaginative insight, no one could deny that. But imagination is cheap.

Anyone can say: "What we need is a new weapon, and we can make it from such-and-such unprecedented materials." But it will remain an idle fantasy until somebody shows up who can figure out *how* to make the needed weapon.

So, having enslaved his engineer, van Rijn strolled around, jollying some of the Flock and bullying some of the others—and when he had them all working their idiotic heads off, he rolled up in a blanket and went to sleep!

XVII

Wace stood on the deck of the *Rijstaffel* and watched his enemy come over the world's rim.

Slowly, he reached into the pouch at his side. His hand closed on a chunk of stale bread and a slab of sausage. It was the last Terrestrial food remaining: for Earth-days, now, he had gone on a still thinner ration than before, so that he could enter this battle with something in his stomach.

He found that he didn't want it after all.

Surprisingly little cold breathed up from underfoot. The warm air over the Sea of Achan wafted the ice-chill away. He was less astonished that there had been no appreciable melting in the week he estimated they had been creeping southward; he knew the thermal properties of water.

Behind him, primitive square sails, lashed to yardarms of green wood on overstrained one-piece masts, bellied in the north wind. These ice ships were tubby, but considerably less so than a Drak'ho raft; and with some unbelievable talent for tyranny, van Rijn had gotten reluctant Lannachska to work under frigid sea water, cutting the bottoms into a vaguely streamlined shape. Now, given the power of a Diomedean breeze, Lannach's war fleet waddled through Achan waves at a good five knots.

Though the hardest moment, Wace reflected, had not been while they worked their hearts out to finish the craft. It had come afterward, when they were almost ready to leave and the winds turned contrary. For a period measured in Earth-days, thousands of Lannachska huddled soul-sick under freezing rains, ranging after fish and bird rookeries to feed cubs that cried with hunger. Councilors and clan leaders had argued that this was a war on the Fates: there could be no choice but to give up and seek out Swampy Kilnu. Somehow, blustering, whining, pleading, promising—in a few cases, bribing with what he had won at dice—van Rijn had held them on Dawrnach.

Well—it was over with.

The merchant came out of the little stone cabin, walked over the gravel-strewn deck past crouching war-engines and heaped missiles, till he reached the bows where Wace stood.

"Best you eat," he said. "Soon gives no chance."

"I'm not hungry," said Wace.

"So, no?" Van Rijn grabbed the sandwich out of his fingers. "Then, by damn, I am!" He began cramming it between his teeth.

Once again he wore a double set of armor, but he had chosen one weapon only for this occasion, an outsize stone ax with a meter-long handle. Wace carried a smaller tomahawk and a shield. Around the humans, it bristled with armed Lannachska.

"They're making ready to receive us, all right," said Wace. His eyes sought out the gaunt enemy war-canoes, beating upwind.

"You expected a carpet with acres and acres, like they say in America? I bet you they spotted us from the air hours ago. Now they send messengers hurry-like back to their army in Lannach." Van Rijn held up the last fragment of meat, kissed it reverently, and ate it.

Wace's eyes traveled backward. This was the flagship—chosen as such when it turned out to be the fastest—and had the forward position in a long wedge. Several score grayish-white, ragged-sailed, helter-skelter little vessels wallowed after. They were outnumbered and outgunned by the Drak'ho rafts, of course; they just had to hope the odds weren't too great. The much lower freeboard did not matter to a winged race, but it would be important that their crews were not very skilled sailors—

But at least the Lannachska were fighters. Winged

tigers by now, thought Wace. The southward voyage had rested them, and trawling had provided the means to feed them, and the will to battle had kindled again. Also, though they had a smaller navy, they probably had more warriors, even counting Delp's absent army.

And they could afford to be reckless. Their females and young were still on Dawrnach—with Sandra, grown so white and quiet—and they had no treasures along to worry about. For cargo they bore just their weapons and their hate.

From the clouds of airborne, Tolk the Herald came down. He braked on extended wings, slithered to a landing, and curved back his neck swan-fashion to regard the humans.

"Does it all go well down here?" he asked.

"As well as may be," said van Rijn. "Are we still bearing on the pest-rotten Fleet?"

"Yes. It's not many buaska away now. Barely over your sea-level horizon, in fact; you'll raise it soon. They're using sail and oars alike, trying to get out of our path, but they'll not achieve it if we keep this wind and those canoes don't delay us."

"No sign of the army in Lannach?"

"None yet. I daresay what's-his-name...the new admiral that we heard about from those prisoners...has messengers scouring the mountains. But that's a big land up there. It will take time to locate him." Tolk snorted professional scorn. "Now I would have had constant liaison, a steady two-way flow of Whistlers."

"Still," said van Rijn, "we must expect them soon, and then gives hell's safety valve popping off."

"Are you certain we can—"

"I am certain of nothings. Now get back to Trolwen and oversee."

Tolk nodded and hit the air again.

Dark purplish water curled in white feathers, beneath a high heaven where clouds ran like playful mountains, tinted rosy by the sun. Not many kilometers off, a small island rose sheer; through a telescope, Wace could count the patches of yellow blossom nodding under tall bluish conifers. A pair of young Whistlers dipped and soared over his head, dancing like the clan banners being unfurled in the sky. It was hard to understand that the slim carved boats racing so near bore fire and sharpened stones.

"Well," said van Rijn, "here begins our fun. Good St. Dismas, stand by me now."

"St. George would be a little more appropriate, wouldn't he?" asked Wace.

"You may think so. Me, I am too old and fat and cowardly to call on Michael or George or Olaf or any like those soldierly fellows. I feel more at home, me, with saints not so bloody energetic, Dismas or my own good namesake who is so kind to travelers."

"And is also the patron of highway men," remarked Wace. He wished his tongue wouldn't get so thick and dry on him. He felt remote, somehow...not really afraid...but his knees were rubbery.

"Ha!" boomed van Rijn. "Good shootings, boy!"

The forward ballista on the *Rijstaffel*, with a whine and a thump, had smacked a half-ton stone into the nearest canoe. The boat cracked like a twig; its crew whirled up, a squad from Trolwen's aerial command pounced, there was a moment's murderous confusion and then the Drak'honai had stopped existing.

Van Rijn grabbed the astonished ballista captain by the hands and danced him over the deck, bawling out,

"Du bist mein Sonnenschein, mein einzig Sonnenschein, du machst mir fröhlich—"

Another canoe swung about, close-hauled. Wace saw its flamethrower crew bent over their engine and hurled himself flat under the low wall surrounding the ice deck.

The burning stream hit that wall, splashed back, and spread itself on the sea. It could not kindle frozen water, nor melt enough of it to notice. Sheltered amidships, a hundred Lannacha archers sent an arrow-sleet up, to arc under heaven and come down on the canoe.

Wace peered over the wall. The flamethrower pumpman seemed dead, the hoseman was preoccupied with a transfixed wing . . . no steersman either, the canoe's boom slatted about in a meaningless arc while its crew huddled—"Dead ahead!" he roared. "Ram them!"

The Lannacha ship trampled the dugout underfoot.

Drak'ho canoes circled like wolves around a buffalo herd, using their speed and maneuverability. Several darted between ice vessels, to assail from the rear; others went past the ends of the wedge formation. It was not quite a one-sided battle—arrows, catapult bolts, flung stones, all hurt Lannachska; oil jugs arced across the water, exploding on ice decks; now and then a fire stream ignited a sail.

But winged creatures with a few buckets could douse burning canvas. During that entire phase of the engagement, only one Lannacha craft was wholly dismasted, and its crew simply abandoned it, parceling themselves out among other vessels. Nothing else could catch fire, except live flesh, which has always been the cheapest article in war.

Several canoes, converging on a single ship, tried to board. They were nonetheless outnumbered, and paid heavily for the attempt. Meanwhile Trolwen, with absolute air mastery, swooped and shot and hammered.

Drak'ho's canoes scarcely hindered the attack. The dugouts were rammed, broken, set afire, brushed aside by their unsinkable enemy.

By virtue of being first, of having more or less punched through the line, the *Rijstaffel* met little opposition. What there was, was beaten off by catapult, ballista, fire pot, and arrows: long-range gunnery. The sea itself burned and smoked behind; ahead lay the great rafts.

When those sails and banners came into view, Wace's dragon crewmen began to sing the victory song of the Flock.

"A little premature, aren't they?" he cried above the racket.

"Ah," said van Rijn quietly, "let them make fun for now. So many will soon be down, blind among the fishes, *nie?*"

"I suppose—" Hastily, as if afraid of what he had done

merely to save his own life, Wace said: "I like that melody, don't you? It's rather like some old American folk songs. *John Harty*, say."

"Folk songs is all right if you should want to play you are Folk in great big capitals," snorted van Rijn. "I stick with Mozart, by damn."

He stared down into the water, and a curious wistfulness tinged his voice. "I always hoped maybe I would understand Bach some day, before I die, old Johann Sebastian who talked with God in mathematics. I have not the brains, though, in this dumb old head. So maybe I ask only one more chance to listen at *Eine Kleine Nachtmusik*."

There was an uproar in the Fleet. Slowly and ponderously, churning the sea with spider-leg oars, the rafts were giving up their attempt at evasion. They were pulling into war formation.

Van Rijn waved angrily at a Whistler. "Quick! You get upstairs fast, and tell that crockhead Trolwen not to bother air-covering us against the canoes. Have him attack the rafts. Keep them busy, by hell! Don't let messengers flappity-flap between enemy captains so they can organize!"

As the young Lannacha streaked away, the merchant tugged his goatee—almost lost by now in a dirt-stiffened beard—and snarled: "Great hairy honeypots! How long do I have to do all the thinkings? Good St. Nicholas, you bring me an officer staff with brains between the ears, instead of clabbered oatmeal, and I build you a cathedral on Mars! You hear me?"

"Trolwen is in the midst of a fight up there," protested Wace. "You can't expect him to think of everything."

"Maybe not," conceded van Rijn grudgingly. "Maybe I am the only one in the galaxy who makes no mistakes."

Horribly near, the massed rafts became a storm when Trolwen took his advice. Bat-winged devils sought each other's lives through one red chaos. Wace thought his own ships' advance must be nearly unnoticed in that whirling, shrieking destruction.

"They're *not* getting integrated!" he said, beating his

fist on the wall. "Before God, they're not!"

A Whistler landed, coughing blood; there was a monstrous bruise on his side. "Over yonder...Tolk the Herald says...empty spot...drove wedge in Fleet—" The thin body arced and then slid inertly to the deck. Wace stooped, taking the unhuman youth in his arms. He heard blood gurgle in lungs pierced by the broken ends of ribs.

"Mother, mother," gasped the Whistler. "He hit me with an ax. Make it stop hurting, mother."

Presently he died.

Van Rijn cursed his awkward vessel into a course change—not more than a few degrees, it wasn't capable of more, but as the nearer rafts began to loom above the ice deck, it could be seen that there was a wide gap in their line. Trolwen's assault had so far prevented its being closed. Red-stained water, littered with dropped spears and bows, pointed like a hand toward the admiral's floating castle.

"In there!" bawled van Rijn. "Clobber them! Eat them for breakfast!"

A catapult bolt came whirring over the wall, ripped through his sleeve and showered ice chips where it struck. Then three streams of liquid fire converged on the *Rijstaffel.*

Flame fingers groped their way across the deck, one Lannacha lay screaming and charring where they had touched him, and found the sails. It was no use to pour water this time: oil-drenched, mast and rigging and canvas became one great torch.

Van Rijn left the helmsman he had been swearing at and bounded across the deck, slipped where some of it had melted, skated on his broad bottom till he fetched up against a wall, and crawled back to his feet calling down damnation on the cosmos. Up to the starboard shrouds he limped, and his stone ax began gnawing the cordage. "Here!" he yelled. "Fast! Help me, you jellybones! Quick, have you got fur on the brain, quick before we drift past!"

Wace, directing the ballista crew, which was stoning a nearby raft, understood only vaguely. Others were more ready than he. They swarmed to van Rijn and hewed. He himself sought the racked oil bombs and broke one at the foot of the burning mast.

Its socket melted, held up only by the shrouds, the enormous torch fell to port when the starboard lines were slashed. It struck the raft there; flames ran from it, beating back frantic Drak'ho crewmen who would push it loose; rigging caught; timbers began to char. As the *Rijstaffel* drifted away, that enemy vessel turned into a single bellowing pyre.

Now the ice ship was nearly uncontrollable, driven by momentum and chance currents deeper into the confused Fleet. But through the gap which van Rijn had so ardently widened, the rest of the Lannacha craft pushed. War-flames raged between floating monsters—but wood will burn and ice will not.

Through a growing smoke-haze among darts and arrows that rattled down from above, on a deck strewn with dead and hurt but still filled by the revengeful hale, Wace trod to the nearest bomb crew. They were preparing to ignite another raft as soon as the ship's drift brought them into range.

"No," he said.

"What?" The captain turned a sooty face to him, crest adroop with weariness. "But sir, they'll be pumping fire at us!"

"We can stand that," said Wace. "We're pretty well sheltered by our walls. I don't want to burn that raft. I want to capture it!"

The Diomedean whistled. Then his wings spread and his eyes flared and he asked: "May I be the first on board it?"

Van Rijn passed by, hefting his ax. He could not have heard what was said, but he rumbled: "*Ja.* I was just about to order this. We can use us a transportation that maneuvers."

The word went over the ship. Its slippery deck darkened with armed shapes that waited. Closer and closer, the wrought ice-floe bore down on the higher and more massive raft. Fire, stones, and quarrels reached out for the Lannachska. They endured it, grimly. Wace sent a Whistler up to Trolwen to ask for help; a flying detachment silenced the Drak'ho artillery with arrows.

Trolwen still had overwhelming numerical superiority. He could choke the sky with his warriors, pinning the Drak'honai to their decks to await sea-borne assault. So far, thought Wace, Diomedes' miserly gods had been smiling on him. It couldn't last much longer.

He followed the first Lannacha wave, which had flown to clear a bridgehead on the raft. He sprang from the ice-floe when it bumped to a halt, grasped a massive timber, and scrambled up the side. When he reached the top and unlimbered his tomahawk and shield, he found himself in a line of warriors. Smoke from the burnings elsewhere stung his eyes; only indistinctly did he see the defending Drak'honai, pulled into ranks ahead of him and up on the higher decks.

Had the yelling and tumbling about overhead suddenly redoubled?

A stumpy finger tapped him. He turned around to meet van Rijn's porcine gaze.

"Whoof and whoo! What for a climb that was! Better I should have stayed, *nie?* Well, boy, we are on our own now. Tolk just sent me word, the whole Drak'ho Expeditionary Force is in sight and lolloping hereward fast."

XVIII

Briefly, Wace felt sick. Had it all come to this, a chipped flint in his skull after Delp's army had beaten off the Lannachska?

Then he remembered standing on the cold black beach of Dawrnach, shortly before they sailed, and wondering aloud if he would ever again speak with Sandra. "I'll have the easy part if we lose," he had said. "It'll be over quickly enough for me. But you—"

She gave him a look that brimmed with pride, and answered: "What makes you think you can lose?"

He hefted his weapon. The lean winged bodies about him hissed, bristled, and glided ahead.

These were mostly troopers from the Mannenach attempt; every ice ship bore a fair number who had been taught the elements of ground fighting. And on the whole trip south to find the Fleet, van Rijn and the Lannacha captains had exhorted them: "Do not join our aerial forces. Stay on the decks when we board a raft. This whole plan hinges on how many rafts we can seize or destroy. Trolwen and his air squadrons will merely be up there to support *you*."

The idea took root reluctantly in any Diomedean brain. Wace was not at all certain it wouldn't die within the next hour, leaving him and van Rijn marooned on hostile timbers while their comrades soared up to a pointless sky battle. But he had no choice, save to trust them now.

He broke into a run. The screech that his followers let out tore at his eardrums.

Wings threshed before him. Instinctively, the un-trained Drak'ho lines were breaking up. Through geological eras, the only sane thing for a Diomedean to do had been to get above an attacker. Wace stormed on where they had stood.

Lifting from all the raft, enemy sailors stooped on these curious unflying adversaries. A Lannacha forgot himself, flapped up, and was struck by three meteor bodies. He was hurled like a broken puppet into the sea. The Drak'honai rushed downward.

And they met spears which snapped up like a picket fence. No few of Lannach's one-time ground troopers had rescued their basketwork shields from the last retreat and were now again transformed into artificial turtles. The rest fended off the aerial assault—and the archers made ready.

Wace heard the sinister whistle rise behind him, and saw fifty Drak'honai fall.

Then a dragon roared in his face, striking with a knife-toothed rake. Wace caught the blow on his shield. It shuddered in his left arm, numbing the muscles. He lashed out a heavy-shod foot, caught the hard belly and heard the wind leave the Drak'ho. His tomahawk rose and fell with a dull chopping sound. The Diomedean fluttered away, pawing at a broken wing.

Wace hurried on. The Drak'honai, stunned by the boarding party's tactics, were now milling around overhead out of bowshot. Females snarled in the forecastle doors, spreading wings to defend their screaming cubs. They were ignored: the object was to capture the raft's artillery.

Someone up there must have seen what was intended. His hawk-shriek and hawk-stoop were ended by a Lannacha arrow; but then an organized line peeled off the Drak'honai mass, plummeted to the forecastle deck, and took stance before the main battery of flamethrowers and ballistae.

"So!" rumbled van Rijn. "They make happy fun games after all. We see about this!"

He broke into an elephantine trot, whirling the great mallet over his head. A slingstone bounced off his leather-decked abdomen, an arrow ripped along one cheek, blowgun darts pincushioned his double cuirass. He got a boost from two winged guards, up the sheer ladderless bulkhead of the forecastle. Then he was in among the defenders.

"Je maintiendrai!" he bawled, and stove in the head of the nearest Drak'ho. *"God send the right!"* he shouted, stamping on the shaft of a rake that clawed after him. *"Fram, fram, Kristmenn, Krossmenn, Kongsmenn!"* he bellowed, drumming on the ribs of three warriors who ramped close. *"Heineken's Bier!"* he trumpeted, turning to wrestle with a winged shape that fastened onto his back, and wringing its neck.

Wace and the Lannachska joined him. There was an interval with hammer and thrust and the huge bone-breaking buffets of wing and tail. The Drak'honai broke. Van Rijn sprang to the flamethrower and pumped. "Aim the hose!" he panted. "Flush them out, you rust-infested heads!" A gleeful Lannacha seized the ceramic nozzle, pressed the hardwood ignition piston, and squirted burning oil upward.

Down on the lower decks, ballistae began to thump, catapults sang and other flamethrowers licked. A party from the ice ship reassembled one of their wooden machine guns and poured darts at the last Drak'ho counterassault.

A female shape ran from the forecastle. "It's our husbands they kill!" she shrieked. "Destroy them!"

Van Rijn leaped off the upper deck, a three-meter fall. Planks thundered and groaned when he hit them. Puffing, waving his arms, he got ahead of the frantic creature. "Get back!" he yelled in her own language. "Back inside! Shoo! Scat! Want to leave your cubs unprotected! I eat young Drak'honai! With horseradish!"

She wailed and scuttled back to shelter. Wace let out a gasp. His skin was sodden with sweat. It had not been too serious a danger, perhaps... in theory, a female mob could have been massacred under the eyes of its young... but who could bring himself to that? Not Eric Wace, certainly. Better give up and take one's spear thrust like a gentleman.

He realized, then, that the raft was his.

Smoke still thickened the air too much for him to see very well what was going on elsewhere. Now and then, through a breach in it, appeared some vision: a raft set unquenchably afire, abandoned; an ice vessel, cracked, dismasted, arrow-swept, still bleakly slugging it out; another Lannacha ship laying to against a raft, another boarding party; the banner of a Lannacha clan blowing in sudden triumph on a foreign masthead. Wace had no idea how the sea fight as a whole was going—how many ice craft had been raked clean, deserted by discouraged crews, seized by Drak'ho counterattack, left drifting uselessly remote from the enemy.

It had been perfectly clear, he thought—van Rijn had said it bluntly enough to Trolwen and the Council—that the smaller, less well equipped, virtually untrained Lannacha navy would have no chance whatsoever of decisively whipping the Fleet. The crucial phase of this battle was not going to involve stones or flames.

He looked up. Beyond the spars and lines, where the

haze did not reach, heaven lay unbelievably cool. The formations of war, weaving in and about, were so far above him that they looked like darting swallows.

Only after minutes did his inexpert eyes grasp the picture.

With most of his force down among the rafts, Trolwen was ridiculously outnumbered in the air as soon as Delp arrived. On the other hand, Delp's folk had been flying for hours to get here; they were no match individually for well-rested Lannachska. Realizing this, each commander used his peculiar advantage: Delp ordered unbreakable mass charges, Trolwen used small squadrons which swooped in, snapped wolfishly, and darted back again. The Lannachska retreated all the time, except when Delp tried to send a large body of warriors down to relieve the rafts. Then the entire, superbly integrated air force at Trolwen's disposal would smash into that body. It would disperse when Delp brought in reinforcements, but it had accomplished its purpose—to break up the formation and checkrein the seaward movement.

So it went, for some timeless time in the wind under the High Summer sun. Wace lost himself, contemplating the terrible beauty of death winged and disciplined. Van Rijn's voice pulled him grudgingly back to luckless unflying humanness.

"Wake up! Are you making dreams, maybe, like you stand there with your teeth hanging out and flapping in the breeze? Lightnings and Lucifer! If we want to keep this raft, we have to make some use with it, by damn. You boss the battery here and I go tell the helmsman what to do. So!" He huffed off, like an ancient steam locomotive in weight and noise and sootiness.

They had beaten off every attempt at recapture, until the expelled crew went wrathfully up to join Delp's legions. Now, awkwardly handling the big sails, or ordered protestingly below to the sweeps, van Rijn's gang got their new vessel into motion. It grunted its way across a roiled, smoky waste of water, until a Drak'ho craft loomed before it. Then the broadsides cut loose, the arrows went like sleet, and crew locked with crew in troubled air midway between the thuttering rafts.

Wace stood his ground on the foredeck, directing the fire of its banked engines: stones, quarrels, bombs, oilstreams, hurled across a few meters to shower splinters and char wood as they struck. Once he organized a bucket brigade, to put out the fire set by an enemy hit. Once he saw one of his new catapults, and its crew, smashed by a two-ton rock, and forced the survivors to lever that stone into the sea and rejoin the fight. He saw how sails grew tattered, yards sagged drunkenly, bodies heaped themselves on both vessels after each clumsy round. And he wondered, in a dim part of his brain, why life had no more sense, anywhere in the known universe, than to be forever tearing itself.

Van Rijn did not have the quality of crew to win by sheer bombardment, like a neolithic Nelson. Nor did he especially want to try boarding still another craft; it was all his little tyro force could do to man and fight this one. But he pressed stubbornly in, holding the helmsmen to their collision course, going below-decks himself to keep exhausted Lannachska at their heavy oars. And his raft wallowed its way through a firestorm, a stonestorm, a storm of living bodies, until it was almost on the enemy vessel.

Then horns hooted among the Drak'honai, their sweeps churned water and they broke from their place in the Fleet's formation to disengage.

Van Rijn let them go, vanishing into the hazed masts and cordage that reached for kilometers around him. He stumped to the nearest hatch, went down through the poop-deck cabins and so out on the main deck. He rubbed his hands and chortled. "Aha! We gave him a little scare, eh, what say? He'll not come near any of our boats soon again, him!"

"I don't understand, Councilor," said Angrek, with immense respect. "We had a smaller crew, with far less skill. He ought to have stayed put, or even moved in on us. He could have wiped us out, if we didn't abandon ship altogether."

"Ah!" said van Rijn. He wagged a sausagelike finger.

"But you see, my young and innocent one, he is carrying females and cubs, as well as many valuable tools and other goods. His whole life is on his raft. He dare not risk its destruction; we could so easy set it hopeless afire, even if we can't make capture. Ha! It will be a frosty morning in hell, when they outthink Nicholas van Rijn, by damn!"

"Females—" Angrek's eyes shifted to the forecastle. A lickerish light rose in them.

"After all," he murmured, "it's not as if they were *our* females—"

A score or more Lannachska were already drifting in that same direction, elaborately casual—but their wings were held stiff and their tails twitched. It was noteworthy that more of the recent oarsmen were in that group than any other class.

Wace came running to the forecastle's edge. He leaned over it, cupped his hands and shouted: "Freeman van Rijn! Look upstairs!"

"So." The merchant raised pouched little eyes, blinked, sneezed, and blew his craggy nose. One by one, the Lannachska resting on scarred bloody decks lifted their own gaze skyward. And a stillness fell on them.

Up there, the struggle was ending.

Delp had finally assembled his forces into a single irresistible mass and taken them down as a unit to sea level. There they joined the embattled raft crews—one raft at a time. A Lannachska boarding party, so suddenly and grossly outnumbered, had no choice but to flee, abandon even its own ice ship, and go up to Trolwen.

The Drak'honai made only one attempt to recapture a raft which was fully in Lannacha possession. It cost them gruesomely. The classic dictum still held, that purely airborne forces were relatively impotent against a well-defended unit of the Fleet.

Having settled in this decisive manner exactly who held every single raft, Delp reorganized and led a sizable portion of his troops aloft again to engage Trolwen's augmented air squadrons. If he could clear them away, then, given the craft remaining to Drak'ho plus total sky domination, Delp could regain the lost vessels.

But Trolwen did not clear away so easily. And, while naval fights went on below, a vicious combat traveled through the clouds. Both were indecisive.

Such was the overall view of events, as Tolk related it to the humans an hour or so later. All that could be seen from the water was that the sky armies were separating. They hovered and wheeled, dizzyingly high overhead, two tangled masses of black dots against ruddy-tinged cloud banks. Doubtless threats, curses, and boasts were tossed across the wind between them, but there were no more arrows.

"What is it?" gasped Angrek. "What's happening up there?"

"A truce, of course," said van Rijn. He picked his teeth with a fingernail, hawked, and patted his abdomen complacently. "They was making nowheres, so finally Tolk got someone through to Delp and said let's talk this over, and Delp agreed."

"But—we can't—you can't bargain with a Draka! He's not . . . he's *alien!*"

A growl of goose-pimpled loathing assent went along the weary groups of Lannachska.

"You can't reason with a filthy wild animal like that," said Angrek. "All you can do is kill it. Or it will kill you!"

Van Rijn cocked a brow at Wace, who stood on the deck above him, and said in Anglic: "I thought maybe we could tell them now that this truce is the only objective of all our fighting so far—but maybe not just yet, *nie?*"

"I wonder if we'll ever dare admit it," said the younger man.

"We will have to admit it, this very day, and hope we do not get stuffed alive with red peppers for what we say. After alls, we did make Trolwen and the Council agree. But then, they are very hard-boiled-egg heads, them." Van Rijn shrugged. "Comes now the talking. So far we have had it soft. This is the times that fry men's souls. Ha! Have you got the nerve to see it through?"

XIX

Approximately one tenth of the rafts lumbered out of the general confusion and assembled a few kilometers away. They were joined by such ice ships as were still in service. The decks of all were jammed with tensely waiting warriors. These were the vessels held by Lannach.

Another tenth or so still burned, or had been torn and beaten by stonefire until they were breaking up under Achan's mild waves. These were the derelicts, abandoned by both nations. Among them were many dugouts, splintered, broken, kindled, or crewed only by dead Drak'honai.

The remainder drew into a mass around the admiral's castle. This was no group of fully manned, fully equipped rafts and canoes; no crew had escaped losses, and a good many vessels were battered nearly into uselessness. If the Fleet could get half their normal fighting strength back into action, they would be very, very lucky.

Nevertheless, this would be almost three times as many units as the Lannachska now held *in toto*. The numbers of males on either side were roughly equal; but, with more cargo space, the Drak'honai had more ammunition. Each of their vessels was also individually superior: better constructed than an ice ship, better crewed than a captured raft.

In short, Drak'ho still held the balance of power.

As he helped van Rijn down into a seized canoe, Tolk said wryly: "I'd have kept my armor on if I were you, Eart'a. You'll only have to be laced back into it, when the truce ends."

"Ah." The merchant stretched monstrously, puffed out his stomach, and plumped himself down on a seat. "Let us suppose, though, the armistice does not break. Then I will have been wearing that bloody-be-smeared corset all for nothings."

"I notice," added Wace, "neither you nor Trolwen are cuirassed."

The commander smoothed his mahogany fur with a nervous hand. "That's for the dignity of the Flock," he muttered. "Those muck-walkers aren't going to think I'm afraid of them."

The canoe shoved off, its crew bent to the oars, it skipped swiftly over wrinkled dark waters. Above it dipped and soared the rest of the agreed-on Lannacha guard, putting on their best demonstration of parade flying for the edification of the enemy. There were about a hundred all told. It was comfortlessly little to take into the angered Fleet.

"I don't expect to reach any agreement," said Trolwen. "No one can—with a mind as foreign as theirs."

"The Fleet peoples are just like you," said van Rijn. "What you need is more brotherhood, by damn. You should bash in their heads without this race prejudice."

"Just like *us?*" Trolwen bristled. His eyes grew flat glass-yellow. "See here, Eart'a—"

"Never mind," said van Rijn. "So they do not have a rutting season. So you think this is a big thing. All right. I got some thinkings to make of my own. Shut up."

The wind ruffled waves and strummed idly on rigging. The sun struck long copper-tinged rays through scudding cloudbanks, to walk on the sea with fiery footprints. The air was cool, damp, smelling a little of salty life. It would not be an easy time to die, thought Wace. Hardest of all, though, to forsake Sandra, where she lay dwindling under the ice cliffs of Dawrnach. *Pray for my soul, beloved, while you wait to follow me. Pray for my soul.*

"Leaving personal feelings aside," said Tolk, "there's much in the commander's remarks. That is, a folk with lives as alien to ours as the Drakska will have minds equally alien. I don't pretend to follow the thoughts of you, Eart'ska: I consider you my friends, but let's admit it, we have very little in common. I only trust you because your immediate motive—survival—has been made so clear to me. When I don't quite follow your reasoning, I can safely assume that it is at least well-intentioned.

"But the Drakska, now—how can they be trusted? Let's say that a peace agreement is made. How can we know they'll keep it? They may have no concept of honor at all, just as they lack all concept of sexual decency. Or, even if they do intend to abide by their oaths, are we sure the words of the treaty will mean the same thing to them as to us? In my capacity of Herald, I've seen many semantic misunderstandings between tribes with different languages. So what of tribes with different instincts?

"Or I wonder...can we even trust ourselves to keep such a pledge? We do not hate anyone merely for having fought us. But we hate dishonor, perversion, uncleanliness. How can we live with ourselves, if we make peace with creatures whom the gods must loathe?"

He sighed and looked moodily ahead to the nearing rafts.

Wace shrugged. "Has it occurred to you, they are thinking very much the same things about you?" he retorted.

"Of course they are," said Tolk. "That's yet another hailstorm in the path of negotiations."

Personally, thought Wace, *I'll be satisfied with a temporary settlement. Just let them patch up their differences long enough for a message to reach Thursday Landing. (How?) Then they can rip each other's throats out for all I care.*

He glanced around him at the slim winged forms, and thought of work and war, torment and triumph—yes, and now and then some laughter or a fragment of song—shared. He thought of high-hearted Trolwen, philosophic Tolk, earnest young Angrek, he thought of brave kindly Delp and his wife Rodonis, who was so much more a lady than many a human female he had known. And the small furry cubs which tumbled in the dust or climbed into his lap... *No,* he told himself, *I'm wrong. It means a great deal to me, after all, that this war should be permanently ended.*

The canoe slipped in between towering raft walls. Drak'ho faces looked stonily down on it. Now and then someone spat into its wake. They were all very quiet.

The unwieldy pile of the flagship loomed ahead. There were banners strung from the mastheads, and a guard in bright regalia formed a ring enclosing the main deck. Just before the wooden castle, sprawled on furs and cushions,

Admiral T'heonax and his advisory council waited. To one side stood Captain Delp with a few personal guards, in war-harness still sweaty and unkempt.

Total silence lay over them as the canoe came to a halt and made fast to a bollard. Trolwen, Tolk, and most of the Lannacha troopers flew straight up to the deck. It was minutes later, after much pushing, panting, and swearing, that the humans topped that mountainous hull.

Van Rijn glowered about him. "What for hospitality!" he snorted in the Drak'ho language. "Not so much as one little rope let down to me, who is pushing my poor old tired bones to an early grave all for your sakes. Before Heaven, it is hard! It is hard! Sometimes I think I give up, me, and retire. Then where will the galaxy be? Then you will all be sorry, when it is too late."

T'heonax gave him a sardonic stare. "You were not the best behaved guest the Fleet has had, Eart'ho," he answered. "I've a great deal to repay you. Yes. I have not forgotten."

Van Rijn wheezed across the planks to Delp, extending his hand. "So our intelligences was right, and it was you doing all the works," he blared. "I might have been sure. Nobody else in this Fleet has so much near a gram of brains. I, Nicholas van Rijn, compliment you with regards."

T'heonax stiffened and his councilors, rigid in braid and sash, looked duly shocked at this ignoring of the admiral. Delp hung back for an instant. Then he took van Rijn's hand and squeezed it, quite in the Terrestrial manner.

"Lodestar help me, it is good to see your villainous fat face again," he said. "Do you know how nearly you cost me my . . . everything? Were it not for my lady—"

"Business and friendship we do not mix," said van Rijn airily. "Ah, yes, good Vrouw Rodonis. How is she and all the little ones? Do they still remember old Uncle Nicholas and the bedtime stories he was telling them, like about the—"

"If you please," said T'heonax in an elaborate voice, "we will, with your permission, carry on. Who shall interpret? Yes, I remember you now, Herald." An ugly look. "Your attention, then. Tell your leader that this parley was arranged by my field commander, Delp hyr Orikan, without even sending a messenger down here to consult me. I would have opposed it had I known. It was neither prudent nor necessary. I shall have to have these decks scrubbed where barbarians have trod. However, since the Fleet is bound by its honor—you do have a word for honor in your language, don't you—I will hear what your leader has to say."

Tolk nodded curtly and put it into Lannachamael. Trolwen sat up, eyes kindling. His guards growled, their hands tightened on their weapons. Delp shuffled his feet unhappily, and some of Theonax's captains looked away in an embarrassed fashion.

"Tell him," said Trolwen after a moment, with bitter precision, "that we will let the Fleet depart from Achan at once. Of course, we shall want hostages."

Tolk translated. T'heonax peeled lips back from teeth and laughed. "They sit here with their wretched handful of rafts and say this to us?" His courtiers tittered an echo.

But his councilors, who captained his flotillas, remained grave. It was Delp who stepped forward and said: "The admiral knows I have taken my share in this war. With these hands, wings, this tail, I have killed enemy males; with these teeth, I have drawn enemy blood. Nevertheless I say now, we'd better at least listen to them."

"What?" T'heonax made round eyes. "I *hope* you are joking."

Van Rijn rolled forth. "I got no time for fumblydiddles," he boomed. "You hear me, and I put it in millicredit words so some two-year-old cub can explain it to you. Look out there!" His arm waved broadly at the sea. "We have rafts. Not so many, perhaps, but enough. You make terms with us, or we keep on fighting. Soon it is you who do not have enough rafts. So! Put that in your pipe and stick it!"

Wace nodded. Good. Good, indeed. Why had that

Drak'ho vessel run from his own lubber-manned prize? It was willing enough to exchange long-range shots, or to grapple sailor against sailor in the air. It was not willing to risk being boarded, wrecked, or set ablaze by Lannach's desperate devils.

Because it was a home, a fortress, and a livelihood—the only way to make a living that this culture knew. If you destroyed enough rafts, there would not be enough fish-catching or fish-storing capacity to keep the folk alive. It was as simple as that.

"We'll sink you!" screamed T'heonax. He stood up, beating his wings, crest aquiver, tail held like an iron bar. "We'll drown every last whelp of you!"

"Possible so," said van Rijn. "This is supposed to scare us? If we give up now, we are done for anyhow. So we take you along to hell with us, to shine our shoes and fetch us cool drinks, *nie?*"

Delp said, with trouble in his gaze: "We did not come to Achan for love of destruction, but because hunger drove us. It was you who denied us the right to take fish which you yourselves never caught. Oh, yes, we did take some of your land too, but the water we must have. We can *not* give that up."

Van Rijn shrugged. "There are other seas. Maybe we let you haul a few more nets of fish before you go."

A captain of the Fleet said slowly: "My lord Delp has voiced the crux of the matter. It hints at a solution. After all, the Sea of Achan has little or no value to you Lannach'honai. We did, of course, wish to garrison your coasts, and occupy certain islands which are sources of timber and flint and the like. And naturally, we wanted a port of our own in Sagna Bay, for emergencies and repairs. These are questions of defense and self-sufficiency, not of immediate survival like the water. So perhaps—"

"*No!*" cried T'heonax.

It was almost a scream. It shocked them into silence. The admiral crouched panting for a moment, then snarled at Tolk: "Tell your leader...I, the final authority...I refuse. I say we can crush your joke of a navy with small loss to ourselves. We have no reason to yield anything to you. We may allow you to keep the uplands of Lannach. That is the greatest concession you can hope for."

"Impossible!" spat the Herald. Then he rattled the translation off for Trolwen, who arched his back and bit the air.

"The mountains will not support us," explained Tolk more calmly. "We have already eaten them bare—that's no secret. We must have the lowlands. And we are certainly not going to let you hold any land whatsoever, to base an attack on us in a later year."

"If you think you can wipe us off the sea now, without a loss that will cripple you also, you may try," added Wace.

"I say we can!" stormed T'heonax. "And will!"

"My lord—" Delp hesitated. His eyes closed for a second. Then he said quite dispassionately: "My lord admiral, a finish fight now would likely be the end of our nation. Such few rafts as survived would be the prey of the first barbarian islanders that chanced along."

"And a retreat into The Ocean would *certainly* doom us," said T'heonax. His forefinger stabbed. "Unless you can conjure the trech and the fruitweed out of Achan and into the broad waters."

"That is true, of course, my lord," said Delp.

He turned and sought Trolwen's eyes. They regarded each other steadily, with respect.

"Herald," said Delp, "tell your chief this. We are not going to leave the Sea of Achan. We cannot. If you insist that we do so, we'll fight you and hope you can be destroyed without too much loss to ourselves. We have no choice in that matter.

"But I think maybe we can give up any thought of occupying either Lannach or Holmenach. You can keep all the solid land. We can barter our fish, salt, sea harvest, handicrafts, for your meat, stone, wood, cloth, and oil. It would in time become profitable for both of us."

"And incidental," said van Rijn, "you might think of this bit too. If Drak'ho has no land, and Lannach has no ships, it will be sort of a little hard for one to make war on another, *nie?* After a few years, trading and getting rich off each other, you get so mutual dependent war is just impossible. So if you agree like now, soon your troubles are over, and then comes Nicholas van Rijn with Earth trade goods for all, like Father Christmas my prices are so reasonable. What?"

"Be still!" shrieked T'heonax.

He grabbed the chief of his guards by a wing and pointed at Delp. "Arrest that traitor!"

"My lord—" Delp backed away. The guard hesitated. Delp's warriors closed in about their captain, menacingly. From the listening lower decks there came a groan.

"The Lodestar hear me," stammered Delp, "I only suggested . . . I know the admiral has the final say—"

"And my say is, 'No.'" declared T'heonax, tacitly dropping the matter of arrest. "As admiral and Oracle, I forbid it. There is no possible agreement between the Fleet and these . . . these vile . . . filthy, dirty, animal—" He dribbled at the lips. His hands curved into claws, poised above his head.

. A rustle and murmur went through the ranked Drak'honai. The captains lay like winged leopards, still cloaked with dignity, but there was terror in their eyes. The Lannachska, ignorant of words but sensitive to tones, crowded together and gripped their weapons more tightly.

Tolk translated fast, in a low voice. When he had finished, Trolwen sighed.

"I hate to admit it," he said, "but if you turn that *marswa's* words around, they are true. Do you really, seriously think two races as different as ours could live side by side? It would be too tempting to break the pledges. They could ravage our land while we were gone on migration, take all our towns again . . . or we could come north once more with barbarian allies, bought with the promise of Drak'ho plunder—We'd be back at each other's throats, one way or another, in five years. Best to have it out now. Let the gods decide who's right and who's too depraved to live."

Almost wearily, he bunched his muscles, to go down fighting if T'heonax ended the armistice this moment.

Van Rijn lifted his hands and his voice. It went like a bass drum, the length and breadth and depth of the castle raft. And nocked arrows were slowly put back into their quivers.

"Hold still! Wait just a bloody minute, by damn. I am not through talking yet."

He nodded curtly at Delp. "You have some sense, you. Maybe we can find a few others with brains not so much like a spoonful of moldy tea sold by my competitors. I am going to say something now. I will use Drak'ho language. Tolk, you make a running translation. This no one on the planet has heard before. I tell you Drak'ho and Lannacha are *not* alien! They are the same identical stupid race!"

Wace sucked in his breath. "What?" he whispered in Anglic. "But the breeding cycles—"

"Kill me that fat worm!" shouted T'heonax.

Van Rijn waved an impatient hand at him. "Be quiet, you. I make the talkings. So! Sit down, both you nations, and listen to Nicholas van Rijn!"

XX

The evolution of intelligent life on Diomedes is still largely conjectural; there has been no time to hunt fossils. But on the basis of existing biology and general principles, it is possible to reason out the course of millennial events.

Once upon a time in the planet's tropics there was a small continent or large island, thickly forested. The equatorial regions never know the long days and nights of high latitudes: at equinox the sun is up for six hours to cross the sky and set for another six; at solstice there is a twilight, the sun just above or below the horizon. By Diomedean standards these are ideal conditions which will support abundant life. Among the species at this past epoch was a small, bright-eyed arboreal carnivore. Like Earth's flying squirrel, it had developed a membrane on which to glide from branch to branch.

But a low-density planet has a queasy structure.

Continents rise and sink with indecent speed, a mere few hundreds of thousands of years. Ocean and air currents are correspondingly deflected; and, because of the great axial tilt and the larger fluid masses involved, Diomedean currents bear considerably more heat or cold than do Earth's. Thus, even at the equator, there were radical climatic shifts.

A period of drought shriveled the ancient forests into scattered woods separated by great dry pampas. The flying pseudo-squirrel developed true wings to go from copse to copse. But being an adaptable beast, it began also to prey on the new grass-eating animals which herded over the plains. To cope with the big ungulates, it grew in size. But then, needing more food to fuel the larger body, it was forced into a variety of environments, seashore, mountains, swamps—yet by virtue of mobility remained interbred rather than splitting into new species. A single individual might thus face many types of country in one lifetime, which put a premium on intelligence.

At this stage, for some unknown reason, the species—or a part of it, the part destined to become important—was forced out of the homeland. Possibly diastrophism broke the original continent into small islands which would not support so large an animal population; or the drying-out may have progressed still further. Whatever the cause, families and flocks drifted slowly northward and southward through hundreds of generations.

There they found new territories, excellent hunting—but a winter which they could not survive. When the long darkness came, they must perforce return to the tropics to wait for spring. It was not the inborn, automatic reaction of Terrestrial migratory birds. This animal was already too clever to be an instinct machine; its habits were *learned*. The brutal natural selection of the annual flights stimulated this intelligence yet more.

Now the price of intelligence is a very long childhood in proportion to the total lifespan. Since there is no action-pattern built into the thinker's genes, each generation must learn everything afresh, which takes time. Therefore, no species can become intelligent unless it or its environment first produces some mechanism for keeping the parents together, so that they may protect the young during the extended period of helpless infancy and ignorant childhood. Mother love is not enough; Mother will have enough to do, tending the suicidally inquisitive cubs, without having to do all the food-hunting and guarding as well. Father must help out. But what will keep Father around, once his sexual urge has been satisfied?

Instinct can do it. Some birds, for example, employ both parents to rear the young. But elaborate instinctive compulsions are incompatible with intelligence. Father has to have a good selfish reason to stay, if Father has brains enough to *be* selfish.

In the case of man, the mechanism is simple: permanent sexuality. The human is never satisfied at any time of year. From this fact we derive the family, and hence the possibility of prolonged immaturity, and hence our cerebral cortex.

In the case of the Diomedean, there was migration. Each flock had a long and dangerous way to travel every year. It was best to go in company, under some form of organization. At journey's end in the tropics, there was the abandon of the mating season—but soon the unavoidable trip back home, for the equatorial islands would not support many visitors for very long.

Out of this primitive annual grouping—since it was not blindly instinctive, but the fruit of experience in a gifted animal—there grew loose permanent associations. Defensive bands became co-operative bands. Already the exigencies of travel had caused male and female to specialize their body types, one for fighting, one for burden-bearing. It was, therefore, advantageous that the sexes maintain their partnership the whole year around.

The animal of permanent family—on Diomedes, as a rule, a rather large family, an entire matrilineal clan—with the long gestation, the long cubhood, the constant change and challenge of environment, the competition for mates each midwinter with alien bands having alien ways: this animal had every evolutionary reason to start thinking. Out of such a matrix grew language, tools, fire, organized nations, and those vague unattainable yearnings we call "culture."

Now while the Diomedean had no irrevocable pattern of inborn behavior, he did tend everywhere to follow certain modes of life. They were the easiest. Analogously, humankind is not required by instinct to formalize and regulate its matings as marriage, but human societies have almost invariably done so. It is more comfortable for all concerned. And so the Diomedean migrated south to breed.

But he did not have to!

When breeding cycles exist, they are controlled by some simple foolproof mechanism. Thus, for many birds on Earth it is the increasing length of the day in springtime which causes mating: the optical stimulus triggers hormonal processes which reactivate the dormant gonads. On Diomedes, this wouldn't work; the light cycle varies too much with latitude. But once the proto-intelligent Diomedean had gotten into migratory habits—and therefore must breed only at a certain time of the year, if the young were to survive—evolution took the obvious course of making that migration itself the governor.

Ordinarily a hunter, with occasional meals of nuts or fruit or wild grain, the Diomedean exercised in spurts. Migration called for prolonged effort; it must have taken hundreds or thousands of generations to develop the flying muscles alone, time enough to develop other adaptations as well. So this effort stimulated certain glands, which operated through a complex hormonal system to waken the gonads. (An exception was the lactating female, whose mammaries secreted an inhibiting agent.) During the great flight, the sex hormone concentration built up—there was no time or energy to spare for its dissipation. Once in the tropics, rested and fed, the Diomedean made up for lost opportunities. He made up so thoroughly that the return trip had no significant effect on his exhausted glands.

Now and then in the homeland, fleetingly, after some unusual exertion, one might feel stirrings toward the opposite sex. One suppressed that, as rigorously as the human suppresses impulses to incest, and for an even more practical reason: a cub born out of season meant death on migration for itself as well as its mother. Not that the average Diomedean realized this overtly; he just accepted the taboo, founded religions and ethical systems and neuroses on it. However, doubtless the vague, lingering year-round attractiveness of the other sex had been an unconscious reason for the initial development of septs and flocks.

When the migratory Diomedean encountered a tribe which did not observe his most basic moral law, he knew physical horror.

Drak'ho's Fleet was one of several which have now been discovered by traders. They may all have originated as groups living near the equator and thus not burdened by the need to travel; but this is still guesswork. The clear fact is that they began to live more off the sea than the land. Through many centuries they elaborated the physical apparatus of ships and tackle, until it had become their entire livelihood.

It gave more security than hunting. It gave a home which could be dwelt in continuously. It gave the possibility of constructing and using elaborate devices, accumulating large libraries, sitting and thinking or debating a problem—in short, the freedom to encumber oneself with a true civilization, which no migrator had except to the most limited degree. On the bad side, it meant grindingly hard labor and aristocratic domination.

This work kept the deckhand sexually stimulated; but warm shelters and stored sea food had made his birthtime independent of the season. Thus the sailor nations grew into a very humanlike pattern of marriage and child-raising: there was even a concept of romantic love.

The migrators, who thought him depraved, the sailor considered swinish. Indeed, neither culture could imagine how the other might even be of the same species.

And how shall one trust the absolute alien?

XXI

"It is these ideological pfuities that make the real nasty wars," said van Rijn. "But now I have taken off the ideology and we can sensible and friendly settle down to swindling each other, *nie?*"

He had not, of course, explained his hypothesis in such detail. Lannach's philosophers had some vague idea of evolution, but were weak on astronomy; Drak'ho science was almost the reverse. Van Rijn had contented himself with very simple, repetitious words, sketching what must be the only reasonable explanation of the well-known reproductive differences.

He rubbed his hands and chortled into a tautening silence. "So! I have not made it all sweetness. Even I cannot do that overnights. For long times to come yet, you each think the others go about this in disgusting style. You make filthy jokes about each other ... I know some good ones you can adapt. But you know, at least, that you are of the same race. Any of you could have been a solid member of the other nation, *nie?* Maybe, come changing times, you start switching around your ways to live. Why not experiment a little, ha? No, no, I see you can not like that idea yet, I say no more."

He folded his arms and waited, bulky, shaggy, ragged, and caked with the grime of weeks. On creaking planks, under a red sun and a low sea wind, the scores of winged warriors and captains shuddered in the face of the unimagined.

Delp said at last, so slow and heavy it did not really break that drumhead silence: "Yes. This makes sense. I believe it."

After another minute, bowing his head toward stone-rigid T'heonax: "My lord, this does change the situation. I think—it will not be as much as we hoped for, but better than I feared—We can make terms, they to have all the land and we to have the Sea of Achan. Now that I know they are not ... devils ... animals—Well, the normal guarantees, oaths and exchange of hostages and so on— should make the treaty firm enough."

Tolk had been whispering in Trolwen's ear. Lannach's commander nodded. "That is much my own thought," he said.

"Can we persuade the Council and the clans, Flockchief?" muttered Tolk.

"Herald, if we bring back an honorable peace, the Council will vote our ghosts godhood after we die."

Tolk's gaze shifted back to T'heonax, lying without movement among his courtiers. And the grizzled fur lifted along the Herald's back.

"Let us first return to the Council alive, Flockchief," he said.

T'heonax rose. His wings beat the air, cracking noises like an ax going through bone. His muzzle wrinkled into a lion mask, long teeth gleamed wetly forth, and he roared:

"No! I've heard enough! This farce is at an end!"

Trolwen and the Lannacha escort did not need an interpreter. They clapped hands to weapons and fell into a defensive circle. Their jaws clashed shut automatically, biting the wind.

"My lord!" Delp sprang fully erect.

"Be still!" screeched T'heonax. "You've said far too much." His head swung from side to side. "Captains of the Fleet, you have heard how Delp hyr Orikan advocates making peace with creatures lower than the beasts. Remember it!"

"But my lord—" An older officer stood up, hands aloft in protest. "My lord admiral, we've just had it shown to us, they aren't beasts . . . it's only a different—"

"Assuming the Eart'ho spoke truth, which is by no means sure, what of it?" T'heonax fleered at van Rijn. "It only makes the matter worse. We know beasts can't help themselves but these Lannach'honai are dirty by choice. And you would let them live? You would . . . would *trade* with them . . . enter their towns . . . let your young be seduced into their—No!"

The captains looked at each other. It was like an audible groan. Only Delp seemed to have the courage to speak again.

"I humbly beg the admiral to recall, we've no real choice. If we fight them to a finish, it may be our own finish too."

"Ridiculous!" snorted T'heonax. "Either you are afraid or they've bribed you."

Tolk had been translating *sotto voce* for Trolwen. Now, sickly, Wace heard the commander's grim reply to his Herald: "If he takes that attitude, a treaty is out of the question. Even if he made it, he'd sacrifice his hostages to us—not to speak of ours to him—just to renew the war whenever he felt ready. Let's get back before I myself violate the truce!"

And there, thought Wace, *is the end of the world. I will die under flung stones, and Sandra will die in Glacier Land. Well . . . we tried.*

He braced himself. The admiral might not let this embassy depart.

Delp was looking around from face to face. "Captains of the Fleet," he cried, "I ask your opinion . . . I implore you, persuade my lord admiral that—"

"The next treasonable word uttered by anyone will cost him his wings," shouted T'heonax. "Or do you question my authority?"

It was a bold move, thought Wace in a distant part of his thuttering brain—to stake all he had on that one challenge. But of course, T'heonax was going to get away with it; no one in this caste-ridden society would deny his absolute power, not even Delp the bold. Reluctant they might be, but the captains would obey.

The silence grew shattering.

Nicholas van Rijn broke it with a long, juicy Bronx cheer.

The whole assembly started. T'heonax leaped backward and for a moment he was like a bat-winged tomcat.

"What was that?" he blazed.

"Are you deaf?" answered van Rijn mildly. "I said—" He repeated, with tremolo.

"What do you mean?"

"It is an Earth term," said van Rijn. "As near as I can render it, let me see . . . well, it means you are a—" The rest was the most imaginative obscenity Wace had heard in his life.

The captains gasped. Some drew their weapons. The Drak'ho guards on the upper decks gripped bows and spears. "Kill him!" screamed T'heonax.

"No!" Van Rijn's bass exploded on their ears. The sheer volume of it paralyzed them. "I am an embassy, by damn! You hurt an embassy and the Lodestar will sink you in hell's boiling seas!"

It checked them. T'heonax did not repeat his order; the guards jerked back toward stillness; the officers remained poised, outraged past words.

"I have somethings to say you," van Rijn continued, only twice as loud as a large foghorn. "I speak to all the Fleet, and ask you yourselves, why this little pip squeaker does so stupid. He makes you carry on a war where both sides lose—he makes you risk your lives, your wives and cubs, maybe the Fleet's own surviving—why? Because he is afraid. He knows, a few years cheek by jowl next to the Lannach'honai, and even more so trading with my company at my fantastic low prices, things begin to change. You get more into thinking by your own selves. You taste freedom. Bit by bit, his power slides from him. And he is too much a coward to live on his own selfs. *Nie*, he has got to have guards and slaves and all of you to make bossing over, so he proves to himself he is not just a little jellypot but a real true Leader. Rather he will have the Fleet ruined, even die himself, than lose this propup, him!"

T'heonax said, shaking: "Get off my raft before I forget there is an armistice."

"Oh, I go, I go," said van Rijn. He advanced toward the admiral. His tread reverberated in the deck. "I go back and make war again if you insist. But only one small question I ask first." He stopped before the royal presence and prodded the royal nose with a hairy forefinger. "Why you make so much fuss about Lannacha home lifes? Could be maybe down underneath you hanker to try it yourself?"

He turned his back, then, and bowed.

Wace did not see just what happened. There were guards and captains between. He heard a screech, a bellow from van Rijn, and then a hurricane of wings was before him.

Something—He threw himself into the press of bodies. A tail crashed against his ribs. He hardly felt it; his fist jolted, merely to get a warrior out of the way and see—

Nicholas van Rijn stood with both hands in the air as a score of spears menaced him. "The admiral bit me!" he wailed. "I am here like an embassy, and the pig bites me! What kind of relations between countries is that, when heads of state bite foreign ambassadors, ha? Does an Earth president bite diplomats? This is uncivilized!"

T'heonax backed off, spitting, scrubbing the blood from his jaws. "Get out," he said in a strangled voice. "Go at once."

Van Rijn nodded. "Come, friends," he said. "We find us places with better manners."

"Freeman... Freeman, where did he—" Wace crowded close.

"Never mind where," said van Rijn huffily.

Trolwen and Tolk joined them. The Lannacha escort fell into step behind. They walked at a measured pace across the deck, away from the confusion of Drak'honai under the castle wall.

"You might have known it," said Wace. He felt exhausted, drained of everything except a weak anger at his chief's unbelievable folly. "This race is carnivorous. Haven't you seen them snap when they get angry? It's . . . a reflex—You might have known!"

"Well," said van Rijn in a most virtuous tone, holding both hands to his injury, "he did not *have* to bite. I am not responsible for his lack of control or any consequences of it, me. All good lawyer saints witness I am not."

"But the ruckus—we could all have been killed!"

Van Rijn didn't bother to argue about that.

Delp met them at the rail. His crest drooped. "I am sorry it must end thus," he said. "We could have been friends."

"Perhaps it does not end just so soon," said van Rijn.

"What do you mean?" Tired eyes regarded him without hope.

"Maybe you see pretty quick. Delp"—van Rijn laid a paternal hand on the Drak'ho's shoulder—"you are a good young chap. I could use a one like you, as a part-time agent for some tradings in these parts. On fat commissions, natural. But for now, remember you are the one they all like and respect. If anything happens to the admiral, there will be panic and uncertainty . . . they will turn to you for advice. If you act fast at such a moment, you can be admiral yourself! Then maybe we do business, ha?"

He left Delp gaping and swung himself with apish speed down into the canoe. "Now, boys," he said, "row like hell."

They were almost back to their own fleet when Wace saw clotted wings whirl up from the royal raft. He gulped. "Has the attack . . . has it begun already?" He cursed himself that his voice should be an idiotic squeak.

"Well, I am glad we are not close to them." Van Rijn, standing up as he had done the whole trip, nodded complacently. "But I think not this is the war. I think they are just disturbed. Soon Delp will take charge and calms them down."

"But—*Delp*?"

Van Rijn shrugged. "If Diomedean proteins is deadly to us," he said, "ours should not be so good for them, ha? And our late friend T'heonax took a big mouthful of me. It all goes to show, these foul tempers only lead to trouble. Best you follow my example. When I am attacked, I turn the other cheek."

XXII

Thursday Landing had little in the way of hospital facilities: an autodiagnostician, a few surgical and therapeutical robots, the standard drugs, and the post xenobiologist to double as medical officer. But a six weeks' fast did not have serious consequences, if you were strong to begin with and had been waited on hand, foot, wing, and tail by two anxious nations, on a planet none of whose diseases could affect you. Treatment progressed rapidly with the help of bioaccelerine, from intravenous glucose to thick rare steaks. By the sixth Diomedean day, Wace had put on a noticeable amount of flesh and was weakly but fumingly aprowl in his room.

"Smoke, sir?" asked young Benegal. He had been out on trading circuit when the rescue party arrived; only now was he getting the full account. He offered cigarettes with a most respectful air.

Wace halted, the bathrobe swirling about his knees. He reached, hesitated, then grinned and said: "In all that time without tobacco, I seem to've lost the addiction. Question is, should I go to the trouble and expense of building it up again?"

"Well, no, sir—"

"Hey! Gimme that!" Wace sat down on his bed and took a cautious puff. "I certainly am going to pick up all my vices where I left off, and doubtless add some new ones."

"You, uh, you were going to tell me, sir . . . how the station here was informed—"

"Oh, yes. That. It was childishly simple. I figured it out in ten minutes, once we got a breathing spell. Send a fair-sized Diomedean party with a written message, plus of course one of Tolk's professional interpreters to help them inquire their way on this side of The Ocean. Devise a big life raft, just a framework of light poles which could be dovetailed together. Each Diomedean carried a single piece; they assembled it in the air and rested on it whenever necessary. Also fished from it: a number of Fleet experts went along to take charge of that angle. There was enough rain for them to catch in small buckets to drink—I knew there would be, since the Drak'honai stay at sea for indefinite periods, and also this is such a rainy planet anyhow.

"Incidentally, for reasons which are now obvious to you, the party had to include some Lannacha females. Which means that the messengers of both nationalities have had to give up some hoary prejudices. In the long run, that's going to change their history more than whatever impression we Terrestrials might have made, by such stunts as flying them home across The Ocean in a single day. From now on, willy-nilly, the beings who went on that trip will be a subversive element in both cultures; they'll be the seedbed of Diomedean internationalism. But that's for the League to gloat about, not me."

Wace shrugged. "Having seen them off," he finished, "we could only crawl into bed and wait. After the first few days, it wasn't so bad. Appetite disappears."

He stubbed out the cigarette with a grimace. It was making him dizzy.

"When do I get to see the others?" he demanded. "I'm strong enough now to feel bored. I want company, dammit."

"As a matter of fact, sir," said Benegal, "I believe Freeman van Rijn said something about"—a thunderous *"Skulls and smallpox!"* bounced in the corridor outside—"visiting you today."

"Run along then," said Wace sardonically. "You're too young to hear this. We blood brothers, who have defied death together, we sworn comrades, and so on and so forth, are about to have a reunion."

He got to his feet as the boy slipped out the back door. Van Rijn rolled in the front entrance.

His Jovian girth was shrunken flat, he had only one chin, and he leaned on a gold-headed cane. But his hair was curled into oily black ringlets, his mustaches and goatee waxed to needle points, his lace-trimmed shirt and cloth-of-gold vest were already smeared with snuff, his legs were hairy tree trunks beneath a batik sarong, he wore a diamond mine on each hand and a silver chain about his neck which could have anchored a battleship. He waved a ripe Trichinopoly cigar above a four-decker sandwich and roared:

"So you are walking again. Good fellow! The only way you get well is not sip dishwater soup and take it easily, like that upgebungled horse doctor has the nerve to tell me to do." He purpled with indignation. "Does one thought get through that sand in his synapses, what it is costing me every hour I wait here? What a killing I can make if I get home among those underhand competition jackals before the news reaches them Nicholas van Rijn is alive after all? I have just been out beating the station engineer over his thick flat mushroom he uses for a head, telling him if my spaceship is not ready to leave tomorrow noon I will hitch him to it and say giddap. So you will come back to Earth with us your own selfs, *nie?*"

Wace had no immediate reply. Sandra had followed the merchant in.

She was driving a wheelchair, and looked so white and thin that his heart cracked over. Her hair was a pale frosty cloud on the pillow, it seemed as if it would be cold to touch. But her eyes lived, immense, the infinite warm green of Earth's gentlest seas; and she smiled at him.

"My lady—" he whispered.

"Oh, she comes too," said van Rijn, selecting an apple from the fruit basket at Wace's bedside. "We all continue our interrupted trip, maybe with not so much fun and games aboard—" He drooped one little obsidian eye at her, lasciviously. "Those we save for later on Earth when we are back to normal, ha?"

"If my lady has the strength to travel—" stumbled Wace. He sat down, his knees would bear him no longer.

"Oh, yes," she murmured. "It is only a matter of following the diet as written for me and getting much rest."

"Worst thing you can do, by damn," grumbled van Rijn, finishing the apple and picking up an orange.

"It isn't suitable," protested Wace. "We lost so many servants when the skycruiser ditched. She'd only have—"

"A single maid to attend me?" Sandra's laugh was ghostly, but it held genuine amusement. "After now I am to forget what we did and endured, and be so correct and formal with you, Eric? That would be most silly, when we have climbed the ridge over Salmenbrok together, not?"

Wace's pulse clamored. Van Rijn, strewing orange peel on the floor, said: "Out of hard lucks, the good Lord can pull much money if He chooses. I cannot know every man in the company, so promising youngsters like you do go sometimes to waste on little outposts like here. Now I will take you home to Earth and find a proper paying job for you."

If *she* could remember one chilled morning beneath Mount Oborch, thought Wace, he, for the sake of his manhood, could remember less pleasant things, and name them in plain words. It was time.

He was still too weak to rise—he shook a little—but he caught van Rijn's gaze and said in a voice hard with anger:

"That's the easiest way to get back your self-esteem, of course. Buy it! Bribe me with a sinecure to forget how Sandra sat with a paintbrush in a coalsack of a room, till she fainted from exhaustion, and how she gave us her last food... how I myself worked my brain and my heart out, to pull us all back from that jailhouse country and win a war to boot—No, don't interrupt. I know you had some part in it. You fought during that naval engagement: because you had no choice, no place to hide. You found a nice nasty way to dispose of an inconvenient obstacle to the peace negotiations. You have a talent for that sort of thing. And you made some suggestions.

"But what did it amount to? It amounted to your saying to me: 'Do this! Build that!' And I had to do it, with nonhuman helpers and stone-age tools, I had to design it, even! Any fool could once have said, 'Take me to the Moon.' It took brains to figure out how!

"Your role, your 'leadership,' amounted to strolling around, gambling and chattering, playing cheap politics, eating like a hippopotamus while Sandra lay starving on Dawrnach—and claiming all the credit! And now I'm supposed to go to Earth, sit down in a gilded pigpen of an office, spend the rest of my life thumb-twiddling... and keep quiet when you brag. Isn't that right? You take your sinecure—"

Wace saw Sandra's eyes on him, grave, oddly compassionate, and jerked to a halt.

"I quit," he ended.

Van Rijn had swallowed the orange and returned to his sandwich during Wace's speech. Now he burped, licked his fingers, took a fresh puff of his cigar, and rumbled quite mildly:

"If you think I give away sinecures, you are being too optimist. I am offering you a job with importance for no reason except I think you can do it better than some knucklebone heads on Earth. I will pay you what the job is worth. And by damn, you will work your promontory off."

Wace gulped after air.

"Go ahead and insult me, public if you wish," said van Rijn. "Just not on company time. Now I go find me who it was put the bomb in that cruiser and take care of him. Also maybe the cook will fix me a little Italian hero sandwich. Death and dynamite, they want to starve me to bones here, them!"

He waved a shaggy paw and departed like an amiable earthquake.

Sandra wheeled over and laid a hand on Wace's. It was a cool touch, light as a leaf falling in a northern October, but it burned him. As if from far off, he heard her:

"I awaited this to come, Eric. It is best you understand now. I, who was born to govern . . . my whole life has been a long governing, not? . . . I know what I speak of. There are the fake leaders, the balloons, with talent only to get in people's way. Yes. But he is not one of them. Without him, you and I would sleep dead beneath Achan."

"But—"

"You complain he made you do the hard things that used your talent, not his? Of course he did. It is not the leader's job to do everything himself. It is his job to order, persuade, wheedle, bully, bribe—just that, to make people do what must be done, whether or not they think it is possible.

"You say, he spent time loafing around talking, making jokes and a false front to impress the natives? Of course! Somebody had to. We were monsters, strangers, beggars as well. Could you or I have started as a deformed beggar and ended as all but king?

"You say he bribed—with goods from crooked dice— and blustered, lied, cheated, politicked, killed both open and sly? Yes. I do not say it was right. I do not say he did not enjoy himself, either. But can you name another way to have gotten our lives back? Or even to make peace for those poor warring devils?"

"Well . . . well—" The man looked away, out the window to the stark landscape. It would be good to dwell inside Earth's narrower horizon.

"Well, maybe," he said at last, grudging each word. "I . . . I suppose I was too hasty. Still—we played our parts too, you know. Without us, he—"

"I think, without us, he would have found some other way to come home," she interrupted. "But we without him, no."

He jerked his head back. Her face was burning a deeper red than the ember sunlight outside could tinge it.

He thought, with sudden weariness: *After all, she is a woman, and women live more for the next generation than men can. Most especially she does, for the life of a planet may rest on her child, and she is an aristocrat in the old pure meaning of the word. He who fathers the next Duke of Hermes may be aging, fat, and uncouth; callous and conscienceless; unable to see her as anything but a boisterous episode. It doesn't matter, if the woman and the aristocrat see him as a man.*

Well-a-day, I have much to thank them both for.

"I—" Sandra looked confused, almost trapped. Her look held an inarticulate pleading. "I think I had best go and let you rest." After a moment of his silence: "He is not yet so strong as he claims. I may be needed."

"No," said Wace with an enormous tenderness. "The need is all yours. Good-by, my lady."

As a dewdrop may reflect the glade wherein it lies, even so does the story which follows give a glimpse into some of the troubles which Technic civilization was bringing upon itself, among many others. Ythrians, be not overly proud; only look back, from the heights of time, across Ythrian history, and then forward to the shadow of God across the future.

This tale appears at first glance to have no bearing on the fate-to-be of Avalon. Yet consider: It shows a kindred spirit. Ythri was not the sole world that responded to the challenge which, wittingly or no, humans and starflight had cried. Like the countless tiny influences which, together, draw a hurricane now this way, now that, the actions of more individuals than we can ever know did their work upon history. Also, Paradox and Trillia are not galactically distant from us; they may yet come to be of direct import.

The tale was brought back to Ythri lifetimes ago by the xenologist Fluoch of Mistwood. Arinnian of Stormgate, whose human name is Christopher Holm and who has rendered several Ythrian works into Anglic, prepared this version for the book you behold.

A LITTLE KNOWLEDGE

They found the planet during the first Grand Survey. An expedition to it was organized very soon after the report appeared; for this looked like an impossibility.

It orbited its G9 sun at an average distance of some three astronomical units, thus receiving about one-eighteenth the radiation Earth gets. Under such a condition (and others, e.g., the magnetic field strength which was present) a subjovian ought to have formed; and indeed it had fifteen times the terrestrial mass. But—that mass was concentrated in a solid globe. The atmosphere was only half again as dense as on man's home, and breathable by him.

"Where 'ave h'all the H'atoms gone?" became the standing joke of the research team. Big worlds are supposed to keep enough of their primordial hydrogen and helium to completely dominate the chemistry. Paradox, as it was unofficially christened, did retain some of the latter gas, to a total of eight percent of its air. This posed certain technical problems which had to be solved before anyone dared land. However, land the men must; the puzzle they confronted was so delightfully baffling.

A nearly circular ocean basin suggested an answer which studies of its bottom seemed to confirm. Paradox had begun existence as a fairly standard specimen, complete with four moons. But the largest of these, probably a captured asteroid, had had an eccentric orbit. At last perturbation brought it into the upper atmosphere, which at that time extended beyond Roche's limit. Shock waves, repeated each time one of these ever-deeper grazings was made, blew vast quantities of gas off into space: especially the lighter molecules. Breakup of the moon hastened this process and made it more violent, by presenting more solid surface. Thus at the final crash, most of those meteoroids fell as one body, to form that gigantic astrobleme. Perhaps metallic atoms, thermally ripped free of their ores and splashed as an incandescent fog across half the planet, locked onto the bulk of what hydrogen was left, if any was.

Be that as it may, Paradox now had only a mixture of what had hitherto been comparatively insignificant impurities, carbon dioxide, water vapor, methane, ammonia, and other materials. In short, except for a small amount of helium, it had become rather like the young Earth. It got less heat and light, but greenhouse effect kept most of its water liquid. Life evolved, went into the photosynthesis business, and turned the air into the oxynitrogen common on terrestrials.

The helium had certain interesting biological effects. These were not studied in detail. After all, with the hyperdrive opening endless wonders to them, spacefarers tended to choose the most obviously glamorous. Paradox lay a hundred parsecs from Sol. Thousands upon thousands of worlds were more easily reached; many were more pleasant and less dangerous to walk on. The expedition departed and had no successors.

First it called briefly at a neighboring star, on one of whose planets were intelligent beings that had developed a promising set of civilizations. But, again, quite a few such lay closer to home.

The era of scientific expansion was followed by the era of commercial aggrandizement. Merchant adventurers began to appear in the sector. They ignored Paradox, which had nothing to make a profit on, but investigated the inhabited globe in the nearby system. In the language dominant there at the time, it was called something like Trillia, which thus became its name in League Latin. The speakers of that language were undergoing their equivalent of the First Industrial Revolution, and eager to leap into the modern age.

Unfortunately, they had little to offer that was in demand elsewhere. And even in the spacious terms of the Polesotechnic League, they lived at the far end of a long haul. Their charming arts and crafts made Trillia marginally worth a visit, on those rare occasions when a trader was on such a route that the detour wasn't great. Besides, it was as well to keep an eye on the natives. Lacking the means to buy the important gadgets of Technic society, they had set about developing these for themselves.

Bryce Harker pushed through flowering vines which covered an otherwise doorless entrance. They rustled back into place behind him, smelling like allspice, trapping gold-yellow sunlight in their leaves. That light also slanted through ogive windows in a curving wall, to glow off the grain of the wooden floor. Furniture was sparse: a few stools, a low table bearing an intricately faceted piece of rock crystal. By Trillian standards the ceiling was high; but Harker, who was of average human size, must stoop.

Witweet bounced from an inner room, laid down the book of poems he had been reading, and piped, "Why, be welcome, dear boy—Oo-oo-ooh!"

He looked down the muzzle of a blaster.

The man showed teeth. "Stay right where you are," he commanded. The vocalizer on his breast rendered the sounds he made into soprano cadenzas and arpeggios, the speech of Lenidel. It could do nothing about his vocabulary and grammar. His knowledge did include the fact that, by omitting all honorifics and circumlocutions without apology, he was uttering a deadly insult.

That was the effect he wanted—deadliness.

"My, my, my dear good friend from the revered Solar Commonwealth," Witweet stammered, "is this a, a jest too subtle for a mere pilot like myself to comprehend? I will gladly laugh if you wish, and then we, we shall enjoy tea and cakes. I have genuine Lapsang Soochong tea from Earth, and have just found the most darling recipe for sweet cakes—"

"Quiet!" Harker rapped. His glance flickered to the windows. Outside, flower colors exploded beneath reddish tree trunks; small bright wings went fluttering past; The Waterfall That Rings Like Glass Bells could be heard in the distance. Annanna was akin to most cities of Lenidel, the principal nation on Trillia, in being spread through an immensity of forest and parkscape. Nevertheless, Annanna had a couple of million population, who kept busy. Three aircraft were crossing heaven. At any moment, a pedestrian or cyclist might come along The Pathway Of The Beautiful Blossoms And The Bridge That Arches Like A Note Of Music, and wonder why two humans stood tense outside number 1337.

Witweet regarded the man's skinsuit and boots, the pack on his shoulders, the tightly drawn sharp features behind the weapon. Tears blurred the blue of Witweet's great eyes. "I fear you are engaged in some desperate undertaking which distorts the natural goodness that, I feel certain, still inheres," he quavered. "May I beg the honor of being graciously let help you relieve whatever your distress may be?"

Harker squinted back at the Trillian. *How much do we really know about his breed, anyway? Damned nonhuman thing—Though I never resented his existence till now—* His pulse knocked; his skin was wet and stank, his mouth was dry and cottony-tasting.

Yet his prisoner looked altogether helpless. Witweet was an erect biped; but his tubby frame reached to barely a meter, from the padded feet to the big, scalloped ears. The two arms were broomstick thin, the four fingers on either hand suggested straws. The head was practically spherical, bearing a pug muzzle, moist black nose, tiny mouth, quivering whiskers, upward-slanting tufty brows. That, the tail, and the fluffy silver-gray fur which covered the whole skin, had made Olafsson remark that the only danger to be expected from this race was that eventually their cuteness would become unendurable.

Witweet had nothing upon him except an ornately embroidered kimono and a sash tied in a pink bow. He surely owned no weapons, and probably wouldn't know what to do with any. The Trillians were omnivores, but did not seem to have gone through a hunting stage in their evolution. They had never fought wars, and personal violence was limited to an infrequent scuffle.

Still, Harker thought, *they've shown the guts to push into deep space. I daresay even an unarmed policeman— Courtesy Monitor—could use his vehicle against us, like by ramming.*

Hurry!

"Listen," he said. "Listen carefully. You've heard that most intelligent species have members who don't mind using brute force, outright killing, for other ends than self-defense. Haven't you?"

Witweet waved his tail in assent. "Truly I am baffled by that statement, concerning as it does races whose achievements are of incomparable magnificence. However, not only my poor mind, but those of our most eminent thinkers have been engaged in fruitless endeavors to—"

"Dog your hatch!" The vocalizer made meaningless noises and Harker realized he had shouted in Anglic. He went back to Lenidellian-equivalent. "I don't propose to waste time. My partners and I did not come here to trade as we announced. We came to get a Trillian spaceship. The project is important enough that we'll kill if we must. Make trouble, and I'll blast you to greasy ash. It won't bother me. And you aren't the only possible pilot we can work through, so don't imagine you can block us by sacrificing yourself. I admit you are our best prospect. Obey, cooperate fully, and you'll live. We'll have no reason to destroy you." He paused. "We may even send you home with a good piece of money. We'll be able to afford that."

The bottling of his fur might have made Witweet impressive to another Trillian. To Harker, he became a ball of fuzz in a kimono, an agitated tail and a sound of coloratura anguish. "But this is insanity...if I may say that to a respected guest....One of *our* awkward, lumbering, fragile, unreliable prototype ships—when you came in a vessel representing centuries of advancement—? Why, why, why, in the name of multiple sacredness, why?"

"I'll tell you later," the man said. "You're due for a routine supply trip to, uh, Gwinsai Base, starting tomorrow, right? You'll board this afternoon, to make final inspection and settle in. We're coming along. You'd be leaving in about an hour's time. Your things must already be packed. I didn't cultivate your friendship for nothing, you see! Now, walk slowly ahead of me, bring your luggage back here and open it so I can make sure what you've got. Then we're on our way."

Witweet stared into the blaster. A shudder went through him. His fur collapsed. Tail dragging, he turned toward the inner rooms.

Stocky Leo Dolgorov and ash-blond Einar Olafsson gusted simultaneous oaths of relief when their leader and his prisoner came out onto the path. "What took you that time?" the first demanded. "Were you having a nap?"

"Nah, he entered one of their bowing, scraping, and unction-smearing contests." Olafsson's grin held scant mirth.

"Trouble?" Harker asked.

"N-no...three, four passersby stopped to talk—we told them the story and they went on," Dolgorov said. Harker nodded. He'd put a good deal of thought into that excuse for his guards' standing around—that they were about to pay a social call on Witweet but were waiting until the pilot's special friend Harker had made him a gift. A lie must be plausible, and the Trillian mind was not human.

"We sure hung on the hook, though." Olafsson started as a bicyclist came around a bend in the path and fluted a string of complimentary greetings.

Dwarfed beneath the men, Witweet made reply. No

gun was pointed at him now, but one rested in each of the holsters near his brain. (Harker and companions had striven to convince everybody that the bearing of arms was a peaceful but highly symbolic custom in *their* part of Technic society, that without their weapons they would feel more indecent than a shaven Trillian.) As far as Harker's wire-taut attention registered, Witweet's answer was routine. But probably some forlornness crept into the overtones, for the neighbor stopped.

"Do you feel quite radiantly well, dear boy?" he asked.

"Indeed I do, honored Pwiddy, and thank you in my prettiest thoughts for your ever-sweet consideration," the pilot replied. "I . . . well, these good visitors from the starfaring culture of splendor have been describing some of their experiences—oh, I simply must relate them to you later, dear boy!—and naturally, since I am about to embark on another trip, I have been made pensive by this." Hands, tail, whiskers gesticulated. *Meaning what?* wondered Harker in a chill; and clamping jaws together: *Well, you knew you'd have to take risks to win a kingdom.* "Forgive me, I pray you of your overflowing generosity, that I rush off after such curt words. But I have promises to keep, and considerable distances to go before I sleep."

"Understood." Pwiddy spent a mere five minutes bidding farewell all around before he pedaled off. Meanwhile several others passed by. However, since no well-mannered person would interrupt a conversation even to make salute, they created no problem.

"Let's go." It grated in Dolgorov's throat.

Behind the little witch-hatted house was a pergola wherein rested Witweet's personal flitter. It was large and flashy—large enough for three humans to squeeze into the back—which fact had become an element in Harker's plan. The car that the men had used during their stay on Trillia, they abandoned. It was unmistakably an off-planet vehicle.

"Get started!" Dolgorov cuffed at Witweet.

Olafsson caught his arm and snapped: "Control your emotions! Want to tear his head off?"

Hunched over the dashboard, Witweet squeezed his

eyes shut and shivered till Harker prodded him. "Pull out of that funk," the man said.

"I . . . I beg your pardon. The brutality so appalled me—" Witweet flinched from their laughter. His fingers gripped levers and twisted knobs. Here was no steering by gestures in a light-field, let alone simply speaking an order to an autopilot. The overloaded flitter crawled skyward. Harker detected a flutter in its grav unit, but decided nothing was likely to fail before they reached the spaceport. And after that, nothing would matter except getting off this planet.

Not that it was a bad place, he reflected. Almost Earthlike in size, gravity, air, deliciously edible life forms—an Earth that no longer was and perhaps never had been, wide horizons and big skies, caressed by light and rain. Looking out, he saw woodlands in a thousand hues of green, meadows, river-gleam, an occasional dollhouse dwelling, grain-fields ripening tawny and the soft gaudiness of a flower ranch. Ahead lifted The Mountain Which Presides Over Moonrise In Lenidel, a snowpeak pure as Fuji's. The sun, yellower than Sol, turned it and a few clouds into gold.

A gentle world for a gentle people. Too gentle.

Too bad. For them.

Besides, after six months of it, three city-bred men were about ready to climb screaming out of their skulls. Harker drew forth a cigarette, inhaled it into lighting and filled his lungs with harshness. *I'd almost welcome a fight*, he thought savagely.

But none happened. Half a year of hard, patient study paid richly off. It helped that the Trillians were—well, you couldn't say lax about security, because the need for it had never occurred to them. Witweet radioed to the portmaster as he approached, was informed that everything looked okay, and took his flitter straight through an open cargo lock into a hold of the ship he was to pilot.

The port was like nothing in Technic civilization, unless on the remotest, least visited of outposts. After all, the Trillians had gone in a bare fifty years from propeller-driven aircraft to interstellar spaceships. Such concentration on research and development had necessarily been at the expense of production and exploitation. What few vessels they had were still mostly experimental. The scientific bases they had established on planets of next-door stars needed no more than three or four freighters for their maintenance.

Thus a couple of buildings and a ground-control tower bounded a stretch of ferrocrete on a high, chilly plateau; and that was Trillia's spaceport. Two ships were in. One was being serviced, half its hull plates removed and furry shapes swarming over the emptiness within. The other, assigned to Witweet, stood on landing jacks at the far end of the field. Shaped like a fat torpedo, decorated in floral designs of pink and baby blue, it was as big as a Dromond-class hauler. Yet its payload was under a thousand tons. The primitive systems for drive, control, and life support took up that much room.

"I wish you a just too, too delightful voyage," said the portmaster's voice from the radio. "Would you honor me by accepting an invitation to dinner? My wife has, if I may boast, discovered remarkable culinary attributes of certain sea weeds brought back from Gwinsai; and for my part, dear boy, I would be so interested to hear your opinion of a new verse form with which I am currently experimenting."

"No . . . I thank you, no, impossible, I beg indulgence—" It was hard to tell whether the unevenness of Witweet's response came from terror or from the tobacco smoke that had kept him coughing. He almost flung his vehicle into the spaceship.

Clearance granted, *The Serenity of the Estimable Philosopher Ittypu* lifted into a dawn sky. When Trillia was a dwindling cloud-marbled sapphire among the stars, Harker let out a breath. "We can relax now."

"Where?" Olafsson grumbled. The single cabin barely allowed three humans to crowd together. They'd have to take turns sleeping in the hall that ran aft to the engine room. And their voyage was going to be long. Top pseudovelocity under the snail-powered hyperdrive of this craft would be less than one light-year per day.

"Oh, we can admire the darling murals," Dolgorov fleered. He kicked an intricately painted bulkhead.

Witweet, crouched miserable at the control board, flinched. "I beg you, dear, kind sir, do not scuff the artwork," he said.

"Why should you care?" Dolgorov asked. "You won't be keeping this junkheap."

Witweet wrung his hands. "Defacement is still very wicked. Perhaps the consignee will appreciate my patterns? I spent *such* a time on them, trying to get every teensiest detail correct."

"Is that why your freighters have a single person aboard?" Olafsson laughed. "Always seemed reckless to me, not taking a backup pilot at least. But I suppose two Trillians would get into so fierce an argument about the interior décor that they'd each stalk off in an absolute snit."

"Why, no," said Witweet, a trifle calmer. "We keep personnel down to one because more are not really needed. Piloting between stars is automatic, and the crewbeing is trained in servicing functions. Should he suffer harm en route, the ship will put itself into orbit around the destination planet and can be boarded by others. An extra would thus uselessly occupy space which is often needed for passengers. I am surprised that you, sir, who have set a powerful intellect to prolonged consideration of our astronautical practices, should not have been aware—"

"I was, I was!" Olafsson threw up his hands as far as the overhead permitted. "Ask a rhetorical question and get an oratorical answer."

"May I, in turn, humbly request enlightenment as to your reason for... sequestering... a spacecraft ludicrously inadequate by every standard of your oh, so sophisticated society?"

"You may." Harker's spirits bubbled from relief of tension. They'd pulled it off. They really had. He sat down—the deck was padded and perfumed—and started a cigarette. Through his bones beat the throb of the gravity drive: energy wasted by a clumsy system. The weight it made underfoot fluctuated slightly in a rhythm that felt wavelike.

"I suppose we may as well call ourselves criminals," he said; the Lenidellian word he must use had milder connotations. "There are people back home who wouldn't leave us alive if they knew who'd done certain things. But we never got rich off them. Now we will."

He had no need for recapitulating except the need to gloat: "You know we came to Trillia half a standard year ago, on a League ship that was paying a short visit to buy art. We had goods of our own to barter with, and announced we were going to settle down for a while and look into the possibility of establishing a permanent trading post with a regular shuttle service to some of the Technic planets. That's what the captain of the ship thought too. He advised us against it, said it couldn't pay and we'd simply be stuck on Trillia till the next League vessel chanced by, which wouldn't likely be for more than a year. But when we insisted, and gave him passage money, he shrugged," as did Harker.

"You have told me this," Witweet said. "I thrilled to the ecstasy of what I believed was your friendship."

"Well, I did enjoy your company," Harker smiled. "You're not a bad little osco. Mainly, though, we concentrated on you because we'd learned you qualified for our uses—a regular freighter pilot, a bachelor so we needn't fuss with a family, a chatterer who could be pumped for any information we wanted. Seems we gauged well."

"We better have," Dolgorov said gloomily. "Those trade goods cost us everything we could scratch together. I took a steady job for two years, and lived like a lama, to get my share."

"And now we'll be living like fakirs," said Olafsson. "But afterward—afterward!"

"Evidently your whole aim was to acquire a Trillian ship," Witweet said. "My bemusement at this endures."

"We don't actually want the ship as such, except for

demonstration purposes," Harker said. "What we want is the plans, the design. Between the vessel itself, and the service manuals aboard, we have that in effect."

Witweet's ears quivered. "Do you mean to publish the data for scientific interest? Surely, to beings whose ancestors went on to better models centuries ago—if, indeed, they ever burdened themselves with something this crude—surely the interest is nil. Unless . . . you think many will pay to see, in order to enjoy mirth at the spectacle of our fumbling efforts?" He spread his arms. "Why, you could have bought complete specifications most cheaply; or, indeed, had you requested of me, I would have been bubbly-happy to obtain a set and make you a gift." On a note of timid hope: "Thus you see, dear boy, drastic action is quite unnecessary. Let us return. I will state you remained aboard by mistake—"

Olafsson guffawed. Dolgorov said, "Not even your authorities can be that sloppy-thinking." Harker ground out his cigarette on the deck, which made the pilot wince, and explained at leisured length:

"We want this ship precisely because it's primitive. Your people weren't in the electronic era when the first human explorers contacted you. They, or some later visitors, brought you texts on physics. Then your bright lads had the theory of such things as gravity control and hyperdrive. But the engineering practice was something else again.

"You didn't have plans for a starship. When you finally got an opportunity to inquire, you found that the idealistic period of Technic civilization was over and you must deal with hardheaded entrepreneurs. And the price was set 'way beyond what your whole planet could hope to save in League currency. That was just the price for diagrams, not to speak of an actual vessel. I don't know if you are personally aware of the fact—it's no secret—but this is League policy. The member companies are bound by an agreement.

"They won't prevent anyone from entering space on his own. But take your case on Trillia. You had learned in a general way about, oh, transistors, for instance. But that did not set you up to manufacture them. An entire industrial complex is needed for that and for the million other necessary items. To design and build one, with the inevitable mistakes en route, would take decades at a minimum, and would involve regimenting your entire species and living in poverty because every bit of capital has to be reinvested. Well, you Trillians were too sensible to pay that price. You'd proceed more gradually. Yet at the same time, your scientists, all your more adventurous types were burning to get out into space.

"I agree your decision about that was intelligent too. You saw you couldn't go directly from your earliest hydrocarbon-fuelled engines to a modern starship—to a completely integrated system of thermonuclear power-plant, initiative-grade navigation and engineering computers, full-cycle life support, the whole works, using solid-state circuits, molecular-level and nuclear-level transitions, forcefields instead of moving parts—an *organism*, more energy than matter. No, you wouldn't be able to build that for generations, probably.

"But you could go ahead and develop huge, clumsy, but workable fission-power units. You could use vacuum tubes, glass rectifiers, kilometers of wire, to generate and regulate the necessary forces. You could store data on tape if not in single molecules, retrieve with a cathode-ray scanner if not with a quantum-field pulse, compute with miniaturized gas-filled units that react in microseconds if not with photon interplays that take a nanosecond.

"You're like islanders who had nothing better than canoes till someone happened by in a nuclear-powered submarine. They couldn't copy that, but they might invent a reciprocating steam engine turning a screw—they might attach an airpipe so it could submerge—and it wouldn't impress the outsiders, but it would cross the ocean too, at its own pace; and it would overawe any neighboring tribes."

He stopped for breath.

"I see," Witweet murmured slowly. His tail switched back and forth. "You can sell our designs to sophonts in a proto-industrial stage of technological development. The idea comes from an excellent brain. But why could you not simply buy the plans for resale elsewhere?"

"The damned busybody League." Dolgorov spat.

"The fact is," Olafsson said, "spacecraft—of advanced type—have been sold to, ah, less advanced peoples in the past. Some of those weren't near industrialization, they were Iron Age barbarians, whose only thought was plundering and conquering. They could do that, given ships which are practically self-piloting, self-maintaining, self-everything. It's cost a good many lives and heavy material losses on border planets. But at least none of the barbarians have been able to duplicate the craft thus far. Hunt every pirate and warlord down, and that ends the problem. Or so the League hopes. It's banned any more such trades."

He cleared his throat. "I don't refer to races like the Trillians, who're obviously capable of reaching the stars by themselves and unlikely to be a menace when they do," he said. "You're free to buy anything you can pay for. The price of certain things is set astronomical mainly to keep you from beginning overnight to compete with the old-established outfits. They prefer a gradual phasing-in of newcomers, so they can adjust.

"But aggressive, warlike cultures, that'd not be interested in reaching a peaceful accommodation—they're something else again. There's a total prohibition on supplying their sort with anything that might lead to them getting off their planets in less than centuries. If League agents catch you at it, they don't fool around with rehabilitation like a regular government. They shoot you."

Harker grimaced. "I saw once on a telescreen interview," he remarked, "Old Nick van Rijn said he wouldn't shoot that kind of offenders. He'd hang them. A rope is reusable."

"And this ship *can* be copied," Witweet breathed. "A low industrial technology, lower than ours, could tool up to produce a modified design, in a comparatively short time, if guided by a few engineers from the core civilization."

"I trained as an engineer," Harker said. "Likewise Leo; and Einar spent several years on a planet where one royal family has grandiose ambitions."

"But the horror you would unleash!" wailed the Trillian. He stared into their stoniness. "You would never dare go home," he said.

"Don't want to anyway," Harker answered. "Power, wealth, yes, and everything those will buy—we'll have more than we can use up in our lifetimes, at the court of the Militants. Fun, too." He smiled. "A challenge, you know, to build a space navy from zero. I expect to enjoy my work."

"Will not the, the, the Polesotechnic League . . . take measures?"

"That's why we must operate as we have done. They'd learn about a sale of plans, and then they wouldn't stop till they'd found and suppressed our project. But a non-Technic ship that never reported in won't interest them. Our destination is well outside their sphere of normal operations. They needn't discover any hint of what's going on—till an interstellar empire too big for them to break is there. Meanwhile, as we gain resources, we'll have been modernizing our industry and fleet."

"It's all arranged," Olafsson said. "The day we show up in the land of the Militants, bringing the ship we described to them, we'll become princes."

"Kings, later," Dolgorov added. "Behave accordingly, you xeno. We don't need you much. I'd soon as not boot you through an airlock."

Witweet spent minutes just shuddering.

The Serenity, etc. moved on away from Trillia's golden sun. It had to reach a weaker gravitational field than a human craft would have needed, before its hyperdrive would function.

Harker spent part of that period being shown around, top to bottom and end to end. He'd toured a sister ship before, but hadn't dared ask for demonstrations as thorough as he now demanded. "I want to know this monstrosity we've got, inside out," he said while personally tearing down and rebuilding a cumbersome oxygen renewer. He could do this because most equipment was paired, against the expectation of eventual in-flight down time.

In a hold, among cases of supplies for the research team on Gwinsai, he was surprised to recognize a lean cylindroid, one hundred twenty centimeters long. "But here's a Solar-built courier!" he exclaimed.

Witweet made eager gestures of agreement. He'd been falling over himself to oblige his captors. "For messages in case of emergency, magnificent sir," he babbled. "A hyperdrive unit, an autopilot, a radio to call at journey's end till someone comes and retrieves the enclosed letter—"

"I know, I know. But why not build your own?"

"Well, if you will deign to reflect upon the matter, you will realize that anything we could build would be too slow and unreliable to afford very probable help. Especially since it is most unlikely that, at any given time, another spaceship would be ready to depart Trillia on the instant. Therefore this courier is set, as you can see if you wish to examine the program, to go a considerably greater distance—though nevertheless not taking long, your human constructions being superlatively fast—to the planet called, ah, Oasis...an Anglic word meaning a lovely, cool, refreshing haven, am I correct?"

Harker nodded impatiently. "Yes, one of the League companies does keep a small base there."

"We have arranged that they will send aid if requested. At a price, to be sure. However, for our poor economy, as ridiculous a hulk as this is still a heavy investment, worth insuring."

"I see. I didn't know you bought such gadgets—not that there'd be a pegged price on them; they don't matter any more than spices or medical equipment. Of course, I couldn't find out every detail in advance, especially not things you people take so for granted that you didn't think to mention them." On impulse, Harker patted the round head. "You know, Witweet, I guess I do like you. I will see you're rewarded for your help."

"Passage home will suffice," the Trillian said quietly, "though I do not know how I can face my kinfolk after having been the instrument of death and ruin for millions of innocents."

"Then don't go home," Harker suggested. "We can't release you for years in any case, to blab our scheme and our coordinates. But we could smuggle in whatever and whoever you wanted, same as for ourselves."

The head rose beneath his palm as the slight form straightened. "Very well," Witweet declared.

That fast? jarred through Harker. *He is nonhuman, yes, but—* The wondering was dissipated by the continuing voice:

"Actually, dear boy, I must disabuse you. We did not buy our couriers, we salvaged them."

"What? Where?"

"Have you heard of a planet named, by its human discoverers, Paradox?"

Harker searched his memory. Before leaving Earth he had consulted every record he could find about this entire stellar neighborhood. Poorly known though it was to men, there had been a huge mass of data—suns, worlds. . . . "I think so," he said. "Big, isn't it? With, uh, a freaky atmosphere."

"Yes." Witweet spoke rapidly. "It gave the original impetus to Technic exploration of our vicinity. But later the men departed. In recent years, when we ourselves became able to pay visits, we found their abandoned camp. A great deal of gear had been left behind, presumably because it was designed for Paradox only and would be of no use elsewhere, hence not worth hauling back. Among these machines we came upon a few couriers. I suppose they had been overlooked. Your civilization can afford profligacy, if I may use that term in due respectfulness."

He crouched, as if expecting a blow. His eyes glittered in the gloom of the hold.

"Hm." Harker frowned. "I suppose by now you've stripped the place."

"Well, no." Witweet brushed nervously at his rising fur. "Like the men, we saw no use in, for example, tractors designed for a gravity of two-point-eight terrestrial. They can operate well and cheaply on Paradox, since their fuel is crude oil, of which an abundant supply exists near the campsite. But we already had electric-celled grav motors, however archaic they are by your standards. And we do not need weapons like those we found, presumably for protection against animals. We certainly have no intention of colonizing Paradox!"

"Hm." The human waved, as if to brush off the chattering voice. "Hm." He slouched off, hands in pockets, pondering.

In the time that followed, he consulted the navigator's bible. His reading knowledge of Lenidellian was fair. The entry for Paradox was as laconic as it would have been in a Technic reference; despite the limited range of their operations, the Trillians had already encountered too many worlds to allow flowery descriptions. Star type and coordinates, orbital elements, mass density, atmospheric composition, temperature ranges, and the usual rest were listed. There was no notation about habitability, but none was needed. The original explorers hadn't been poisoned or come down with disease; Trillian metabolism was similar to theirs.

The gravity field was not too strong for this ship to make landing and, later, ascent. Weather shouldn't pose any hazards, given reasonable care in choosing one's path; that was a weakly energized environment. Besides, the vessel was meant for planetfalls, and Witweet was a skilled pilot in his fashion. . . .

Harker discussed the idea with Olafsson and Dolgorov. "It won't take but a few days," he said, "and we might pick up something really good. You know I've not been too happy about the Militants' prospects of building an ample industrial base fast enough to suit us. Well, a few machines like this, simple things they can easily copy but designed by good engineers . . . could make a big difference."

"They're probably rustheaps," Dolgorov snorted. "That was long ago."

"No, durable alloys were available then," Olafsson said. "I like the notion intrinsically, Bryce. I don't like the thought of our tame xeno taking us down. He might crash us on purpose."

"That sniveling faggot?" Dolgorov gibed. He jerked his head backward at Witweet, who sat enormous-eyed in the pilot chair listening to a language he did not understand. "By accident, maybe, seeing how scared he is!"

"It's a risk we take at journey's end," Harker reminded them. "Not a real risk. The ship has some ingenious failsafes built in. Anyhow, I intend to stand over him the whole way down. If he does a single thing wrong, I'll kill him. The controls aren't made for me, but I can get us aloft again, and afterward we can re-rig."

Olafsson nodded. "Seems worth a try," he said. "What can we lose except a little time and sweat?"

Paradox rolled enormous in the viewscreen, a darkling world, the sky-band along its sunrise horizon redder than Earth's, polar caps and winter snowfields gashed by the teeth of mountains, tropical forest and pampas a yellow-brown fading into raw deserts on one side and chopped off on another side by the furious surf of an ocean where three moons fought their tidal wars. The sun was distance-dwarfed, more dull in hue than Sol, nevertheless too bright to look near. Elsewhere, stars filled illimitable blackness.

It was very quiet aboard, save for the mutter of powerplant and ventilators, the breathing of men, their restless shuffling about in the cramped cabin. The air was blued and fouled by cigarette smoke; Witweet would have fled into the corridor, but they made him stay, clutching a perfume-dripping kerchief to his nose.

Harker straightened from the observation screen. Even at full magnification, the rudimentary electro-optical system gave little except blurriness. But he'd practiced on it, while orbiting a satellite, till he felt he could read those wavering traces.

"Campsite and machinery, all right," he said. "No details. Brush has covered everything. When were your people here last, Witweet?"

"Several years back," the Trillian wheezed. "Evidently vegetation grows apace. Do you agree on the safety of a landing?"

"Yes. We may snap a few branches, as well as flatten a lot of shrubs, but we'll back down slowly, the last hundred meters, and we'll keep the radar, sonar, and gravar sweeps going." Harker glanced at his men. "Next thing is to compute our descent pattern," he said. "But first I want to spell out again, point by point, exactly what each of us is to do under exactly what circumstances. I don't aim to take chances."

"Oh, no," Witweet squeaked. "I beg you, dear boy, I beg you the prettiest I can, please don't."

After the tension of transit, landing was an anticlimax. All at once the engine fell silent. A wind whistled around the hull. Viewscreens showed low, thick-boled trees; fronded brownish leaves; tawny undergrowth; shadowy glimpses of metal objects beneath vines and amidst tall, whipping stalks. The sun stood at late afernoon in a sky almost purple.

Witweet checked the indicators while Harker studied them over his head. "Air breathable, of course," the pilot said, "which frees us of the handicap of having to wear smelly old spacesuits. We should bleed it in gradually, since the pressure is greater than ours at present and we don't want earaches, do we? Temperature—" He shivered delicately. "Be certain you are wrapped up snug before you venture outside."

"You're venturing first," Harker informed him.

"What? Oo-ooh, my good, sweet, darling friend, no, please, no! It is *cold* out there, scarcely above freezing. And once on the ground, no gravity generator to help, why, weight will be tripled. What could I possibly, possibly do? No, let me stay inside, keep the home fires burning—I mean keep the thermostat at a cozy temperature—and, yes, I will make you the nicest pot of tea—"

"If you don't stop fluttering and do what you're told, I'll tear your head off," Dolgorov said. "Guess what I'll use your skin for."

"Let's get cracking," Olafsson said. "I don't want to stay in this Helheim any longer than you."

They opened a hatch the least bit. While Paradoxian air seeped in, they dressed as warmly as might be, except for Harker. He intended to stand by the controls for the first investigatory period. The entering gases added a whine to the wind-noise. Their helium content made speech and other sounds higher pitched, not quite natural; and this would have to be endured for the rest of the journey, since the ship had insufficient reserve tanks to flush out the new atmosphere. A breath of cold got by the heaters, and a rank smell of alien growth.

But you could get used to hearing funny, Harker thought. And the native life might stink, but it was harmless. You couldn't eat it and be nourished, but neither could its germs live off your body. If heavy weapons had been needed here, they were far more likely against large, blundering herbivores than against local tigers.

That didn't mean they couldn't be used in war.

Trembling, eyes squinched half-shut, tail wrapped around his muzzle, the rest of him bundled in four layers of kimono, Witweet crept to the personnel lock. Its outer valve swung wide. The gangway went down. Harker grinned to see the dwarfish shape descend, step by step under the sudden harsh hauling of the planet.

"Sure you can move around in that pull?" he asked his companions.

"Sure," Dolgorov grunted. "An extra hundred-fifty kilos? I can backpack more than that, and then it's less well distributed."

"Stay cautious, though. Too damned easy to fall and break bones."

"I'd worry more about the cardiovascular system,"

Olafsson said. "One can stand three gees a while, but not for a very long while. Fluid begins seeping out of the cell walls, the heart feels the strain too much—and we've no gravanal along as the first expedition must have had."

"We'll only be here a few days at most," Harker said, "with plenty of chances to rest inboard."

"Right," Olafsson agreed. "Forward!"

Gripping his blaster, he shuffled onto the gangway. Dolgorov followed. Below, Witweet huddled. Harker looked out at bleakness, felt the wind slap his face with chill, and was glad he could stay behind. Later he must take his turn outdoors, but for now he could enjoy warmth, decent weight—

The world reached up and grabbed him. Off balance, he fell to the deck. His left hand struck first, pain gushed, he saw the wrist and arm splinter. He screamed. The sound came weak as well as shrill, out of a breast laboring against thrice the heaviness it should have had. At the same time, the lights in the ship went out.

Witweet perched on a boulder. His back was straight in spite of the drag on him, which made his robes hang stiff as if carved on an idol of some minor god of justice. His tail, erect, blew jauntily in the bitter sunset wind; the colors of his garments were bold against murk that rose in the forest around the dead spacecraft.

He looked into the guns of three men, and into the terror that had taken them behind the eyes; and Witweet laughed.

"Put those toys away before you hurt yourselves," he said, using no circumlocutions or honorifics.

"You bastard, you swine, you filthy treacherous xeno, I'll kill you," Dolgorov groaned. "Slowly."

"First you must catch me," Witweet answered. "By virtue of being small, I have a larger surface-to-volume ratio than you. My bones, my muscles, my veins and capillaries and cell membranes suffer less force per square centimeter than do yours. I can move faster than you, here. I can survive longer."

"You can't outrun a blaster bolt," Olafsson said.

"No. You can kill me with that—a quick, clean death which does not frighten me. Really, because we of Lenidel observe certain customs of courtesy, use certain turns of speech—because our males in particular are encouraged to develop esthetic interests and compassion—does that mean we are cowardly or effeminate?" The Trillian clicked his tongue. "If you supposed so, you committed an elementary logical fallacy which our philosophers name the does-not-follow."

"Why shouldn't we kill you?"

"That is inadvisable. You see, your only hope is quick rescue by a League ship. The courier can operate here, being a solid-state device. It can reach Oasis and summon a vessel, which, itself of similar construction, can also land on Paradox and take off again... in time. This would be impossible for a Trillian craft. Even if one were ready to leave, I doubt the Astronautical Senate would permit the pilot to risk descent.

"Well, rescuers will naturally ask questions. I cannot imagine any story which you three men, alone, might concoct that would stand up under the subsequent, inevitable investigation. On the other hand, I can explain to the League's agents that you were only coming along to look into trade possibilities and that we were trapped on Paradox by a faulty autopilot which threw us into a descent curve. I can do this *in detail*, which you could not if you killed me. They will return us all to Trillia, where there is no death penalty."

Witweet smoothed his wind-ruffled whiskers. "The alternative," he finished, "is to die where you are, in a most unpleasant fashion."

Harker's splinted arm gestured back the incoherent Dolgorov. He set an example by holstering his own gun. "I ... guess we're outsmarted," he said, word by foul-tasting word. "But what happened? Why's the ship inoperable?"

"Helium in the atmosphere," Witweet explained calmly. "The monatomic helium molecule is ooh-how-small. It diffuses through almost every material. Vacuum tubes, glass rectifiers, electronic switches dependent on pure gases, any such device soon becomes poisoned. You, who were used to a technology that had long left this kind of thing behind, did not know the fact, and it did not occur to you as a possibility. We Trillians are, of course, rather acutely aware of the problem. I am the first who ever set foot on Paradox. You should have noted that my courier is a present-day model."

"I see," Olafsson mumbled.

"The sooner we get our message off, the better," Witweet said. "By the way, I assume you are not so foolish as to contemplate the piratical takeover of a vessel of the Polesotechnic League."

"Oh, no!" said they, including Dolgorov, and the other two blasters were sheathed.

"One thing, though," Harker said. A part of him wondered if the pain in him was responsible for his own abnormal self-possession. Counterirritant against dismay? Would he weep after it wore off? "You bargain for your life by promising to have ours spared. How do we know we want your terms? What'll they do to us on Trillia?"

"Entertain no fears," Witweet assured him. "We are not vindictive, as I have heard some species are; nor have we any officious concept of 'rehabilitation.' Wrongdoers are required to make amends to the fullest extent possible. You three have cost my people a valuable ship and whatever cargo cannot be salvaged. You must have technological knowledge to convey, of equal worth. The working conditions will not be intolerable. Probably you can make restitution and win release before you reach old age.

"Now, come, get busy. First we dispatch that courier, then we prepare what is necessary for our survival until rescue."

He hopped down from the rock, which none of them would have been able to do unscathed, and approached them through gathering cold twilight with the stride of a conqueror.

A book such as this would be rattlewing indeed did it not tell anything about Falkayn himself. Yet there seems no lift in repeating common knowledge or reprinting tales which, in their different versions, are as popular and available as ever aforetime.

Therefore Hloch reckons himself fortunate in having two stories whereof the fullness is well-nigh unknown, and which furthermore deal with events whose consequences are still breeding winds.

The first concerns Merseia. Although most folk, even here on far Avalon, have caught some awareness of yonder world and the strange fate that stooped upon it, the part that the Founder-to-be took has long been shadowed, as has been the very fact that he was there at all. For reasons of discretion, he never spoke publicly of the matter, and his report was well buried in League archives. Among his descendants, only a vague tradition remained that he had passed through such air.

Hearing this, Rennhi set herself to hunt down the truth. On Falkayn's natal planet Hermes she learned that, several years after the Babur War, he and van Rijn had quietly transferred many data units thither, putting them in care of the Grand Ducal house and his own immediate kin. The feeling was that they would be more secure than

in the Solar System, now when a time of storms was so
clearly brewing. After the League broke up, there was no
decipherment program anymore, and the units lay
virtually forgotten in storage. Rennhi won permission to
transfer the molecular patterns. Once home again, she
instigated a code-breaking effort. It was supported by the
armed forces in hopes of snatching useful information,
for by that time war with the Empire had become a
thunderhead threat.

This hope was indirectly fulfilled. Nothing in the
records had military value, but the cracking of a
fiendishly clever cipher developed cryptographic capabilities. Nor does much in them have any particular bearing
on Avalon. Nearly everything deals with details of
matters whose bones grew white centuries ago. Interrupted by hostilities, the study has only been completed lately.

A few treasures did come forth, bright among them a
full account of what happened on Merseia. Hloch and
Arinnian together have worked it into narrative form.

DAY OF BURNING

For who knows how long, the star had orbited quietly in the wilderness between Betelgeuse and Rigel. It was rather more massive than average—about half again as much as Sol—and shone with corresponding intensity, white-hot, corona and prominences a terrible glory. But there are no few like it. A ship of the first Grand Survey noted its existence. However, the crew were more interested in a neighbor sun which had planets, and could not linger long in that system either. The galaxy is too big; their purpose was to get some hint about this spiral arm which we inhabit. Thus certain spectroscopic omens escaped their notice.

No one returned thither for a pair of centuries. Technic civilization had more than it could handle, let alone comprehend, in the millions of stars closer to home. So the fact remained unsuspected that this one was older than normal for its type in its region, must indeed have wandered in from other parts. Not that it was very ancient, astronomically speaking. But the great childless suns evolve fast and strangely.

By chance, though, a scout from the Polesotechnic League, exploring far in search of new markets, was passing within a light-year when the star exploded.

Say instead (insofar as simultaneity has any meaning across interstellar distances) that the death agony had occurred some months before. Ever more fierce, thermonuclear reaction had burned up the last hydrogen at the center. Unbalanced by radiation pressure, the outer layers collapsed beneath their own weight. Forces were released which triggered a wholly different order of atomic fusions. New elements came into being, not only those which may be found in the planets but also the short-lived transuranics; for a while, technetium itself dominated that anarchy. Neutrons and neutrinos flooded forth, carrying with them the last balancing energy. Compression turned into catastrophe. At the brief peak, the supernova was as radiant as its entire galaxy.

So close, the ship's personnel would have died had she not been in hyperdrive. They did not remain there. A dangerous amount of radiation was still touching them between quantum microjumps. And they were not equipped to study the phenomenon. This was the first chance in our history to observe a new supernova. Earth was too remote to help. But the scientific colony on Catawrayannis could be reached fairly soon. It could dispatch laboratory craft.

Now to track in detail what was going to happen, considerable resources were demanded. Among these were a place where men could live and instruments be made to order as the need for them arose. Such things could not well be sent from the usual factories. By the time they arrived, the wave front carrying information about rapidly progressing events would have traveled so far that inverse-square enfeeblement would create maddening inaccuracies.

But a little beyond one parsec from the star—an excellent distance for observation over a period of years—was a G-type sun. One of its planets was terrestroid to numerous points of classification, both physically and biochemically. Survey records showed that the most advanced culture on it was at the verge of an industrial-scientific revolution. Ideal!

Except, to be sure, that Survey's information was less than sketchy, and two centuries out of date.

"No."

Master Merchant David Falkayn stepped backward in startlement. The four nearest guards clutched at their pistols. Peripherally and profanely, Falkayn wondered what canon he had violated now.

"Beg, uh, beg pardon?" he fumbled.

Morruchan Long-Ax, the Hand of the Vach Dathyr, leaned forward on his dais. He was big even for a Merseian, which meant that he overtopped Falkayn's rangy height by a good fifteen centimeters. Long, shoulder-flared orange robes and horned miter made his bulk almost overwhelming. Beneath them, he was approximately anthropoid, save for a slanting posture counterbalanced by the tail which, with his booted feet, made a tripod for him to sit on. The skin was green, faintly scaled, totally hairless. A spiky ridge ran from the top of his skull to the end of that tail. Instead of earflaps, he had deep convolutions in his head. But the face was manlike, in a heavy-boned fashion, and the physiology was essentially mammalian.

How familiar the mind was, behind those jet eyes, Falkayn did not know.

The harsh basso said: "You shall not take the rule of this world. If we surrendered the right and freehold they won, the God would cast back the souls of our ancestors to shriek at us."

Falkayn's glance flickered around. He had seldom felt so alone. The audience chamber of Castle Afon stretched high and gaunt, proportioned like nothing men had ever built. Curiously woven tapestries on the stone walls, between windows arched at both top and bottom, and battle banners hung from the rafters, did little to stop echoes. The troopers lining the hall, down to a hearth whose fire could have roasted an elephant, wore armor and helmets with demon masks. The guns which they added to curved swords and barbed pikes did not seem out of place. Rather, what appeared unattainably far was a glimpse of ice-blue sky outside.

The air was chill with winter. Gravity was little higher than Terrestrial, but Falkayn felt it dragging at him.

He straightened. He had his own sidearm, no chemical slugthrower but an energy weapon. Adzel, abroad in the city, and Chee Lan aboard the ship, were listening in via the transceiver on his wrist. And the ship had power to level all Ardaig. Morruchan must realize as much.

But he had to be made to cooperate.

Falkayn picked his words with care: "I pray forgiveness, Hand, if perchance in mine ignorance I misuse thy... uh... your tongue. Naught was intended save friendliness. Hither bring I news of peril impending, for the which ye must busk yourselves betimes lest ye lose everything ye possess. My folk would fain show your folk what to do. So vast is the striving needed, and so scant the time, that perforce ye must take our counsel. Else can we be of no avail. But never will we act as conquerors. 'Twere not simply an evil deed, but 'twould boot us naught, whose trafficking is with many worlds. Nay, we would be brothers, come to help in a day of sore need."

Morruchan scowled and rubbed his chin. "Say on, then," he replied. "Frankly, I am dubious. You claim Valenderay is about to become a supernova—"

"Nay, Hand, I declare it hath already done so. The light therefrom will smite this planet in less than three years."

The time unit Falkayn actually used was Merseian, a trifle greater than Earth's. He sweated and swore to himself at the language problem. The Survey xenologists had gotten a fair grasp of Eriau in the several months they spent here, and Falkayn and his shipmates had acquired it by synapse transform while en route. But now it turned out that, two hundred years back, Eriau had been in a state of linguistic overturn. He wasn't even pronouncing the vowels right.

He tried to update his grammar. "Would ye, uh, I mean if your desire is... if you want confirmation, we can take you or a trusty member of your household so near in our vessel that the starburst is beheld with living eyes."

"No doubt the scientists and poets will duel for a berth on that trip," Morruchan said in a dry voice. "But I believe you already. You yourself, your ship and companions, are proof." His tone sharpened. "At the same time, I am no Believer, imagining you half-divine because you come from outside. Your civilization has a technological head start on mine, nothing else. A careful reading of the records from that other brief period when aliens dwelt among us shows they had no reason more noble than professional curiosity. And that was fitful; they left, and none ever returned. Until now.

"So: what do you want from us?"

Falkayn relaxed a bit. Morruchan seemed to be his own kind despite everything, not awestruck, not idealistic, not driven by some incomprehensible nonhuman motivation, but a shrewd and skeptical politician of a pragmatically oriented culture.

Seems to be, the man cautioned himself. *What do I really know about Merseia?*

Judging by observation made in orbit, radio monitoring, initial radio contact, and the ride here in an electric groundcar, this planet still held a jumble of societies, dominated by the one which surrounded the Wilwidh Ocean. Two centuries ago, local rule had been divided among aristocratic clans. He supposed that a degree of continental unification had since been achieved, for his request for an interview with the highest authority had gotten him to Ardaig and a confrontation with this individual. But could Morruchan speak for his entire species? Falkayn doubted it.

Nevertheless, you had to start somewhere.

"I shall be honest, Hand," he said. "My crew and I are come as naught but preparers of the way. Can we succeed, we will be rewarded with a share in whatever gain ensueth. For our scientists wish to use Merseia and its moons as bases wherefrom to observe the supernova through the next dozen years. Best for them would be if your folk could provide them with most of their needs, not alone food but such instruments as they tell you how to fashion. For this they will pay fairly; and in addition, ye will acquire knowledge.

"Yet first must we assure that there remaineth a Merseian civilization. To do that, we must wreak huge works. And ye will pay us for our toil and goods supplied to that end. The price will not be usurious, but it will allow us a profit. Out of it, we will buy whatever Merseian wares can be sold at home for further profit." He smiled. "Thus all may win and none need fear. The Polesotechnic League compriseth nor conquerors nor bandits, naught save merchant adventurers who seek to make their"— more or less—"honest living."

"Hunh!" Morruchan growled. "Now we bite down to the bone. When you first communicated and spoke about a supernova, my colleagues and I consulted the astronomers. We are not altogether savages here; we have at least gone as far as atomic power and interplanetary travel. Well, our astronomers said that such a star reaches a peak output about fifteen billion times as great as Korych. Is this right?"

"Close enough, Hand, if Korych be your own sun."

"The only nearby one which might burst in this manner is Valenderay. From your description, the brightest in the southern sky, you must be thinking of it too."

Falkayn nodded, realized he wasn't sure if this gesture meant the same thing on Merseia, remembered it did, and said: "Aye, Hand."

"It sounded terrifying," Morruchan said, "until they pointed out that Valenderay is three and a half light-years distant. And this is a reach so enormous that no mind can swallow it. The radiation, when it gets to us, will equal a mere one-third of what comes daily from Korych. And in some fifty-five days" (Terrestrial) "it will have dwindled to half . . . and so on, until before long we see little except a bright nebula at night.

"True, we can expect troublesome weather, storms, torrential rains, perhaps some flooding if sufficient of the south polar ice cap melts. But that will pass. In any case, the center of civilization is here, in the northern hemisphere. It is also true that, at peak, there will be a dangerous amount of ultraviolet and X radiation. But Merseia's atmosphere will block it.

"Thus." Morruchan leaned back on his tail and bridged the fingers of his oddly humanlike hands. "The peril you speak of scarcely exists. What do you really want?"

Falkayn's boyhood training, as a nobleman's son on Hermes, rallied within him. He squared his shoulders. He was not unimpressive, a tall, fair-haired young man with blue eyes bright in a lean, high-cheekboned face. "Hand," he said gravely, "I perceive you have not yet had time to consult your folk who are wise in matters—"

And then he broke down. He didn't know the word for "electronic."

Morruchan refrained from taking advantage. Instead, the Merseian became quite helpful. Falkayn's rejoinder was halting, often interrupted while he and the other worked out what a phrase must be. But, in essence and in current language, what he said was:

"The Hand is correct as far as he goes. But consider what will follow. The eruption of a supernova is violent beyond imagining. Nuclear processes are involved, so complex that we ourselves don't yet understand them in detail. That's why we want to study them. But this much we do know, and your physicists will confirm it.

"As nuclei and electrons recombine in that supernal fireball, they generate asymmetrical magnetic pulses. Surely you know what this does when it happens in the detonation of an atomic weapon. Now think of it on a stellar scale. When those forces hit, they will blast straight through Merseia's own magnetic field, down to the very surface. Unshielded electric motors, generators, transmission lines...oh, yes, no doubt you have surge arrestors, but your circuit breakers will be tripped, intolerable voltages will be induced, the entire system will be wrecked. Likewise telecommunications lines. And computers. If you use transistors—ah, you do—the flipflop between p and n type conduction will wipe every memory bank, stop every operation in its tracks.

"Electrons, riding that magnetic pulse, will not be long in arriving. As they spiral in the planet's field, their synchrotron radiation will completely blanket whatever electronic apparatus you may have salvaged. Protons should be slower, pushed to about half the speed of light. Then come the alpha particles, then the heavier matter: year after year after year of cosmic fallout, most of it radioactive, to a total greater by orders of magnitude than any war could create before civilization was destroyed. Your planetary magnetism is no real shield. The majority of ions are energetic enough to get through. Nor is your atmosphere any good defense. Heavy nuclei, sleeting through it, will produce secondary radiation that does reach the ground.

"I do not say this planet will be wiped clean of life. But I do say that, without ample advance preparation, it will suffer ecological disaster. Your species might or might not survive; but if you do, it will be as a few starveling primitives. The early breakdown of the electric system on which your civilization is now dependent will have seen to that. Just imagine. Suddenly no more food moves into the cities. The dwellers go forth as a ravening horde. But if most of your farmers are as specialized as I suppose, they won't even be able to support themselves. Once fighting and famine have become general, no more medical service will be possible, and the pestilences will start. It will be like the aftermath of an all-out nuclear strike against a country with no civil defense. I gather you've avoided that on Merseia. But you certainly have theoretical studies of the subject, and—I have seen planets where it did happen.

"Long before the end, your colonies throughout this system will have been destroyed by the destruction of the apparatus that keeps the colonists alive. And for many years, no spaceship will be able to move.

"Unless you accept our help. We know how to generate force screens, small ones for machines, gigantic ones which can give an entire planet some protection. Not enough—but we also know how to insulate against the energies that get through. We know how to build engines and communications lines which are not affected. We know how to sow substances which protect life against hard radiation. We know how to restore mutated genes. In short, we have the knowledge you need for survival.

"The effect will be enormous. Most of it you must carry out yourselves. Our available personnel are too few, our lines of interstellar transportation too long. But we can supply engineers and organizers.

"To be blunt, Hand, you are very lucky that we learned of this in time, barely in time. Don't fear us. We have no ambitions toward Merseia. If nothing else, it lies far beyond our normal sphere of operation, and we have millions of more profitable planets much closer to home. We want to save you, because you are sentient beings. But it'll be expensive, and a lot of the work will have to be done by outfits like mine, which exist to make a profit. So, besides a scientific base, we want a reasonable economic return.

"Eventually, though, we'll depart. What you do then is your own affair. But you'll still have your civilization. You'll also have a great deal of new equipment and new knowledge. I think you're getting a bargain."

Falkayn stopped. For a while, silence dwelt in that long dim hall. He grew aware of odors which had never been on Earth or Hermes.

Morruchan said at last, slowly: "This must be thought on. I shall have to confer with my colleagues, and others. There are so many complications. For example, I see no good reason to do anything for the colony on Ronruad, and many excellent reasons for letting it die."

"What?" Falkayn's teeth clicked together. "Meaneth the Hand the next outward planet? But meseems faring goeth on apace throughout this system."

"Indeed, indeed," Morruchan said impatiently. "We depend on the other planets for a number of raw materials, like fissionables, or complex gases from the outer worlds. Ronruad, though, is of use only to the Gethfennu."

He spoke that word with such distaste that Falkayn postponed asking for a definition. "What recommendations I make in my report will draw heavily upon the Hand's wisdom," the human said.

"Your courtesy is appreciated," Morruchan replied: with how much irony, Falkayn wasn't sure. He was taking the news more coolly than expected. But then, he was of a different race from men, and a soldierly tradition as well. "I hope that, for now, you will honor the Vach Dathyr by guesting us."

"Well—" Falkayn hesitated. He had planned on returning to his ship. But he might do better on the spot. The Survey crew had found Merseian food nourishing to men, in fact tasty. One report had waxed ecstatic about the ale.

"I thank the Hand."

"Good. I suggest you go to the chambers already prepared, to rest and refresh yourself. With your leave, a messenger will come presently to ask what he should bring you from your vessel. Unless you wish to move it here?"

"Uh, best not . . . policy—" Falkayn didn't care to take chances. The Merseians were not so far behind the League that they couldn't spring a nasty surprise if they wanted to.

Morruchan raised the skin above his brow ridges but made no comment. "You will dine with me and my councillors at sunset," he said. They parted ceremoniously.

A pair of guards conducted Falkayn out, through a series of corridors and up a sweeping staircase whose bannister was carved into the form of a snake. At the end, he was ushered into a suite. The rooms were spacious, their comfort-making gadgetry not greatly below Technic standards. Reptile-skin carpets and animal skulls mounted on the crimson-draped walls were a little disquieting, but what the hell. A balcony gave on a view of the palace gardens, whose austere good taste was reminiscent of Original Japanese, and on the city.

Ardaig was sizeable, must hold two or three million souls. This quarter was ancient, with buildings of gray stone fantastically turreted and battlemented. The hills which ringed it were checkered by the estates of the wealthy. Snow lay white and blue-shadowed between. Ramparted with tall modern structures, the bay shone like gunmetal. Cargo ships moved in and out, a delta-wing jet whistled overhead. But he heard little traffic noise; nonessential vehicles were banned in the sacred Old Quarter.

"Wedhi is my name, Protector," said the short Merseian in the black tunic who had been awaiting him. "May he consider me his liegeman, to do as he commands." Tail slapped ankles in salute.

"My thanks," Falkayn said. "Thou mayest show me how one maketh use of facilities." He couldn't wait to see a bathroom designed for these people. "And then, mayhap, a tankard of beer, a textbook on political geography, and privacy for some hours."

"The Protector has spoken. If he will follow me?"

The two of them entered the adjoining chamber, which was furnished for sleeping. As if by accident, Wedhi's tail brushed the door. It wasn't automatic, merely hinged, and closed under the impact. Wedhi seized Falkayn's hand and pressed something into the palm. Simultaneously, he caught his lips between his teeth. A signal for silence?

With a tingle along his spine, Falkayn nodded and stuffed the bit of paper into a pocket.

When he was alone, he opened the note, hunched over in case of spy eyes. The alphabet hadn't changed.

Be wary, star dweller. Morruchan Long-Ax is no friend. If you can arrange for one of your company to come tonight in secret to the house at the corner of Triau's Street and Victory Way which is marked by twined fylfots over the door, the truth shall be explained.

As darkness fell, the moon Neihevin rose full, Luna size and copper color, above eastward hills whose forests glistened with frost. Lythyr was already up, a small pale crescent. Rigel blazed in the heart of that constellation named the Spear Bearer.

Chee Lan turned from the viewscreen with a shiver and an unladylike phrase. "But I am not equipped to do that," said the ship's computer.

"The suggestion was addressed to my Gods," Chee answered.

She sat for a while, brooding on her wrongs. Ta-chih-chien-pih—O_2 Eridani A II or Cynthia to humans—felt even more distant than it was, warm ruddy sunlight and rustling leaves around treetop homes lost in time as well as space. Not only the cold outside daunted her. Those Merseians were so bloody *big!*

She herself was no larger than a medium-sized dog, though the bush of her tail added a good deal. Her arms, almost as long as her legs, ended in delicate six-fingered hands. White fur fluffed about her, save where it made a bluish mask across the green eyes and round, blunt-muzzled face. Seeing her for the first time, human females were apt to call her darling.

She bristled. Ears, whiskers, and hair stood erect. What was she—descendant of carnivores who chased their prey in five-meter leaps from branch to branch, xenobiologist by training, trade pioneer by choice, and pistol champion because she liked to shoot guns—what was she doing, feeling so much as respect for a gaggle of slewfooted bald barbarians? Mainly she was irritated. While standing by aboard the ship, she'd hoped to complete her latest piece of sculpture. Instead, she must hustle into that pustulent excuse for weather, and skulk through a stone garbage dump that its perpetrators called a city, and hear some yokel drone on for hours about some squabble between drunken cockroaches which he thought was politics... and pretend to take the whole farce seriously!

A narcotic cigarette soothed her, however ferocious the puffs in which she consumed it. "I guess the matter is important, at that," she murmured. "Fat commissions for me if the project succeeds."

"My programming is to the effect that our primary objective is humanitarian," said the computer. "Though I cannot find that concept in my data storage."

"Never mind, Muddlehead," Chee replied. Her mood had turned benign. "If you want to know, it relates to those constraints you have filed under Law and Ethics. But no concern of ours, this trip. Oh, the bleeding hearts do quack about Rescuing a Promising Civilization, as if the galaxy didn't have too chaos many civilizations already. Well, if they want to foot the bill, it's their taxes. They'll have to work with the League, because the League has most of the ships, which it won't hire out for nothing. And the League has to start with us, because trade pioneers are supposed to be experts in making first contacts and we happened to be the sole such crew in reach. Which is our good luck, I suppose."

She stubbed out her cigarette and busied herself with preparations. There was, for a fact, no alternative. She'd had to admit that, after a three-way radio conversation with her partners. (They didn't worry about eavesdroppers, when not a Merseian knew a word of Anglic.) Falkayn was stuck in what's-his-name's palace. Adzel was loose in the city, but he'd be the last one you'd pick for an undercover mission. Which left Chee Lan.

"Maintain contact with all three of us," she ordered the ship. "Record everything coming in tonight over my two-way. Don't stir without orders—in a galactic language— and don't respond to any native attempts at a communication. Tell us at once whatever unusual you observe. If you haven't heard from any of us for twenty-four hours at a stretch, return to Catawrayannis and report."

No answer being indicated, the computer made none.

Chee buckled on a gravity harness, a tool kit, and two guns, a stunner and a blaster. Over them she threw a black mantle, less for warmth than concealment. Dousing the lights, she had the personnel lock open just long enough to let her through, jumped, and took to the air.

It bit her with chill. Flowing past, it felt liquid. An enormous silence dwelt beneath heaven; the hum of her grav was lost. Passing above the troopers who surrounded *Muddlin' Through* with armor and artillery—a sensible precaution from the native standpoint, she had to agree, sensibly labelled an honor guard—she saw the forlorn twinkle of campfires and heard a snatch of hoarse song. Then a hovercraft whirred near, big and black athwart the Milky Way, and she must change course to avoid being seen.

For a while she flew above snow-clad wilderness. On an unknown planet, you didn't land downtown if you could help it. Hills and woods gave way at length to a cultivated plain where the lights of villages huddled around tower-jagged castles. Merseia—this continent, at least—appeared to have retained feudalism even as it swung into an industrial age. Or had it?

Perhaps tonight she would find out.

The seacoast hove in view, and Ardaig. That city did not gleam with illumination and brawl with traffic as most Technic communities did. Yellow windows strewed its night, like fireflies trapped in a web of phosphorescent paving. The River Oiss gleamed dull where it poured through town and into the bay, on which there shone a double moonglade. No, triple; Wythna was rising now. A murmur of machines lifted skyward.

Chee dodged another aircraft and streaked down for the darkling Old Quarter. She landed behind a shuttered bazaar and sought the nearest alley. Crouched there, she peered forth. In this section, the streets were decked with a hardy turf which ice had blanketed, and lit by widely spaced lamps. A Merseian went past, riding a horned gwydh. His tail was draped back across the animal's rump; his cloak fluttered behind him to reveal a quilted jacket reinforced with glittering metal discs, and a rifle slanted over his shoulder.

No guardsman, surely; Chee had seen what the military wore, and Falkayn had transmitted pictures of Morruchan's household troops to her via a hand scanner. He had also passed on the information that those latter doubled as police. So why was a civilian going armed? It bespoke a degree of lawlessness that fitted ill with a technological society...unless that society was in more trouble than Morruchan had admitted. Chee made certain her own guns were loose in the holsters.

The clop-clop of hooves faded away. Chee stuck her head out of the alley and took bearings from street signs. Instead of words, they used colorful heraldic emblems. But the Survey people had compiled a good map of Ardaig, which Falkayn's gang had memorized. The Old Quarter ought not to have changed much. She loped off, seeking cover whenever she heard a rider or pedestrian approach. There weren't many.

This corner! Squinting through murk, she identified the symbol carved in the lintel of a lean gray house. Quickly, she ran up the stairs and rapped on the door. Her free hand rested on the stunner.

The door creaked open. Light streamed through. A Merseian stood silhouetted against it. He carried a pistol himself. His head moved back and forth, peering into the night. "Here I am, thou idiot," Chee muttered.

He looked down. A jerk went through his body. "*Huya!* You are from the star ship?"

"Nay," Chee sneered, "I am come to inspect the plumbing." She darted past him, into a wainscoted corridor. "If thou wouldst preserve this chickling secrecy of thine, might one suggest that thou close yon portal?"

The Merseian did. He stood a moment, regarding her in the glow of an incandescent bulb overhead. "I thought you would be...different."

"They were Terrans who first visited this world, but surely thou didst not think every race in the cosmos is formed to those ridiculous specifications. Now I've scant time to spare for whatever griping ye have here to do, so lead me to thine acher."

The Merseian obeyed. His garments were about like ordinary street clothes, belted tunic and baggy trousers, but a certain precision in their cut—as well as blue-and-gold stripes and the double fylfot embroidered on the sleeves—indicated they were a livery. Or a uniform? Chee felt the second guess confirmed when she noted two others, similarly attired, standing armed in front of a door. They saluted her and let her through.

The room beyond was baronial. Radiant heating had been installed, but a fire also roared on the hearth. Chee paid scant attention to rich draperies and carven pillars. Her gaze went to the two who sat awaiting her.

One was scarfaced, athletic, his tailtip restlessly aflicker. His robe was blue and gold, and he carried a short ceremonial spear. At sight of her, he drew a quick breath. The Cynthian decided she'd better be polite. "I hight Chee Lan, worthies, come from the interstellar expedition in response to your kind invitation."

"*Khraich.*" The aristocrat recovered his poise and touched finger to brow. "Be welcome. I am Dagla, called Quick-to-Anger, the Hand of the Vach Hallen. And my comrade: Olgor hu Freylin, his rank Warmaster in the Republic of Lafdigu, here in Ardaig as agent for his country."

That being was middle-aged, plump, with skin more dark and features more flat than was common around the Wilwidh Ocean. His garb was foreign too, a sort of toga with metal threads woven into the purple cloth. And he was soft-spoken, imperturbable, quite without the harshness of these lands. He crossed his arms—gesture of greeting?—and said in accented Eriau:

"Great is the honor. Since the last visitors from your high civilization were confined largely to this region, perhaps you have no knowledge of mine. May I therefore say that Lafdigu lies in the southern hemisphere, occupying a goodly part of its continent. In those days we were unindustrialized, but now, one hopes, the situation has altered."

"Nay, Warmaster, be sure our folk heard much about Lafdigu's venerable culture and regretted they had no time to learn therefrom." Chee got more tactful the bigger the lies she told. Inwardly, she groaned: *Oh, no! We haven't troubles enough, there has to be international politicking too!*

A servant appeared with a cut-crystal decanter and goblets. "I trust that your race, like the Terran, can partake of Merseian refreshment?" Dagla said.

"Indeed," Chee replied. "'Tis necessary that they who voyage together use the same stuffs. I thank the Hand."

"But we had not looked for, *hurgh*, a guest your size," Olgor said. "Perhaps a smaller glass? The wine is potent."

"This is excellent." Chee hopped onto a low table, squatted, and raised her goblet two-handed. "Galactic custom is that we drink to the health of friends. To yours, then, worthies." She took a long draught. The fact that alcohol does not affect the Cynthian brain was one she had often found it advantageous to keep silent about.

Dagla tossed off a yet larger amount, took a turn around the room, and growled: "Enough formalities, by your leave, Shipmaster." She discarded her cloak. "Shipmistress?" He gulped. His society had a kitchen-church-and-kids attitude toward females. "We—*kh-h-h*—we've grave matters to discuss."

"The Hand is too abrupt with our noble guest," Olgor chided.

"Nay, time is short," Chee said. "And clearly the business hath great weight, sith ye went to the length of suborning a servant in Morruchan's very stronghold."

Dagla grinned. "I planted Wedhi there eight years ago. He's a good voice-tube."

"No doubt the Hand of the Vach Hallen hath surety of all his own servitors?" Chee purred.

Dagla frowned. Olgor's lips twitched upward.

"Chances must be taken." Dagla made a chopping gesture. "All we know is what was learned from your first radio communications, which said little. Morruchan was quick to isolate you. His hope is plainly to let you hear no more of the truth than he wants. To use you! Here, in this house, we may speak frankly with each other."

As frankly as you two klongs choose, Chee thought. "I listen with care," she said.

Piece by piece, between Dagla and Olgor, the story emerged. It sounded reasonable, as far as it went.

When the Survey team arrived, the Wilwidh culture stood on the brink of a machine age. The scientific method had been invented. There was a heliocentric astronomy, a post-Newtonian, pre-Maxwellian physics, a dawning chemistry, a well-developed taxonomy, some speculations about evolution. Steam engines were at work on the first railroads. But political power was fragmented among the Vachs. The scientists, the engineers, the teachers were each under the patronage of one or another Hand.

The visitors from space had too much sense of responsibility to pass on significant practical information. It wouldn't have done a great deal of good anyway. How do you make transistors, for instance, before you can refine ultrapure semimetals? And why should you want to, when you don't yet have electronics? But the humans had given theoretical and experimental science a boost by what they related—above all, by the simple and tremendous fact of their presence.

And then they left.

A fierce, proud people had their noses rubbed in their own insignificance. Chee guessed that here lay the root of most of the social upheaval which followed. And belike a more urgent motive than curiosity or profit began to drive the scientists: the desire, the need to catch up, to bring Merseia in one leap onto the galactic scene.

The Vachs had shrewdly ridden the wave. Piecemeal they shelved their quarrels, formed a loose confederation, met the new problems well enough that no movement arose to strip them of their privileges. But rivalry persisted, and cross purposes, and often a reactionary spirit, a harking back to olden days when the young were properly respectful of the God and their elders.

And meanwhile modernization spread across the planet. A country which did not keep pace soon found itself under foreign domination. Lafdigu had succeeded best. Chee got a distinct impression that the Republic was actually a hobnail-booted dictatorship. Its own imperial ambitions clashed with those of the Hands. Nuclear war was averted on the ground, but space battles had erupted from time to time, horribly and inconclusively.

"So here we are," Dagla said. "Largest, most powerful, the Vach Dathyr speak loudest in this realm. But others press upon them, Hallen, Ynvory, Rueth, yes, even landless Urdiolch. You can see what it would mean if any one of them obtained your exclusive services."

Olgor nodded. "Among other things," he said, "Morruchan Long-Ax would like to contrive that my country is ignored. We are in the southern hemisphere. We will get the worst of the supernova blast. If unprotected, we will be removed from his equations."

"In whole truth, Shipmistress," Dagla added, "I don't believe Morruchan wants your help. *Khraich*, yes, a minimum, to forestall utter collapse. But he has long ranted against the modern world and its ways. He'd not be sorry to see industrial civilization reduced so small that full-plumed feudalism returns."

"How shall he prevent us from doing our work?" Chee asked. "Surely he is not fool enough to kill us. Others will follow."

"He'll bet the knucklebones as they fall," Dagla said. "At the very least, he'll try to keep his position—that you work through him and get most of your information from his sources—and use it to increase his power. At the expense of every other party!"

"We could predict it even in Lafdigu, when first we heard of your coming," Olgor said. "The Strategic College dispatched me here to make what alliances I can. Several Hands are not unwilling to see my country continue as a force in the world, as the price for our help in diminishing their closer neighbors."

Chee said slowly: "Meseems ye make no few assumptions about us, on scant knowledge."

"Shipmistress," said Olgor, "civilized Merseia has had two centuries to study each word, each picture, each legend about your people. Some believe you akin to gods—or demons—yes, whole cults have flowered from the expectation of your return, and I do not venture to guess what they will do now that you are come. But there have also been cooler minds; and that first expedition was honest in what it told, was it not?

"Hence: the most reasonable postulate is that none of the starfaring races have mental powers we do not. They simply have longer histories. And as we came to know how many the stars are, we saw how thinly your civilization must be spread among them. You will not expend any enormous effort on us, in terms of your own economy. You cannot. You have too much else to do. Nor have you time to learn everything about Merseia and decide every detail of what you will effect. The supernova will flame in our skies in less than three years. You must cooperate with whatever authorities you find, and take their words for what the crucial things are to save and what others must be abandoned. Is this not truth?"

Chee weighed her answer. "To a certain degree," she said carefully, "ye have right."

"Morruchan knows this," Dagla said. "He'll use the knowledge as best he can." He leaned forward, towering above her. "For our part, we will not tolerate it. Better the world go down in ruin, to be rebuilt by us, than that the Vach Dathyr engulf what our ancestors wrought. No planetwide effort can succeed without the help of a majority. Unless we get a full voice in what decisions are made, we'll fight."

"Hand, Hand," reproved Olgor.

"Nay, I take no offense," Chee said. "Rather, I give thanks for so plain a warning. Ye will understand, we bear ill will toward none on Merseia, and have no partisanship—" *in your wretched little jockeyings.* "If ye have prepared a document stating your position, gladly will we ponder on the same."

Olgor opened a casket and took out a sheaf of papers bound in something like snakeskin. "This was hastily written," he apologized. "At another date we would like to give you a fuller account."

" 'Twill serve for the nonce." Chee wondered if she should stay a while. No doubt she could learn something further. But chaos, how much propaganda she'd have to strain out of what she heard! Also, she'd now been diplomatic as long as anyone could expect. Hadn't she?

They could call the ship directly, she told them. If Morruchan tried to jam the airwaves, she'd jam him, into an unlikely posture. Olgor looked shocked. Dagla objected to communication which could be monitored. Chee sighed. "Well, then, invite us hither for a private talk," she said. "Will Morruchan attack you for that?"

"No . . . I suppose not . . . but he'll get some idea of what we know and what we're doing."

"My belief was," said Chee in her smoothest voice, "that the Hand of the Vach Hallen wished naught save an end to these intrigues and selfishnesses, an openness in which Merseians might strive together for the common welfare."

She had never cherished any such silly notion, but Dagla couldn't very well admit that his chief concern was to get his own relatives on top of everybody else. He made wistful noises about a transmitter which could not be detected by Merseian equipment. Surely the galactics had one? They did, but Chee wasn't about to pass on stuff with that kind of potentialities. She expressed regrets—nothing had been brought along—so sorry—goodnight, Hand, goodnight, Warmaster.

The guard who had let her in escorted her to the front door. She wondered why her hosts didn't. Caution, or just a different set of mores? Well, no matter. Back to the ship. She ran down the frosty street, looking for an alley from which her takeoff wouldn't be noticed. Someone might get trigger happy.

An entrance gaped between two houses. She darted into darkness. A body fell upon her. Other arms clasped tight, pinioning. She yelled. A light gleamed briefly, a sack was thrust over her head, she inhaled a sweet-sick odor and whirled from her senses.

Adzel still wasn't sure what was happening to him, or how it had begun. There he'd been, minding his own

business, and suddenly he was the featured speaker at a
prayer meeting. If that was what it was.

He cleared his throat. "My friends," he said.

A roar went through the hall. Faces and faces and faces
stared at the rostrum which he filled with his four and a
half meters of length. A thousand Mersians must be
present: clients, commoners, city proletariat, drably
clad for the most part. Many were female; the lower
classes didn't segregate sexes as rigidly as the upper. Their
odors made the air thick and musky. Being in a new part
of Ardaig, the hall was built plain. But its proportions, the
contrasting hues of paneling, the symbols painted in
scarlet across the walls, reminded Adzel he was on a
foreign planet.

He took advantage of the interruption to lift the
transceiver hung around his neck up to his snout and
mutter plaintively, "David, what *shall* I tell them?"

"Be benevolent and noncommittal," Falkayn's voice
advised. "I don't think mine host likes this one bit."

The Wodenite glanced over the seething crowd, to the
entrance. Three of Morruchan's household guards stood
by the door and glowered.

He didn't worry about physical attack. Quite apart
from having the ship for a backup, he was too formidable
himself: a thousand-kilo centauroid, his natural armorplate shining green above and gold below, his spine more
impressively ridged than any Merseian's. His ears were
not soft cartilage but bony, a similar shelf protected his
eyes, his rather crocodilian face opened on an alarming
array of fangs. Thus he had been the logical member of
the team to wander around the city today, gathering
impressions. Morruchan's arguments against this had
been politely overruled. "Fear no trouble, Hand,"
Falkayn said truthfully. "Adzel never seeketh any out. He
is a Buddhist, a lover of peace who can well afford
tolerance anent the behavior of others."

By the same token, though, he had not been able to
refuse the importunities of the crowd which finally
cornered him.

"Have you got word from Chee?" he asked.

"Nothing yet," Falkayn said. "Muddlehead's monitoring, of course. I imagine she'll contact us tomorrow. Now don't you interrupt me either, I'm in the middle of an interminable official banquet."

Adzel raised his arms for silence, but here that gesture was an encouragement for more shouts. He changed position, his hooves clattering on the platform, and his tail knocked over a floor candelabrum. "Oh, I'm sorry," he exclaimed. A red-robed Merseian named Gryf, the chief nut of this organization—Star Believers, was that what they called themselves?—picked the thing up and managed to silence the house.

"My friends," Adzel tried again. "Er...my friends, I am, er, deeply appreciative of the honor ye do me in asking for some few words." He tried to remember the political speeches he had heard while a student on Earth. "In the great fraternity of intelligent races throughout the universe, surely Merseia hath a majestic part to fulfill."

"Show us—show us the way!" howled from the floor. "The way, the truth, the long road futureward!"

"Ah...yes. With pleasure." Adzel turned to Gryf. "But perchance first your, er, glorious leader should explain to me the purposes of this—this—" What was the word for "club"? Or did he want "church"?

Mainly he wanted information.

"Why, the noble galactic jests," Gryf said in ecstasy. "You know we are those who have waited, living by the precepts the galactics taught, in loyal expectation of their return which they promised us. We are your chosen instrument for the deliverance of Merseia from its ills. Use us!"

Adzel was a planetologist by profession, but his large bump of curiosity had led him to study in other fields. His mind shuffled through books he had read, societies he had visited...yes, he identified the pattern. These were cultists, who'd attached a quasi-religious significance to what had actually been quite a casual stopover. Oh, the jewel in the lotus! What kind of mess had ensued?

He had to find out.

"That's, ah, very fine," he said. "Very fine indeed. Ah . . . how many do ye number?"

"More than two million, Protector, in twenty different nations. Some high ones are among us, yes, the Heir of the Vach Isthyr. But most belong to the virtuous poor. Had they all known the Protector was to walk forth this day— Well, they'll come as fast as may be, to hear your bidding."

An influx like that could make the pot boil over, Adzel foresaw. Ardaig had been restless enough as he quested through its streets. And what little had been learned about basic Merseian instincts, by the Survey psychologists, suggested they were a combative species. Mass hysteria could take ugly forms.

"No!" the Wodenite cried. The volume nearly blew Gryf off the podium. Adzel moderated his tone. "Let them stay home. Calm, patience, carrying out one's daily round of duties, those are the galactic virtues."

Try telling that to a merchant adventurer! Adzel checked himself. "I fear we have no miracles to offer."

He was about to say that the word he carried was of blood, sweat, and tears. But no. When you dealt with a people whose reactions you couldn't predict, such news must be released with care. Falkayn's first radio communications had been guarded, on precisely that account.

"This is clear," Gryf said. He was not stupid, or even crazy, except in his beliefs. "We must ourselves release ourselves from our oppressors. Tell us how to begin."

Adzel saw Morruchan's troopers grip their rifles tight. *We're expected to start some kind of social revolution?* he thought wildly. *But we can't! It's not our business. Our business is to save your lives, and for that we must not weaken but strengthen whatever authority can work with us, and any revolution will be slow to mature, a consequence of technology—Dare I tell them this tonight?*

Pedantry might soothe them, if only by boring them to

sleep. "Among those sophonts who need a government,"
Adzel said, "the basic requirement for a government
which is to function well is that it be legitimate, and the
basic problem of any political innovator is how to
continue, or else establish anew, a sound basis for that
legitimacy. Thus newcomers like mineself cannot—"

He was interrupted (later he was tempted to say
"rescued") by a noise outside. It grew louder, a harsh
chant, the clatter of feet on pavement. Females in the
audience wailed. Males snarled and moved toward the
door. Gryf sprang from the platform, down to what Adzel
identified as a telecom, and activated the scanner. It
showed the street, and an armed mob. High over them,
against snow-laden roofs and night sky, flapped a yellow
banner.

"Demonists!" Gryf groaned. "I was afraid of this."

Adzel joined him. "Who be they?"

"A lunatic sect. They imagine you galactics mean, have
meant from the first, to corrupt us to our destruction. . . . I
was prepared, though. See." From alleys and doorways
moved close-ranked knots of husky males. They carried
weapons.

A trooper snapped words into the microphone of a
walkie-talkie. Sending for help, no doubt, to quell the
oncoming riot. Adzel returned to the rostrum and filled
the hall with his pleas that everyone remain inside.

He might have succeeded, by reverberation if not
reason. But his own transceiver awoke with Falkayn's
voice: "Get here at once! Chee's been nabbed!"

"What? Who did it? Why?" The racket around became
of scant importance.

"I don't know. Muddlehead just alerted me. She'd left
this place she was at. Muddlehead received a yell, sounds
of scuffling, then no more from her. I'm sending him aloft,
to try and track her by the carrier wave. He says the source
is moving. You move too, back to Afon."

Adzel did. He took part of the wall with him.

Korych rose through winter mists that turned gold as
they smoked past city towers and above the river.

Kettledrums rolled their ritual from Eidh Hill. Shutters came down off windows and doors, market circles began to fill, noise lifted out of a hundred small workshops. Distantly, but deeper and more portentous, sounded the buzz of traffic and power from the new quarters, hoot of ships on the bay, whine of jets overhead, thunder of rockets as a craft left the spaceport for the moon Seith.

Morruchan Long-Ax switched off the lights in his confidence chamber. Dawnglow streamed pale through glass, picking out the haggardness of faces. "I am weary," he said, "and we are on a barren trail."

"Hand," said Falkayn, "it had better not be. Here we stay until we have reached some decision."

Morruchan and Dagla glared. Olgor grew expressionless. They were none of them accustomed to being addressed thus. Falkayn gave them stare for stare, and Adzel lifted his head from where he lay coiled on the floor. The Merseians slumped back onto their tails.

"Your whole world may be at stake, worthies," Falkayn said. "My people will not wish to spend time and treasure, aye, some lives, if they look for such ungrateful treatment."

He picked up the harness and kit which lay on Morruchan's desk and hefted them. Guided by Muddle-head, searchers from this household had found the apparatus in a ditch outside town and brought it here several hours ago. Clearly Chee's kidnappers had suspected a signal was being emitted. The things felt pitifully light in his hand.

"What more can be said?" Olgor argued. "We have each voiced a suspicion that one of the others engineered the deed to gain a lever for himself. Or yet a different Vach, or another nation, may have done it; or the Demonists; or even the Star Believers, for some twisted reason." He turned to Dagla. "Are you certain you have no inkling who that servant of yours may have been working for?"

"I told you before, no," said the Hallen chief. "It's not our way in this country to pry into lives. I know only that Dwyr entered my service a few years ago, and gave satisfaction, and now has also vanished. So I presume he was a spy for someone else, and told his masters of a chance to seize a galactic. A telecom call would be easy to make, and they needed only to cover the few possible routes she could take on leaving me."

"In sum," Morruchan declared, "he acted just like your spy who betrayed my doings to you."

"Enough, worthies," Falkayn sighed. "Too stinking often this night have we tracked the same ground. Perchance investigation will give some clues to this Dwyr, whence he came and so forth. But such taketh time. We must needs look into every possibility at once. Including your very selves. Best ye perform a mutual checking."

"And who shall do the like for you?" Morruchan asked.

"What meaneth the Hand?"

"This might be a trick of your own."

Falkayn clutched his hair. "For what conceivable reason?" He wanted to say more, but relations were strained already.

"How should I know?" Morruchan retorted. "You are unknowns. You *say* you have no imperial designs here, but your agents have met with rivals of mine, with a cult whose main hope is to upset the order of things—and with how many else? The Gethfennu?"

"Would the Hand be so gracious as to explain to me who those are?" said Adzel in an oil-on-the-waves voice.

"We described them already," Dagla answered.

"Then 'twas whilst I was out, Hand, directing our ship in its search and subsequent return to base. Indulge a humble fool's request, I beg you."

The idea of someone equipped like Adzel calling himself a humble fool took the Merseians so much aback that they forgot to stay angry. Falkayn added: "I'd not mind hearing about them again. Never suspected I their existence erenow."

"They are the criminal syndicate, spread across the world and on into space," Morruchan said. "Thieves, assassins, harlots, tricksters, corrupters of all good."

He went on, while Falkayn analyzed his words. No doubt the Gethfennu were a bad influence. But Morruchan was too prejudiced, and had too little historical sense, to see why they flourished. The industrial revolution had shaken foundation stones loose from society. Workers flocking to the cities found themselves cut off from the old feudal restrictions . . . and securities. Cultural and material impoverishment bred lawlessness. Yet the baronial tradition survived, in a distorted form; gangs were soon gathered into a network which offered members protection and purpose as well as loot.

The underground kingdom of the Gethfennu could not be destroyed by Vachs and nations divided against each other. It fought back too effectively, with money and influence more often than with violence. And, to be sure, it provided some safety valve. A commoner who went to one of its gambling dens or joyhouses might get fleeced, but he would not plot insurrection.

So a tacit compromise was reached, the kind that many planets have known, Earth not least among them. Racketeering and vice were held to a tolerable level, confined to certain areas and certain classes, by the gang lords. Murder, robbery, and shakedown did not touch the aristocratic palace or the high financial office. Bribery did, in some countries, and thereby the Gethfennu was strengthened.

Of late, its tentacles had stretched beyond these skies. It bought into established interplanetary enterprises. And then there was Ronruad, the next planet out. Except for scientific research, it had scant intrinsic value, but bases upon it were of so great strategic importance that they had occasioned wars. Hence the last general peace treaty had neutralized it, placed it outside any jurisdiction. Soon afterward, the Gethfennu took advantage of this by building a colony there, where anything went. A spaceship line, under the syndicate's open-secret control, offered passenger service. Luridor became the foremost town for respectable Merseians to go in search of unrestrained, if expensive fun. It also became a hatchery of trouble, and Falkayn could understand why Morruchan didn't want it protected against the supernova.

Neither, he found, did Dagla. Probably few if any Hands did. Olgor was less emphatic, but agreed that, at best, Ronruad should get a very low priority.

"The Gethfennu may, then, have seized Chee Lan for ransom?" Adzel said.

"Perhaps," Dagla said. "Though the ransom may be that you galactics help them. If they've infiltrated Hand Morruchan's service too, they could know what the situation is."

"In that case," Falkayn objected, "they are scarcely so naive as to think—"

"I will investigate," Morruchan promised. "I may make direct inquiry. But channels of communication with the Gethfennu masters are devious, therefore slow."

"In any event," Falkayn said bleakly, "Adzel and I do not propose to leave our partner in the grip of criminals— for years, after which they may cut her throat."

"You do not know they have her," Olgor reminded him.

"True. Yet may we prowl somewhat through space, out toward their colony. For little can we do on Merseia, where our knowledge is scant. Here must ye search, worthies, and contrive that all others search with you."

The command seemed to break Morruchan's thin-stretched patience. "Do you imagine we've nothing better to do than hunt for one creature? We, who steer millions?"

Falkayn lost his temper likewise. "If ye wish to keep on doing thus, best ye make the finding of Chee Lan your foremost concern!"

"Gently, gently," Olgor said. "We are so tired that we are turning on allies. And that is not well." He laid a hand on Falkayn's shoulder. "Galactic," he said, "surely you can understand that organizing a systemwide hunt, in a world as diverse as ours, is a greater task than the hunt itself. Why, no few leaders of nations, tribes, clans, factions will not believe the truth if they are told. Proving it to them will require diplomatic skill. Then there are others whose main interest will be to see if they cannot somehow maneuver this affair to give them an advantage over us. And yet others hope you do go away and never return; I do not speak merely of the Demonists."

"If Chee be not returned safely," Falkayn said, "those last may well get their wish."

Olgor smiled. The expression went no deeper than his lips. "Galactic," he murmured, "let us not play word games. Your scientists stand to win knowledge and prestige here, your merchants a profit. They will not allow an unfortunate incident, caused by a few Merseians and affecting only one of their fold...they will not let that come between them and their objectives. Will they?"

Falkayn looked into the ebony eyes. His own were the first to drop. Nausea caught at his gullet. The Warmaster of Lafdigu had identified his bluff and called it.

Oh, no doubt these who confronted him would mount some kind of search. If nothing else, they'd be anxious to learn what outfit had infiltrated agents onto their staffs, and to what extent. No doubt, also, various other Merseians would cooperate. But the investigation would be ill-coordinated and lackadaisical. It would hardly succeed against beings as wily as those who captured Chee Lan.

These three here—nigh the whole of Merseia—just didn't give a damn about her.

She awoke in a cell.

It was less than three meters long, half that in width and height: windowless, doorless, comfortless. A coat of paint did not hide the basic construction, which was of large blocks. Their unresponsiveness to her fist-pounding suggested a high density. Brackets were bolted into the walls, to hold equipment of different sorts in place. Despite non-Technic design, Chee recognized a glow-lamp, a thermostated air renewer, a waste unit, an acceleration couch...space gear, by Cosmos!

No sound, no vibration other than the faint whirr of the air unit's fan, reached her. The walls were altogether blank. After a while, they seemed to move closer. She chattered obscenities at them.

But she came near weeping with relief when one block slid aside. A Merseian face looked in. Behind was polished metal. Rumble, clangor, shouted commands resounded through what must be a spaceship's hull, from what must be a spaceport outside.

"Are you well?" asked the Merseian. He looked still tougher than average, but he was trying for courtesy, and he wore a neat tunic with insignia of rank.

Chee debated whether to make a jump, claw his eyes out, and bolt for freedom. No, not a chance. But neither was she going to embrace him. "Quite well, I thank thee," she snarled, "if thou'lt set aside trifles such as that thy heart-rotten varlets have beaten and gassed me, and I am athirst and anhungered. For this outrage, methinks I'll summon my mates to blow thy pesthole of a planet from the universe it defileth."

The Merseian laughed. "You can't be too sick, with that kind of spirit. Here are food and water." He passed her some containers. "We blast off soon for a voyage of a few days. If I can supply you with anything safe, I will."

"Where are we bound? Who art thou? What meaneth—"

"*Hurh*, little one, I'm not going to leave this smugglehole open very long, for any spillmouth to notice. Tell me this instant what you want, so I can try to have it sent from the city."

Later Chee swore at herself, more picturesquely than she had ever cursed even Adzel. Had she specified the right things, they might have been a clue for her partners. But she was too foggy in the head, too dazed by events. Automatically, she asked for books and films which might help her understand the Merseian situation better. And a grammar text, she added in haste. She was tired of sounding like a local Shakespeare. The Merseian nodded and pushed the block back in place. She heard a faint click. Doubtless a tongue-and-groove lock, operated by a magnetic key.

The rations were revivifying. Before long, Chee felt in shape to make deductions. She was evidently in a secret compartment, built into the wall of a radiation shelter. Merseian interplanetary vessels ran on a thermonuclear-powered ion drive. Those which made landings—ferries tending the big ships, or special jobs such as this presumably was—set down in deep silos and departed from them, so that electromagnetic fields could contain the blast and neutralize it before it poisoned the neighborhood. And each craft carried a blockhouse for crew and passengers to huddle in, should they get caught by a solar storm. Altogether, the engineering was superb. Too bad it would go by the board as soon as gravity drive and force screens became available.

A few days, at one Merseian gee: hm, that meant an adjacent planet. Not recalling the present positions, Chee wasn't sure which. A lot of space traffic moved in the Korychan System, as instruments had shown while *Muddlin' Through* approached. From a distance, in magniscreens, she had observed some of the fleet, capacious cargo vessels and sleek navel units.

Her captor returned with the materials she had requested and a warning to strap in for blastoff. He introduced himself genially as Iriad the Wayfarer, in charge of this dispatch boat.

"Who are thou working for?" Chee demanded.

He hesitated, then shrugged. "The Gethfennu." The block glided back to imprison her.

Lift was nothing like the easy upward floating of a galactic ship. Acceleration rammed Chee down into her couch and sat on her chest. Thunder shuddered through the very blockhouse. Eternal minutes passed before the pressure slacked off and the boat fell into steady running.

After that, for a timeless time, Chee had nothing to do but study. The officers brought her rations. They were a mixed lot, from every part of Merseia; some did not speak Eriau, and none had much to say to her. She considered tinkering her life support apparatus into a weapon, but without tools the prospect was hopeless. So for amusement she elaborated the things she would like to do to Iriad, come the day. Her partners would have flinched.

Once her stomach, the only clock she had, told her she was far overdue for a meal. When finally her cell was opened, she leaped forward in a whirlwind of abuse. Iriad stepped back and raised a pistol. Chee stopped and said: "Well, what happened? Hadn't my swill gotten moldly enough?"

Iriad looked shaken. "We were boarded," he said low.

"How's that?" Acceleration had never varied.

"By . . . your people. They laid alongside, matching our vector as easily as one runner might pace another. I did not know what armament they had, so—He who came aboard was a dragon."

Chee beat her fists on the shelter deck. Oh, no, no, no! Adzel had passed within meters of her, and never suspected . . . the big, ugly, vacuum-skulled bumblemaker!

Iriad straightened. "But Haguan warned me it might happen," he said with a return of self-confidence. "We know somewhat about smuggling. And you are not gods, you galactics."

"Where did they go?"

"Away. To inspect other vessels. Let them."

"Do you seriously hope to keep me hidden for long?"

"Ronruad is full of Haguan's boltholes." Iriad gave her her lunch, collected the empty containers, and departed.

He came back several meals later, to supervise her transferral from the cell to a packing crate. Under guns, Chee obeyed his instructions. She was strapped into padding, alongside an air unit, and left in darkness. There followed hours of maneuver, landing, waiting, being unloaded and trucked to some destination.

Finally the box was opened. Chee emerged slowly. Weight was less than half a standard gee, but her muscles were cramped. A pair of workers bore the crate away. Guards stayed behind, with a Merseian who claimed to be a medic. The checkup he gave her was expert and sophisticated enough to bear him out. He said she should rest a while, and they left her alone.

Her suite was interior but luxurious. The food brought her was excellent. She curled in bed and told herself to sleep.

Eventually she was taken down a long, panelled corridor and up a spiral ramp to meet him who had ordered her caught.

He squatted behind a desk of dark, polished wood that looked a hectare in area. Thick white fur carpeted the room and muffled footsteps. Pictures glowed, music sighed, incense sweetened the air. Windows gave a view outside; this part of the warren projected aboveground. Chee saw ruddy sand, strange wild shrubbery, a dust storm walking across a gaunt range of hills and crowned with ice crystals. Korych stood near the horizon, shrunken, but fierce through the tenuous atmosphere. A few stars also shone in that purple sky. Chee recognized Valenderay, and shivered a little. So bright and steady it looked; and yet, at this moment, death was riding from it on the wings of light.

"Greeting, galactic." The Eriau was accented differently from Olgor's. "I am Haguan Eluatz. Your name, I gather, is Chee Lan."

She arched her back, bottled her tail, and spat. But she felt very helpless. The Merseian was huge, with a belly that bulged forward his embroidered robe. He was not of the Wilwidh stock, his skin was shiny black and heavily scaled, his eyes almond-shaped, his nose a scimitar.

One ring-glittering hand made a gesture. Chee's guards slapped tails to ankles and left. The door closed behind them. But a pistol lay on Haguan's desk, next to an intercom.

He smiled. "Be not afraid. No harm is intended you. We regret the indignities you have suffered and will try to make amends. Sheer necessity forced us to act."

"The necessity for suicide?" Chee snorted.

"For survival. Now why don't you make yourself comfortable on yonder couch? We have talk to forge, we two. I can send for whatever refreshment you desire. Some arthberry wine, perhaps?"

Chee shook her head, but did jump onto the seat.

"Suppose you explain your abominable behavior," she said.

"Gladly." Haguan shifted the weight on his tail. "You may not know what the Gethfennu is. It came into being after the first galactics had departed. But by now—" He continued for a while. When he spoke of a systemwide syndicate, controlling millions of lives and uncounted wealth, strong enough to build its own city on this planet and clever enough to play its enemies off against each other so that none dared attack that colony: he was scarcely lying. Everything that Chee had seen confirmed it.

"Are we in this town of yours now?" she asked.

"No. Elsewhere on Ronruad. Best I not be specific. I have too much respect for your cleverness."

"And I have none for yours."

"*Khraich?* You must. I think we operated quite smoothly, and on such short notice. Of course, an organization like ours must always be prepared for anything. And we have been on special alert ever since your arrival. What little we have learned—" Haguan's gaze went to the white point of Valenderay and lingered. "That star, it is going to explode. True?"

"Yes. Your civilization will be scrubbed out unless—"

"I know, I know. We have scientists in our pay." Haguan leaned forward. "The assorted governments on Merseia see this as a millennial chance to rid themselves of the troublesome Gethfennu. We need only be denied help in saving our colony, our shipping, our properties on the home planet and elsewhere. Then we are finished. I expect you galactics would agree to this. Since not everything can be shielded in time, why not include us in that which is to be abandoned? You stand for some kind of law and order too, I suppose."

Chee nodded. In their mask of dark fur, her eyes smoldered emerald. Haguan had guessed shrewdly. The League didn't much care who it dealt with, but the solid citizens whose taxes were to finance the majority of the rescue operations did.

"So to win our friendship, you take me by force," she sneered half-heartedly.

"What had we to lose? We might have conferred with you, pleaded our cause, but would that have wrought good for us?"

"Suppose my partners recommend that no help be given your whole coprophagous Merseian race."

"Why, then the collapse comes," Haguan said with chilling calm, "and the Gethfennu has a better chance than most organizations of improving its relative position. But I doubt that any such recommendation will be made, or that your overlords would heed it if it were.

"So we need a coin to buy technical assistance. You."

Chee's whiskers twitched in a smile of sorts. "I'm scarcely that big a hostage."

"Probably not," Haguan agreed. "But you are a source of information."

The Cynthian's fur stood on end with alarm. "Do you have some skewbrained notion that I can tell you how to do everything for yourself? I'm not even an engineer!"

"Understood. But surely you know your way about in your own civilization. You know what the engineers can and cannot do. More important, you know the planets, the different races and cultures upon them, the mores, the laws, the needs. You can tell us what to expect. You can help us get interstellar ships—hijacking under your advice should succeed, being unlooked for—and show us how to pilot them, and put us in touch with someone who, for pay, will come to our aid."

"If you suppose for a moment that the Polesotechnic League would tolerate—"

Teeth flashed white in Haguan's face. "Perhaps it won't, perhaps it will. With so many stars, the diversity of peoples and interests is surely inconceivable. The Gethfennu is skilled in stirring up competition among others. What information you supply will tell us how, in this particular case. I don't really visualize your League, whatever it is, fighting a war—at a time when every resource must be devoted to saving Merseia—to prevent someone else rescuing us."

He spread his hands. "Or possibly we'll find a different approach," he finished. "It depends on what you tell and suggest."

"How do you know you can trust me?"

Haguan said like iron: "We judge the soil by what crops it bears. If we fail, if we see the Gethfennu doomed, we can still enforce our policy regarding traitors. Would you care to visit my punishment facilities? They are quite extensive. Even though you are of a new species, I think we could keep you alive and aware for many days."

Silence dwelt a while in that room. Korych slipped under the horizon. Instantly the sky was black, strewn with the legions of the stars, beautiful and uncaring.

Haguan switched on a light, to drive away that too enormous vision. "If you save us, however," he said, "you will go free with a very good reward."

"But—" Chee looked sickly into sterile years ahead of her. And the betrayal of friends, and scorn if ever she returned, a lifetime's exile. "You'll keep me till then?"

"Of course."

No success. No ghost of a clue. She was gone into an emptiness less fathomable than the spaces which gaped around their ship.

They had striven, Falkayn and Adzel. They had walked into Luridor itself, the sin-bright city on Ronruad, while the ship hovered overhead and showed with a single, rock-fusing flash of energy guns what power menaced the world. They had ransacked, threatened, bribed, beseeched. Sometimes terror met them, sometimes the inborn arrogance of Merseia's lords. But nowhere and never had anyone so much as hinted he knew who held Chee Lan or where.

Falkayn ran a hand through uncombed yellow locks. His eyes stood bloodshot in a sunken countenance. "I still think we should've taken that casino boss aboard and worked him over."

"No," said Adzel. "Apart from the morality of the

matter, I feel sure that everyone who has any information is hidden away. That precaution is elementary. We're not even certain the outlaw regime is responsible."

"Yeh. Could be Morruchan, Dagla, Olgor, or colleagues of theirs acting unbeknownst to them, or any of a hundred other governments, or some gang of fanatics, or—Oh, *Judas!*"

Falkayn looked at the after viewscreen. Ronruad's tawny-red crescent was dwindling swiftly among the constellations, as the ship drove at full acceleration back toward Merseia. It was a dwarf planet, an ocherous pebble that would not make a decent splash if it fell into one of the gas giants. But the least of planets is still a world: mountains, plains, valleys, arroyos, caves, waters, square kilometers by the millions, too vast and varied for any mind to grasp. And Merseia was bigger yet; and there were others, and moons, asteroids, space itself.

Chee's captors need but move her around occasionally, and the odds against a fleetful of League detectives finding her would climb for infinity.

"The Merseians themselves are bound to have some notion where to look, what to do, who to put pressure on," he mumbled for the hundredth time. "We don't know the ins and outs. Nobody from our cultures ever will—five billion years of planetary existence to catch up with! We've got to get the Merseians busy. I mean really busy."

"They have their own work to do," Adzel said.

Falkayn expressed himself at pungent length on the value of their work. "How about those enthusiasts?" he wondered when he had calmed down a trifle. "The outfit you were talking to."

"Yes, the Star Believers should be loyal allies," Adzel said. "But most of them are poor and, ah, unrealistic. I hardly expect them to be of help. Indeed, I fear they will complicate our problem by starting pitched battles with the Demonists."

"You mean the antigalactics?" Falkayn rubbed his chin. The bristles made a scratchy noise, in the ceaseless gentle thrum that filled the cabin. He inhaled the sour smell of his own weariness. "Maybe they did this."

"I doubt that. They must be investigated, naturally—a major undertaking in itself—but they do not appear sufficiently well organized."

"Damnation, if we don't get her back I'm going to push for letting this whole race stew!"

"You will not succeed. And in any event, it would be unjust to let millions die for the crime of a few."

"The millions jolly well ought to be tracking down the few. It's possible. There have to be some leads somewhere. If every single one is followed—"

The detector panel flickered. Muddlehead announced: "Ship observed. A chemical carrier, I believe, from the outer system. Range—"

"Oh, dry up," Falkayn said, "and blow away."

"I am not equipped to—"

Falkayn stabbed the voice cutoff button.

He sat for a while, then, staring into the stars. His pipe went out unnoticed between his fingers. Adzel sighed and laid his head down on the deck.

"Poor little Chee," Falkayn whispered at last. "She came a long way to die."

"Most likely she lives," Adzel said.

"I hope so. But she used to go flying through trees, in an endless forest. Being caged will kill her."

"Or unbalance her mind. She is so easily infuriated. If anger can find no object, it turns to feed on itself."

"Well . . . you were always squabbling with her."

"It meant nothing. Afterward she would cook me a special dinner. Once I admired a painting of hers, and she thrust it into my hands and said, 'Take the silly thing, then,' like a cub that is too shy to say it loves you."

"Uh-huh."

The cutoff button popped up. "Course adjustment required," Muddlehead stated, "in order to avoid dangerously close passage by ore carrier."

"Well, do it," Falkayn rasped, "and I wish those bastards joy of their ores. Destruction, but they've got a lot of space traffic!"

"Well, we are in the ecliptic plane, and as yet near Ronruad," Adzel said. "The coincidence is not great."

Falkyan clenched his hands. The pipestem snapped. "Suppose we strafe the ground," he said in a cold strange voice. "Not kill anyone. Burn up a few expensive installations, though, and promise more of the same if they don't get off their duffs and start a real search for her."

"No. We have considerable discretion, but not that much."

"We could argue with the board of inquiry later."

"Such a deed would produce confusion and antagonism, and weaken the basis of the rescue effort. It might actually make rescue impossible. You have observed how basic pride is to the dominant Merseian cultures. An attempt to browbeat them, with no face-saving formula possible, might compel them to refuse galactic assistance. We would be personally, criminally responsible. I cannot permit it, David."

"So we can't do anything, not anything, to—"

Falkayn's words chopped off. He smashed a fist down on the arm of his pilot chair and surged to his feet. Adzel rose also, sinews drawn taut. He knew his partner.

Merseia hung immense, shining with oceans, blazoned with clouds and continents, rimmed with dawn and sunset and the deep sapphire of her sky. Her four small moons made a diadem. Korych flamed in plumage of zodiacal light.

Space cruiser *Yonuar*, United Fleet of the Great Vachs, swung close in polar orbit. Officially she was on patrol to stand by for possible aid to distressed civilian vessels. In fact she was there to keep an eye on the warcraft of Lafdigu, Wolder, the Nersan Alliance, any whom her masters mistrusted. And, yes, on the new-come galactics, if they returned hither. The God alone knew what they intended. One must tread warily and keep weapons close to hand.

On his command bridge, Captain Tryntaf Fangryf-

Tamer gazed into the simulacrum tank and tried to imagine what laired among those myriad suns. He had grown up knowing that others flitted freely between them while his people were bound to this one system, and hating that knowledge. Now they were here once again...why? Too many rumors flew about. But most of them centered on the ominous spark called Valenderay.

Help; collaboration; were the Vach Isthyr to become mere clients of some outworld grotesque?

A signal fluted. The intercom said: "Radar Central to captain. Object detected on an intercept path." The figures which followed were unbelievable. No meteoroid, surely, despite an absence of jet radiation. Therefore, the galactics! His black uniform tunic grew taut around Tryntaf's shoulders as he hunched forward and issued orders. Battle stations: not that he was looking for trouble, but he was prudent. And if trouble came, he'd much like to see how well the alien could withstand laser blasts and nuclear rockets.

She grew in his screens, a stubby truncated raindrop, ridiculously tiny against the sea-beast hulk of *Yonuar*. She matched orbit so fast that Tryntaf heard the air suck in through his lips. Doom and death, why wasn't that hull broken apart and the crew smeared into a red layer? Some kind of counterfield....The vessel hung a few kilometers off and Tryntaf sought to calm himself. They would no doubt call him, and he must remain steady of nerve, cold of brain.

For his sealed orders mentioned that the galactics had left Merseia in anger, because the whole planet would not devote itself to a certain task. The Hands had striven for moderation; of course they would do what they reasonably could to oblige their guests from the stars, but they had other concerns too. The galactics seemed unable to agree that the business of entire worlds was more important than their private wishes. Of necessity, such an attitude was met with haughtiness, lest the name of the Vachs, of all the nations, be lowered.

Thus, when his outercom screen gave him an image,

Tryntaf kept one finger on the combat button. He had some difficulty hiding his revulsion. Those thin features, shock of hair, tailless body, fuzzed brown skin, were like a dirty caricature of Merseiankind. He would rather have spoken to the companion, whom he could see in the background. That creature was honestly weird.

Nonetheless, Tryntaf got through the usual courtesies and asked the galactic's business in a level tone.

Falkayn had pretty well mastered modern language by now. "Captain," he said, "I regret this and apologize, but you'll have to return to base."

Tryntaf's heart slammed. Only his harness prevented him from jerking backward, to drift across the bridge in the dreamlike flight of zero gravity. He swallowed and managed to keep his speech calm. "What is the reason?"

"We have communicated it to different leaders," said Falkayn, "but since they don't accept the idea, I'll also explain to you personally.

"Someone, we don't know who, has kidnapped a crew member of ours. I'm sure that you, Captain, will understand that honor requires we get her back."

"I do," Tryntaf said, "and honor demands that we assist you. But what has this to do with my ship?"

"Let me go on, please. I want to prove that no offense is intended. We have little time to make ready for the coming disaster, and few personnel to employ. The contribution of each is vital. In particular, the specialized knowledge of our vanished teammate cannot be dispensed with. So her return is of the utmost importance to all Merseians."

Tryntaf grunted. He knew the argument was specious, meant to provide nothing but an acceptable way for his people to capitulate to the strangers' will.

"The search for her looks hopeless when she can be moved about in space," Falkayn said. "Accordingly, while she is missing, interplanetary traffic must be halted."

Tryntaf rapped an oath. "Impossible."

"Contrariwise," Falkayn said. "We hope for your

cooperation, but if your duty forbids this, we too can enforce the decree."

Tryntaf was astonished to hear himself, through a tide of fury, say just: "I have no such orders."

"That is regrettable," Falkayn said. "I know your superiors will issue them, but that takes time and the emergency will not wait. Be so good as to return to base."

Tryntaf's finger poised over the button. "And if I don't?"

"Captain, we shouldn't risk damage to your fine ship—"

Tryntaf gave the signal.

His gunners had the range. Beams and rockets vomited forth.

Not one missile hit. The enemy flitted aside, letting them pass, as if they were thrown pebbles. A full-power ray struck: but not her hull. Energy sparked and showered blindingly off some invisible barrier.

The little vessel curved about like an aircraft. One beam licked briefly from her snout. Alarms resounded. Damage Control cried, near hysteria, that armorplate had been sliced off as a knife might cut soft wood. No great harm done; but if the shot had been directed at the reaction-mass tanks—

"How very distressing, Captain," Falkayn said. "But accidents will happen when weapons systems are overly automated, don't you agree? For the sake of your crew, for the sake of your country whose ship is your responsiblity, I do urge you to reconsider."

"Hold fire," Tryntaf gasped.

"You will return planetside, then?" Falkayn asked.

"I curse you, yes," Tryntaf said with a parched mouth.

"Good. You are a wise male, Captain. I salute you. Ah . . . you may wish to notify your fellow commanders elsewhere, so they can take steps to assure there will be no further accidents. Meanwhile, though, please commence re-entry."

Jets stabbed into space. *Yonuar*, pride of the Vachs, began her inward spiral.

And aboard *Muddlin' Through*, Falkayn wiped his brow and grinned shakily at Adzel. "For a minute," he said, "I was afraid that moron was going to slug it out."

"We could have disabled his command with no casualties," Adzel said, "and I believe they have lifecraft."

"Yes, but think of the waste; and the grudge." Falkayn shook himself. "Come on, let's get started. We've a lot of others to round up."

"Can we—a lone civilian craft—blockade an entire globe?" Adzel wondered. "I do not recall that it has ever been done."

"No, I don't imagine it has. But that's because the opposition has also had things like grav drive. These Merseian rowboats are something else again. And we need only watch this one planet. Everything funnels through it." Falkayn stuffed tobacco into a pipe. "Uh, Adzel, suppose you compose our broadcast to the public. You're more tactful than I am."

"What shall I say?" the Wodenite asked.

"Oh, the same guff as I just forked out, but dressed up and tied with a pink ribbon."

"Do you really expect this to work, David?"

"I've pretty high hopes. Look, all we'll call for is that Chee be left some safe place and we be notified where. We'll disavow every intention of punishing anybody, and we can make that plausible by pointing out that the galactics have to prove they're as good as their word if their mission is to have any chance of succeeding. If the kidnappers don't oblige—Well, first, they'll have the entire population out on a full-time hunt after them. And second, they themselves will be suffering badly from the blockade meanwhile. Whoever they are. Because you wouldn't have as much interplanetary shipping as you do, if it weren't basic to the economy."

Adzel shifted in unease. "We must not cause anyone to starve."

"We won't. Food isn't sent across space, except gourmet items; too costly. How often do I have to explain to you, old thickhead? What we will cause is that everybody loses money. Megacredits per diem. And Very Important Merseians will be stranded in places like Luridor, and they'll burn up the maser beams ordering their subordinates to remedy that state of affairs. And factories will shut down, spaceports lie idle, investments crumble, political and military balances get upset. . . . You can fill in the details."

Falkayn lit his pipe and puffed a blue cloud. "I don't expect matters will go that far, actually," he went on. "The Merseians are as able as us to foresee the consequences. Not a hypothetical disaster three years hence, but money and power eroding away right now. So they'll put it first on their agenda to find those kidnappers and take out resentment on them. The kidnappers will know this and will also, I trust, be hit in their personal breadbasket. I bet in a few days they'll offer to swap Chee for an amnesty."

"Which I trust we will honor," Adzel said.

"I told you we'll have to. Wish we didn't."

"Please don't be so cynical, David. I hate to see you lose merit."

Falkayn chuckled. "But I make profits. Come on, Muddlehead, get busy and find us another ship."

The teleconference room in Castle Afon could handle a sealed circuit that embraced the world. On this day it did.

Falkayn sat in a chair he had brought, looking across a table scarred by the daggers of ancestral warriors, to the mosaic of screens which filled the opposite wall. A hundred or more Merseian visages lowered back at him. On that scale, they had no individuality. Save one: a black countenance ringed by empty frames. No lord would let his image stand next to that of Haguan Eluatz.

Beside the human, Morruchan, Hand of the Vach Dathyr, rose and said with frigid ceremoniousness: "In the name of the God and the blood, we are met. May we be well met. May wisdom and honor stand shield to shield—" Falkayn listened with half an ear. He was busy rehearsing his speech. At best, he was in for a cobalt bomb's worth of trouble.

No danger, of course, *Muddlin' Through* hung plain in sight above Ardaig. Television carried that picture around Merseia. And it linked him to Adzel and Chee Lan, who waited at the guns. He was protected.

But what he had to say could provoke a wrath so great that his mission was wrecked. He must say it with infinite care, and then he must hope.

"—obligation to a guest demands we hear him out," Morruchan finished brusquely.

Falkayn stood up. He knew that in those eyes he was a monster, whose motivations were not understandable and who had proven himself dangerous. So he had dressed in his plainest gray zipsuit, and was unarmed, and spoke in soft words.

"Worthies," he said, "forgive me that I do not use your titles, for you are of many ranks and nations. But you are those who decide for your whole race. I hope you will feel free to talk as frankly as I shall. This is a secret and informal conference, intended to explore what is best for Merseia.

"Let me first express my heartfelt gratitude for your selfless and successful labors to get my teammate returned unharmed. And let me also thank you for indulging my wish that the, uh, chieftain Haguan Eluatz participate in this honorable assembly, albeit he has no right under law to do so. The reason shall soon be explained. Let me, finally, once again express my regret at the necessity of stopping your space commerce, for however brief a period, and my thanks for your cooperation in this emergency measure. I hope that you will consider any losses made good, when my people arrive to help you rescue your civilization.

"Now, then, it is time we put away whatever is past and look to the future. Our duty is to organize that great task. And the problem is, how shall it be organized? The galactic technologists do not wish to usurp any Merseian authority. In fact, they could not. They will be too few, too foreign, and too busy. If they are to do their work in the short time available, they must accept the guidance of the powers that be. They must make heavy use of existing facilities. That, of course, must be authorized by those who control the facilities. I need not elaborate. Experienced leaders like yourselves, worthies, can easily grasp what is entailed."

He cleared his throat. "A major question, obviously, is: with whom shall our people work most closely? They have no desire to discriminate. Everyone will be consulted, within the sphere of his time-honored prerogatives. Everyone will be aided, as far as possible. Yet, plain to see, a committee of the whole would be impossibly large and diverse. For setting overall policy, our people require a small, unified Merseian council, whom they can get to know really well and with whom they can develop effective decision-making procedures.

"Furthermore, the resources of this entire system must be used in a coordinated way. For example, Country One cannot be allowed to hoard minerals which Country Two needs. Shipping must be free to go from any point to any other. And all available shipping must be pressed into service. We can furnish radiation screens for your vessels, but we cannot furnish the vessels themselves in the numbers that are needed. Yet at the same time, a certain amount of ordinary activity must continue. People will still have to eat, for instance. So—how do we make a fair allocation of resources and establish a fair system of priorities?

"I think these considerations make it obvious to you, worthies, that an international organization is absolutely essential, one which can *impartially* supply information, advice, and coordination. If it has facilities and workers of its own, so much the better.

"Would that such an organization had legal existence! But it does not, and I doubt there is time to form one. If, you will pardon me for saying so, worthies, Merseia is burdened with too many old hatreds and jealousies to join overnight in brotherhood. In fact, the international group must be watched carefully, lest it try to aggrandize itself or diminish others. We galactics can do this with one organization. We cannot with a hundred.

"So." Falkayn longed for his pipe. Sweat prickled his skin. "I have no plenipotentiary writ. My team is merely supposed to make recommendations. But the matter is so urgent that whatever scheme we propose will likely be adopted, for the sake of getting on with the job. And we have found one group which transcends the rest. It pays no attention to barriers between people and people. It is large, powerful, rich, disciplined, efficient. It is not exactly what my civilization would prefer as its chief instrument for the deliverance of Merseia. We would honestly rather it went down the drain, instead of becoming yet more firmly entrenched. But we have a saying that necessity knows no law."

He could feel the tension gather, like a thunderstorm boiling up; he heard the first rageful retorts; he said fast, before the explosion came: "I refer to the Gethfennu."

What followed was indescribable.

But he was, after all, only warning of what his report would be. He could point out that he bore a grudge of his own, and was setting it aside for the common good. He could even, with considerable enjoyment, throw some imaginative remarks about ancestry and habits in the direction of Haguan—who grinned and looked smug. In the end, hours later, the assembly agreed to take the proposal under advisement. Falkayn knew what the upshot would be. Merseia had no choice.

The screens blanked.

Wet, shaking, exhausted, he looked across a stillness into the face of Morruchan Long-Ax. The Hand loomed over him. Fingers twitched longingly near a pistol butt. Morruchan said, biting off each word: "I trust you realize what you are doing. You're not just perpetuating that gang. You're conferring legitimacy on them. They will be able to claim they are now a part of recognized society."

"Won't they, then, have to conform to its laws?" Falkayn's larynx hurt, his voice was husky.

"Not them!" Morruchan stood brooding a moment. "But a reckoning will come. The Vachs will prepare one, if nobody else does. And afterward—Are you going to teach us how to build stargoing ships?"

"Not if I have any say in the matter," Falkayn replied.

"Another score. Not important in the long run. We're bound to learn a great deal else, and on that basis . . . well, galactic, our grandchildren will see."

"Is ordinary gratitude beneath your dignity?"

"No. There'll be enough soft-souled dreambuilders, also among my race, for an orgy of sentimentalism. But then you'll go home again. I will abide."

Falkayn was too tired to argue. He made his formal farewells and called the ship to come get him.

Later, hurtling through the interstellar night, he listened to Chee's tirade: "—I still have to get back at those greasepaws. They'll be sorry they ever touched me."

"You don't aim to return, do you?" Falkayn asked.

"Pox, no!" she said. "But the engineers on Merseia will need recreation. The Gethfennu will supply some of it, gambling especially, I imagine. Now if I suggest our lads carry certain miniaturized gadgets which can, for instance, control a wheel—"

Adzel sighed. "In this splendid and terrible cosmos," he said, "why must we living creatures be forever perverse?"

A smile tugged at Falkayn's mouth. "We wouldn't have so much fun otherwise," he said.

Men and not-men were still at work when the supernova wave-front reached Merseia.

Suddenly the star filled the southern night, a third as brilliant as Korych, too savage for the naked eye to look at. Blue-white radiance flooded the land, shadows were etched sharp, trees and hills stood as if illuminated by lightning. Wings beat upward from forests, animals cried through the troubled air, drums pulsed and prayers lifted in villages which once had feared the dark for which they now longed. The day that followed was lurid and furious.

Over the months, the star faded, until it became a knife-keen point and scarcely visible when the sun was aloft. But it waxed in beauty, for its radiance excited the gas around it, so that it gleamed amidst a whiteness which deepened at the edge to blue-violet and a nebular lacework which shone with a hundred faerie hues. Thence also, in Merseia's heaven, streamed huge shuddering banners of aurora, whose whisper was heard even on the ground. An odor of storm was blown on every wind.

Then the nuclear rain began. And nothing was funny any longer.

Also in the records left on Hermes was information about an episode which had long been concealed: how Nicholas van Rijn came to the world which today we know as Mirkheim. The reasons for secrecy at the time are self-evident. Later they did not obtain. However, it is well known that Falkayn was always reluctant to mention his part in the origins of the Supermetals enterprise, and curt-spoken whenever the subject was forced upon him. Given all else there was to strive with in the beginning upon Avalon, it is no flaw of wind that folk did not press their leaders about this, and that the matter dropped from general awareness. Even before then, he had done what he could to suppress details.

Of course, the alatan facts are in every biography of the Founder. Yet this one affair is new to us. It helps explain much which followed, especially his reserve, rare in an otherwise cheerful and outgoing person. In truth, it gives us a firmer grip than we had before upon the reality of him.

The records contain only the ship's log for that voyage, plus some taped conversations, data lists, and the like. However, these make meaningful certain hitherto cryptic references in surviving letters written by Coya to her husband. Furthermore, with the identity of vessel and captain known, it became possible to enlist the aid of the Wryfields Choth on Ythri. Stirrok, its Wyvan, was most helpful in finding Hirharouk's private journal, while his descendants kindly agreed to waive strict rightness and allow it to be read.

From these sources, Hloch and Arinnian have composed the narrative which follows.

LODESTAR

Lightning reached. David Falkayn heard the crack of torn air and gulped a rainy reek of ozone. His cheek stung from the near miss. In his eyes, spots of blue-white dazzle danced across night.

"Get aboard, you two," Adzel said. "I'll hold them."

Crouched, Falkayn peered after a target for his own blaster. He saw shadows move beneath strange constellations—that, and flames which tinged upward-roiling smoke on the far side of the spacefield, where the League outpost was burning. Shrieks resounded. "No, you start," he rasped. "I'm armed, you're not."

The Wodenite's bass remained steady, but an earth-quake rumble entered it. "No more deaths. A single death would have been too much, of folk outraged in their own homes. David, Chee: go."

Half-dragon, half-centaur, four and a half meters from snout to tailtip, he moved toward the unseen natives. Firelight framed the hedge of bony plates along his back, glimmered off scales and belly-scutes.

Chee Lan tugged at Falkayn's trousers. "Come on," she spat. "No stopping that hairy-brain when he wambles off on an idealism binge. He won't board before us, and they'll kill him if we don't move fast." A sneer: "I'll lead the way, if that'll make you feel more heroic."

Her small, white-furred form shot from the hauler
behind which they had taken refuge. (No use trying to get
that machine aloft. The primitives had planned their
attack shrewdly, must have hoarded stolen explosives as
well as guns for years, till they could demolish everything
around the base at the same moment as they fell upon the
headquarters complex.) Its mask-markings obscured her
blunt-muzzled face in the shuddering red light; but her
bottled-up tail stood all too clear.

A Tamethan saw. On long thin legs, beak agape in a
war-yell, he sped to catch her. His weapon was merely a
spear. Sick-hearted, Falkayn took aim. Then Chee darted
between those legs, tumbled the autochthon on his tocus
and bounded onward.

Hurry! Falkayn told himself. Battle ramped around
Adzel. The Wodenite could take a certain number of slugs
and blaster bolts without permanent damage, he knew,
but not many . . . and those mighty arms were pulling their
punches. Keeping to shadow as well as might be, the
human followed Chee Lan.

Their ship loomed ahead, invulnerable to the attackers. Her gangway was descending. So the Cynthian had
entered audio range, had called an order to the main
computer. . . . *Why didn't we tell Muddlehead to use
initiative in case of trouble?* groaned Falkayn's mind.
*Why didn't we at least carry radios to call for its help? Are
we due for retirement? A sloppy trade pioneer is a dead
trade pioneer.*

A turret gun flashed and boomed. Chee must have
ordered that. It was a warning shot, sent skyward, but
terrifying. The man gusted relief. His rangy body sped
upramp, stopped at the open airlock, and turned to peer
back. Combat seemed to have frozen. And, yes, here
Adzel came, limping, trailing blood, but alive. Falkayn
wanted to hug his old friend and weep.

No. First we haul mass out of here. He entered the ship.
Adzel's hoofs boomed on the gangway. It retracted, the
airlock closed, gravity drive purred, and *Muddlin'
Through* ascended to heaven.

—Gathered on the bridge, her crew stared at a downward-viewing screen. The fires had become sparks, the spacefield a scar, in an illimitable night. Far off, a river cut through jungle, shining by starlight like a drawn sword.

Falkayn ran fingers through his sandy hair. "We, uh, well, do you think we can rescue any survivors?" he asked.

"I doubt there are any by now," Adzel said. "We barely escaped: because we have learned, over years, to meet emergencies as a team."

"And if there are," Chee added, "who cares?" Adzel looked reproof at her. She bristled her whiskers. "We saw how those slimesouls were treating the aborigines."

"I feel sure much of the offense was caused simply by ignorance of basic psychology and mores."

"That's no excuse, as you flapping well know. They should've taken the trouble to learn such things. But no, the companies couldn't wait for that. They sent their bespattered factors and field agents right in, who promptly set up a little dunghill of an empire— *Ya-pu-yeh!*" In Chee's home language that was a shocking obscenity, even for her.

Falkayn's shoulders slumped. "I'm inclined to agree," he said. "Besides, we mustn't take risks. We've got to make a report."

"Why?" Adzel asked. "Our own employer was not involved."

"No, thanks be. I'd hate to feel I must quit. . . . This is League business, however. The mutual-assistance rule—"

"And so League warcraft come and bomb some poor little villages?" Adzel's tail drummed on the deck.

"With our testimony, we can hope not. The Council verdict ought to be, those klongs fell flat on their own deeds." Falkayn sighed. "I wish we'd been around here longer, making a regular investigation, instead of just chancing by and deciding to take a few days off on a pleasant planet." He straightened. "Well. To space, Muddlehead, and to—m-m-m, nearest major League base—Irumclaw."

"And you come along to sickbay and let me dress those wounds, you overgrown bulligator," Chee snapped at the Wodenite, "before you've utterly ruined this carpet, drooling blood on it."

Falkayn himself sought a washroom, a change of clothes, his pipe and tobacco, a stiff drink. Continuing to the saloon, he settled down and tried to ease away his trouble. In a viewscreen, the world dwindled which men had named Tametha—arbitrarily, from a native word in a single locality, which they'd doubtless gotten wrong anyway. Already it had shrunk in his vision to a ball, swirled blue and white: a body as big and fair as ever Earth was, four or five billion years in the making, uncounted swarms of unknown life forms, sentiences and civilizations, histories and mysteries, become a marble in a game . . . or a set of entries in a set of data banks, for profit or loss, in a few cities a hundred or more light-years remote.

He thought: *This isn't the first time I've seen undying wrong done. Is it really happening oftener and oftener, or am I just getting more aware of it as I age? At thirty-three, I begin to feel old.*

Chee entered, jumped onto the seat beside him, and reported Adzel was resting. "You do need that drink, don't you?" she observed. Falkayn made no reply. She inserted a mildly narcotic cigarette in an interminable ivory holder and puffed it to ignition.

"Yes," she said, "I get irritated likewise, no end, whenever something like this befouls creation."

"I'm coming to think the matter is worse, more fundamental, than a collection of episodes." Falkayn spoke wearily. "The Polesotechnic League began as a mutual-benefit association of companies, true; but the idea was also to keep competition within decent bounds. That's breaking down, that second aspect. How long till the first does too?"

"What would you prefer to free enterprise? The Terran Empire, maybe?"

"Well, you being a pure carnivore, and coming besides

from a trading culture that was quick to modernize—
exploitation doesn't touch you straight on the nerves,
Chee. But Adzel—he doesn't say much, you know him,
but I've become certain it's a bitterness to him, more and
more as time slides by, that nobody will help his people
advance... because they haven't anything that anybody
wants enough to pay the price of advancement. And—
well, I hardly dare guess how many others. Entire
worldsful of beings who look at yonder stars till it aches in
them, and know that except for a few lucky individuals,
none of them will ever get out there, nor will their
descendants have any real say about the future, no, will
instead remain nothing but potential victims—"

Seeking distraction, Falkayn raised screen magnification and swept the scanner around jewel-blazing
blackness. When he stopped for another pull at his glass,
the view happened to include the enigmatic glow of the
Crab Nebula.

"Take that sentimentalism and stuff it back where it
came from," Chee suggested. "The new-discovered
species will simply have to accumulate capital. Yours did.
Mine did soon after. We can't give a free ride to the whole
universe."

"N-no. Yet you know yourself—be honest—how quick
somebody already established would be to take away that
bit of capital, whether by market manipulations or by
thinly disguised piracy. Tametha's a minor example. All
that those tribesbeings wanted was to trade directly with
Over-the-Mountains." Falkayn's fist clamped hard
around his pipe. "I tell you, lass, the heart is going out of
the League, in the sense of ordinary compassion and
helpfulness. How long till the heart goes out in the sense
of its own survivability? Civilization *needs* more than the
few monopolists we've got."

The Cynthian twitched her ears, quite slowly, and
exhaled smoke whose sweetness blent with the acridity of
the man's tobacco. Her eyes glowed through it, emerald-
hard. "I sort of agree. At least, I'd enjoy listening to the
hot air hiss out of certain bellies. How, though, Davy?
How?"

"Old Nick—he's a single member of the Council, I realize—"

"Our dear employer keeps his hirelings fairly moral, but strictly on the principle of running a taut ship. He told me that himself once, and added, 'Never mind what the ship is taught, ho, ho, ho!' No, you won't make an idealist of Nicholas van Rijn. Not without transmuting every atom in his fat body."

Falkayn let out a tired chuckle. "A new isotope. Van Rijn-235, no, likelier Vr-235,000—"

And then his glance passed over the Nebula, and as if it had spoken to him across more than a thousand parsecs, he fell silent and grew tense where he sat.

This happened shortly after the Satan episode, when the owner of Solar Spice & Liquors had found it needful once more to leave the comforts of the Commonwealth, risk his thick neck on a cheerless world, and finally make a month-long voyage in a ship which had run out of beer. Returned home, he swore by all that was holy and much that was not: Never again!

Nor, for most of the following decade, had he any reason to break his vow. His business was burgeoning, thanks to excellently chosen personnel in established trade sites and to pioneers like the *Muddlin' Through* team who kept finding him profitable new lands. Besides, he had maneuvered himself into the overlordship of Satan. A sunless wandering planet, newly thawed out by a brush with a giant star, made a near-ideal site for the manufacture of odd isotopes on a scale commensurate with present-day demand. Such industry wasn't his cup of tea "or," he declared, "my glass Genever that molasses-on-Pluto-footed butler is supposed to bring me before I crumble away from thirst." Therefore van Rijn granted franchises, on terms calculated to be an ångström short of impossibly extortionate.

Many persons wondered, often in colorful language, why he didn't retire and drink himself into a grave they would be glad to provide, outsize though it must be. When van Rijn heard about these remarks, he would grin and look still harder for a price he could jack up or a competitor he could undercut. Nevertheless, compared to earlier years, this was for him a leisured period. When at last word got around that he meant to take Coya Conyon, his favorite granddaughter, on an extended cruise aboard his yacht—and not a single mistress along for him—hope grew that he was slowing down to a halt.

I can't say I like most of those money-machine merchant princes, Coya reflected, several weeks after leaving Earth; *but I really wouldn't want to give them heart attacks by telling them we're now on a nonhuman vessel, equipped in curious ways but unmistakably battle-ready, bound into a region that nobody is known to have explored.*

She stood before a viewport set in a corridor. A ship built by men would not have carried that extravagance; but to Ythrians, sky dwellers, ample outlook is a necessity of sanity. The air she breathed was a little thinner than at Terrestrial sea level; odors included the slight smokiness of their bodies. A ventilator murmured not only with draft but with a barely heard rustle, the distance-muffled sound of wingbeats from crewfolk off duty cavorting in an enormous hold intended for it. At 0.75 standard weight she still—after this long a trip—felt exhilaratingly light.

She was not presently conscious of that. At first she had reveled in adventure. Everything was an excitement; every day offered a million discoveries to be made. She didn't mind being the sole human aboard besides her grandfather. He was fun in his bearish fashion: had been as far back as she could remember, when he would roll roaring into her parents' home, toss her to the ceiling, half-bury her under presents from a score of planets, tell her extravagant stories and take her out on a sailboat or to a live performance or, later on, around most of the Solar System. . . . Anyhow, to make Ythrian friends, to discover a little of how their psyches worked and how one differed from another, to trade music, memories, and myths, watch their aerial dances and show them some ballet, that was an exploration in itself.

Today, however—They were apparently nearing the

goal for which they had been running in a search helix, whatever it was. Van Rijn remained boisterous; but he would tell her nothing. Nor did the Ythrians know what was sought, except for Hirharouk, and he had passed on no other information than that all were to hold themselves prepared for emergencies cosmic or warlike. A species whose ancestors had lived like eagles could take this more easily than men. Even so, tension had mounted till she could smell it.

Her gaze sought outward. As an astrophysicist and a fairly frequent tourist, she had spent a total of years in space during the twenty-five she had been in the universe. She could identify the brightest individual stars amidst that radiant swarm, lacy and lethal loveliness of shining nebulae, argent torrent of Milky Way, remote glimmer of sister galaxies. And still size and silence, unknownness and unknowability, struck against her as much as when she first fared forth.

Secrets eternal . . . why, of course. They had run at a good pseudovelocity for close to a month, starting at Ythri's sun (which lies 278 light-years from Sol in the direction of Lupus) and aiming at the Deneb sector. That put them, oh, say a hundred parsecs from Earth. Glib calculation. Yet they had reached parts which no record said anyone had ever done more than pass through, in all the centuries since men got a hyperdrive. The planetary systems here had not been catalogued, let alone visited, let alone understood. Space is that big, that full of worlds.

Coya shivered, though the air was warm enough. *You're yonder somewhere, David,* she thought, *if you haven't met the inevitable final surprise. Have you gotten my message? Did it have any meaning to you?*

She could do nothing except give her letter to another trade pioneer whom she trusted. He was bound for the same general region as Falkayn had said *Muddlin' Through* would next go questing in. The crews maintained rendezvous stations. In one such turbulent place he might get news of Falkayn's team. Or he could deposit the letter there to be called for.

Guilt nagged her, as it had throughout this journey. A

betrayal of her grandfather—No! Fresh anger flared. *If he's not brewing something bad, what possible harm can it do him that David knows what little I knew before we left—which is scarcely more than the old devil has let me know to this hour?*

And he did speak of hazards. I did have to force him into taking me along (because the matter seemed to concern you, David, oh, David). If we meet trouble, and suddenly you arrive—

Stop romancing, Coya told herself. *You're a grown girl now.* She found she could control her thoughts, somewhat, but not the tingle through her blood.

She stood tall, slender almost to boyishness, clad in plain black tunic, slacks, and sandals. Straight dark hair, shoulder-length, framed an oval face with a snub nose, mouth a trifle too wide but eyes remarkably big and gold-flecked green. Her skin was very white. It was rather freakish how genes had recombined to forget nearly every trace of her ancestry—van Rijn's Dutch and Malay; the Mexican and Chinese of a woman who bore him a girl-child and with whom he had remained on the same amicable terms afterward as, somehow, he did with most former loves; the Scots (from Hermes, David's home planet) plus a dash of African (via a planet called Nyanza) in that Malcolm Conyon who settled down on Earth and married Beatriz Yeo.

Restless, Coya's mind skimmed over the fact. Her lips could not help quirking. *In short, I'm a typical modern human.* The amusement died. *Yes, also in my life. My grandfather's generation seldom bothered to get married. My father's did. And mine, why, we're reviving patrilineal surnames.*

A whistle snapped off her thinking. Her heart lurched until she identified the signal. "All hands alert."

That meant something had been detected. Maybe not the goal; maybe just a potential hazard, like a meteoroid swarm. In uncharted space, you traveled warily, and van Rijn kept a candle lit before his little Martian sandroot statuette of St. Dismas.

A moment longer, Coya confronted the death and glory beyond the ship. Then, fists knotted, she strode aft. She was her grandfather's granddaughter.

"Lucifer and leprosy!" bellowed Nicholas van Rijn. "You have maybe spotted what we maybe are after, at extreme range of your instruments tuned sensitive like an artist what specializes in painting pansies, a thing we cannot reach in enough hours to eat three good rijstaffels, and you have the bladder to tell me I got to armor me and stand around crisp saying, 'Aye-yi-yi, sir'?" Sprawled in a lounger, he waved a two-liter tankard of beer he clutched in his hairy left paw. The right held a churchwarden pipe, which had filled his stateroom with blue reek.

Hirharouk of the Wryfields Choth, captain of the chartered ranger *Gaiian* (=*Dewfall*), gave him look for look. The Ythrian's eyes were large and golden, the man's small and black and crowding his great hook nose; neither pair gave way, and Hirharouk's answer held an iron quietness: "No. I propose that you stop guzzling alcohol. You do have drugs to induce sobriety, but they may show side effects when quick decision is needed."

While his Anglic was fluent, he used a vocalizer to convert the sounds he could make into clearly human tones. The Ythrian voice is beautifully ringing but less flexible than man's. Was it to gibe or be friendly that van Rijn responded in pretty fair Planha? "Be not perturbed. I am hardened, which is why my vices cost me a fortune. Moreover, a body my size has corresponding capacity." He slapped the paunch beneath his snuff-stained blouse and gaudy sarong. The rest of him was huge in proportion. "This is my way of resting in advance of trouble, even as you would soar aloft and contemplate."

Hirharouk eased and fluted his equivalent of a laugh. "As you wish. I daresay you would not have survived to this date, all the sworn foes you must have, did you not know what you do."

Van Rijn tossed back his sloping brow. Long swarthy ringlets in the style of his youth, except for their

greasiness, swirled around the jewels in his earlobes; his
chins quivered beneath waxed mustaches and goatee; a
bare splay foot smote the densely carpeted deck. "You
mistake me," he boomed, reverting to his private version
of Anglic. "You cut me to the quiche. Do you suppose I,
poor old lonely sinner, *ja*, but still a Christian man with a
soul full of hope, do you suppose *I* ever went after
anything but peace—as many peaces as I could get? No,
no, what I did, I was pushed into, self-defense against sons
of mothers, greedy rascals who I may forgive though God
cannot, who begrudge me what tiny profit I need so I not
become a charge on a state that is only good for grinding
up taxpayers anyway. Me, I am like gentle St. Francis, I
go around ripping off olive branches and covering stormy
seas with oil slicks and watering troubled fish."

He stuck his tankard under a spout at his elbow for a
refill. Hirharouk observed him. And Coya, entering the
disordered luxury of the stateroom, paused to regard
them both.

She was fond of van Rijn. Her doubts about this
expedition, the message she had felt she must try to send
to David Falkayn, had been a sharp blade in her.
Nonetheless she admitted the Ythrian was infinitely more
sightly. Handsomer than her too, she felt, or David
himself. That was especially true in flight; yet, slow and
awkward though they were aground, the Ythrians
remained magnificent to see, and not only because of the
born hunter's inborn pride.

Hirharouk stood some 150 centimeters tall. What he
stood on was his wings, which spanned five and a half
meters when unfolded. Turned downward, they spread
claws at the angle which made a kind of foot; the
backward-sweeping alatan surface could be used for extra
support. What had been legs and talons, geological
epochs ago, were arms and three-fingered two-thumbed
hands. The skin on those was amber-colored. The rest of
him wore shimmering bronze feathers, save where these
became black-edged white on crest and on fan-shaped
tail. His body looked avian, stiff behind its jutting

keelbone. But he was no bird. He had not been hatched. His head, raised on a powerful neck, had no beak: rather, a streamlined muzzle, nostrils at the tip, below them a mouth whose lips seemed oddly delicate against the keen fangs.

And the splendor of these people goes beyond the sunlight on them when they ride the wind, Coya thought. *David frets about the races that aren't getting a chance. Well, Ythri was primitive when the Grand Survey found it. The Ythrians studied Technic civilization, and neither licked its boots nor let it overwhelm them, but took what they wanted from it and made themselves a power in our corner of the galaxy. True, this was before that civilization was itself overwhelmed by* laissez-faire capitalism—

She blinked. Unlike her, the merchant kept his quarters at Earth-standard illumination; and Quetlan is yellower than Sol. He was used to abrupt transitions. She coughed in the tobacco haze. The two males grew aware of her.

"Ah, my sweet bellybird," van Rijn greeted, a habit he had not shaken from the days of her babyhood. "Come in. Flop yourself." A gesture of his pipe gave a choice of an extra lounger, a desk chair, an emperor-size bed, a sofa between the liquor cabinet and the bookshelf, or the deck. "What you want? Beer, gin, whisky, cognac, vodka, arrack, akvavit, half-dozen kinds wine and liqueur, ansa, totipot, slumthunder, maryjane, ops, galt, Xanadu radium, or maybe—" he winced "—a soft drink? A soft, flabby drink?"

"Coffee will do, thanks." Coya drew breath and courage. "*Gunung Tuan,* I've got to talk with you."

"*Ja,* I outspected you would. Why I not told you more before is because—oh, I wanted you should enjoy your trip, not brood like a hummingbird on ostrich eggs."

Coya was unsure whether Hirharouk spoke in tact or truth: "Freeman van Rijn, I came to discuss our situation. Now I return to the bridge. For honor and life... *khr-r-r,* I mean please... hold ready for planlaying as information lengthens." He lifted an arm. "Freelady Conyon, hail and fare you well."

He walked from them. When he entered the bare corridor, his claws clicked. He stopped and did a handstand. His wings spread as wide as possible in that space, preventing the door from closing till he was gone, exposing and opening the gill-like slits below them. He worked the wings, forcing those antlibranchs to operate like bellows. They were part of the "supercharger" system which enabled a creature his size to fly under basically terrestroid conditions. Coya did not know whether he was oxygenating his bloodstream to energize himself for command, or was flushing out human stench.

He departed. She stood alone before her grandfather.

"Do sit, sprawl, hunker, or how you can best relax," the man urged. "I would soon have asked you should come. Time is to make a clean breast, except mine is too shaggy and you do not take off your tunic." His sigh turned into a belch. "A shame. Customs has changed. Not that I would lech in your case, no, I got incest repellent. But the sight is nice."

She reddened and signalled the coffeemaker. Van Rijn clicked his tongue. "And you don't smoke neither," he said. "Ah, they don't put the kind of stuff in youngsters like when I was your age."

"A few of us try to exercise some forethought as well as our consciences," Coya snapped. After a pause: "I'm sorry. Didn't mean to sound self-righteous."

"But you did. I wonder, has David Falkayn influenced you that way, or you him?—Ho-ho, a spectroscope would think your face was receding at speed of light!" Van Rijn wagged his pipestem. "Be careful. He's a good boy, him, except he's not a boy no more. Could well be, without knowing it, he got somewhere a daughter old as you."

"We're friends," Coya said half-furiously. She sat down on the edge of the spare lounger, ignored its attempts to match her contours, twined fingers between knees, and glared into his twinkle. "What the chaos do you expect my state of mind to be, when you wouldn't tell me what we're heading for?"

"You did not have to come along. You shoved in on me, armored in black mail."

Coya did not deny the amiably made statement. She had threatened to reveal the knowledge she had gained at his request, and thereby give his rivals the same clues. He hadn't been too hard to persuade; after warning her of possible danger, he growled that he would be needing an astrophysicist and might as well keep things in the family.

I hope, God, how I hope he believes my motive was a hankering for adventure as I told him! He ought to believe it, and flatter himself I've inherited a lot of his instincts ... No, he can't have guessed my real reason was the fear that David is involved, in a wrong way. If he knew that, he need only have told me, "Blab and be damned," and I'd have had to stay home, silent. As is ... David, in me you have here an advocate, whatever you may have done.

"I could understand your keeping me ignorant while we were on the yacht," she counterattacked. "No matter how carefully picked the crew, one of them might have been a commercial or government spy and might have managed to eavesdrop. But when, when in the Quetlan System we transferred to this vessel, and the yacht proceeded as if we were still aboard, and won't make any port for weeks—why didn't you speak?"

"Maybe I wanted you should for punishment be like a Yiddish brothel."

"What?"

"Jews in your own stew. Haw, haw, haw!" She didn't mile. Van Rijn continued: "Mainly, here again I could not be full-up sure of the crew. Ythrians is fearless and I suppose more honest by nature than men. But that is saying microbial little, *nie?* Here too we might have been overheard and—Well, Hirharouk agreed, he could not either absolute predict how certain of them would react. He tried but was not able to recruit everybody from his own choth." The Planha word designated a basic social unit, more than a tribe, less than a nation, with cultural and religious dimensions corresponding to nothing human. "Some, even, is from different societies and belong to no choths at allses. Ythrians got as much variation as the Commonwealth—no, more, because they not had time yet for technology to make them into homogeneouses."

The coffeemaker chimed. Coya, rose, tapped a cup, sat back down, and sipped. The warmth and fragrance were a point of comfort in an infinite space.

"We had a long trek ahead of us," the merchant proceeded, "and a lot of casting about, before we found what it *might* be we are looking for. Meanwhiles Hirharouk, and me as best I was able, sounded out those crewbeings not from Wryfields, got to understand them a weenie bit and—Hokay, he thinks we can trust them, regardless how the truth shapes up or ships out. And now, like you know, we have detected an object which would well be the simple, easy, small dissolution to the riddle."

"What's small about a supernova?" Coya challenged. "Even an extinct one?"

"When people ask me how I like being old as I am," van Rijn said circuitously, "I tell them, 'Not bad when I consider the alternative.' Bellybird, the alternative here would make the Shenn affair look like a game of peggletymum."

Coya came near spilling her coffee. She had been adolescent when the sensation exploded: that the Polesotechnic League had been infiltrated by agents of a nonhuman species, dwelling beyond the regions which Technic civilization dominated and bitterly hostile to it; that war had barely been averted; that the principal rescuers were her grandfather and the crew of a ship named *Muddlin' Through*. On that day David Falkayn was unknowingly promoted to god (j.g.). She wondered if he knew it yet, or knew that their occasional outings together after she matured had added humanness without reducing that earlier rank.

Van Rijn squinted at her. "You guessed we was hunting for a supernova remnant?" he probed.

She achieved a dry tone: "Since you had me investigate the problem, and soon thereafter announced your plans for a 'vacation trip,' the inference was fairly obvious."

"Any notion why I should want a white dwarf or a black hole instead of a nice glass red wine?"

Her pulse knocked. "Yes, I think I've reasoned it out." *And I think David may have done so before either of us, almost ten years ago. When you, Grandfather, asked me to use in secret—*

—the data banks and computers at Luna Astrocenter, where she worked, he had given a typically cryptic reason. "Could be this leads to a nice gob of profit nobody else's nose should root around in because mine is plenty big enough." She didn't blame him for being close-mouthed, then. The League's self-regulation was breaking down, competition grew ever more literally cutthroat, and governments snarled not only at the capitalists but at each other. The Pax Mercatoria was drawing to an end and, while she had never wholly approved of it, she sometimes dreaded the future.

The task he set her was sufficiently interesting to blot out her fears. However unimaginably violent, the suicides of giant suns by supernova bursts, which may outshine a hundred billion living stars, are not rare cosmic events. The remains, in varying stages of decay—white dwarfs, neutron stars, in certain cases those eldritch not-quite-things known as black holes—are estimated to number fifty million in our galaxy alone. But its arms spiral across a hundred thousand light-years. In this raw immensity, the prospects of finding by chance a body the size of a smallish planet or less, radiating corpse-feebly if at all, are negligible.

(The analogy with biological death and decomposition is not morbid. Those lay the foundation for new life and further evolution. Supernovae, hurling atoms together in fusing fury, casting them forth into space as their own final gasps, have given us all the heavier elements, some of them vital, in our worlds and our bodies.)

No one hitherto had—openly—attempted a more subtle search. The scientists had too much else to do, as discovery exploded outward. Persons who wished to study supernova processes saw a larger variety of known cases than could be dealt with in lifetimes. Epsilon Aurigae, Sirius B, and Valenderay were simply among the most famous examples.

Coya in Astrocenter had at her beck every fact which Technic civilization had ever gathered about the stellar part of the universe. From the known distribution of former supernovae, together with data on other star types, dust, gas, radiation, magnetism, present location and concentrations, the time derivatives of these quantities: using well-established theories of galactic development, it is possible to compute with reasonable probability the distribution of undiscovered dark giants within a radius of a few hundred parsecs.

The problem is far more complex than that, of course; and the best of self-programming computers still needs a highly skilled sophont riding close herd on it, if anything is to be accomplished. Nor will the answers be absolute, even within that comparatively tiny sphere to which their validity is limited. The most you can learn is the likelihood (not the certainty) of a given type of object existing within such-and-such a distance of yourself, and the likeliest (not the indubitable) direction. To phrase it more accurately, you get a hierarchy of decreasingly probable solutions.

This suffices. If you have the patience, and money, to search on a path defined by the equations, you *will* in time find the kind of body you are interested in.

Coya had taken for granted that no one before van Rijn had been that interested. But the completeness of Astrocenter's electronic records extended to noting who had run which program when. The purpose was to avoid duplication of effort, in an era when nobody could keep up with the literature in the smallest specialty. Out of habit rather than logic, Coya called for this information and—

—*I found out that ten years earlier, David wanted to know precisely what you, Grandfather, now did. But he never told you, nor said where he and his partners went afterward, or anything.* Pain: *Nor has he told me. And I have not told you. Instead, I made you take me along; and before leaving, I sent David a letter saying everything I knew and suspected.*

Resolution: *All right, Nick van Rijn! You keep complaining about how moralistic my generation is. Let's see how you like getting some cards off the bottom of the deck!*

Yet she could not hate an old man who loved her.

"What do you mean by your 'alternative'?" she whispered.

"Why, simple." He shrugged like a mountain sending off an avalanche. "If we do not find a retired supernova, being used in a way as original as spinning the peach basket, then we are up against a civilization outside ours, infiltrating ours, same as the Shenna did—except this one got technology would make ours let go in its diapers and scream, 'Papa, Papa, in the closet is a boogeyman!'" Unaccustomed grimness descended on him. "I think, in that case, really is a boogeyman, too."

Chill entered her guts. "Supermetals?"

"What else?" He took a gulp of beer. "Ha, you is guessed what got me started was Supermetals?"

She finished her coffee and set the cup on a table. It rattled loud through a stretching silence. "Yes," she said at length, flat-voiced. "You've given me a lot of hours to puzzle over what this expedition is for."

"A jigsaw puzzle it is indeed, girl, and us sitting with bottoms snuggled in front of the jigsaw."

"In view of the very, very special kind of supernova-and-companion you thought might be somewhere not too far from Sol, and wanted me to compute about—in view of that, and of what Supermetals is doing, sure, I've arrived at a guess."

"Has you likewise taken into account the fact Supermetals is not just secretive about everything like is its right, but refuses to join the League?"

"That's also its right."

"Truly true. Nonetheleast, the advantages of belonging is maybe not what they used to was; but they do outweigh what small surrender of anatomy is required."

"You mean autonomy, don't you?"

"I suppose. Must be I was thinking of women. A stern chaste is a long chaste.... But you never got impure thoughts." Van Rijn had the tact not to look at her while he rambled, and to become serious again immediately: "You better hope, you heathen, and I better pray, the supermetals what the agents of Supermetals is peddling do not come out of a furnace run by anybody except God Himself."

The primordial element, with which creation presumably began, is hydrogen-1, a single proton accompanied by a single electron. To this day, it comprises the overwhelming bulk of matter in the universe. Vast masses of it condensed into globes, which grew hot enough from that infall to light thermonuclear fires. Atoms melted together, forming higher elements. Novae, supernovae— and, less picturesquely but more importantly, smaller suns shedding gas in their red giant phase—spread these through space, to enter into later generations of stars. Thus came planets, life, and awareness.

Throughout the periodic table, many isotopes are radioactive. From polonium (number 84) on, none are stable. Protons packed together in that quantity generate forces of repulsion with which the forces of attraction cannot forever cope. Sooner or later, these atoms will break up. The probability of disintegration—in effect, the half-life—depends on the particular structure. In general, though, the higher the atomic number, the lower the stability.

Early researchers thought the natural series ended at uranium. If further elements had once existed, they had long since perished. Neptunium, plutonium, and the rest must be made artificially. Later, traces of them were found in nature: but merely traces, and only of nuclei whose atomic numbers were below 100. The creation of new substances grew progressively more difficult, because of proton repulsion, and less rewarding, because of vanishingly brief existence, as atomic number increased. Few people expected a figure as high as 120 would ever be reached.

Well, few people expected gravity control or faster-than-light travel, either. The universe is rather bigger and more complicated than any given set of brains. Already in those days, an astonishing truth was soon revealed. Beyond a certain point, nuclei become *more* stable. The periodic table contains an "island of stability," bounded on the near side by ghostly short-lived isotopes like those of 112 and 113, on the far side by the still more speedily fragmenting 123, 124 . . . etc. . . . on to the next "island" which theory says could exist but practice has not reached save on the most infinitesimal scale.

The first is amply hard to attain. There are no easy intermediate stages, like the neptunium which is a stage between uranium and plutonium. Beyond 100, a half-life of a few hours is Methuselan; most are measured in seconds or less. You build your nuclei by main force, slamming particles into atoms too hard for them to rebound—though not so hard that the targets shatter.

To make a few micrograms of, say, element 114, eka-platinum, was a laboratory triumph. Aside from knowledge gained, it had no industrial meaning.

Engineers grew wistful about that. The proper isotope of eka-platinum will not endure forever; yet its half-life is around a quarter million years, abundant for mortal purposes, a radioactivity too weak to demand special precautions. It is lustrous white, dense (31.7), of high melting point (ca. 4700°C.), nontoxic, hard and tough and resistant. You can only get it into solution by grinding it to dust, then treating it with H_2F_2 and fluorine gas, under pressure at 250°.

It can alloy to produce metals with a range of properties an engineer would scarcely dare daydream about. Or, pure, used as a catalyst, it can become a veritable Philosopher's Stone. Its neighbors on the island are still more fascinating.

When Satan was discovered, talk arose of large-scale

manufacture. Calculations soon damped it. The mills which were being designed would use rivers and seas and an entire atmosphere for cooling, whole continents for dumping wastes, in producing special isotopes by the ton. But these isotopes would all belong to elements below 100. Not even on Satan could modern technology handle the energies involved in creating, within reasonable time, a ton of eka-platinum; and supposing this were somehow possible, the cost would remain out of anybody's reach.

The engineers sighed...until a new company appeared, offering supermetals by the ingot or the shipload, at prices high but economic. The source of supply was not revealed. Governments and the Council of the League remembered the Shenna.

To them, a Cynthian named Tso Yu explained blandly that the organization for which she spoke had developed a new process which it chose not to patent but to keep proprietary. Obviously, she said, new laws of nature had been discovered first; but Supermetals felt no obligation to publish for the benefit of science. Let science do its own sweating. Nor did her company wish to join the League, or put itself under any government. If some did not grant it license to operate in their territories, why, there was no lack of others who would.

In the three years since, engineers had begun doing things and building devices which were to bring about the same kind of revolution as did the transistor, the fusion converter, or the neg-gravity generator. Meanwhile a horde of investigators, public and private, went quietly frantic.

The crews who delivered the cargoes and the agents who sold them were a mixed lot, albeit of known species. A high proportion were from backward worlds like Diomedes, Woden, or Ikrananka; some originated in neglected colonies like Lochlann (human) or Catawray-annis (Cynthian). This was understandable. Beings to whom Supermetals had given an education and a chance to better themselves and help out their folk at home would be especially loyal to it. Enough employees hailed from sophisticated milieus to deal on equal terms with League executives.

This did not appear to be a Shenn situation. Whenever an individual's past life could be traced, it proved normal, up to the point when Supermetals engaged him (her, it, yx . . .)—and was not really abnormal now. Asked point blank, the being would say he didn't know himself where the factory was or how it functioned or who the ultimate owners were. He was merely doing a well-paid job for a good, *simpático* outfit. The evidence bore him out.

("I suspect, me, some detectiving was done by kidnaps, drugs, and afterward murder," van Rijn said bleakly. "I would never allow that, but fact is, a few Supermetals people have disappeared. And . . . as youngsters like you, Coya, get more prudish, the companies and governments get more brutish." She answered: "The second is part of the reason for the first.")

Scoutships trailed the carriers and learned that they always rendezvoused with smaller craft, built for speed and agility. Three or four of these would unload into a merchantman, then dash off in unpredictable directions, using every evasive maneuver in the book and a few that the League had thought were its own secrets. They did not stop dodging until their instruments confirmed that they had shaken their shadowers.

Politicians and capitalists alike organized expensive attempts to duplicate the discoveries of whoever was behind Supermetals. Thus far, progress was nil. A body of opinion grew, that that order of capabilities belonged to a society as far ahead of the Technic as the latter was ahead of the neolithic. Then why this quiet invasion?

"I'm surprised nobody but you has thought of the supernova alternative," Coya said.

"Well, it *has* barely been three years," van Rijn answered. "And the business began small. It is still not big. Nothing flashy-splashy: some kilotons arriving annually, of stuff what is useful and will get more useful after more is learned about the properties. Meanwhiles, everybody got lots else to think about, the usual skulduggeries and unknowns and whatnots. Finalwise, remember, I am pustulent—*dood en ondergang*, this Anglic!—I am postulating something which astronomically is hyperimprobable. If you asked a colleague offhand, his first response would be that it isn't possible. His second would be, if he is a sensible man, How would you like to come to his place for a drink?" He knocked the dottle from his pipe. "No doubt somebody more will eventual think of it too, and sic a computer onto the problem of: Is this sort of thing possible, and if so, where might we find one?"

He stroked his goatee. "Howsomever," he continued musingly, "I think a good whiles must pass before the idea does occur. You see, the ordinary being does not care. He buys from what is on the market without wondering where it come from or what it means. Besides, Supermetals has not gone after publicity, it uses direct contacts; and what officials are concerned about Supermetals has been happy to avoid publicity themselves. A big harroo might too easy get out of control, lose them votes or profits or something."

"Nevertheless," Coya said, "a number of bright minds are worrying; and the number grows as the amount of supermetals brought in does."

"*Ja*. Except who wears those minds? Near-as-damn all is corporation executives, politicians, laboratory scientists, military officers, and—now I will have to wash my mouth out with Genever—bureaucrats. In shorts, they is planetlubbers. When they cross space, they go by cozy passenger ships, to cities where everything is known except where is a restaurant fit to eat in that don't charge as if the dessert was eka-platinum à la mode.

"Me, my first jobs was on prospecting voyages. And I traveled plenty after I founded Solar, troublepotshooting on the frontier and beyond in my own personals. I know—every genuine spaceman knows, down in his marrow like no deskman ever can—how God always makes surprises on us so we don't get too proud, or maybe just for fun. To me it came natural to ask myself: What joke might God have played on the theorists this time?"

"I hope it is only a joke," Coya said.

The star remained a titan in mass. In dimensions, it was hardly larger than Earth, and shrinking still, megayear by megayear, until at last light itself could no longer escape and there would be in the universe one more point of elemental blackness and strangeness. That process was scarcely started—Coya estimated the explosion had occurred some 500 millennia ago—and the giant-become-dwarf radiated dimly in the visible spectrum, luridly in the X-ray and gamma bands. That is, each square centimeter emitted a gale of hard quanta; but so small was the area in interstellar space that the total was a mere spark, undetectable unless you came within a few parsecs.

Standing in the observation turret, staring into a viewscreen set for maximum photoamplification, she discerned a wan-white speck amidst stars which thronged the sky and, themselves made to seem extra brilliant, hurt her eyes. She looked away, toward the instruments around her which were avidly gathering data. The ship whispered and pulsed, no longer under hyperdrive but accelerating on negagravity thrust.

Hirharouk's voice blew cool out of the intercom, from the navigation bridge where he was: "The existence of a companion is now confirmed. We will need a long baseline to establish its position, but preliminary indications are of a radius vector between forty and fifty a.u."

Coya marveled at a detection system which could identify the light-bending due to a substellar object at that distance. Any observatory would covet such equipment. Her thought went to van Rijn: *If you paid what it cost, Gunung Tuan, you were smelling big money.*

"So far?" came her grandfather's words. "By damn, a chilly ways out, enough to freeze your astronomy off."

"It had to be," she said. "This was an A-zero: radiation equal to a hundred Sols. Closer in, even a superjovian would have been cooked down to the bare metal—as happened when the sun detonated."

"*Ja*, I knows, I knows, my dear. I only did not foresee things here was on quite this big a scale.... Well, we can't spend weeks at sublight. Go hyper, Hirharouk, first to get your baseline sights, next to come near the planet."

"Hyperdrive, this deep in a gravitational well?" Coya exclaimed.

"Is hokay if you got good engines well tuned, and you bet ours is tuned like a late Beethoven quartet. Music, maestro!"

Coya shook her head before she prepared to continue gathering information under the new conditions of travel.

Again *Dewfall* ran on gravs. Van Rijn agreed that trying to pass within visual range of the ultimate goal, faster than light, when to them it was still little more than a mystery wrapped in conjectures, would be a needlessly expensive form of suicide.

Standing on the command bridge between him and Hirharouk, Coya stared at the meters and displays filling an entire bulkhead, as if they could tell more than the heavens in the screens. And they could, they could, but they were not the Earth-built devices she had been using; they were Ythrian and she did not know how to read them.

Poised on his perch, crested carnivore head lifted against the Milky Way, Hirharouk said: "Data are pouring in as we approach. We should make optical pickup in less than an hour."

"Hum-hum, better call battle stations," the man proposed.

"This crew needs scant notice. Let them slake any soul-thirst they feel. God may smite some of us this day." Through the intercom keened a melody, plangent strings and thuttering drums and shrilling pipes, like nothing Earth had brought forth but still speaking to Coya of hunters high among their winds.

Terror stabbed her. "You can't expect to fight!" she cried.

"Oh, an ordinary business precaution," van Rijn smiled.

"No! We mustn't!"

"Why not, if they are here and do rumblefumbles at us?"

She opened her lips, pulled them shut again, and stood in anguish. *I can't tell you why not. How can I tell you these may be David's people?*

"At least we are sure that Supermetals is not a *whinna* for an alien society," Hirharouk said. Coya remembered vaguely, through the racket in her temples, a demonstration of the *whinna* during her groundside visit to Ythri. It was a kind of veil, used by some to camouflage themselves, to resemble floating mists in the eyes of unflying prey; and this practical use had led to a form of dream-lovely airborne dance; and—*And here I was caught in the wonder of what we have found, a thing which must be almost unique even in this galaxy full of miracles . . . and everything's gotten tangled and ugly and, and, David, what can we do?*

She heard van Rijn: "Well, we are not total-sure. Could be our finding is accidental; or maybe the planet is not like we suppose. We got to check on that, and hope the check don't bounce back in our snoots."

"Nuclear engines are in operation around our quarry," Hirharouk said. "Neutrinos show it. What else would they belong to save a working base and spacecraft?"

Van Rijn clasped hands over rump and paced, slap-slap-slap over the bare deck. "What can we try and predict in advance? Forewarned is forearmed, they say, and the four arms I want right now is a knife, a blaster, a machine gun, and a rover missile, nothing fancy, maybe a megaton."

"The mass of the planet—" Hirharouk consulted a readout. The figure he gave corresponded approximately to Saturn.

"No bigger?" asked van Rijn, surprised.

"Originally, yes," Coya heard herself say. The scientist in her was what spoke, while her heart threshed about like any animal netted by a stooping Ythrian. "A gas giant, barely substellar. The supernova blew most of that away—you can hardly say it boiled the gases off; we have no words for what happened—and nothing was left except a core of nickel-iron and heavier elements."

She halted, noticed Hirharouk's yellow gaze intent on her, and realized the skipper must know rather little of the theory behind this venture. To him she had not been repeating banalities. And he was interested. If she could please him by explaining in simple terms, then maybe later—

She addressed him: "Of course, when the pressure of the outer layers was removed, that core must have exploded into new allotropes, a convulsion which flung away the last atmosphere and maybe a lot of solid matter. Better keep a sharp lookout for meteoroids."

"That is automatic," he assured her. "My wonder is why a planet should exist. I was taught that giant stars, able to become supernovae, do not have them."

"Well, they is still scratching their brains to account for Betelgeuse," van Rijn remarked.

"In this case," Coya told the Ythrian, "the explanation comes easier. True, the extremely massive suns do not in general allow planetary systems to condense around them. The parameters aren't right. However, you know giants can be partners in multiple star systems, and sometimes the difference between partners is quite large. So, after I was alerted to the idea that it might happen, and wrote a program which investigated the possibility in detail, I learned that, yes, under special conditions, a double can form in which one member is a large sun and one a superjovian planet. When I extrapolated backward things like the motion of dust and gas, changes in galactic magnetism, et cetera—it turned out that such a pair could exist in this neighborhood."

Her glance crossed the merchant's craggy features. *You found a clue in the appearance of the supermetals,* she thought. *David got the idea all by himself.* The lean snubnosed face, the Vega-blue eyes came between her and the old man.

*Of course, David may not have been involved. This
could be a coincidence. Please, God of my grandfather
Whom I don't believe in, please make it a coincidence.
Make those ships ahead of us belong not to harmless
miners but to the great and terrible Elder Race.*

She knew the prayer would not be granted. And
neither van Rijn nor Hirharouk assumed that the miners
were necessarily harmless.

She talked fast, to stave off silence: "I daresay you've
heard this before, Captain, but you may like to have me
recapitulate in a few words. When a supernova erupts, it
floods out neutrons in quantities that I, I can put a
number to, perhaps, but I cannot comprehend. In a full
range of energies, too, and the same for other kinds of
particles and quanta—Do you see? Any possible reaction
must happen.

"Of course, the starting materials available, the
reaction rates, the yields, every quantity differs from case
to case. The big nuclei which get formed, like the
actinides, are a very small percentage of the total. The
supermetals are far less. They scatter so thinly into space
that they're effectively lost. No detectable amount enters
into the formation of a star or planet afterward.

"Except—here—here was a companion, a planet-sized
companion, turned into a bare metallic globe. I wouldn't
try to guess how many quintillion tons of blasted-out
incandescent gases washed across it. Some of those
alloyed with the molten surface, maybe some plated out—
and the supermetals, with their high condensation
temperatures, were favored.

"A minute fraction of the total was supermetals, yes,
and a minute fraction of that was captured by the planet,
also yes. But this amounted to—how much?—billions of
tons? Not hard to extract from combination by modern
methods; and a part may actually be lying around pure.
It's radioactive; one must be careful, especially of the
shorter-lived products, and a lot has decayed away by
now. Still, what's left is more than our puny civilization
can ever consume. It took a genius to think this might be!"

She grew aware of van Rijn's eyes upon her. He had

stopped pacing and stood troll-burly, tugging his beard.

A whistle rescued her. Planha words struck from the intercom. Hirharouk's feathers rippled in a series of expressions she could not read; his tautness was unmistakable.

She drew near to the man's bulk. "What next?" she whispered. "Can you follow what they're saying?"

"*Ja*, pretty well; anyhow, better than I can follow words in an opera. Detectors show three ships leaving planetary orbit on an intercept course. The rest stay behind. No doubt those is the working vessels. What they send to us is their men-of-war."

Seen under full screen magnification, the supermetal world showed still less against the constellations than had the now invisible supernova corpse—a ball, dimly reflecting star-glow, its edge sharp athwart distant brightnesses. And yet, Coya thought: a world.

It could not be a smooth sphere. There must be uplands, lowlands, flatlands, depths, ranges and ravines, cliffs whose gloom was flecked with gold, plains where mercury glaciers glimmered; there must be internal heat, shudders in the steel soil, volcanoes spouting forth flame and radioactive ash; eternally barren, it must nonetheless mumble with a life of its own.

Had David Falkayn trod those lands? He would have, she knew, merrily swearing because beyond the ship's generated field he and his space gear weighed five or six times what they ought, and no matter the multitudinous death traps which a place so uncanny must hold in every shadow. Naturally, those shadows had to be searched out; whoever would mine the metals had first to spend years, and doubtless lives, in exploring, and studying, and the development and testing and redevelopment of machinery ... but that wouldn't concern David. He was a charger, not a plowhorse. Having made his discovery, told chosen beings about it, perhaps helped them raise the initial funds and recruit members of races which could better stand high weight than men can—having done that, he'd

depart on a new adventure, or stop off in the Solar
Commonwealth and take Coya Conyon out dancing.

"Iyan wherill-ll cha quellan."

The words, and Hirharouk's response, yanked her
back to this instant. "What?"

"Shush." Van Rijn, head cocked, waved her to silence.
"By damn, this sounds spiky. I should tell you, Shush-
kebab."

Hirharouk related: "Instruments show one of the three
vessels is almost equal to ours. Its attendants are less, but
in a formation to let them take full advantage of their
firepower. If that is in proportion to size, which I see no
reason to doubt, we are outgunned. Nor do they act as if
they simply hope to frighten us off. That formation and its
paths are well calculated to bar our escape spaceward."

"Can you give me details—? No, wait." Van Rijn
swung on Coya. "Bellybird, you took a stonkerish lot of
readings on the sun, and right here is an input-output
panel you can switch to the computer system you was
using. I also ordered, when I chartered the ship, should be
a program for instant translation between Anglic
language, Arabic numerals, metric units, whatever else
kinds of ics is useful—translations back and forth
between those and the Planha sort. Think you could
quick-like do some figuring for us?" He clapped her
shoulder, nearly felling her. "I know you can." His voice
dropped. "I remember your grandmother."

Her mouth was dry, her palms were wet, it thudded in
her ears. She thought of David Falkayn and said, "Yes.
What do you want?"

"Mainly the pattern of the gravitational field, and what
phenomena we can expect at the different levels of
intensity. Plus radiation, electromagnetics, anything else
you got time to program for. But we is fairly well
protected against those, so don't worry if you don't get a
chance to go into details there. Nor don't let outside
talkings distract you—Whoops!" Hirharouk was receiving a fresh report. "Speak of the devil and he gives you
horns."

The other commander had obviously sent a call on a standard band, which had been accepted. As the image screen awoke, Coya felt hammerstruck. *Adzel!*

No . . . no . . . the head belonged to a Wodenite, but not the dear dragon who had given her rides on his back when she was little and had tried in his earnest, tolerant fashion to explain his Buddhism to her when she grew older. Behind the being she made out a raven-faced Ikranankan and a human in the garb of a colony she couldn't identify.

His rubbery lips shaped good Anglic, a basso which went through her bones: "Greeting. Commodore Nadi speaks."

Van Rijn thrust his nose toward the scanner. "Whose commodore?" he demanded like a gravel hauler dumping its load.

For a second, Nadi was shaken. He rallied and spoke firmly: "*Kho*, I know who you are, Freeman van Rijn. What an unexpected honor, that you should personally visit our enterprise."

"Which is Supermetals, *nie?*"

"It would be impolite to suggest you had failed to reach that conclusion."

Van Rijn signalled Coya behind his back. She flung herself at the chair before the computer terminal. Hirharouk perched imperturbable, slowly fanning his wings. The Ythrian music had ended. She heard a rustle and whisper through the intercom, along the hurtling hull.

Words continued. Her work was standardized enough that she could follow them.

"Well, you see, Commodore, there I sat, not got much to do no more, lonely old man like I am except when a girl goes wheedle-wheedle at me, plenty time for thinking, which is not fun like drinking but you can do it alone and it is easier on the kidneys and the hangovers next day are not too much worse. I thought, if the supermetals is not made by an industrial process we don't understand, must be they was made by a natural one, maybe one we do know a little about. That would have to be a supernova. Except a supernova blows everything out into space, and the supermetals is so small, proportional, that they get lost. Unless the supernova had a companion what could catch them?"

"Freeman, pray accept my admiration. Does your perspicacity extend to deducing who is behind our undertaking?"

"*Ja*, I can say, bold and bald, who you undertakers are. A consortium of itsy-bitsy operators, most from poor or primitive societies, pooling what capital they can scrape together. You got to keep the secret, because if they know about this hoard you found, the powerful outfits will horn themselves in and you out; and what chance you get afterward, in courts they can buy out of petty cash? No, you will keep this hidden long as you possible can. In the end, somebody is bound to repeat my sherlockery. But give you several more years, and you will have pumped gigacredits clear profit out of here. You may actual have got so rich you can defend your property."

Coya could all but see the toilers in their darkness—in orbital stations; aboard spacecraft; down on the grave-yard surface, where robots dug ores and ran refineries, and sentient beings stood their watches under the murk and chill and weight and radiation and millionfold perils of Eka-World....

Nadi, slow and soft: "That is why we have these fighting ships, Freeman and Captain."

"You do not suppose," van Rijn retorted cherrily, "I would come this far in my own precious blubber and forget to leave behind a message they will scan if I am not home in time to race for the Micronesia Cup?"

"As a matter of fact, Freeman, I suppose precisely that. The potential gains here are sufficient to justify virtually any risk, whether the game be played for money or . . . something else." Pause. "If you have indeed left a message, you will possess hostage value. Your rivals may be happy to see you a captive, but you have allies and employees who will exert influence. My sincere apologies, Freeman, Captain, everyone aboard your vessel. We will try to make your detention pleasant."

Van Rijn's bellow quivered in the framework. "*Wat

drommel? You sit smooth and calm like buttered granite and say you will make us prisoners?"

"You may not leave. If you try, we will regretfully open fire."

"You are getting on top of yourself. I warn you, always she finds nothing except an empty larder, Old Mother Hubris."

"Freeman, please consider. We noted your hyperdrive vibrations and made ready. You cannot get past us to spaceward. Positions and vectors guarantee that one of our vessels will be able to close in, engage, and keep you busy until the other two arrive." Reluctantly, van Rijn nodded. Nadi continued: "True, you can double back toward the sun. Evidently you can use hyperdrive closer to it than most. But you cannot go in that direction at anywhere near top pseudospeed without certain destruction. We, proceeding circuitously, but therefore able to go a great deal faster, will keep ahead of you. We will calculate the conoid in which your possible paths spaceward lie, and again take a formation you cannot evade."

"You is real anxious we should taste your homebrew, ha?"

"Freeman, I beg you, yield at once. I promise fair treatment—if feasible, compensation—and while you are among us, I will explain why we of Supermetals have no choice."

"Hirharouk," van Rijn said, "maybe you can talk at this slagbrain." He stamped out of scanner reach. The Ythrian threw him a dubious glance but entered into debate with the Wodenite. Van Rijn hulked over Coya where she sat. "How you coming?" he whispered, no louder than a Force Five wind.

She gestured at the summary projected on a screen. Her computations were of a kind she often handled. The results were shown in such terms as diagrams and equations of equipotential surfaces, familiar to a space captain. Van Rijn read them and nodded. "We got enough information to set out on," he decided. "The rest you can figure while we go."

Shocked, she gaped at him. "What? Go? But we're caught!"

"He thinks that. Me, I figured whoever squats on a treasure chest will keep guards, and the guards will not be glimmerwits but smart, trained oscos, in spite of what I called the Commodore. They might well cook for us a cake like what we is now baked in. Ergo, I made a surprise recipe for them." Van Rijn's regard turned grave. "It was for use only if we found we was sailing through dire straits. The surprise may turn around and bite us. Then we is dead. But better dead than losing years in the nicest jail, *nie?*" (And she could not speak to him of David.) "I said this trip might be dangerous." Enormous and feather-gentle, a hand stroked down her hair. "I is very sorry, Beatriz, Ramona." The names he murmured were of her mother and grandmother.

Whirling, he returned to Hirharouk, who matched pride against Nadi's patience, and uttered a few rapid-fire Planha words. The Ythrian gave instant assent. Suddenly Coya knew why the man had chosen a ship of that planet. Hirharouk continued his argument. Van Rijn went to the main command panel, snapped forth orders, and took charge of *Dewfall*.

At top acceleration, she sprang back toward the sun.

Of that passage, Coya afterward remembered little. First she glimpsed the flashes when nuclear warheads drove at her, and awaited death. But van Rijn and Hirharouk had adjusted well their vector relative to the enemy's. During an hour of negagrav flight, no missile could gather sufficient relative velocity to get past defensive fire; and that was what made those flames in heaven.

Then it became halfway safe to go hyper. That must be at a slower pace than in the emptiness between stars; but within an hour, the fleeing craft neared the dwarf. There, as gravitation intensified, she had to resume normal state.

Instead of swinging wide, she opened full thrust almost straight toward the disc.

Coya was too busy to notice much of what happened

around her. She must calculate, counsel, hang into her seat harness as forces tore at her which were too huge for the compensator fields. She saw the undead supernova grow in the viewscreens till its baneful radiance filled them; she heard the ribs of the vessel groan and felt them shudder beneath stress; she watched the tale of the radiation meters mounting and knew how close she came to a dose whose ravages medicine could not heal; she heard orders bawled by van Rijn, fluted by Hirharouk, and whistling replies and storm of wingbeats, always triumphant though *Dewfall* flew between the teeth of destruction. But mainly she was part of the machinery.

And the hours passed and the hours passed.

They could not have done what they did without advance preparation. Van Rijn had foreseen the contingency and ordered computations made whose results were in the data banks. Her job was to insert numbers and functions corresponding to the reality on hand, and get answers by which he and Hirharouk might steer. The work killed her, crowded out terror and sometimes the memory of David.

Appalled, Nadi watched his quarry vanish off his telltales. He had followed on hyperdrive as close as he dared, and afterward at sublight closer than he ought to have dared. But for him was no possibility of plunging in a hairpin hyperbola around yonder incandescence. In all the years he had been stationed here, not he nor his fellows had imagined anyone would ever venture near the roiling remnant of a sun which had once burned brighter than its whole galaxy. Thus there were no precalculations in storage, nor days granted him to program them on a larger device than a ship might carry.

Radiation was not the barrier. It was easy to figure how narrow an approach a crew could endure behind a given amount of armor. But a mass of half a dozen Sols, pressed into the volume of an Earth, has stupendous gravitational power; the warped space around makes the laws of nature take on an eerie aspect. Moreover, a dwarf star spins at a fantastic rate: which generates relativistic forces, describable only if you have determined the precise quantities involved. And pulsations, normally found nowhere outside the atomic nucleus, reach across a million or more kilometers—

After the Ythrian craft whipped around the globe, into weirdness, Nadi had no way of knowing what she did, how she moved. He could not foretell where she would be when she again became detectable. And thus he could plan no interception pattern.

He could do nothing but hope she would never reappear. A ship flying so close, not simply orbiting but flying, would be seized, torn apart, and hauled into the star, unless the pilot and his computers knew exactly what they did.

Or almost exactly. That was a crazily chancy ride. When Coya could glance from her desk, she saw blaze in the screens, Hirharouk clutching his perch with both hands while his wings thundered and he yelled for joy, van Rijn on his knees in prayer. Then they ran into a meteoroid swarm (she supposed) which rebounded off their shield-fields and sent them careening off trajectory; and the man shook his fist, commenced on a mighty oath, glimpsed her and turned it into a Biblical "Damask rose and shittah tree!" Later, when something else went wrong—some interaction with a plasma cloud—he came to her, bent over and kissed her brow.

They won past reef and riptide, lined out for deep space, switched back into hyperdrive and ran on homeward.

Coincidences do happen. The life would be freakish which held none of them.

Muddlin' Through, bound for Eka-World in response to Coya's letter, passed within detection range of *Dewfall*, made contact, and laid alongside. The pioneers boarded.

This was less than a day after the brush with oblivion. And under no circumstances do Ythrians go in for tumultuous greetings. Apart from Hirharouk, who felt he must represent his choth, the crew stayed at rest. Coya, roused by van Rijn, swallowed a stimpill, dressed, and hastened to the flying hold—the sole chamber aboard which would comfortably accommodate Adzel. In its echoing dim space she threw her arms partway around him, took Chee Lan into her embrace, kissed David Falkayn and wept and kissed him and kissed him.

Van Rijn cleared his throat. "A-hem!" he grumbled. "Also bgr-rrm. I been sitting here hours on end, till my end is sore, wondering when everybody elses would come awake and make celebrations by me; and I get word about you three mosquito-ears is coming in, and by my own self I hustle stuff for a party." He waved at the table he had laid, bottles and glasses, platesful of breads, cheeses, sausage, lox, caviar, kanuba, from somewhere a vaseful of flowers. Mozart lilted in the background. "Well, ha, poets tell us love is enduring, but I tell us good food is not, so we take our funs in the right order, *nie?*"

Formerly Falkayn would have laughed and tossed off the first icy muglet of akvavit; he would have followed it with a beer chaser and an invitation to Coya that they see what they could dance to this music. Now she felt sinews tighten in the fingers that enclosed hers; across her shoulder he said carefully: "Sir, before we relax, could you let me know what's happened to you?"

Van Rijn got busy with a cigar. Coya looked a plea at Adzel, stroked Chee's fur where the Cynthian crouched on a chair, and found no voice. Hirharouk told the story in a few sharp words.

"A-a-ah," Falkayn breathed. "Judas priest. Coya, they ran you that close to that hellkettle—" His right hand let go of hers to clasp her waist. She felt the grip tremble and grew dizzy with joy.

"Well," van Rijn hufffed. "I didn't want she should come, my dear tender little bellybird, *ja*, tender like tool steel—"

Coya had a sense of being put behind Falkayn, as a man puts a woman when menace draws near. "Sir," he said most levelly, "I know, or can guess, about that. We can discuss it later if you want. What I'd like to know immediately, please, is what you propose to do about the Supermetals consortium."

Van Rijn kindled his cigar and twirled a mustache. "You understand," he said, "I am not angry if they keep things under the posies. By damn, though, they tried to make me a prisoner or else shoot me to bits of lard what would go into the next generation of planets. And Coya, too, Davy boy, don't forget Coya, except she would make those planets prettier. For that, they going to pay."

"What have you in mind?"

"Oh . . . a cut. Not the most unkindest, neither. Maybe like ten percent of gross."

The creases deepened which a hundred suns had weathered into Falkayn's countenance. "Sir, you don't need the money. You stopped needing more money a long while back. To you it's nothing but a counter in a game. Maybe, for you, the only game in town. Those beings aft of us, however—they are not playing."

"What do they do, then?"

Surprisingly, Hirharouk spoke. "Freeman, you know the answer. They seek to win that which will let their peoples fly free." Standing on his wings, he could not spread gold-bronze plumes; but his head rose high. "In the end, God the Hunter strikes every being and everything which beings have made. Upon your way of life I see His shadow. Let the new come to birth in peace."

From Falkayn's hands, Coya begged: "*Gunung Tuan*, all you have to do is do nothing. Say nothing. You've won your victory. Tell them that's enough for you, that you too are their friend."

She had often watched van Rijn turn red—never before white. His shout came ragged: "*Ja! Ja!* Friend! So nice, so kind, maybe so farsighted—Who, what I thought of like a son, broke his oath of fealty to me? Who broke kinship?"

He suspected, Coya realized sickly, *but he wouldn't admit it to himself till this minute, when I let out the truth.* She held Falkayn sufficiently hard for everyone to see.

Chee Lan arched her back. Adzel grew altogether still. Falkayn forgot Coya—she could feel how he did—and looked straight at his chief while he said, word by word like blows of a hammer: "Do you want a response? I deem best we let what is past stay dead."

Their gazes drew apart. Falkayn's dropped to Coya. The merchant watched them standing together for a soundless minute. And upon him were the eyes of Adzel, Chee, and Hirharouk the sky dweller.

He shook his head. "Hokay," said Nicholas van Rijn, well-nigh too low to hear. "I keep my mouth shut. Always. Now can we sit down and have our party for making you welcome?" He moved to pour from a bottle; and Coya saw that he was indeed old.

The rest would appear to be everyone's knowledge: how at last, inevitably, the secret of Mirkheim's existence was ripped asunder; how the contest for its possession brought on the Babur War; how that struggle turned out to be the first civil war in the Commonwealth and gave the Polesotechnic League a mortal wound. The organization would linger on for another hundred Terran years, but waning and disintegrating; in truth, already it had ceased to be what it began as, the proud upbearer of liberty. Eventually the Commonwealth, too, went under. The Troubles were only quelled with the rise and expansion of the Empire—and its interior peace is often bought with foreign violence, as Ythri and Avalon have learned. Honor be forever theirs whose deathpride preserved for us our right to rule ourselves!

Surely much of that spirit flies through time from David and Coya Conyon/Falkayn. When they led to this planet humans who would found new homes, they were doing more than escaping from the chaos they foresaw; they were raising afresh the ancient banner of freedom. When they obtained the protection and cooperation of Ythri, they knew—it is in their writings—how rich and strong a world must come from the dwelling together of two races so unlike.

Thus far the common wisdom. As for the creation and history of our choth upon Avalon, that is in *The Sky Book of Stormgate*.

Yet Hloch has somewhat more to give you before his own purpose is fully served. As you well know, our unique society did not come easily into being. Especially in the early years, misunderstandings, conflicts, bitterness, even enmity would often strike talons into folk. Have you heard much of this from the human side? Belike not. It is fitting that you learn.

Hloch has therefore chosen two final tales as representative. That they are told from youthful hover-points is, in his mind, very right.

The first of them is the last that Judith Dalmady/ Lundgren wrote for *Morgana*. Though she was then in her high old age, the memories upon which she was drawing were fresh.

WINGLESS

As far as we know—but how much do we really know, in
this one corner of this one galaxy which we have somewhat
explored?—Avalon was the first planet whereon two
different intelligent species founded a joint colony. Thus
much was unforeseeable, not only about the globe itself,
whose mysteries had barely been skimmed by the original
explorers, but about the future of so mixed a people. The
settlers began by establishing themselves in the Hesperian
Islands, less likely to hold fatal surprises than a continent.
And the two races chose different territories.

Relations between them were cordial, of course. Both
looked forward to the day when men and Ythrians would
take over the mainlands and dwell there together. But at
first it seemed wise to avoid possible friction. After all,
they had scarcely anything in common except more or less
similar biochemistries, warm blood, live birth, and the
hope of making a fresh start on an uncorrupted world. Let
them get acquainted gradually, let mutuality develop in
an unforced way.

Hence Nat Falkayn rarely saw winged folk in the early
part of his life. When an Ythrian did, now and then, have
business in Chartertown, it was apt to be with his
grandfather David, or, presently, his father Nicholas:
certainly not with a little boy. Even when an eaglelike

411

being came as a dinner guest, conversation was seldom in Anglic. Annoyed by this, Nat grew downright grindstone about learning the Planha language as his school required. But the effort didn't pay off until he was seventeen Avalonian years old—twelve years of that Mother Earth he had never seen, of which his body bore scarcely an atom.

At that time, the archipelago settlements had grown to a point where leaders felt ready to plant a seed of habitation on the Coronan continent. But much study and planning must go before. Nicholas Falkayn, an engineer, was among those humans who joined Ythrian colleagues in a research and development team. The headquarters of this happened to be at the chief abode of the allied folk, known to its dwellers as Trauvay and to humans as Wingland. He would be working out of there for many cycles of the moon Morgana, each of which equalled not quite half a Lunar month. So he brought his wife and children along.

Nat found himself the only boy around in his own age bracket. However, there was no lack of young Ythrian companions.

"Hyaa-aah!" In a whirl and thunder, Keshchyi left the balcony floor and swung aloft. Sunlight blazed off his feathers. The whistling, trumpeting challenge blew down: "What are you waiting for, you mudfeet?"

Less impetuous than his cousin, Thuriak gave Nat a sharp yellow glance. "Well, are you coming?" he asked.

"I . . . guess so," the human mumbled.

You are troubled, Thuriak said, not with his voice. Infinitely variable, Ythrian plumage can send ripples of expression across the entire body, signs and symbols often more meaningful than words will ever be. Nat had learned some of the conventional attitudes as part of his Planha lessons. But now, during these days of real acquaintance with living creatures, he had come to feel more and more like a deaf-mute.

He could merely say, in clumsy direct speech: "No, I'm fine. Honest I am. Just, uh, well, wondering if I shouldn't at least call my mother and ask—"

His tone trailed off. Thuriak seemed to be registering scorn. And yet this was a gentle, considerate youth, not at all like that overbearing Keshchyi....

If you must, like a nestling. Did that really stand written on the bronze-hued feathers, the black-edged white of crest and tail?

Nat felt very alone. He'd been delighted when these contemporaries of his, with whom he'd talked a bit and played a few games, invited him to spend the Freedom Week vacation at their home. And certainly that whole extended household known as the Weathermaker Choth had shown him politeness, if not intimacy—aside from a few jeering remarks of Keshchyi's, which the fellow probably didn't realize were painful. And his parents had been glad to let him accept. "It's a step toward the future," his father had exclaimed. "Our two kinds are going to have to come to know each other inside out. That's a job for your generation, Nat . . . and here you're beginning on it."

But the Ythrians were alien, and not just in their society. In their bones, their flesh, the inmost molecules of their genes, they were not human. It was no use pretending otherwise.

"Different" did not necessarily mean "inferior." Could it, heartbreakingly, mean "better"? Or "happier"? Had God been in a more joyful mood when He made the Ythrians than when He made man?

Perhaps not. They were pure carnivores, born hunters. Maybe that was the reason why they allowed, yes, encouraged their young to go off and do reckless things, accepting stoically the fact that the unfit and the unlucky would not return alive—

Keshchyi swooped near. Nat felt a gust of air from beneath his wings. "Are you glued in your place?" he shouted. "The tide isn't, I can tell you. If you want to come, then for thunder's sake, move!"

"He's right, you know," said calmer Thuriak. Eagerness quivered across him.

Nat gulped. As if searching for something familiar, anything, his gaze swept around.

He stood on a balcony of that tall stone tower which

housed the core families. Below were a paved courtyard and rambling wooden buildings. Meadows where meat animals grazed sloped downhill in Terrestrial grass and clover, Ythrian starbell and wry, Terrestrial oak and pine, Ythrian braidbark and copperwood, until cultivation gave way to the reddish mat of native susin, the scattered intense green of native chasuble bush and delicate blue of janie. The sun Laura stood big and golden-colored at morning, above a distantly glimpsed mercury line of ocean. Elsewhere wandered a few cottony clouds and the pale, sinking ghost of Morgana. A flock of Avalonian draculas passed across view, their leathery wings awkward beside the plumed splendor of Keshchyi's. No adult Ythrians were to be seen; they ranged afar on their business.

Nat, who was short and slender, with rumpled brown hair above thin features, felt dwarfed in immensity.

The wind murmured, caressed his face with coolness, blew him an odor of leaves and distances, a smoky whiff of Thuriak's body.

Though young, that being stood nearly as tall as one full-grown, which meant that he was about Nat's height. What he stood on was his enormous wings, folded downward, claws at their main joints to serve as a kind of feet. What had been the legs and talons of his birdlike ancestors were, on him, arms and hands. His frame had an avian rigidity and jutting keelbone, but his head, borne proudly on a rather long neck, was almost mammalian beneath its crest—streamlined muzzle, tawny eyes, mouth whose lips looked oddly delicate against the fangs, little brow yet the skull bulging backward to hold an excellent brain.

"Are you off, then?" Thuriak demanded while Keshchyi whistled in heaven. "Or would you rather stay here? It might be best for you, at that."

Blood beat in Nat's temples. *I'm not going to let these creatures sneer at humans!* ran through him. At the same time he knew he was being foolish, that he ought to check with his mother—and knew he wasn't going to, that he couldn't help himself. "I'm coming," he snapped.

Good, said Thuriak's plumage. He brought his hands to the floor and stood on them an instant while he spread those wings. Light shining through made his pinions look molten. Beneath them, the gill-like antlibranch slits, the "biological superchargers" which made it possible for an animal this size to fly under Earthlike conditions, gaped briefly, a row of purple mouths. In a rush and roar of his own, Thuriak mounted.

He swung in dizzying circles, up and up toward his hovering cousin. Shouts went between them. An Ythrian in flight burned more food and air than a human; they said he was more alive.

But I am no Ythrian, Nat thought. Tears stung him. He wiped them away, angrily, with the back of a wrist, and sought the controls of his gravbelt.

It encircled his coveralls at the waist. On his back were the two cylinders of its powerpack. He could rise, he could fly for hours. But how wretched a crutch this was!

Leaving the tower, he felt a slight steady vibration from the drive unit, pulsing through his belly. His fingers reached to adjust the controls, level him off and line him out northward. Wind blew, shrill and harsh, lashing his eyes till he must pull down the goggles on his leather helmet. The Ythrians had transparent third lids.

In the last several days, he had had borne in on him—until at night, on the cot set up for him in the young males' nest, he must stifle his sobs lest somebody hear—borne in on him how much these beings owned their unbounded skies, and how his kind did not.

The machine that carried him went drone, drone. He trudged on a straight course through the air, while his companions dipped and soared and reveled in the freedom of heaven which was their birthright.

The north shore curved to form a small bay. Beyond susin and bush and an arc of dunes, its waters glistened clear blue-green; surf roared furious on the reefs across its mouth. A few youngsters kept sailboats here. Keshchyi and Thuriak were among them.

But . . . they had quietly been modifying theirs for use

on open sea. Today they proposed to take it out.

Nat felt less miserable when he had landed. On foot, he was the agile one, the Ythrians slow and limited. That was a poor tradeoff, he thought grayly. Still, he could be of help to them. Was that the real reason they had invited him to join this maiden venture?

For Keshchyi, yes, no doubt, the boy decided. *Thuriak seems to like me as a person.... Seems* to. His look went across that haughty unhuman countenance, and though it was full of expression, he could read nothing more subtle than a natural excitement.

"Come on!" Keshchyi fairly danced in his impatience. "Launch!" To Nat: "You. Haul on the prow. We'll push on the stern. Jump!"

For a moment of anger, Nat considered telling him to go to hell and returning alone. He knew he wasn't supposed to be here anyway, on a dangerous faring, without having so much as told his parents. The whole idea had been presented to him with such beast-of-prey suddenness.... *No,* he thought. *I can't let them believe I, a human, must be a coward. I'll show 'em better.* He seized the stempost, which curved over the bow in a graceful sculpture of vines and leaves. He bent his back and threw his muscles into work.

The boat moved readily from its shelter and across the beach. It was a slim, deckless, nearly flat-bottomed hull, carvel-built, about four meters long. A single mast rested in brackets. Sand, gritty beneath Nat's thin shoesoles, gave way to a swirl of water around his trouser legs. The boat uttered a chuckling sound as it came afloat.

Keshchyi and Thuriak boarded in a single flap. Nat must make an undignified scramble across the gunwale and stand there dripping. Meanwhile the others raised the mast, secured its stays, began unlashing jib and mainsail. It was a curious rig, bearing a flexible gaff almost as long as the boom. The synthetic cloth rose crackling into the breeze.

"Hoy, wait a minute," Nat said. The Ythrians gave him a blank glance and he realized he had spoken in Anglic. Had they never imagined it worth the trouble to learn his language properly, as he had theirs? He shifted to Planha: "I've been sailing myself, around First Island, and know— uh, what is the word?" Flushing in embarrassment, he fumbled for ways to express his idea.

Thuriak helped him. After an effort, they reached understanding. "You see we have neither keel nor centerboard, and wonder how we'll tack," the Ythrian interpreted. "I'm surprised the sportsmen of your race haven't adopted our design." He swiveled a complexly curved board, self-adjusting on its pivot by means of vanes, upward from either rail. "This interacts with the wind to provide lateral resistance. No water drag. Much faster than your craft. We'll actually sail as a hydrofoil."

"Oh, grand!" Nat marvelled.

His pleasure soured when Keshchyi said in a patronizing tone: "Well, of course, knowledge of the ways of air comes natural to us."

"So we're off," Thuriak laughed. He took the tiller in his right hand and jibsheet in his left; wing-claws gripped a perch-bar. The flapping sails drew taut. The boat bounded forward.

Hunkered in the bottom—there were no thwarts—Nat saw the waters swirl, heard them hiss, felt a shiver of speed and tasted salt on his lips. The boat reached planing speed and skimmed surface in a smooth gallop. The shore fell aft, the surf grew huge and loud ahead, dismayingly fast.

Nat gulped. *No, I will not show them any uneasiness.* After all, he still wore his gravbelt. In case of capsizing or—or whatever—he could flit to shore. The Ythrians could too. Was that why they didn't bother to carry lifejackets along?

The reefs were of some dark coraloid. They made a nearly unbroken low wall across the lagoon entrance. Breakers struck green-bright, smashed across those jagged backs, exploded in foam and bone-rattling thunder. Whirlpools seethed. In them, thick brown nets of atlantis weed, torn loose from a greater mass far out to sea, snaked around and around. Squinting through spindrift, Nat barely made out a narrow opening toward which Thuriak steered.

I don't like this, I don't like it one bit, went through him, chill amidst primal bellows and grunts and hungry suckings.

Thuriak put down the helm. The boat came about in a slash of boom and gaff, a snap of sailcloth, sounds that were buried in the tornado racket. On its new tack, it leaped for the passage. Thuriak fluted his joy. Keshchyi spread plumes which shone glorious in sun and scud-blizzard.

The boat dived in among the reefs. An unseen net of weed caught the rudder. A riptide and a flaw of wind grabbed hold. The hull smashed against a ridge. Sharpnesses went like saws through the planks. The surf took the boat and started battering it to death.

Nat was aloft before he knew what had really happened. He hovered on his thrust-fields, above white and green violence, and stared wildly around. There was Thuriak, riding the air currents, dismay on every feather, but alive, safe... Where was Keshchyi?

Nat yelled the question. Faint through the noise there drifted back to him the shriek: "I don't know, I don't see him, did the gaff whip over him—?" and Thuriak swooped about and about, frantic.

A cry tore from him. "Yonder!" And naked grief: "No, no, oh, Keshchyi, my blood-kin, my friend—"

Nat darted to join the Ythrian. Winds clawed at him; the breakers filled his head with their rage. Through a bitter upflung mist he peered. And he saw—

—Keshchyi, one wing tangled in the twining weed, a-thresh in waves that surged across him, bore him under, cast him back for an instant and swept him bloodily along a reefside.

"We can grab him!" Nat called. But he saw what Thuriak had already seen, that this was useless. The mat which gripped Keshchyi was a dozen meters long and wide. It must weigh a ton or worse. He could not be raised, unless someone got in the water first to free him.

And Ythrians, winged sky-folk, plainly could not swim. It was flatout impossible for them. At most, help from above would keep the victim alive an extra minute or two.

Nat plunged.

Chaos closed on him. He had taken a full breath, and held it as he was hauled down into ice-pale depths. *Keep calm, keep calm, panic is what kills.* The currents were stronger than he was. But he had a purpose, which they did not. He had the brains to use them. Let them whirl him under—he felt his cheek scraped across a stone—for they would cast him back again and—

Somehow he was by Keshchyi. He was treading water, gulping a lungful when he could, up and down, up and down, away and back, always snatching to untangle those cables around the wing, until after a time beyond time, Keshchyi was loose.

Thuriak extended a hand. Keshchyi took it. Dazed, wounded, plumage soaked, he could not raise himself, nor could Thuriak drag him up alone.

A billow hurled Nat forward. His skull flew at the reef where the boat tossed in shards. Barely soon enough, he touched the controls of his gravbelt and rose.

He grabbed Keshchyi's other arm and switched the power output of his unit to Overload. Between them, he and Thuriak brought their comrade to land.

"My life is yours, Nathaniel Falkayn," said Keshchyi in the house. "I beg your leave to honor you."

"Aye, aye," whispered through the rustling dimness where the Weathermaker Choth had gathered.

"Awww..." Nat mumbled. His cheeks felt hot. He wanted to say, "Please, all I ask is, don't tell my parents what kind of trouble I got my silly self into." But that wouldn't be courteous, in this grave ceremony that his friends were holding for him.

It ended at last, however, and he and Thuriak got a chance to slip off by themselves, to the same balcony from which they had started. The short Avalonian day was drawing to a close. Sunbeams lay level across the fields. They shimmered off the sea, beyond which were homes of men. The air was still, and cool, and full of the scent of growing things.

"I have learned much today," Thuriak said seriously.

"Well, I hope you've learned to be more careful in your next boat," Nat tried to laugh. *I wish they'd stop making such a fuss about me,* he thought. *They will in time, and we can relax and enjoy each other. Meanwhile, though—*

"I have learned how good it is that strengths be different, so that they may be shared."

"Well, yes, sure. Wasn't that the whole idea behind this colony?"

And standing there between sky and sea, Nat remembered swimming, diving, surfing, all the years of his life, brightness and laughter of the water that kissed his face and embraced his whole body, the riding on splendid waves and questing into secret twilit depths, the sudden astonishing beauty of a fish or a rippled sandy bottom, sunlight a-dance overhead . . . and he looked at the Ythrian and felt a little sorry for him.

For his last chapter, Hloch returns to A. A. Craig's *Tales of the Great Frontier*. The author was a Terran who traveled widely, gathering material for his historical narratives, during a pause in the Troubles, several lifetimes after the World-Taking. When he visited Avalon, he heard of an incident from the person, then aged, who had experienced it, and made therefrom the story which follows. Though fictionalized, the account is substantially accurate. Though dealing with no large matter, it seems a fitting one wherewith to close.

RESCUE ON AVALON

The Ythrian passed overhead in splendor. Sunlight on feathers made bronze out of his six-meter wingspan and the proudly held golden-eyed head. His crest and tail were white as the snowpeaks around, trimmed with black. He rode the wind like its conqueror.

Against his will, Jack Birnam confessed the sight was beautiful. But it was duty which brought up his binoculars. If the being made a gesture of greeting, he owed his own race the courtesy of a return salute; and Ythrians often forgot that human vision was less keen than theirs. *I have to be especially polite when I'm in country that belongs to them,* the boy thought. Bitterness rushed through him. *And this does, now, it does. Oh, curse our bargaining Parliament!*

Under magnification, he clearly saw the arched carnivore muzzle with its oddly delicate lips; the talons which evolution had made into hands; the claws at the "elbows" of the wings, which served as feet on the ground; the gill-like slits in the body, bellows pumped by the flight muscles, a biological supercharger making it possible for a creature that size to get aloft. He could even see by the plumage that this was a middle-aged male, and of some importance to judge by the ornate belt, pouch, and dagger which were all that he wore.

Though the Ythrian had undoubtedly noticed Jack, he gave no sign. That was likely just his custom. Choths differed as much in their ways as human nations did, and Jack remembered hearing that the Stormgate folk, who would be moving into these parts, were quite reserved. Nevertheless the boy muttered at him, "You can call it dignity if you want. I call it snobbery, and I don't like you either."

The being dwindled until he vanished behind a distant ridge. *He's probably bound for Peace Deep on the far side, to hunt,* Jack decided. *And I wanted to visit there. . . . Well, why not, anyway? I'll scarcely meet him; won't be going down into the gorge myself. The mountains have room for both of us—for a while, till his people come and settle them.*

He hung the glasses on his packframe and started walking again through loneliness.

The loftiest heights on the planet Avalon belong to the Andromeda Range. But that is a name bestowed by humans. Not for nothing do the Ythrians who have joined them in their colonizing venture call that region the Weathermother. Almost exactly two days—twenty-two hours—after he had spied the stranger, a hurricane caught Jack Birnam. Born and raised here, he was used to sudden tempests. The rapidly spinning globe was always breeding them. Yet the violence of this one astonished him.

He was in no danger. It had not been foolish to set off by himself on a trip into the wilderness. He would have preferred a companion, of course, but none of his friends happened to be free; and he didn't expect he'd ever have another chance to visit the beloved land. He knew it well. He intended merely to hike, not climb. At age twenty-four (or seventeen, if you counted the years of an Earth where he had never been) he was huskier than many full-grown men. In case of serious difficulty, he need merely send a distress signal by his pocket transceiver. Homing on it, an aircar from the nearest rescue station in the foothills should reach him in minutes.

If the sky was fit to fly in!

When wind lifted and clouds whirled like night out of the north, he made his quick preparations. His sleeping bag, with hood and breathing mask for really foul conditions, would keep him warm at lower temperatures than occurred anywhere on Avalon. Unrolled and erected over it as a kind of pup tent, a sheet of duraplast would stop hailstones or blown débris. The collapsible alloy frame, light but equally sturdy, he secured to four pegs whose explosive heads had driven them immovably into bedrock. This shelter wasn't going anywhere. When he had brought himself and his equipment inside, he had nothing to do but wait out the several shrieking hours which followed.

Nonetheless, he was almost frightened at the fury, and half-stunned by the time it died away.

Crawling forth, he found the sun long set. Morgana, the moon, was full, so radiant that it crowded most stars out of view. Remote snowfields glittered against blue-black heaven; boulders and shrubs on the ridgetop where Jack was camped shone as if turned to silver, while a nearby stream flowed like mercury. The cluck and chuckle of water, the boom of a more distant cataract, were the only sounds. After the wind-howl, this stillness felt almost holy. The air was chill but carried odors of plant life, sharp trefoil, sweet livewell, and janie. Breath smoked ghostly.

After his long lying motionless, he couldn't sleep. He decided to make a fire, cook a snack and coffee, watch dawn when it came. Here above timberline, the low, tough vegetation wasn't much damaged. But he was sure to find plenty of broken-off wood. The trees below must have suffered far worse. He'd see in the morning. At present, to him those depths were one darkness, hoar-frosted by moonlight.

His transceiver beeped. He stiffened. That meant a general broadcast on the emergency band. Drawing the flat object from his coverall, he flipped its switch for two-way. A human voice lifted small: "—Mount Farview area.

Andromeda Rescue Station Four calling anyone in the Mount Farview area. Andromeda—"

Jack brought the instrument to his mouth. "Responding," he said. Inside his quilted garment, he shivered with more than cold. "John Birnam responding to ARS Four. I . . . I'm a single party, on foot, but if I can help—"

The man at the other end barked: "Where are you, exactly?"

"It doesn't have a name on the map," Jack replied, "but I'm on the south rim of a big canyon which starts about twenty kilometers east-north-east of Farview's top. I'm roughly above the middle of the gorge, that'd be, uh, say thirty kilometers further east."

It does have a name, though, went through his mind. *I named it Peace Deep, five years ago when I first came on it, because the forest down there is so tall and quiet. Wonder what the Ythrians will call it, after I can't come here anymore?*

"Got you," answered the man. He must have an aerial survey chart before him. "John Birnam, you said? I'm Ivar Holm. Did you come through the storm all right?"

"Yes, thanks, I was well prepared. Are you checking?"

"In a way." Holm spoke grimly. "Look, this whole sector's in bad trouble. The prediction on that devil-wind was totally inadequate, a gross underestimate. Not enough meteorological monitors yet, I suppose. Or maybe the colonies are too young to've learned every trick that Avalon can play. Anyhow, things are torn apart down here in the hills—farms, villages, isolated camps—aircars smashed or crashed, including several that belonged to this corps. In spite of help being rushed in from outside, we'll be days in finding and saving the survivors. Our pilots and medics are going to have to forget there ever was such a thing as sleep."

"I . . . I'm sorry," Jack said lamely.

"I was praying someone would be in your vicinity. You see, an Ythrian appears to have come to grief thereabouts."

"An Ythrian!" Jack whispered.

"Not just any Ythrian, either. Ayan, the Wyvan of Stormgate."

"What?"

"Don't you know about that?" It was very possible. Thus far, the two races hadn't overlapped a great deal. Within the territories they claimed, they had been too busy adapting themselves and their ways to a world that was strange to them both. Jack, whose family were sea ranchers, dwelling on the coast five hundred kilometers westward, had seldom encountered one of the other species. Even a well-educated person might be forgiven for a certain vagueness about details of an entire set of alien societies.

"In the Stormgate choth," Holm said, "'Wyvan' comes as close to meaning 'Chief' or 'President' as you can get in their language. And Stormgate, needing more room as its population grows, has lately acquired this whole part of the Andromedas."

"I know," Jack couldn't help blurting in a refreshed rage. "The Parliament of Man and the Great Khruath of the Ythrians made their nice little deal, and never mind those of us who spent all the time we could up here because we love the country!"

"Huh? What're you talking about? It was a fair exchange. They turned over some mighty good prairie to us. We don't live by hunting and ranching the way they do. We can't use alps for anything except recreation—and not many of us ever did—and why are you and I wasting time, Birnam?"

Jack set his teeth. "Go on, please."

"Well. Ayan went to scout the new land personally, alone. That's Ythrian style. You must be aware what a territorial instinct their race has got. Now I've received a worried call from Stormgate headquarters. His family says he'd have radioed immediately after the blow, if he could, and asked us to relay a message that he wasn't hurt. But he hasn't. Nor did he ever give notice of precisely where he'd be, and no Ythrian on an outing uses enough gear to be readily spotted from the air."

"A low-power sender won't work out of that particular

forest," Jack said. "Too much ironleaf growing there."

"Sunblaze!" Holm groaned. "Things never do go wrong one at a time, do they?" He drew breath. "Ordinarily we'd have a fleet of cars out searching, regardless of the difficulty. We can't spare them now, especially since he may well be dead. Nevertheless—You spoke as if you had a clue to his whereabouts."

Jack paused before answering slowly, "Yes, I believe I do."

"What? Quick, for mercy's sake!"

"An Ythrian flew by me a couple of days ago, headed the same way I was. Must've been him. Then when I arrived on this height, down in the canyon I saw smoke rising above the treetops. Doubtless a fire of his. I suppose he'd been hunting and—Well, I didn't pay close attention, but I could point the site out approximately. Why not send a team to where I am?"

Holm kept silent a while. The moonlight seemed to grow more cold and white.

"Weren't you listening, Birnam?" he said at last. "We need every man and every vehicle we can get, every minute they can be in action. According to my map, that gorge is heavily wooded. Do you mean we should tie up two or three men and a car for hours or days, searching for the exact place—when the chances of him being alive look poor, and . . . you're right on the scene?

"Can't you locate him? Find what the situation is, do what you can to help, and call back with precise information. Given that, we can snake him right out of there, without first wasting man-hours that should go to hundreds of people we know we can save. How about it?"

Now Jack had no voice.

"Hello?" Holm's cry was tiny in the night. "Hello?"

Jack gripped the transceiver till his knuckles stood bloodless. "I'm not sure what I can manage," he said.

"How d'you mean?"

"I'm allergic to Ythrians."

"*Huh?*"

"Something about their feathers or—It's gotten extremely bad in the last year or two. If I come near one, soon I can hardly breathe. And I didn't bring my antiallergen, this trip. Never expected to need it."

"Your condition ought to be curable."

"The doctor says it is, but that requires facilities we don't have on Avalon. RNA transformation, you know. My family can't afford to send me to a more developed planet. I just avoid those creatures."

"You can at least go look, can't you?" Holm pleaded. "I appreciate the risk, but if you're extra careful—"

"Oh, yes," Jack said reluctantly. "I can do that."

With the starkness of his folk, Ayan had shut his mind to pain while he waited for rescue or death. From time to time he shrilled forth hunting calls, and these guided Jack to him after the boy reached the general location. They had grown steadily weaker, though.

Far down a steep slope, the Ythrian sprawled rather than lay, resting against a chasuble bush. Everywhere around him were ripped branches and fallen boles, a tangle which had made it a whole day's struggle for Jack to get here. Sky, fading toward sunset, showed through rents in the canopy overhead. Mingled with green and gold of other trees was the shimmering, glittering purple foliage of ironleaf.

The alatan bone in Ayan's left wing was bent at an ugly angle. That fracture made it alike impossible for him to fly or walk. Gaunt, exhausted, he still brought his crest erect as the human blundered into view. Hoarseness thickened the accent of his Anglic speech: "Welcome indeed!"

Jack stopped three meters off, panting, sweating despite the chill, knees wobbly beneath him. He knew it was idiotic, but could think of nothing else than: "How ... are you, ... sir?" *And why call him "sir," this land-robber?*

"In poor case," dragged out of Ayan's throat. "Well it is that you arrived. I would not have lasted a second night. The wind cast a heavy bough against my wing and broke it. My rations and equipment were scattered; I do not think you could find them yourself." The three fingers and two thumbs of a hand gestured at the transceiver clipped on his belt. "Somehow this must also have been disabled. My calls for help have drawn no response."

"They wouldn't, here." Jack pointed to the sinister loveliness which flickered in a breeze above. "Didn't you know? That's called ironleaf. It draws the metal from the soil and concentrates pure particles, to attract pollinating bugs by the shininess. Absorbs radio waves. Nobody should go into an area like this without a partner."

"I was unaware—even as the weather itself caught me by surprise. The territory is foreign to me."

"It's home country to *me*." Fists clenched till nails bit into palms.

Ayan's stare sharpened upon Jack. Abruptly he realized how peculiar his behavior must seem. The Ythrian needed help, and the human only stood there. Jack couldn't simply leave him untended; he would die.

The boy braced himself and said in a hurry: "Listen. Listen good, because maybe I won't be able to repeat this. I'll have to scramble back up to where I can transmit. Then they'll send a car that I can guide to you. But I can't go till morning. I'd lose my way, or break my neck, groping in the dark through this wreckage the storm's made. First I'll do what's necessary for you. We better plan every move in advance."

"Why?" asked Ayan quietly.

"Because you make me sick! I mean—allergy—I'm going to get asthma and hives, working on you. Unless we minimize my exposure, I may be too ill to travel tomorrow."

"I see." For all his resentment, Jack was awed by the self-control. "Do you perchance carry anagon in your first-aid kit? No? Pity. I believe that is the sole painkiller which works on both our species. *Hrau*. You can toss me your filled canteen and some food immediately. I am near collapse from both thirst and hunger."

"It's human-type stuff, you realize," Jack warned. While men and Ythrians could eat many of the same things, each diet lacked certain essentials of the other. For that matter, native Avalonian life did not hold adequate nutrition for either colonizing race. The need to maintain separate ecologies was a major reason why they tended to live apart. *I can't ever return,* Jack thought. *Even if the new dwellers allowed me to visit, my own body wouldn't.*

"Calories, at least," Ayan reminded him. "Though I have feathers to keep me warmer than your skin would, last night burned most of what energy I had left."

Jack obliged. "Next," he proposed, "I'll start a fire and cut enough wood to last you till morning."

Was Ayan startled? That alien face wasn't readable. It looked as if the Ythrian was about to say something and then changed his mind. The boy went on: "What sort of preliminary care do you yourself need?"

"Considerable, I fear," said Ayan. Jack's heart sank. "Infection is setting in, and I doubt you carry an antibiotic safe for use on me; so my injuries must be thoroughly cleansed. The bone must be set and splinted, however roughly. Otherwise—I do not wish to complain, but the pain at every slightest movement is becoming quite literally unendurable. I barely managed to keep the good wing flapping, thus myself halfway warm, last night. Without support for the broken one, I could not stay conscious to tend the fire."

Jack forgot that he hated this being. "Oh, gosh, no! I wasn't thinking straight. You take my bag. I can, uh, sort of fold you into it."

"Let us see. Best we continue planning and preparations."

Jack nodded jerkily. The time soon came when he must take a breath, hold it as long as possible, and go to the Ythrian.

It was worse than his worst imagining.

At the end, he lay half-strangled, eyes puffed nearly shut, skin one great burning and itch, wheezed, wept, and shuddered. Crouched near the blaze, Ayan looked at him across the meters of cold, thickening dusk which again separated them. He barely heard the nonhuman voice:

"You need that bedroll more than I do, especially so when you must have strength back by dawn to make the return trip. Take your rest."

Jack crept to obey. He was too wretched to realize what the past hour must have been like for Ayan.

* * * * *

First light stole bleak between trees. The boy wakened to a ragged call: "*Khrraah, khrraah, khrraah,* human—" For a long while, it seemed, he fought his way through mists and cobwebs. Suddenly, with a gasp, he came to full awareness.

The icy air went into his lungs through a throat much less swollen than before. Bleariness and ache still possessed his head, but he could think, he could see. . . .

Ayan lay by the ashes of the fire. He had raised himself on his hands to croak aloud. His crest drooped, his eyes were glazed. "*Khrraah*—"

Jack writhed from his bag and stumbled to his feet. "What happened?" he cried in horror.

"I . . . fainted . . . only recovered this moment—Pain, weariness, and . . . lack of nourishment—I feared I might collapse but hoped I would not—"

It stabbed through Jack: *Why didn't I stop to think? Night before last, pumping that wing—the biological supercharger kindling his metabolism beyond anything a human can experience—burning not just what fuel his body had left, but vitamins that weren't in the rations I could give him—*

"Why didn't you insist on the bedding?" the human cried in anguish of his own. "I could've stayed awake all right!"

"I was not certain you could," said the harsh whisper. "You appeared terribly ill, and . . . it would have been wrong, that the young die for the old. . . . I know too little about your kind—" The Ythrian crumpled.

"And I about yours." Jack sped to him, took him in his arms, brought him to the warm bag and tucked him in with enormous care. Presently Ayan's eyes fluttered open, and Jack could feed him.

The asthma and eruptions weren't nearly as bad as earlier. Jack hardly noticed, anyway. When he had made sure Ayan was resting comfortably, supplies in easy reach, he himself gulped a bite to eat and started off.

It would be a stiff fight, in his miserable shape, to get past the ironleaf before dark. He'd do it, though. He knew he would.

The doctors kept him one day in the hospital. Recovered, he borrowed protective garments and a respirator, and went to the Ythrian ward to say goodbye.

Ayan lay in one of the frames designed for his race. He was alone in his room. Its window stood open to a lawn and tall trees—Avalonian king's-crown, Ythrian wind-nest, Earthly oak—and a distant view of snowpeaks. Light spilled from heaven. The air sang. Ayan looked wistfully outward.

But he turned his head and, yes, smiled as Jack entered, recognizing him no matter how muffled up he was. "Greeting, galemate," he said.

The boy had spent his own time abed studying usages of Stormgate. He flushed; for he could have been called nothing more tender and honoring than "galemate."

"How are you?" he inquired awkwardly.

"I shall get well, because of you." Ayan grew grave. "Jack," he murmured, "can you come near me?"

"Sure, as long's I'm wearing this." The human approached. Talons reached out to clasp his gloved hand.

"I have been talking with Ivar Holm and others," Ayan said very low. "You resent me, my whole people, do you not?"

"Aw, well—"

"I understand. We were taking from you a place you hold dear. Jack, you, and any guests of yours, will forever be welcome there, to roam as you choose. Indeed, the time is over-past for our two kinds to intermingle freely."

"But . . . I mean, thank you, sir," Jack stammered, "but I can't."

"Your weakness? Yes-s-s." Ayan uttered the musical Ythrian equivalent of a chuckle. "I suspect it is of largely psychosomatic origin, and might fade of itself when your anger does. But naturally, my choth will send you off-planet for a complete cure."

Jack could only stare and stutter.

Ayan lifted his free hand. "Thank us not. We need the closeness of persons like you, who would not abandon even an enemy."

"But you aren't!" burst from Jack. "I'll be proud to call you my friend!"

To those who have traveled with him this far, Hloch gives thanks. It is his hope that he has aided you to a little deeper sight, and thereby done what honor he was able to his choth and to the memory of his mother, Rennhi the wise.

Countless are the currents which streamed together at Avalon. Here we have flown upon only a few. Of these, some might well have been better chosen. Yet it seems to Hloch that all, in one way or another, raise a little higher than erstwhile his knowledge of that race with which ours is to share this world until God the Hunter descends upon both. May this be true for you as well, O people.

Now *The Earth Book of Stormgate* is ended. From my tower I see the great white sweep of the snows upon Mount Anrovil. I feel the air blow in and caress my feathers. Yonder sky is calling. I will go.

Fair winds forever.